Three "Kids" on a Mule

To
Debra
Thanks.
William Meador

Three "Kids" on a Mule

William Meador

Writers Club Press
San Jose New York Lincoln Shanghai

Three "Kids" on a Mule

Writers Club Press
an imprint of iUniverse.com, Inc.

For information address:
iUniverse.com, Inc.
5220 S 16th, Ste. 200
Lincoln, NE 68512
www.iuniverse.com

ISBN: 0-595-17816-2

Printed in the United States of America

FOREWORD

This is one of the stories of the Kidd and Carter families, whose saga stretched from Virginia, Kentucky and Tennessee to Texas and the Territory of New Mexico. Some of them came to Texas before Independence but returned east to fight in the Civil War. They were farmers, ranchers, freighters, miners, soldiers, army officers, blackguards and even preachers. Their epic of moving to West Texas and to The Territory of New Mexico has been told by mouth from generation to generation. Some information has come from diaries, genealogy studies and a little from history. But, more importantly this story is about courage, tenacity and the belief in country and God.

CHAPTER ONE

As Robert brushed the flank of the mule, he looked out of the barn at the beautiful fall day. He could see the Double Mountains thirty miles to the southwest. They were sharp and clear on this fall day. Robert thought to himself, "Fall is still in the air and is a great time of the year. The mornings dawn crisp, and the days are still warm enough that you don't need a coat." He gazed up at the North Central Texas sky and wondered how it could be so crystal clear and blue. Looking down the lane he could see the heavy foliage on the trees. The trees lining the lane were covered in a variety of colors due to unusually heavy rain during the spring and summer. He could feel the promise of good times in the air, as the holidays were close at hand. He spoke to the mule, "This is the best time of the year." The mule turned his head and looked at Robert with big, soft brown eyes.

Robert wanted to shout for joy. Thanksgiving was only a few days away. School will be out for four days, and if it stays warm the family would go to Grandma's and Grandpa's for turkey dinner and a visit. They live in the next county. It is an overnight trip, and most of the time the family stays for two or three additional nights. It is more fun to visit Grandpa and Grandma than anything in the world. They have lots of fowl to chase, animals to ride and cliffs above the Brazos River to climb.

Papa would scold us for chasing the fowl, but there were flocks and flocks, and they seemed to enjoy the game, especially the turkeys and the guineas. All of the grandchildren, about twenty from five families, would play hide and seek among the bushes and trees. This was where all the chickens, turkeys, peacocks and guineas roosted. That is, they roosted there at night and pecked for worms and grasshoppers in the daytime. Grandpa used the great flock of guineas to keep the bugs out of his fields.

Grandpa and Papa are called the best farmers in two counties. They always had good crops, and their fields are clear of weeds and Johnson grass. Papa said that he had had the best harvest in a number of years, and if we were good, that Christmas would be special this year. I can hardly wait for the holidays! My two sisters, Minnie, thirteen, and Lizzie, seven, have each other to keep company. But, as an only boy of ten with two sisters, it's a pain. They sure don't know how to do the things boys like to do. The trip to Grandpa's is going to be really special because there would be about eleven other boys to go hunting, riding and maybe swimming with, if the weather stayed warm.

I would get to ride a horse at Grandpa's. He has enough horses, that, by riding double, all of the boys could go hunting on horseback. Of course, Papa did not use horses for working the place. He did not believe they were worth owning. He had only mules. Great, big, strong mules. Papa says that a mule is far smarter than a horse. Just for example, a mule will not founder if you leave feed out. Nor, will he drink, when thirsty till he makes himself sick. Guess that was the only difference in Grandpa and Papa. Well, there was one other difference. Papa will bust my back side when I don't mind. But Grandpa will only scold me, and then give me a good talking to. Boy, I'd rather have the busting than the talking to any day. Oh, it was going.....

"Robert, are you through grooming that mule?"

"Almost, Papa," I answered. Boy, there is sure a lot of work to do around here. I need to be hunting or fishing. Any ten year old, especially one that is almost eleven, needs to be out exploring and not doing chores. Why, there might be some Indians out there, and I could find them. I could report them to the sheriff. I would be a hero and get to have a horse. And if I had a horse I could take him to Grandpa's for Thanksgiving.

"Well, quit day dreaming about Grandpa's or whatever and get your chores finished. Hear?"

How in the world did Papa know when I had stopped doing a chore and was watching a hawk or thinking about something away off across some other place? He must have somebody snitching on me. Or, he had eyes in the back of his head, just like my schoolteacher.

Papa is a big man. Over six feet and all muscles. He could lift bales of hay all day and then laugh at night when younger men complained about being tired. His eyes are blue and his hair blond. My grandpa said we all came from some place called Holland, wherever that is. Papa's smile could melt butter, that is what Mama says. He is gentle with Lizzie and Minnie, my sisters. You can see his love for the three women in his life, Mama, Minnie and Lizzie.

"Yes, Papa", I shouted back, as I finished with the last few strokes on Old Number One's coat. The mules were really putting on heavy coats for the winter. The currying of the animals has become very slow and hard. Manes and tails are tangled and full of burrs and trash. Papa said this was going to be a very hard winter. All of the animals are putting on lots of heavy coats. Papa would allow, "God's way of telling us to get ready for a bad season, and His way of protecting the animals."

Now, Old Number One was the mule that Papa got first. He wasn't old by mule years, just first and smart as a whip. Papa has four mules all numbered, one, two, three and four. They are all a deep brown with big dark eyes. When you called on the numbers, that mule's ears would perk up, and he was ready do to your bidding. Mama says that Papa should give the mules proper names, as they work so hard and were so gentle. Papa allows that a number is just as good a name to a mule. Mama just smiles her disapproval and says nothing, but pets and feeds them little bits of fruit or vegetables.

"Robert, come to supper and bring your father and sisters!" called Mama.

"Yes, 'um," I called back to my Mama on the back porch of our house. I looked back at the most beautiful mother in the world. She is grace, dignity, pure sunshine and a blond beauty. Her hair is long and shiny, like the sun. Her smile could light up a room and does light up the hearts of our family. When Papa and Mama look at each other and us, we see pure love. That is what our home is built on. The love and care of two good people.

"Robert, I don't see your sisters, so go down through the orchard and garden and look for them. They were to pick some fruit and vegetables, but they are still gone."

"Yes, 'um," I called back, again. Now you have to know my two sisters to understand their actions and ideas. My sister Minnie is thirteen, and at thirteen all she thinks about is, yuck, boys and romance. She day-dreams worse than me. I would not tell her, but she is really pretty, with her long blond hair and blue eyes. She is almost a reflection of our mother. Her blond hair is just like Mama's and Papa's. When she smiles you see love and happiness. Her blue eyes just shine. She is already the most popular girl at school and, though I hate to admit it she is one of the smartest. Lord, she is smart. There is one more thing about my sister that I really like. She has the voice of an angel. That is what Papa says and that must be the truth. She sings with Mama and one of my aunts, and they are good. Minnie is becoming more and more like Mama, in looks and in manners. I would not tell her, but she will be beautiful.

Lizzie is a smaller duplication of both of them, blond and blue eyed. It is startling that they all look so much alike. Lizzie, bubbles all the time. She does not walk, she runs. Lizzie does not talk, she explodes. She is never still, she moves and wiggles and squirms. She is life. She is pure life and joy. The joy of my Mama and Papa.

I guess I'm not the only one that thinks Minnie is pretty. All of the boys at school and church sure do hang around a lot. They do dumb things trying to get her attention. She thinks all of their stunts are childish and stupid, with her being one of the brightest students in school. By the way, little Lizzie is just as pretty and probably as smart as Minnie. She sure tries to copy Minnie and sure does whatever Minnie tells her. Reads all the time and likes homework like it was candy.

Mrs. Wilson, her teacher, says, "That Minnie needs to go to a finishing school and get a teaching diploma." But Mama just nods and says. "We will see when she finishes school here." We only have ten grades and Minnie, at thirteen, is in the eighth grade. Boy is she smart! Makes life a little rough on me, a dumb old boy. I'm anything but smart, ten years old and in the fifth grade.

Oh, Papa taught me lots on the farm, about outdoors and about nature. He thinks that a boy should know as much about the outdoors as is possible. Papa taught me how to plow, harness the mules, check hooves, curry animals, doctor sick critters and a hundred other things on the farm. Then the most important teaching, at least to me, is the outdoors, mainly how to hunt, camp out and fish. I think that I am very near as good as Papa.

Schooling and books are just not my thing. Mrs. Stout says, "Robert, if you could write down all you think about, you would be famous. It is just that you don't think about school or school work. All you think about is hunting, fishing or riding some big mule and trying to act like a Texas Ranger. Robert, all of the Indians are gone from this part of the world, so stop playing like you are a ranger and chasing imaginary Indians."

As I leave the rear of the barn I can hear the girls laughing down in the garden. I waved to get their attention and then called, "Mama says that supper is ready and come to the house."

Minnie replies, "Come help us carry the baskets. They are full and heavy." She is wearing one of Mama's creations. Ah...what was it that Mama called it, a pinafore. What ever that is. It was light pink with a white apron. Mama says it makes her look like something out of book.

More than likely like a little Dutch girl. I giggled behind my hand because I didn't want Papa to bust me one.

Lizzie and I are wearing our usual blue and white overalls, faded blue shirts and old brown floppy hats. Mama says Lizzie is going to have to start wearing dresses and acting like a girl. She couldn't be tomboy forever.

"Ugh, you girls are sissies. Can't carry some baskets up to the house. You lazy…"

"Robert, get your body down here and help or I'll …" Just then a rattlesnake began to rattle under a tomato vine only a few feet from Lizzie. Both girls let out screams that would raise the dead. Before any of us can move, Ol' Bullet, my dog, rushed in between Lizzie and the snake. Then in a flash he had the snake by the back of the head and killed it with a snap of his jaws.

Papa came running out of the barn hollering, "What's happening! What's wrong? Is someone hurt?" He rushed over and scooped up Lizzie, who was crying.

"No," I replied. "Just Ol' Bullet to the rescue. He killed a snake that scared the girls." Ol' Bullet was named for his speed, not what he looked like. He was ugly to put it gently. He was big and strong and weighed about sixty pounds, all muscle. His front feet turned in just a little like a bulldog and he was broad across the chest. A black and brown evil monster with four white feet, who loved Lizzie, Minnie and me in that order.

"It is all right, Lizzie. Just let me wipe your eyes and everything is fine." As Papa wiped her eyes and held her close he said, "Lizzie, don't let anything ever happen to Papa's little angel. Your mother would just die if you got bit by a rattlesnake."

Lizzie at first just sobbed and then said with her bottom lip stuck out, "Bad snake! Ol' Bullet took care of me, Papa. Ol' Bullet loves me!"

"That's right, Baby, but you girls should take Ol' Bullet with you when you come down here. Snakes are snakes and they are looking for a place to hibernate for the winter. They are crawling all over. I killed two today down in the west field. Keep one of the dogs close. Best if you take Ol' Bullet all the time. O.K.?"

"O.K. Papa," Lizzie said. "I don't like snakes, they scare me." She continued to shake as we headed back to the house. Minnie and I carried the four laden baskets. Ol' Bullet seemed to march ahead as if he was on guard for more snakes. Maybe that was just my imagination, but his head was carried a little higher.

Mother, wringing her apron, met us about half way across the yard, "What was all of the commotion down there at the barn?"

Lizzie blurted out, "Ol' Bullet killed a snake and saved my life." She was over her scare and still wanted to be the center of attention.

"Girls, didn't I tell you to take a dog with you down in that garden?" Mama scolded.

"Yes, Mama," answered Minnie, "I was just in a hurry and was thinking about Thanksgiving." Her head hung in shame for her actions and what could have been the outcome if Ol' Bullet had not been so quick.

"Well, girls, I'm just glad Robert and his dog showed up at the right time. You sure would have been unhappy if you had been snake bit. Plus, you could have missed Thanksgiving with Grandpa and Grandma. But, still worse, you could have died from the poison. You know the only doctor is twenty miles from us, and sometimes there is not much that can be done by the time he arrives. Only last month the Cable boy died from a snake bite."

Both girls chorused, "Yes, Mama." Minnie continued, "Mama it was my fault for not taking a dog. I just want next week to pass so we can go visiting."

"Well, it is only one week 'til Thanksgiving, and then we'll go. Now, in the house for supper and bed. Tomorrow, we will go to town and do some shopping for the few things I need to take to Grandma's for Thanksgiving dinner. Minnie, we will order your Christmas play dress if Mr. Gallager does not have something appropriate. Now scoot!"

We three kids ran ahead of Mama and Papa full of chatter and plans for tomorrow. As we went up the porch, I teased Minnie by saying, "And the next day is Sunday, and Minnie can see her boy friend, Samuel." I danced away laughing and ran into the house.

Minnie ran in the house behind me hollering at the top of her lungs, "Mama, Robert's teasing me about boys again."

Papa laughing called, "Robert, leave your sister alone." Then laughed some more and said, "Daughter, you sure do get a lot of attention at church and school. Just the price you will have to pay for being beautiful like your mother."

Mama's face turned pink, but she smiled at Papa and her eyes were very bright. Mama gazed up at Papa with those beautiful blue eyes that were full of love.

"Minnie, your father is right, now quit fussing and help me with supper. Lizzie, set the table. Robert, bring the milk from the cooler and let's eat." We all sat at our appointed places and bowed our heads for Papa to say Grace.

Thanksgiving day finally arrived, and what a glorious day! We would have the whole weekend at Grandpa's and Grandma's. At dinnertime we ate and ate, till our sides were about to bust. Then we went back and ate some more. Grandma always had a table fit for kings. Grandma laid out the standard turkey and dressing, but she also had several wild meats and lots of things like sweet potato pie and mince meat pies. I could eat about one pie per day. When you are ten going on eleven and there is that amount of food you sure can eat. But some of my cousins sure gave me a run for the money. Grandma thought that she was going to run out of food but smiled every moment, as she helped grandchildren heap their plates with more food and more pie.

Grandma and Grandpa are about the greatest people in the world. Everybody that knows them says they are the most God- fearing and hardest working people in the county. They are kind and gentle with all of the grandchildren. Despite their age, they still stand straight and have a spring in their steps. A little gray has appeared in Grandpa's hair, but Grandma's hair is still blond and beautiful. Grandma has added a few pounds over the years, while Grandpa is just as lean and muscular as he was in his younger days.

Then after dinner we had a singing. With our family of about thirty there are some good fiddle players, some fair guitar players and lots of great voices.

Just like at church, we sang hymns with beautiful harmony. When we got tired of singing hymns, we turned to patriotic songs and folk songs. When the family sang those patriotic songs you wanted to jump up and shout. At times I bet they could hear us in the next county. When we sang the "*Battle Hymn of the Republic*," the men got all teary. Most of them had served in the war. They served with the North and that did not set well with some of our neighbors who served for the South. Anyway, we sang that song and a lot more. Our Uncle John was an officer in the Union Army and had served out west, fighting Indians. Two other brothers, besides Papa had been regular soldiers. No heroes, just soldiers serving their country.

We sang right 'til supper and then up to bedtime. We had mixed quartets, trios and solos, but the very best was Mama, Minnie and Aunt Pearl. Boy, was it good! No matter what they sang or how many songs, the family wanted them to do some more. They finally just gave out. Oh, it was pretty! I saw Grandma wipe her eyes several times, and the men that are Deacons in the church kept saying, "Amen!, Amen!"

On Friday night after Thanksgiving the men moved all of the furniture out of the living room except the chairs. Then they rolled up the rug, and the family did round and square dances until they were all exhausted. The "dancing" was over about midnight. I think the best part was when Grandpa got out his harmonica. He played and did the jig. That is, he danced until Grandma put her foot down and made him stop. She was afraid he was going to have a heart attack. Boy, is he good! I told you, he acts young!

Each family brought tents for the men and boys to use for sleeping. The women could all stay in the house. Then of course, there was the barn. On the first night we boys put up a fuss to stay in the barn. Just the boys. Boy, was that a mistake. Papa and an uncle finally came in the barn about one o'clock and spent the rest of the night to just settle us down. One of the uncles stayed with us each night after that, so everyone could get some rest. We are a loud bunch.

Sunday morning dawned bright and clear. The entire family went to the First Baptist Church. We dressed up in our Sunday go to meeting clothes. Grandpa and Grandma are in hog heaven with the entire family in attendance. Of course there was a lot of singing, and our family did most of the specials that day. When Mama, Minnie and Aunt Pearl sang, the Deacons in the church sure got to "Amen'n" long and loud.

On the way home I got several tongue lashings about one thing and then another. Ate like a horse (not a mule), acted like an Indian, chased the fowl, sang too loud and off key and wouldn't go to sleep at bed time, and on and on. Papa laid down so much law that I will be in the dog house for several years. But, let me tell you, it will be worth every moment. I don't think Papa means all he says. Because every once in while, he starts chuckling about something we boys did. I think that he will, on purpose, forget all the law he laid down. I believe he is remembering some of the things he and his brothers and cousins used to do. I've heard some stories.

Mama started reminding us of our parts in the Christmas program. We had to learn lines and do acting stuff. I was not happy about being in the play. I had to wear some old thing that made me look like a shepherd or something. An old blanket with a towel around my head. Now Minnie was always the star. She played Mary and had lots of lines and sang a couple of songs. I wondered what the church would do when all of us grew up or moved. We had done the play for years, well, I know for ten years, because I was the baby Jesus for a year or two, and then Lizzie was the baby. Understand that our church is a lot smaller than where

Grandpa and Grandma go to church. They have lots of kids to do parts. Not us. We have to use every kid in some part. We even joined up with the Methodists down the road to have a play and enough actors. It was fun to be with my two friends from the Methodist Church. These two friends are brothers and about my age. So, every chance that came along we are glad to be together. Well, there are a couple of other good things that made the whole mess bearable. We are out of class to rehearse and the stockings filled with candy and fruit.

It was time for the play, and I was as nervous as a cat. We began serious rehearsals right after Thanksgiving, and the program was on December twenty. Believe it or not, the show came off without a hitch. No lines missed and no mistakes. The audience went wild, and we gave curtain call after curtain call. They acted like they had never seen, nor heard, the Nativity story before. On the way home Papa cleared up the mystery for me. "Son, your sister was magnificent and has an excellent voice. But, when your mother joined her in the singing of *"Silent Night"*, the audience was spellbound. Our girls have never sounded better."

The ride home in the wagon, under a clear sky and bright stars, made the Christmas Story even more real. Mother and Minnie hummed or sang softly all the way home. It was late, but Mother allowed us stay awake and have hot drinks and talk about the program. Lizzie slept some on the way home and wanted to stay awake, but slowly she surrendered to the sandman.

Mama turned to us and announced, "I will have a surprise for you on Christmas Day. I have been saving the surprise just for that day." We all tried to pry the surprise out of her, but to no avail. She just said, "This will be a great surprise for all of you." And with a mischievous smile on her face and twinkle in her eye she commanded, "No guessing or prodding to find out. Just go to bed, and you will find out on Christmas Day. Now, the lot of you, off to bed and sleep."

We awoke the next day, December 21, to cloudy skies and a northern wind. Papa bundled up against the weather and tended to the animals. I went out during the best part of the day and helped Papa, but during the high wind I stayed indoors. The dirt was getting so bad in the air that Papa strung up a rope from the house to the barn. By nightfall the wind had become a howling, vicious, raging beast.

On December 22, the wind was so high and the dirt and dust so thick, you could not see the barn from the house. Papa's idea of stringing a rope from the house to the barn, so he could travel back and forth, was a God-sent idea. Mama commented, "I sure am glad that you put the rope up before the storm became so bad. It's bad enough inside, but, to go out in this blinding dirt could be very dangerous."

"Papa, how about the stock?" asked Mama.

"The mules and the milk cow will be all right in the barn and the chickens are in a stout coup and should be safe. Now you can see why the animals have such a thick coat this year."

Mama looked out one of the windows at the howling storm and asked, "What about the cows in the pasture?"

"They are out of the wind down in the ravine back of the barn. They have plenty of hay for a few days. If the storm continues I will need to go down there."

"But, Papa how will you be able to see for all of the dust?" asked Minnie.

"From the rear door of the barn to the ravine is only about twenty yards. I can string some more rope out as I go, and then follow it back to the barn."

December 23, was a day of terror. The wind howled and screamed around the farmhouse. The house shook and rattled. At times it seemed it would blow away. The hard gusts made the house shake on it's foundation. Dust was so thick that you could not see the edge of the porch. Part of the reason you could not see very far, was that the dirt was so thick that it was almost like night outside. Papa carried a lantern with him when he went to the barn.

Upon his return from the barn he said, "The wind knocked me off my feet twice and blew out the lantern. I just crept along holding onto the rope. Had to re-light the lantern in the barn. The mules were rolling their eyes at every new gust. Another gust of wind would blow something up against the barn, and the mules would shy and dance around. Their skins were quivering with every new blast. The dogs have taken refuge in the barn and they whimper when some large bang occurs. At noon, if at all possible, I will go on down to the ravine and check on the stock."

We kids were scared to death. We did not cry, just sat wide eyed, hunched over and crowded together. The wind became so violent that about mid-evening Papa and Mama took us down into the storm cellar. The entrance and stairs into the cellar are on the screened-in back porch. We were out in the wind and dirt that long but the silence of the cellar was well worth the short trip. We dug the dirt out of eyes and mouths and settled down. Mama had brought books and sewing to help pass the time. She laughed and said, "You kids can read your books by the lantern like Abe Lincoln did when he was a boy. Only, he had to use a candle."

"Time to check the stock", commented Papa as he looked at his pocket watch. There was no way to tell time otherwise down in the cellar. "Anything you want from the house, Mama?"

"No, not for now, I brought our supper in the basket. I was afraid that we would be here for some time, and I prepared for just such an event. We will need things for breakfast, but we will take care of that in the morning."

"Good planning, Mama. I just wonder how the rest of the family is fairing, especially Grandpa and Grandma." As he pulled on his coat he asked, "Where are my gloves?"

"Here Papa". Lizzie had been playing with them, and as she handed them to him, she looked up into his eyes and with a pleading voice said, "Papa, please see how the dogs are doing. You know that Ol' Bullet saved my life."

"Why, Baby, that was before Thanksgiving. Does that still bother you?"

"Oh! No!, Papa, but Bullet needs to be loved and looked after just like we do."

"Very well, Angel, your wish is my command."

Lizzie jumped up and grabbed Papa's leg and demanded, "Really?"

"Your wish is my command."

"Then make the wind stop blowing!"

"Well, Angel, that is in the hand of the Almighty. But, Mama and I will say a prayer for Him to protect us and our families and all the animals. Will that do?"

"Yes, Papa."

"Then, you help your mother, and I'll be back in a while."

He eased the cellar door open and went up the stairs to the second door on the surface. For a few moments, when each door was opened you could hear the howling wind. As soon as both doors were closed, it was completely silent. We had spent time in the cellar over the years during bad clouds and tornadoes, but, this straight wind was far more terrifying than any of the other storms. The hard sudden gust made you jump almost out of your skin. Certainly not as destructive as a tornado, but could be just as hair-raising.

In perhaps an hour Papa returned, frozen to the bone and covered with dirt. "The animals are doing pretty good. But, the buildings are taking a beating. I had to nail up some boards on the barn The house has lost some shingles and a couple of window shutters. They were blown out against the barn. I don't think the chicken house is damaged much, but I could not see it very well and did not try to go to it. I did go down in the ravine using a rope. The cows are down in there. Best I could count they're all there. Just laying there. Mostly with their eyes closed against the dust and dirt. I'm not sure, but the windmill and the watertower may have blown over. I just could not see them in the dark. We still have water in the cistern and can repair the mill and the tower."

"The children have had their supper, so wash a little and eat. I have made beds for all of us," said Mama. She turned to us and said, "As soon as Papa eats, it will be bedtime." Mama raised her hand to stop the chorus of objections. "We need to rest and pray for the storm to blow out tonight, so we can go to candlelight service tomorrow night at the church. We have not missed that service in too many years to miss one now. So, get ready for bed."

The next morning the squeaking hinges on the cellar door awoke everyone. Papa was opening the door, and that was the first time we had heard the squeak over the storm. "Papa, the storm is gone, we heard the hinges!" exclaimed Minnie.

"That's right, it is really still and quiet out here, Minnie."

Slowly, he climbed the stairs and opened the door. We all rushed up the stairs to stare in disbelief at the scene that stretched before us. The sun was out in a bright shining blue sky. The temperature had to be below freezing. Frost was on some of the roofs. Trees were blown out of the ground. The windmill and the watertower were blown over. The chicken coop was turned over, and the chickens were trapped inside. Dirt was piled and drifted against everything.

The silence was eerie and like death. Not a thing moved. No sound came from the chicken coop or from any critter on the face of the earth. Mama broke the silence, "Everyone back in the cellar so you will stay warm. We will build a fire in the fireplace and get the house warm and then you can all come in to the fire."

By noon we were in the house working to clean up the mess. Well, I mean the girls were cleaning and helping Mama, and I was helping Papa. I took the mules out to exercise and cleaned the barn stalls from three days of mule apples. I also picked up all the broken branches and trash that had blown into the yard. Papa repaired several broken items and drew water from the cistern to water the mules and other animals. The water down in the pasture had to have the ice broken on the surface so the cows could drink. Papa harnessed two of the mules, tied them to the chicken coop and righted it. The chickens raised a fuss for a few moments and discovered that their world was right side up again and settled down. We filled their water trough and put out grain and corn, and all was well in the coop.

By late afternoon, the minor damaged things had been repaired, and the house was cleaned and back in order. We gathered around the fireplace and had hot drinks, while Mama and Papa discussed going to the midnight candle service at the church. Mama's argument was we had not missed a service in years, so we needed to go. Plus, if everybody stayed home there would not be a service. Papa's argument was that it was too cold. Mama finally ended the discussion by saying, "We are going. These children have been out in colder weather than this. If the wind was still blowing, it might be a different story. Also, we need to see how the neighbors have come through this storm. We have an obligation to be there and to the church. And, Papa, you will need to give help to some of the members that have damage to their places, because you know when they find out about the windmill and the tower, they are going to come over and want to help repair them. Papa, you have always helped out in the community, and people respect that. You are a leader in this church and community, and the people here look up to you for your leadership. So, no more talk, we are going and that is final!"

Papa's jaw dropped just a little, but he recovered and exclaimed, "Children, did you hear your mother? Why are you sitting around here doing nothing. Let's get busy and get ready to go!" He got up and went off in the other room muttering to himself, "Lord, help me if I ever make that woman mad at me. I do believe that was the longest speech she has ever made." When we loaded in the wagon the girls and Mama were visions. Papa and I just had on our new blue overalls and white shirts, but the women! I stood and looked first at Mama, she was wearing a white dress that I had not seen. With her blond hair she looked like an angel. Minnie had on a blue dress with a blue cape. The boys were going to go crazy tonight. Lizzie had on a pink dress with little white bows. Papa spread blankets over them to help keep them warm. He beamed at them and said, "Can't let our girls get cold. Robert, aren't our girls pretty?" I just nodded, "Yes."

The candlelight service was better than ever this year. The church was completely packed. Everyone for miles came that night. Some because of the storm, others to see how neighbors made out, but we found out that most came to hear Minnie, Mama and Aunt Pearl sing. Word had spread and those that were not at the Christmas program wanted to hear them, and those that were at the program were anxious to hear them again. But, before they sang, the congregation sang carols and heard the story of the birth of Jesus read from the Bible.

The three did about six songs. Some of the kids including the two of us had rehearsed some Bible story scenes, kind'a a repeat of some of the things we had done at the school program. The story of the Child was depicted as each song was sung. Then the preacher, in his new black frock, had all of the candles blown out until there was only one candle burning. He held the candle high in the air and said, "Into the darkness of this world a Child came and brought light as the Savior of man. His light spread and the word of the Child brought light to those in darkness." Then he turned and began to light candles all around. Then those in turn, turned and lighted the candles next to them. Slowly the light spread all over the church. Soon the building was again bright and just at the stroke of midnight, we sang *"Joy to the World"*.

The ride home, all bundled up and snuggled down in all those blankets, was heaven. Riding in the cold after the service was a journey that we children would never forget. First, we sang carols and talked about the candlelight service. We talked about the problems that the wind had caused for a lot of neighbors. We were in far better shape than some of them. One family had had their home blown away. Several families had lost all or some of their stock. The stock had turned tail to the wind and just vanished in the dark dirty elements. Walked all the way to Kingdom Come in three days of wind. Some may have frozen, others drowned in the river and still others just kept walking south, away from home and the wind. Lots of work for some of the families to get back on their feet. The preacher had offered a prayer of thanks that no one was killed or hurt. He asked, "Lord the Almighty One, please help these people, Your servants and worshipers."

"Good man, the preacher," said Papa. "He looked right religious tonight."

Mama punched Papa in the ribs and said. "Papa, don't make fun."

Papa replied, "The preacher was in good form and his sermon was better than most. And yes, he is a very good man."

"Yes, he is. And by the way, I am glad we went to the service for two reasons. First, all of the good program, the good singing and the candle-light service. But, just as important the preacher knew he could call on you," Papa was to head up a committee, a committee to do the work and to help folks to get on their feet. "See now, aren't you glad that you went? Right? Children, no one can get things done like your Papa!"

Then Minnie suddenly remembered, "This is Christmas, Mother. You have promised us all a present and a surprise." We all begged to know what was the present Mama had for all of us. She hushed us, and we rode along for a ways. Then in the quiet of that cold starry Christmas night Mama said, "Come late spring we will be having a new baby." There was complete, I mean complete silence for a moment. All you could hear was the clomping of the mules hooves on the road, and then every one began to holler with the joy of a new family member. Papa hugged Mama and we kids yelled for joy. Maybe it would be a boy and I would have somebody on my side.

From Christmas to the New Year the men worked long and hard repairing all the damage done by the three day storm. Our windmill and tower was up, repaired and working as good as ever. The house that had been blown away in the storm was the only thing not rebuilt. Those poor folks just loaded their belongings and went to her folks for the rest of the winter. Said they would return in the spring and start over, but

Papa felt they were just whipped too bad and would not be back. Most of the damage done by the storm was to small buildings and barns, so the men found that by working as a crew, all the work was done by the New Year.

Word came that Grandpa and Grandma had faired very well, with only minor damage to their property. The worst damage in the area seemed to be in our county and the center of all the damage was our community. Our community is made up of one store, two churches, a blacksmith-stable with its corral and the school. Oh, by the way, what we call our community, besides the four establishments, is composed of about ten families in a five mile radius of the church. Then, there are another twenty families living within about ten miles of the church.

If everyone came to a meeting from all the area there would be around three hundred and fifty people present. We use the school as a meeting place for civic matters and the church for all other events. The church would hold about two hundred and it was full at the candlelight service. Lots of the people who come to holiday events stay with family or friends or just camp out, as it is too far in a wagon to return home that day. Some of the people were caught out in the three day storm and had to stay with neighbors until it was over. When they got on home, they found all kinds of difficulties and problems. But, people that live way out in the country just depend on their own abilities and make repairs and go on with life. All of the people in closer helped each other.

There is one other event that occurs in our community once a year that I really do like. The two week summer brush arbor camp revival. Out of thirty plus families just about everyone comes. They may not stay for the whole two weeks. They may stay a while and then go home, but come back for the final few days. But, you can be sure that no one really wants to miss a thing. Because, once in a while the "Holy Spirit" would break loose at the meeting, and for a ten year old it was a show. Shouting and speaking in tongues sure made for an interesting meeting. Now the Baptists did not go for this sort or behavior very much and the

Methodist were aghast. But when you have Holy Rollers and Assembly of God in a revival just about anything could happen. And the Baptists sure did want the other folks to come and put their money in the collection plate, when it was collection time.

Now, everyone would bring tents and camp for the two weeks. In the afternoon we boys could hunt and ride horses, or sometimes, as it was summer, we would ride down to the river in the afternoon for a good swim. The men would come along, and it was a great time for the young boys to hear the men talk church, work, family and crops. Of course, we went to camp meeting in the morning and then at night. Sure got lots of preaching and Bible study. Really was hard on boys from about nine up to fifteen or sixteen to sit in a Bible class and preaching in the morning, and then have to come back to preaching again that night. Now preaching and singing could last up to two hours or more. I came to the place many a time that my mind could not absorb another word. Especially, when my backside was numb all the way up to my shoulders.

The New Year came without fanfare. The weather had stayed dry and, had turned cold and bitter, but I had the warm memories of Thanksgiving and Christmas. New Year did not cause much celebration at our house. Some folks had parties and lots of merriment. Papa thought those parties were almost sinful, because there was some drinking and such. So, we passed on those invitations and stayed home. Besides, Papa was worn out from all the work repairing the damage done from the three day dust storm.

At suppertime on the third of January we celebrated Lizzie's eighth birthday. She had wanted a store bought doll for a couple of years. So with the good bumper crop Papa and Mama had decided to give her a doll they had seen in Mr. Gallager's store. Papa had been to town several times helping do the repairs, and he had slipped it home one night. Lizzie's eyes became big and round when she saw the big box the doll was in. She just sat there holding the box, while we all encouraged her to open the present. She kept saying over and over, "It's so pretty. I can't rip the paper off, it's too pretty." Finally, with a bunch of coaxing and help from Mama, they removed the paper, Lizzie wanted to save the wrapping. When the lid came off, she just stared in disbelief. Then she squealed, grabbed the doll and danced around the room. She only stopped dancing long enough to hug first Mama, and then Papa, before whirling away again. When she finally settled down, Mama brought out a cake with eight candles, and we sang "Happy Birthday" to her. Her eyes shone like bright lights, and her face was just beaming.

Mama rose from the supper table and looked at her family. "This is the best time of the year. We have Thanksgiving in November, Christmas in December, Lizzie's birthday in January, Robert's in February and Minnie's in March. We will have birthday parties for Robert and Minnie to look forward to in the next two months. I love having a celebration in those five months. It makes the winter shorter and some bright spots in these cold, hard months."

We all chimed in with our thoughts on the holidays and birthdays.

Just at dusk and in the midst of our party, we heard hoofbeats in the yard and before anyone could move there was pounding on the door.

"Trouble!" exclaimed Papa as he jumped to his feet. This was only an omen and hint at the trouble about to visit our family.

He jerked the door open to find Mr. Fuller, the blacksmith, in a highly agitated state twisting his hat in both hands and shifting from foot to foot. He addressed Mama, "Oh, you must come quick. Your sister Pearl is taken deathly ill." Mr. Fuller was a big man. He filled the doorway, but he was as gentle as a kitten. We kids loved to go to his shop for he always had candy and a big smile on his face. But, tonight there was no laughter in his voice or smile on his face.

"Pearl?" We all asked in chorus. Papa exclaimed, "Man, come in out of the weather and to the fire, then you can tell us what has happened."

"Yes, thank you," He entered the house and moved to the fire. He shed his heavy coat and held his hands out to the fire and began rubbing them together. Then he continued, "Aunt Pearl came down late yesterday and has been getting worse ever since. The Preacher has gone for the doctor, but you know it is twenty miles one way, and as cold as it is it will be slow travel. Probably will be tomorrow before they can get back. Twenty miles each way in this weather will be difficult and almost impossible. Your sister seems to be worse every single passing hour." Moisture filled Mr. Fowler's eyes as he looked at Mama, "She was asking for you, so I came as quick as possible."

Without hesitation or thought Mama jumped up from the table and gave Mr. Fowler's arm a squeeze. "We thank you so sincerely. It has been a hardship on you to come out in this weather. Papa, I'll get my things, and you can take me to Aunt Pearl's," said Mama.

Papa hesitated for a few moments and then said, "Mr. Fuller, Mama is right, and I know you are tired from that twelve mile ride. Will you stay here with the children tonight? I'll take Mama in and come back in the morning. It will be too late for us to make a round trip tonight. I'll go by and tell your wife that you are spending the night at our place. You can use the extra bedroom, and it will be a great favor to us."

"I would be glad to spend the night, and you are right that is a long cold ride," replied Mr. Fuller. "You will be late getting there, and to come back tonight is too much to ask, so ya'll just go and don't worry about a thing. These children will help me do any chores that need to be done." He beamed and with a twinkle in his eye said, "I understand it is some-body's birthday. So we will go ahead with the party. Again, don't you worry, these children are like my grandchildren."

Mr. Fuller was almost like another grandpa. He was near Grandpa's age, and we all looked up to him as a leader in the church and the community. He always treated any child with kindness and affection. Every child loved and liked to be with him. He had taken our minds off of Aunt Pearl with the mention of the birthday. Some of the festive atmosphere returned to the room in spite of the urgency that pushed Mama and Papa to hurry to town.

"We can give Mr. Fowler some of my cake," exclaimed Lizzie.

While Mr. Fowler warmed by the fire and had a piece of cake, Mama and Papa made ready for the cold trip to town. In a few minutes they were ready to go.

Papa had put Mr. Fowler's horses in the barn and hitched two of the mules to the small wagon. The small wagon had a set of hoops and a canvas cover that gave some protection from the elements.

Mama and Papa both hugged each one of us and gave us a kiss. "Be good and mind Mr. Fowler." We all nodded, silenced by the fact that they were both leaving in such bad weather. Plus, we had never been separated from our parents. Papa bundled Mama in the wagon and called to us, "Mind Mr. Fowler and do your chores. Don't worry I will be home in the morning." As they drove off, Mama threw us a kiss.

Next morning Papa did not come back to the farm. During the night another storm had blown in from the north. The first one in December had lots of dust and dirt, but the second storm of the season, and the first one of the year, had brought snow and more snow. By morning there was at least a foot of snow on the flat places and three and four feet in the drifts.

It was hard to get to the barn and pens due to the ice and snow, but Mr. Fowler and I managed to tend the stock. The temperature continued to drop all day, and by the second night of the storm it was below zero and the wind had increased.

The second morning the wind was whipping the snow into a blinding nightmare. Mr. Fowler once again helped me with feeding the animals close to the house and in the barn. But, any livestock in the field had to fend alone and seek the best shelter they could find. I was sure glad a rope had been strung from the house to the barn. Another one was strung from the barn to the chicken coop and pens.

As we finished the chores late that second afternoon I asked, "How long do you think this storm will last, Mr. Fowler?"

"No way to know, Robert. I have seen these storms blow through in a day or two and then again I have seen them last for two weeks. Snowed every day, and the wind never stopped for a moment. I saw three feet of snow on the flat ground one time, and we could not get out of the house for over a week after the storm. Lots of folks died in that storm."

"Mr. Fowler, how long ago was that storm?"

"About five years ago the best I remember. I had been home from the war between the States about five or six years when we decided to move to Texas. So we decide to move to east Texas, and as the army was clearing out the Indians in this part of the state, we decided to moved on out here about two years later. That storm came roaring down from the North Pole that first year out here. Darn near convinced me to go back to our home in Kentucky or at least move south."

"Why, did you stay?" I asked, as I put out feed for the animals.

"Well, Robert, by that time, some of our family had moved to Texas, just like your family. By then, it just seemed best to stay out here. Had the blacksmith shop and livery. The town seemed to be growing and business was pretty good. But best of all we had some grandchildren out here and did not want to leave them. Just like your Grandpa, Robert."

"I sure wish Mama and Papa would come home."

"They probably can't travel due to the snow and ice, Robert. That snow is deep and would be hard pulling for even those two big mules."

Night came quickly and lanterns were lit so the final chores could be finished. The ropes were a good guide back to the house. Inside Minnie had a big fire going and a supper of hot soup ready to eat. One thing about Minnie, she had learned how to be a good cook from Mama. Boy, was I glad. We were really hungry from wading around in the snow.

The conversation, as at each meal, turned to the question of how soon would Mama and Papa be back. Lizzie was beginning to become a little whinny for her parents. Minnie did not complain about having to do the house chores for all of us, but you could tell she was really wanting them to come home. Now, Mr. Fowler had been talking to me about not letting the girls know how I felt, so I could keep them cheered up. So, I just bit down on my lip and did my best to not let my feelings show.

The third morning dawned cloudy, still and colder. Colder, if that was possible. All the outside water was frozen solid. To water the animals, water from the cistern had to be drawn and carried. Walking in the deep snow was almost an impossible task. If you waited too long the water in a bucket would freeze before being poured for the animals. Snow was now at least two feet deep and still a light sleet was coming down. About noon, the sleet stopped and the temperature rose. The cloud cover helped the afternoon to warm. But still no word from our parents. No word from town and no word on Aunt Pearl. Worry was beginning to show on our faces, and Mr. Fowler kept looking down the road, watching to see if someone would appear. As night came it began to snow again. Large, round and wet flakes that stuck to everything. Then about midnight the snow stopped and the temperature dropped some more. Dropped to below zero for the second time, and this time it froze all of the snow and the earth solid beneath.

On the fourth morning we awoke to a bright sun and a world covered in solid ice. The snow and ice was perhaps two feet thick. You could see to go to the barn and the pens, but you really had to be careful with every step or you would fall. That is when trouble struck for the second time. Mr. Fowler fell and broke his leg. We finally got him into the house, after a lot of slipping and sliding on the ice. Gee, he sure was a big man! We made him as comfortable as possible, but could not decide what to do next.

As the day wore on we three kids almost panicked. Mr. Fowler needed someone to set his leg as he was in a lot of pain. The doctor could be anywhere, in our town or still home. If the preacher got to the doctor before the snowstorm started, then they could be anywhere between the doctor's home and Aunt Pearl's. Mr. Fowler figured that the preacher and the doctor never started back due to the storm. That the storm hit, and the preacher, if he got to the doctor's, probably could not leave immediately. They would have waited till the next morning to start, but the storm hit and they may not have been able to travel.

On the fifth morning after I completed the chores, we three huddled out of earshot of Mr. Fowler. "Robert, is there enough food and water for the animals for a day or two?" asked Minnie.

"Gee, Minnie, I don't know. If the water freezes the animals will suffer. I guess you could take them some if you were really careful. We sure don't need you to break a leg."

"I will wear those rubber boots of Papa's over my boots. That will help me stay warm and keep me from sliding so much. Mr. Fowler is wearing leather sole boots and they slip real easy. I heard him saying he wished he had worn his rubber boots and that he could not understand his forgetting to wear them in this weather. Robert, we have got to have help. You are the only one that can get to town. By riding bareback on a mule with a blanket around you, the warmth from the mule will keep you warm. We will use that big horse blanket and you can cover all but your hands and face. You have good warm gloves and boots and with the blanket, you should manage. O.K.?"

"All right, Minnie. Pack me something to eat 'cause it may take me through noon to get to town, if I can."

"Robert, don't you say 'if'. You have got to find help."

"Don't worry. I'll get Number One and be ready to go in a few minutes. And don't tell Mr. Fowler. He would try to stop me."

In a matter of minutes I had put back on my warm boots, hat, scarf and coat. I chose Old Number One because if I became lost or something happened, Old Number One would go on to town because that was the way he was headed. If headed for home, that is where he would go.

I stopped by the porch and took the canvas sack that contained the food that Minnie had packed for the trip. "I'll hurry all I can and don't worry, Minnie."

"Just be careful, Robert. We need you to find somebody!" I waved and rode east down the lane and toward town.

I rode about two hours and covered close to three miles. At the fork in the road I met Carl Schmitt. Mr. Schmitt's farm lay about a mile north and on the other fork of the road.

"Robert, what in the world are you doing out in this weather?" He asked as he stopped the team of horses pulling a buckboard wagon.

I reined to a stop. "Mr. Schmitt, we need help out at the farm. Mama and Papa went to town to be with Aunt Pearl, who is sick. Mr. Fowler came to bring them word of her illness, and he stayed with us. Yesterday morning he fell and broke his leg. And, Mama and Papa haven't come back, and it's been five days! Minnie and Lizzie are at home with Mr. Fowler!" The words rushed out.

"Good Lord, boy!" He exclaimed. "You do need help. I've started to town. Why, don't you go to my house and wait for me. I'll go to town and get help and come back for you. You will be safe and warm at my farm."

"Can't I go with you? I want to see Mama and Papa." "How long have you been out in this cold, Robert?" "About three hours, I guess, Mr. Schmitt."

"With this cold and temperature as low as it is, I think you should go to my house and get warm. It's a lot colder than you realize."

"Oh, Mr. Schmitt!"

"Please, Robert. I can make better time alone and I can have your Papa back in no time, and then we will all go to your house. All right?"

"I'm really not cold with this big horse blanket around me and sitting on this warm mule, but I'll do as you ask." I replied out of respect to my elders, but I really wanted to go on to town. It was only a few more miles.

"Thank you, Robert," said Mr. Schmitt as he slapped the rumps of the horses and started to town.

I turned Old Number One north and rode slowly toward Mr. Schmitt's Farm. I worried all the way up the slope toward the Schmitt farm. The day was more than half gone and it would soon start getting dark. Mr. Schmitt would make fair time, but I doubted that he could go all the way to town and then back to the farm tonight.

I went about one half mile when I stopped on the ridge. I reined the mule around to see how far Mr. Schmitt had gone. Just as Mr. Schmitt got to a corner in the road where trees would hide him from sight, another team and wagon came into view. The two wagons and their drivers stood in stark outline against the bright snow and ice. Suddenly Mr. Schmitt stood up in the wagon and began to wave for me to come back.

Mr. Schmitt reined his team around and followed the other wagon back toward me. I kicked the mule in the ribs and started down the slope to meet them at the fork. It took only a short time for us to all meet at the junction in the road.

"Robert, you remember Mr. Higgins, the blacksmith?" asked Mr. Schmitt. "He is from the Cottonwood community."

"Yes Sir," I replied.

"Mr. Higgins just came through town hunting the doctor and the preacher. He took the wrong fork in the road and came down our road instead."

Mr. Higgins looked at Robert careful and then said, "Boy, can you take some hard news, I mean really bad news?"

I swallowed, as I was doing everything I could to appear brave, but my heart was sinking, and I feared the worse, "Yes Sir."

"Your Aunt Pearl died three days ago. Your Mama and Papa were with her all the time. She was a great teacher and a fine Christian lady."

I looked down at the back of the mule to keep the men from seeing tears in my eyes. Before I could say anything in reply Mr. Schmitt said, "Robert, there is more and it's not good. Your Papa is down, really sick. Your Mama is down, but not as sick. There are sick all over the area. It is a flu epidemic."

I sat on the mule stunned to the bone and dead of heart. My mind did not want to accept the fact that Aunt Pearl was dead, and that my parents were very ill. I finally looked up at the men and saw they were watching me very close. "What is going to happen now?" I asked softly.

"Robert, Mr. Higgins is going on to your place and help. He thinks he can set Mr. Fowler's leg, and he can be of help with the chores. We have all got to get in out of the elements before night. Now, do you feel up to riding back to the farm? You have got to brave and tell your sisters."

Very feebly I answered, "Yes, Sir." My heart had tuned to stone, and I could not feel the cold anyway. For that matter I was so numb I could not feel anything at all.

"Good, then I will go to town and check on your parents. I'll be to your place tomorrow. Mr. Higgins can help you tonight and in the morning after chores are done he is going to see if he can find the doctor. I gave him directions on how to find the main road. With everything under snow, I'm surprised that he wasn't lost long before now."

I turned Old Number One toward home and let him have his head. One fact for sure, Old Number One would never get lost. Mules were smarter than horses and most people.

Mr. Schmitt turned his team toward town, and Mr. Higgins followed me down the lane toward the farm. Time seemed to stand still in my mind. Suddenly we were at the house. The girls came running out of the house, having heard the hoof beats and the wagon.

"Robert, where are Mama and Papa, and what are you doing back?" called Minnie.

"Let me put the animals in the barn, and then I will come in and tell you what has happened. This is Mr. Higgins from the Cottonwood community, and he will be spending the night with us."

Mr. Higgins spoke up, "Howdy, young ladies. Robert, let me put your mule and my horses up, and you go on in where it is warm. You need to get by the fire You have been out in the cold a long time. While you warm up, you can catch them up on the news."

I had been trying to put off telling the girls, but now there was no way around having to tell them. "Thank you, Mr. Higgins. Guess I'm getting a little cold." Really, I didn't know if it was the cold, or being numb with fear. Fear of what was going to happen to our parents.

I slid down off the mule and handed Mr. Higgins the reins and the big horse blanket. Hr. Higgins clucked at his team and started them off around the house to the barn. I went up the steps and followed the girls inside.

Both girls were full of questions, but I held them off by saying, "Let me get out of this coat and my boots off." I kept my head down trying to get control before I looked into the eyes of my sisters. Then when I raised my head I could not stop the tears. They just ran down my cheeks. The girls stared at me wide eyed, but kept their silence. Finally I said very softly, "Aunt Pearl is dead." With that announcement both girls burst in tears, even before I could finish my sentence about our parents.

Then Minnie, through her tears asked, "Where are Mama and Papa?"

My head dropped on my chest and I said, with a whisper, "Papa is very ill, and Mama is down with the influenza. That is what made Aunt Pearl die, and Mama and Papa are very sick."

Lizzie blurted out, "Are Mama and Papa going to die?"

With all the effort I could muster, I said, "Lizzie, I don't know." Then I gushed out the rest in an effort to get it all said, "I met Mr. Schmitt at the fork of the road that goes to their farm. That is about the time Mr. Higgins showed up looking for the main road. Mr. Schmitt has gone to town to see about our parents and will be out here in the morning. Mr. Higgins is going to try to set Mr. Fowler's leg. Tomorrow, Mr. Higgins is going to look for the doctor." My voice broke, and I could not say anything further for several minutes. I never cried out loud, but tears kept running down my cheeks and finally I choked up and said no more.

There was a knock on the front door. "Oh, poor Mr. Higgins," said Minnie, "I forgot he was out in the cold." She rushed to the door and let him in. "I'm sorry, Mr. Higgins, please come to the fire and warm." Suddenly Minnie was in control of her emotions and of the situation.

"Let me fix you and Robert something hot to drink, and then you can look at Mr. Fowler's leg. He has been in lots of pain, but has said little about it."

While, Mr. Higgins removed his hat, coat and gloves, he asked. "Are you young people O.K.? I mean, about your folks and your aunt?"

Minnie replied first, "Oh, Mr. Higgins this is such a shock and so sudden. I'm numb."

Lizzie, through sad eyes looked at Mr. Higgins and asked, "Did you see Mama and Papa?"

"No, young lady, they would not let me in to see them. Said they were too sick, and that I might get whatever made them sick. I'm, sorry."

The only sound that filled the room was the fire crackling and some soft sobs.

After a short time Mr. Higgins said, "Let's have a look at Mr. Fowler's leg." Minnie, having regained her composure went ahead of Mr. Higgins into the bedroom where Mr. Fowler was lying on the bed. He was so big and heavy that the girls could not do anything but cover him and keep him warm. Mr. Higgins followed her into the bedroom and introduced himself to Mr. Fowler. "Mr. Fowler, I'm not a doctor, but in the war I was in a medical unit and helped the doctor on lots of cases. I think I can set that leg, but understand if we don't get it straight and it heals crooked, you may have a limp."

"Man, do the best you can. I don't have many options, and you look like a honest man. At least you did not beat around the bush. You came out and gave it to me straight. If you can stop the pain, I can endure a crooked leg. So, get on with it."

Mr. Higgins spoke to Minnie, "I know you folks are good solid teetotalers. Most good Baptists are, but do you have any whiskey in the house for medical use?"

"Yes, we do have a bottle. Just a minute, and I'll get it." In a moment she was back with the bottle of whiskey and handed it to Mr. Higgins.

Mr. Higgins looked at the three of us and said, "I think it will be best if you wait in the other room."

Mr. Fowler spoke up, "He is right kids. This gentleman is going to help me, and you need to go to the living room." We three filed out slowly and Minnie turned at the door. "If you need help you call me, I have helped Papa with lots of animal doctoring. It does not bother me, and he says I am better than lots of men. I have never set a leg or it would have already been done!" She tossed her hair and shut the door behind her.

"Boy, I'll bet she will be a tough one to handle when she is grown and married. Poor man that crosses her. Now Mr. Fowler, I bet you are a good teetotaling Baptist deacon. Am I right?"

"Mr. Higgins, you are quite correct, but that whiskey is for medical use, so hand me the bottle. Let me shed my righteous indignities about drinking, and let's get on with the setting of this leg."

"Mr. Fowler, one thing about you Baptists, you are practical. But, I like being a Methodist better. A drink now and then is fine, and even a little dancing, but you folks make it hard on a man getting some of the grit out of his craw. Now, bottoms up on that bottle because this may hurt like Hell's brimstone."

Mr. Fowler was taking swig after swig of the whiskey in an effort to kill the pain when Mr. Higgins set the bone. As Mr. Fowler drank, Mr. Higgins worked the boot off and cut away the pants leg. After about fifteen minutes and almost a whole bottle, Mr. Fowler's speech was very slurred, and he was very happy. "O.K., my good Methodist friend, set this thing before this fine glow wears off."

Mr. Higgins answered, "Fine, but first let me have a shot of the whiskey." Mr. Fowler handed him the bottle and Mr. Higgins took a big jolt.

Mr. Higgins gave Mr. Fowler a rope that he had tied to the bedstead and said, "Hold on with all your strength. When we are ready I will count to three and then pull. Let's hope for the best my good Baptist friend, and this leg will be good as new." With that order, Mr. Higgins took Mr. Fowler's ankle in his hands and said, "Hold on now, and I'll count to three. One, two..." at that point Mr. Higgins jerked with all his might, and the bone popped into place. "Three."

Mr. Fowler had only grunted when the bone popped in place. "Mr. Higgins."

"Yes, Mr. Fowler."

"I hope your bone setting is better than your counting."

"I do too, Sir. Now let me splint this leg with these two short slats I found in the closet. I bet they were from an infant's bed. Just right for splints. I forgot to look for something in the barn, I was so darn cold, but the Lord does provide. Hey, my good Baptist friend?"   "Thank the Lord for whiskey and bed slats, my good Methodist friend."

"How is the pain?"

"Feels one hundred percent better."

"By the way, my good Baptist friend, thank the Lord for a so, so moderate Methodist."

"A-MEN." And with that Mr. Fowler passed out.

The next morning dawned bright, still and clear. The temperature was standing right at zero and by mid-morning Mr. Higgins was on his way. Mr. Fowler on the other hand had a hangover larger than all outdoors. He was gracious to everyone, but sure was glad when we left him alone, and it was quiet. We waved goodbye to Mr. Higgins as he drove off. Minnie had fixed him enough food for a couple of days. We also told him that when someone came by we would try to get word to his family about where he was, and what was happening.

All day we watched down the lane for Mr. Schmitt. The hours drug along and time just almost stood still. Mr. Fowler was better by afternoon and had eaten a good meal and was resting. About every half hour he would call out, "See anyone, yet?"

"No, Mr. Fowler," we would reply. He was just as anxious to hear from town as we were. He had family, and when he had heard about the flu epidemic he was very concerned.

We had just about given up hope that anyone was coming that afternoon, when a wagon appeared down the lane. It was Mr. Schmitt. I grabbed my coat and hat, ran down the road to meet him. He did not look me in the eye or say much. Just drove on without asking me if I wanted to ride. Very strange manner for Mr. Schmitt and his gentle mannerisms, and I became very uneasy.

He drew the team up to the house as Minnie and Lizzie burst from the house shouting "Where are Mama and Papa? Are they O.K.? When are they coming home?"

Mr. Schmitt climbed down from the wagon and looked at each one of us. "Let's go in the house, children, I'm cold to the bone." By that time Mr. Fowler, with aid of a chair for a cane, came into the living room. All of us gathered around the fireplace. We gazed into the fire and waited for Mr. Schmitt to give us the news from town. Mr. Schmitt finally broke his silence, "That was the longest ride I have ever made. The cold sure can hurt, but what I have to tell all of you is going to hurt more. Children, you must be brave. Your Father died about sundown yesterday, and your Mama passed away a few hours later. When we told her that he was dead, all the light went out of her eyes and she just stopped wanting to live."

Silence filled the room. The only sound was the crackling of the fire. After a while Minnie asked with a dull voice, "Where are Mama and Papa?"

"Sugar, they are out in the wagon."

That broke the silence. All three of us broke down and cried. Minnie tried to comfort the two of us, but the wailing was uncontrollable. The two men dried our eyes over and over and tried words of condolence, but nothing could kill the pain the three of us felt. Both men had a great deal of difficulty not breaking down.

Lizzie was the first to stop crying and demanded, "We can't leave Mama and Papa out in the cold, we need to bring them in to the fire."

Mr. Fowler gathered her up in his arms and said, "Little one, they can't feel the cold. They are fine where they are."

Suddenly Minnie wailed, "Oh, the baby. Mama was gong to have a baby in the spring." We all started crying even harder.

Mr. Schmitt stood and drew on his coat, "I'll put them in the smoke house for now. They will be fine there. After the storm passes, we will have to wait for the ground to thaw so we can dig graves for them. We will come back and carry them to the cemetery at that time." He returned in about an hour. "I fed the animals and put my team in the barn. Do you have enough room for me to spend the night?"

"Certainly, Mr. Schmitt." Minnie replied. Then, having regained some control over her crying, she asked, "What will happen next?"

"Minnie, my wife and some of the women will be here tomorrow, and I will take Mr. Fowler back to town so he can be with his family." Never had Mr. Schmitt called Mr. Fowler by his first name, but he turned to him and said, "Henry, I have bad news for you, too. The influenza has struck all over the county. Your wife is terribly ill and your oldest daughter is not expected to live. I'm sorry to have tell you this way, but I don't guess there is a easy way. Sorry, my friend."

Mr. Fowler sat looking into the fire for long time and then whispered, "Thank you, Karl." Both men extended their right hands and shook hands. Concern and pain for the other passed between those two men. The compassion shared was apparent in their eyes. Eyes were moist with grief and concern for the other. "What about your family, Karl?"

"They are fine for now, but the illness seems to travel in the air and has hit almost every home."

Minnie rose and asked, "Would you like some supper?" She moved off without waiting for an answer and motioned for Lizzie to go with her. Soon we heard Lizzie setting the table and Minnie singing softly, *"What a Friend We Have In Jesus."*

I could only remember Mama and Papa riding off in the wagon. They both waved, and Mama threw us a kiss. We will never see them again.

CHAPTER TWO

The cold persisted night and day. There had been more snow, which had just added to the misery. Reports of the number of dead came with every visitor and passer by. The influenza had struck every home in the country. The doctor never came, the preacher finally found him. Found him and his entire family dead. The doctor had shot himself. There was a note that said he could not face life after the loss of his family and the inability to help the people that had depended on him for healing. Healing that he could not bring to his own family, much less others.

The influenza had taken many lives, some directly, some indirectly. Death came in the form of illness, suicide or freezing. Several families had frozen when they became too weak to attend to each other, or too weak to fix food and keep a fire going. The combination was too much for the body to withstand. The final count will never be known, but the unofficial count was over two hundred. Almost two thirds of the community and surrounding farms were affected. Some members of the community just vanished. They probably tried to get help, became too weak and froze to death out in the open. They would become lost and disoriented in the blizzard, causing them to wander off into gullies and ravines looking for shelter. There they would die and never be found. Many succumbed to the cold when everyone was too weak to keep a fire or even fix a meal. A few had nervous breakdowns or just went crazy. Bad all around.

The cold outside numbed the body, but the cold in the heart and mind did more to devitalize the spirit than all the cold in the world. More than a week had passed since Mr. Schmitt had brought the bodies of Mama and Papa back to the farm. Life staggered on for us three children, but there was no joy or merriment around the house. Chores were done automatically and listlessly. I didn't remember doing just little things. Things that should have stuck in my mind. I would bring in the eggs and then go back and try to do it all over again. I would take the bucket to milk the cow and discover that she had already been milked. Back in the house I would ask who had milked the cow. But no one paid attention to my strange behavior.

Minnie moved about the house in a trance. Her motions were dreamlike and without focus. She had cried off and on real hard for a day or two, and then the tears had stopped, and she ceased to be a child anymore. Her face was drawn and her eyes dull. She had taken charge of the house and the meals, but never a smile and hardly a word passed her lips. I saw her several times just standing and looking out the window at the smokehouse. Staring at space and some object that I could not see. Minnie would set the table, serve food and clean up without saying one word. I, like my sisters, did not need much food during these days. More was thrown out, than we ate.

Lizzie sat in a trance and talked to her doll in monotones. She stroked the doll's hair and hummed softly to it, or spoke in monosyllables. She only moved when told to come eat, go to bed or do this or that. She ate little when she was told to go to the table for a meal. But, the worse part was the dead and vacant look in her eyes. Lizzie was not the bouncing, bubbling ball of energy that had stormed through the house only a few days ago. She was listless and unseeing. I walked right up to her to hand her a cup of hot milk, and she made no move of recognition. I put the cup in her hand, and she just sat there staring at it, not knowing what it was or what to do.

I, at first, tried to be a "man" and do the chores, take charge and most of all not cry. Despite everything I did, when I was in the barn alone with Ol' Bullet, all I could do was cry. The hardest part was passing the smokehouse time after time each day. The knowing that Mama and Papa were in there, frozen solid, dead and waiting a burial. Waiting for the weather to warm enough that graves could be dug for a double funeral. I had dreams, dreams that were horrible, but I could not remember the next day. I would wake up in the middle of the night in a cold sweat and shaking all over. My life was a shambles. My Mama and Papa were not going to join us around the supper table ever again.

I felt each day as if I would die. I would never hear my Mama's laughter. Never hear her sing with Minnie and Aunt Pearl, not ever again. Never hear Papa's voice call out to me when I was daydreaming. His laughter would never fill the house. Never.... never....oh, why did this happen to us? I knew that Minnie and Lizzie were hurting, but I did not know how to talk to them, or how they could talk to me. The silence just became deeper and deeper.

We had no family to come and help, only neighbors and some people from the church. It would be difficult for them, for they had deaths and illness to tend to at home. Mr. Fowler had gone home, only to take the flu and die within one week. Mr. Higgins froze searching for the doctor. Mr. Schmitt lost several members of his family.

The school did not reopen with the new year, and none of the churches were holding services. The preacher had stopped trying to go to every home that had a death. He sent word that when the earth thawed, graves would be dug, and graveside services would be held.

People were afraid to gather in large groups. Some said the illness was passed either at the school Christmas program or at the church midnight service. Actually, the influenza invaded the community through several people who had gone outside the area for business or to visit relatives. It would be learned later the illness had spread across the whole area in a matter of days to touch the majority of the people.

About two weeks after losing Mama and Papa, along with Aunt Pearl, we learned that Grandpa and Grandma were stricken with the deadly influenza and had died. Out grief just magnified and life became grimmer. We would learn later that all of our family had been hit, and hit hard. At the Thanksgiving dinner there had been five families beside Grandpa and Grandma. Of those thirty odd people, only fifteen were left. Three in our family, Uncle Nate and his wife and three children, Aunt Bess and three children and Aunt Margie and two children. The flu had taken all the men, but Uncle Nate and Uncle John,. We had lost two grandparents, two uncles, three aunts and fourteen cousins, plus our parents. The irony of it all was that we were not alone. Every family would visit some cemetery when the weather warmed.

The loneliness of each day grew and grew. We three spoke little or not at all. There just wasn't anything we could say. Then a new shock hit me. I found that Minnie had been going out to the smokehouse and sitting and talking with Mama and Papa. When I could ask her, "Why are you going out to the smokehouse?", she replied, "I just feel close to them there. I can talk and ask questions about how to take care of things. I had forgotten how to make lye soap, but when I went out and sat with Mother, I remembered. Robert, I know that they are dead and can't talk to me, but it is a comfort. They look so peaceful."

"Minnie, you never wear any of the clothes that Mama made for you. You only wear overalls and a shirt like Lizzie and me. Why?"

"Robert, I just can't wear them. They make me think of Mama and Papa too much."

This was the most she had said for over three weeks. At least all in one statement. I looked at her real close and asked, "Minnie what will become of us? Where will we go? Who would want us? We don't have any family to stay with, and I sure don't want to go to an orphan's home We can't be separated!" We hung onto one another and the tears came. For Minnie it was the first cry in days. For me, it was just another cry in many every day.

"Robert, I just don't know. I heard some say that the only relatives we have, close by are Uncle Nate and Aunt Pettie. But, I don't want to live with them. They were real strange at the Thanksgiving get-together. Papa, said that Uncle Nate was always trying to borrow money from some member of the family or borrow grain, tools or animals. Things you would never see again, if you loaned them to him."

"Isn't there anyone else we can live with?"

"There is Uncle John and his family in the New Mexico Territory. I don't know if they would take us in. But, we sure don't want to live with Uncle Nate."

For once in our lives, Minnie and I totally agreed on one subject. But another thing had happened in the last few minutes. We were talking. Talking about our future and what might happen. Oh, there was one more thing we agreed on, to stay away from these relatives if at all possible.

Then out of the blue, the weather changed and warmed. Here it was the end of January, and the weather had changed to almost springlike. The winds went to the Southwest, and warm days returned. The winds were like you have in March, not at the beginning of February. All of the adults said, "Watch out, that Old Man Winter is teasing us and will come storming in just when we least expect it."

In a matter of a few days all of the ice and snow had melted. The earth thawed and the very event that we dreaded the most was upon us. Two men from the church came to inform us that a group from the church would be out the next day. We would need to be ready, and they would take Mama and Papa to the cemetery for burial.

Fairly early the next morning some of the ladies and two men from the church arrived. They took Mama and Papa in the house and dressed them and placed them in pine boxes. They had brought the pine boxes with them from town. When they finished, the two pine boxes were loaded in one of our wagons. Old Number One and Number Two were hitched to the wagon , and we were ready to go. We kids rode in the second wagon, the one that had brought the two men and the women to the farm. We were told that we needed to hurry because with the warm weather the bodies would begin to smell. We were also told to wear black to the funeral. But, we did not have black. All I had was blue coveralls and the girls just had plain dresses, except for their Christmas dresses, and they couldn't wear them. So the ladies said just wear your heavy coats and keep them buttoned.

They told us that there had been graveside services all over the country. The preacher was almost exhausted from riding from cemetery to cemetery. A couple of the men had taken a surrey and were taking him from service to service. He would be at our cemetery for that day only, and was waiting on us.

When we arrived we got another shock. There stood Uncle Nate and Aunt Pettie, all dressed up in black and trying to look pious and humble. They had been notified several days ahead, because they had to come about thirty miles. A telegraph message to the sheriff at the countyseat had notified them, so they had plenty of time to arrive.

Uncle Nate is about five feet six inches tall and weighs well over two hundred pounds. Aunt Pettie is a little shorter, by five inches at least. She could not have been over five feet. It was hard to tell which one was the biggest around. They were large. That was the word Papa used to be polite. They were decked out in black, following the code of proper dress, not like us. Minnie whispered, "Those clothes look brand new!"

Aunt Pettie's dress had lots of ruffles and things, all in black. With a prim little black hat and veil. The dress, many sizes smaller would have been great on somebody else. On her it looked like a great big black hog out of the mud. Papa would kill me for thinking things like that. She even carried a stylish umbrella, also black.

Uncle Nate was prancing about, trying to look important. He would shuffle from one group of mourners to another group, always talking in subdued tones. He gave orders to the preachers and then to the mortician, back and forth, jumping around like a fat toad. The mourners all tried to be engaged in conversation when he approached. He didn't even notice, he just flitted on and looked for a sympathetic ear.

To make things worse, they had rented a black buggy from somewhere and even had a driver. They were putting on airs that made you choke. You could hear the whispers, "Wonder where she got the black wagon canvas"….. "He looks like a big black balloon"… "They look like matching black bookends." Uncle Nate and Aunt Pettie were full of themselves, and the mourners were making fun of them.

They came three days early and dropped in on Aunt Bess unannounced. Just like them to be pushy. Aunt Bess was very unhappy about them barging in on her. She had her own grief with the losses in her family. Sure, Uncle Nate had lost his parents, Grandpa and Grandma, but Aunt Bess had lost a husband, her parents, three children and the greatest Mother-in-law and Father-in-law in the world.

The services were simple and short. Mrs. Barton played the pump organ, that had been brought out from the church. The preacher removed his hat, and the crowd of people became quiet. He was much sadder than the last time we saw him. He read some of Mama's and Papa's favorite scripture and had a prayer. Then he looked over the group and said, "Each one of you knew these two fine Christians. They attended church diligently, and with that same diligence they attended their farm, their children and their families. You can't find a man or a woman that was more willing to give of time and help than these two. They will be missed by friends and family." He turned from the group and lifted his face toward heaven and worded a prayer, "Lord, we commend the souls of these, your servants, into Your hands. We pray for the members of the family left in this mortal world. We further pray for all the souls that You have taken from our midst. We give thanks for their contributions to the schools, churches, communities and families. We give You the praise for all blessings, love, kindness and Your gift of salvation through Your Son, the Lord Jesus Christ. Amen!"

He turned back to the group and announced, "Mrs. Barton is going to play some of the favorite songs that Aunt Pearl, Minnie and her Mama sang for us so many times. We will miss that music and those angelic voices. But, two of those are singing in the heavenly Father's choir today. Singing of joy and no more tribulation. Now let the music, like angel wings, surround you and give you comfort."

The organ music softly filled the our ears, hearts and the space around us. The soft warm wind and the music seemed to mingle. The music was like the wings of angels. Soft and then stronger, filling the air. Some of the group hummed along, but most just stood and wiped tears from their eyes. After some time the preacher spoke once more. "Food has been taken to Aunt Bess's and you are invited to come over and visit with the family and eat before going home."

The three of us just sat in some chairs by the grave, watched and listened to the service. Our tears were all gone for now, but later I was sure there would be some hard moments. Minnie just smiled, so lovely and sweetly to everyone. Just like Mama in her mannerisms. Lizzie and I held on to each other for dear life and did not mutter one word. We hardly noticed Aunt Marjie and Aunt Bess when they sat with us, or when they led us to the wagons. They tried to distract us from the filling of the graves, but we pulled away. Both of us ran back to the graves. We stood close to the graves and watched them slowly filled with dirt. It was hard to see the graves as the tears begin to flow from my eyes. I could not look at Minnie or Lizzie. My vision was too blurred.

When the men started covering the graves, Mr. Barton , the county sheriff, handed Uncle Nate a shovel. "I'm sure out of respect for your brother you will want to help cover these graves!"

Uncle Nate started to object and "I'm, ...Ah...now...just...a... moment."

Mr. Barton broke in, and in a voice of iron he said to him, "Shovel! Damn you! You either shovel or never set foot in this county again. These men have dug graves for all of your family, and you have not turned a finger to help. Don't give me any arguments about being in mourning, too fat, too far from home or anything! SHOVEL!"

Everyone stood open mouthed and shocked. Never had anyone heard Mr. Barton speak in that tone of voice. Uncle Nate took the shovel and grumbling under his breath, he began to shovel soil back into one of the graves. He was so fat that after a few shovels, he shed his coat and then his vest, but he did as he was told and shoveled dirt until both graves were covered.

After the graves were filled, those attending the service came around and shook hands with us, Aunt Marjie and her children, and Aunt Bess and her children. To our surprise they did not offer to shake the hands of Uncle Nate, Aunt Pettie or their children. Each one expressed some words of comfort to us and declined the invitation to come over to Aunt Bess's. They did not want to attend a large gathering or be around Uncle Nate, I guess.

We loaded into our wagon and Aunt Marjie's wagon. Aunt Bess and Aunt Marjie along with their children, had come to the funeral in Aunt Marjie's. Aunt Bess got into our wagon and we started down the lane toward town and her house. To get our minds on something else Aunt Bess said, "Now, we have got to decided what to do with your farm. I know your Mama and Papa would want you to have the place." I looked back at the cemetery one last time. The two mounds of dirt looked so lonesome. That was the last time I would see my Mama's and Papa's graves for many years.

To make things worse, if they could be, as we rode back to Aunt Bess's I realized that today was my birthday. I was eleven. I bit down on my lip and pulled my head and face down in my big coat. I didn't want anyone to see my tears. I sure wasn't going to mention that this was my birthday. Not on the day we had buried Mama and Papa.

By the time we arrived at Aunt Bess's, we knew something was eating at her. She had remained silent the rest of the way to her house. Silence was not a part of Aunt Bess's character or nature. When we all got in the house, we realized she was in a fury, and then we found out what had put a burr under her saddle blanket.

"I have held my peace up until now, but, Aunt Marjie, did you know that Uncle Nate and Aunt Pettie spent some time over at Grandpa's and Grandma's place on their way here. That is twenty miles out of the way, but they sure have looked everything over. They even spent a night or so there. Looking over the property and planning, 'WHAT THEY', were going to do with 'THEIR PROPERTY.'"

Aunt Marjie's mouth dropped open, "They did what? They have been over there digging through all of Grandpa's and Grandma's things? What did they cart off?"

"Nothing that I could tell, from what they unloaded from the wagon when they came barging in here. I looked in the wagon, and it was empty. They could have something in their bags, but I doubt they are that brazen."

"Oh, I would not put anything past that crowd. Sneaky, is what I call them. Can't trust them out of your sight." Boy, Papa had had them pegged right, and Aunt Marjie just put our feelings into words. Sneaky, under handed and besides all that, they both are bossy.

"Well, I've got a little surprise for them when they get here. Mr. and Mr. Barton are coming over. Judge Long from the countyseat has been here for several days trying to help families clear up titles. He is making quitclaim deeds and will record the transfers at the courthouse. He will be here in a few minutes. He saw us go by the Hall place, and he said he would watch and follow us. We will wait for," she spat out, "Uncle Nate and his greedy bunch of jackals, and we will have supper. Then my surprise!"

Let me tell you a little about my two aunts. That is what they are, my two aunts. They are not related in anyway, other than they are sisters-in-law. But, they walk alike, they talk alike and they look alike. They are even both dark headed and have blue eyes They are both stout women, not fat, just stout. When they hug you, they almost squeeze all the breath out you. Papa figured that if his mules got down and could not plow, he would harness the two of them up, and they could do the job. Boy, did that make Mama mad to hear talk about her sisters-in-law that way!

There was a knock at the door. "Robert, will you see who is at the door?" I ran to the door and opened it for a short man with white hair. Snow white. "You must be Robert," he said as he stuck out his hand and shook mine. "I'm Judge Long. I knew your Mama and Papa very well. I knew your entire family. Mighty good people. What a loss!" He proceeded into the house. Everybody knew the judge. He was a chubby jolly man with his cane and his case for papers. He never went anyplace without them. He was dressed in a black suit and hat. He looked very imposing, even if he was only five feet five inches tall. He walked with dignity and purpose. The ladies all said he was the perfect gentleman.

Just as I started to close the door, the sheriff and his wife pulled up in a buckboard. They waved, and I held the door for them. They crowded into the house to a chorus of greetings and back slapping. Even at the time of funerals, you can only be sad for so long. At least that is what I thought. Boy, how little did I know about anything.

Mr. Burton is a giant of a man, but his wife was very small and dainty. When he came in the door he filled the frame. When she came in, it was like a child had entered the house. Only in size that is. She is a charming and beautiful lady.

In a few minutes Uncle Nate and Aunt Pettie, in all their finery, came in the house with their brood, and without as much as knocking. Walked in, just like they owned Aunt Bess's place. Uncle Nate was leading the column of moochers. He strutted in and with a loud voice demanded, "When do we eat?" Aunt Pettie followed, and voiced her opinion, "I hope it is soon." Their four kids were a sneaky looking foursome. They kept looking in drawers and shelves on the sly. They were real mousy, and when they looked at you, it was out of the corner of their eyes. Like they were hiding something.

Glen, the oldest, by all reports was dumb. He was not in school and had quit in the fifth grade. He went around pulling one ear and mumbling to himself. He slouched and kind of slid his feet along as if they were too heavy to pick up. His brother, George, was about my age and was known in the family as a bully. Around adults he was the perfect gentleman, but away from the adults, he became loud and bossy. Just like his parents. Then there were the twins. They were little whiny brats. Their clothes never quite fit, and their hair always needed to be combed. They just sat around and looked sad and pitiful. Never moving much and being very quiet, 'til they started whining. All four were creepy, sneaky and dirty. They had not put on the finery that their parents were displaying. I know it was winter, but when did they have their last bath? Ugh! Oh, yeah, when they ate, they used their hands most of the time, like they did not know what a knife and a fork were. Ugh!

Aunt Bess ignored the fact that they did not knock and began to make over them and pour sweet attention on them, like she had found a long lost relative. The judge and Mr. and Mrs. Barton were taken aback a little, due to what Aunt Bess had said to them on a previous meeting. But, she sure sugared them up and set the stage for her little surprise. Little surprise! Ha! Ha! I'll bet it was going to be a BIG surprise, Aunt Bess had planned for them. She was having too much fun, and Uncle Nate and Aunt Pettie were eyeing her with suspicion. But, she continued carrying off her plan all through the evening meal.

"Now, let's all settle down in the living room and have coffee and some hot chocolate for the children." She served Uncle Nate and his wife first and then his children. Boy, was she laying it on. I didn't know what she was up to, but she sure had our attention. Even Lizzie had caught on that there was something very unusual about to happen. Minnie was hurrying around helping Aunt Bess set the stage. Aunt Bess's children and Aunt Marjie's children were as quiet as church mice. That should have been a giveaway, if anything was going to get your attention. The judge and Mr. and Mrs. Barton were hiding their mouths behind their hands to keep from snickering out loud.

Then she dropped the bomb right in Uncle Nate's lap, just after he got all settled and was acting like a king. He had already announced, that as the only living man in the family, he would be looking after Grandpa's and Grandma's affairs. And as the only man he would supervise Aunt Bess and Aunt Marjie as to how they should handle their affairs. Further, he would take over Mama's and Papa's place and see to the disposition of the property. Boy, that last idea sure scared the three of us. Our eyes got big and our hearts sped up....Uncle Nate looking after us!

Well, to say the least the next few minutes were probably, due to the circumstances, one of my fondest memories. On another day I would have been rolling in the floor, but as it was, all we could do was be quiet, watch and wait for the show.

The BOMB was dropped. "Uncle Nate are you comfortable?" Aunt Bess asked.

"Why yes, Aunt Bess. Certainly was an excellent supper, and the dessert was out of this world." Boy, he should know! He had three pieces, and now he was really full, full of pie and of himself. His biggest trouble was his mouth was too far from the table, due to his large stomach. He kept getting crumbs all over his black vest.

Even Aunt Pettie was all puffed up with importance, now that her husband was going to be important. She had tried to act so refined at the supper table. She kept crooking her little finger when she picked up her cup. If her children had had half of the table manners she tried to display, they would have been angels.

Aunt Bess moved over by the judge and asked him, "Judge Long, would you please read the documents you brought with you? Matter of fact, perhaps you would just go over all the documents you have."

"My pleasure, Aunt Bess!" He almost bowed to her and cleared his throat. Taking several papers from his case he spread them out on a small table and said, "Now, just where should I begin? Haa, yes...let's start with this one." He adjusted his reading glasses and smoothed down his white mustache.

Uncle Nate suddenly sat up straight, "Is this something you and I should go over privately, Judge?" He looked very startled.

"No, I don't think that will be necessary. Now, this is the last will and testament of Grandpa and Grandma. They recorded this will at the courthouse some three years ago."

Uncle Nate sputtered, "I never knew that there was a will, I should have been notified!" He semi-rose from his chair.

"Why?" asked the judge, looking at Uncle Nate over his glasses.

"Why? Why, I am the only living male in this family, and all matters should be taken up with me!" Uncle Nate put his two hands together like a church steeple and tried to look important.

"Hardly!" blasted the judge. "Now, just keep still and keep quiet, or the sheriff will escort you out of the room. Am I clear, Sir?"

BOY! OH, Boy! You should have seen the look on Uncle Nate's face and that open mouth of his wife's! You could have tossed an orange into that cave. They were stunned speechless with such stern instructions from the judge. They exchanged glances and looked sick, for some reason.

"Now, if we are ready, I'll read the will. As I said, this is the recorded, legal, last will and testament of Grandpa and Grandma Carter." The judge glanced all around the room.

I, William Henry Carter and my wife Elizabeth Frances Brown Carter, both being of sound mind and of good health, do swear and attest to the following in this joint will:

In the event that I, William Henry Carter should precede my wife in death, then all my worldly goods I bestow upon her, except $100 I give to the Baptist church where I am a member. She may divide and dispose of our joint property in a later will as she sees fit.

In the event that I, Elizabeth Frances Brown Carter should precede my husband in death, then all my worldly goods I bestow upon him, except

$100 I give to the Baptist Church where I am a member. He may divide and dispose of our joint property in a later will as he sees fit.

In the event we should both pass into death together, we desire that the following items go to our family members:

Grandma's Bible goes to Minnie.

$200 will be given to the Baptist Church.

All our clothes will be given to the church to give to the needy.

Then all of our land, equipment, tools, animals and stock shall be sold and divided between the living heirs of our issue, or the descendants of those heirs.

We hereby appoint the court to be executor of our estate.

Herein signed by:

William Henry Carter	*Elizabeth Frances Brown Carter*
husband	*wife*

Recorded volume 12 Page 284

Witnessed by:

Henry Ward Long, Judge	*Sally Rose Mills, County Clerk*

With a sigh, the judge appeared to be relishing the moment, "Well, now, that takes care of the reading of the will. As the court is appointed the executor in this will and as I am the judge, I appoint myself as executor."

Uncle Nate jumped to his feet and hollered, "That's not legal, this is not right. I should be executor and be handling my parents' affairs. There must be a later will or some document."

The sheriff rose from his chair and towered over Uncle Nate, "Uncle Nate, sit down and be quiet, or I'll place you under arrest for disturbing the peace!"

That startled Uncle Nate. He turned white, his mouth gaped open. He looked up at the sheriff and over at the judge and slowly sank into his chair.

"Now, to the will of Aunt Bess's and Aunt Marjie's husbands. They leave everything to you individually. You both have read the wills, and if there is no discussion, I see no need to reread them. Do you both agree here in front of witnesses?"

Both aunts answered, "We agree." They would be fairly rich widow ladies after Grandma's and Grandpa's farm was sold. The sale price would be divided equally between the five sons or their heirs. That would include Uncle Nate, Papa's heirs, Uncle John and the two Aunts, as they were heirs of the other two brothers.

The judge turned to Minnie, Lizzie and me, smiled and then said, "Children, the Court is appointing me as your guardian. That is I'm appointing myself. We will help you with the sale of the property, if that is what you want. We will do whatever we can do to help you. You can keep what you want from the place or not even sell it. I know you are all minors, but you have friends and some family that would do anything for you. What would you like to do? Do you have any ideas?"

Minnie spoke first, "No Judge, but if you will let us, we would like to talk it over." There was a very deep line across her forehead and sadness in her eyes.

"That is fine, Minnie. Some of the church men and women have agreed to stay with you at the farm for awhile to let you make some decisions. They can't do that forever, but for a short while."

Then I blurted out, "I want to go to the New Mexico Territory to our Uncle John's." I was afraid that we would wind up going to Uncle Nate's. We knew that the two aunts would take us in, but they had all they could handle.

"But, son, that is over a hundred miles away, and he does not even know that his parents, brothers and family members have passed away. Much less that you are going to show up on his door step." There was real concern in his voice.

"I know, but can't we write him or something to let him know what has happened, and what we want to do?" I was persistent.

The sheriff interjected, "Son, we tried to wire him….we think that all of the lines are down due to the storms. That is a long ways out there, and it is still pretty wild."

"But, can't we at least write him?" I insisted.

"That is an idea, Robert," The judge agreed, "so, let's give it a few days. I will be back over from the countyseat, and I will come by the place to see if you still feel that way."

Sheriff Burton, shaking his head yes, added, "If you like, I can try to send more wires to the Territory." Then he added, "That is, when everyone is in agreement that you want to go out there."

Uncle Nate slowly rose from his chair, to gain attention, and commented, "I would like to voluntarily state that I will stay on the farm with Minnie, Robert and Lizzie until they decide. My oldest boy can look after things at home. I will take my family home and then return to help." He seemed truly contrite and anxious to help. "I might even suggest that the three of them come live with us while we contact Brother John. I will send Brother John a letter telling him all that has happened. We can't ask Aunt Bess or Aunt Marjie to take in three more with all the demands of their families on them" He motioned in an arch, "Further, we can't let the people of this community keep caring for ours. They have done enough already. Sheriff, you were right out at the cemetery. I need to take the responsibility for these children. These two aunts will have their hands full with all the problems that confront them. The people of the community can't look after these three forever. Right?"

Judge Long cocked his head to one side and glanced up at Uncle Nate, "Well, Uncle Nate, you are right about one thing. The community can't look after them forever. Plus, these aunts will certainly have their hands full."

I had a gut feeling that Uncle Nate had been scheming up some way to get in control of the situation. In a low dignified voice he said, "Judge, let me make a suggestion. Let the kids stay out at the place for awhile. Get the neighbors to help 'till I can get back, and then I can look after the place. I can help sell the place, if that is what these three want. Then they can stay with us until we hear from the New Mexico Territory. By and by we will hear from Brother John. I'm sure when he hears that the children want to stay with him, he will send for them, or I can take them to him. Agreed?" I'll bet he has a trump card up his sleeve, I thought.

Minnie exclaimed, "Our minds are made up, Judge."

Everyone looked at her in amazement. "Are you sure, Minnie?"

"We want to sell out and go to Uncle John's" She had read my mind and saw the look on my face. She made her decision, a good decision I thought.

The judge stood and looked at the three of us. "I'm game to help you in any way possible."

"I'll get a letter off as soon as I get home," said Uncle Nate. "Then I'll be back to help. Help with the sale of the farm or whatever." Everyone was a little amazed at this willingness to be so helpful. I thought, I'll bet he is playing for time.

Uncle Nate extended his hand to the judge. "I know you're just doing your job, so no hard feelings. If I can be of service, judge, in helping with the sale of Grandpa's and Grandma's place or any of their personal possessions, I will be available."

The judge slowly returned his handshake and reflected, "Maybe, I've been wrong about you, Uncle Nate, but this is a good chance for you to prove to your family that you have some good qualities down deep."

"Well, Judge, are you ready to go to our house?" asked the sheriff. "We have about an hour's buggy ride to make it home, so what say we call it a day?" He turned and picked up his hat and placing it on his head, he held the door open for his wife. As they went out, he called, "Thanks for the great supper, and call on us if we can be of any help."

The judge followed them out, but before he got into the buggy he said, "I'll get all of these documents recorded and back to you as soon as possible. I will need to check on you three and see if you are behaving. Ha! Ha! You are some of the best young people I've met, so I'm not worried. Now don't you worry about selling the place. I know a couple of men who just might be interested in that property. Well, goodnight all, and God's watch and care over you."

Soon the sound of the buggy faded into the darkness. "Boy, I'm sure glad I don't have that ride at this time of the night," commented Uncle Nate. Thinking he had redeemed his place in the family with one short speech, which was pretty good for him, he said, "Now, we have got to get to bed so I can get the family home tomorrow. I will write a letter to Brother John, rest one day, and then I will be back on the next day. That way the neighbors will not have to help out too long on the place."

I'm still not convinced I thought. There is more to this than meets the eye.

We all agreed that it was bedtime. Took a bit of arranging to bed down that many people, but Aunt Bess is an organizer and soon had a bed for everyone. Shortly the lights were out, and silence filled the house.

I found myself in a small room near the rear of the house in a room next to Uncle Nate and Aunt Pettie. I could hear them, through the thin wall, talking in whispers.

Uncle Nate spoke, "Now, woman just you relax. I know what I'm doing. The deck was stacked against us with the judge and the sheriff in the room. But, listen, we will get our fifth of grandpa's and Grandma's property at the sale. And I can take Brother John's fifth when I take the brats to New Mexico, if we take them out there. We should be able to get most of the kids' folk's animals and equipment. We will talk them into taking as much of their folk's stuff to our home as possible. Then while we wait for an answer to John's letter, it will appear that we are just being helpful. The stock, equipment and work animals, we will just be keeping in good, safe surroundings until John answers that letter. Understand?"

I was right! My gut feeling had been right on target! Uncle Nate was planning and scheming to get his hands on as much of the inheritance as he could!

Aunt Pettie greedily asked, "You mean you will take John's share of the money?"

"I mean, we will see. If I have to go all the way to the New Mexico Territory, there may not be any money for Uncle John or something might just have happened to that money. He doesn't need that money, we do. So why should I get it to him?" The bed springs squeaked in protest when one of them got in the bed.

"And all of the kids' folk's stuff?" whined Aunt Pettie.

"Well, if John does not answer, then we will just call all of it ours, for looking after those three snooty brats," Uncle Nate boasted.

"What will you do about the kids, Nate?" whispered Aunt Pettie.

"Oh, if things are rough and tough, they will run away. Maybe just one at a time, but they might run away for good, or perhaps all three. Now, wouldn't that be too bad?"

"We can make life miserable, you can bet on that," she agreed with glee.

"That's the idea, no letter, get all of their belongings. Plus, if their place sells, we could say that we would be glad to deliver that money to John along with the children. We will just play it slow and easy. When we have John's share of Grandpa's place, all of their belongings and the money from the sale of their place, then we can act! What can we do if they run away?.....Nothing." gloated Uncle Nate.

"Why, Nate, we could almost be rich with all of that," exclaimed Aunt Pettie, dreamily.

"We could sure be well fixed. I figure in the neighborhood of maybe twenty five thousand dollars," added Uncle Nate.

"Oh, Nate, maybe we could leave this part of the country and go someplace that is green and warm all the time." Her words were dreamy at the idea.

"Good idea, woman! Now go to sleep." More bedsprings groaning, as the other one got into the bed.

I was scared to death. I lay there in the darkness, shivering from the cold and from fear. I couldn't stop shaking. I was scared that they would find out that I was just on the other side of the wall from them. Boy, they might cut my throat if they knew that I had overheard their conversation. Who could I tell? No one would believe me. They would just think that I did not want to go home with them and was making all of this up to cause trouble. Worst of all, Uncle Nate would steal it all, if he could.

I finally went to sleep, a very troubled sleep, with all kinds of weird things chasing me. Uncle Nate and Aunt Pettie were after me, and I could not run. Sleep, solid sleep finally came, and I rested till dawn. I was glad that little room had an east window and the light woke me. I put on my clothes, boots and coat and slipped out of the house. It was cold, but it felt good on my hot face. I was really scared.

The next morning I dodged Uncle Nate and his family like the plague. I was afraid that they would see something in my face that would give me away. I had to tell somebody, but there was no one to tell. Oh, my heart beat rapidly, and my face was very hot. I had to tell someone.

Boy, oh boy! What a mess! Three weeks had passed since the funeral, and Uncle Nate had been out on the farm for most of that time. I wondered just what he was doing out there. Stealing things, hiding things, or just going through Mama's an Papa's things. I still had not told anyone about the conversation I had overheard. I tried to tell Minnie, but couldn't get the words out. To make matters worse, she thought I was going crazy or just having nightmares.

She was in the kitchen helping make pies when I tried to tell her. She frowned and said, "You don't know what you are talking about. You must have dreamed it. That's it, you ate too much that night, and you just dreamed you thought you heard all of this. You told me you had a bad dream." Boy, NOW, have I got a bellyache from fright!

The judge will be here today or maybe tomorrow, then I will try to talk to him. How does an eleven year old boy accuse a grown man of being a thief? Or, that he plans to steal from your Grandpa and your Papa? That he is going to try to get you to run away from home? I really doubt that he wrote Uncle John in the Territory of New Mexico. Can I suggest that Uncle Nate was only trying to buy some time so he could come up with some scheme. Who is going to believe an eleven year old big-mouth boy?

The next morning, I had just finished cleaning the barn for Aunt Bess when she called me from the back door, "Robert, come in, the judge and the sheriff are here and want to go over some things with you and your sisters." She held the door open for me, and she whispered, "We will ask them to stay for lunch and perhaps the judge will play you some check-ers". I thought I was hot stuff on the checkerboard.

The judge and the sheriff were sitting as the kitchen table having cof-fee when I went in. The judge was dressed in a brown suit and vest. His hat was white, and it matched his mustache. The sheriff was, as always, dressed in his cowboy looking clothes. Minnie, Lizzie and Aunt Bess were already sitting at the table with them. As I came in, I heard the judge say, "This is the most unbelievable weather. In December we had that sand and dust storm. January, we had all that snow and ice, and the influenza epidemic raged through our countryside."

He took a drink of coffee and continued, "Now, can you believe that for most of February we have only had two or three days of storms, with little or no moisture? Just enough snow to cover the ground, and then it is gone. How could it freeze and be so bad and then within days be so nice?"

My stomping the mud off my feet interrupted him. "Hello, Mr. Robert. How are you doing? I understand from your aunt that you are the best worker in the county. She sure does brag on you, son." Little did he know that Minnie had threaten me within an inch of my life if I did-n't do some of the chores around the place. Good worker, Ha, Ha.

My ears and neck turned red at all of the compliments. "Come over here and sit with me, your aunt and your sisters." I pulled out a chair and sat down. The judge unfolded some papers and looked at the three of us before he continued, "I have gone over these documents with your Aunt Bess, and now I want to go over them with you. There may be something that you don't understand, so don't be bashful, just ask me to explain, if you don't"

"First, your Grandpa's and Grandma's farm has been auctioned off. I have shown the check to your two aunts. The check is made out to the court. Now, I will take it to the bank and then they will make out five checks in return. A fifth each for your aunts, one fifth put in a trust for you kids at the bank, one fifth for your Uncle Nate and one fifth for your Uncle John."

"Judge, what is a trust?" I asked.

"Well, Robert. that's a term used at the bank. If you put money in the bank, and have a receipt for the money, the bank holds that money for you in a special account. The money can't be drawn out, and it is held for you and your sisters. Another term might mean that you trust them to keep the money safe."

"That means, that someone like Uncle Nate could not touch that money?" The judge's eyebrows shot up, and the sheriff's eyes squinted at me. You could read the judge's mind. Why would an eleven year old be asking that kind of question and interrupting?

But, he continued. "That's right, Robert. Only you and your sisters, along with me or your aunts, can draw the money out of the bank. And it means that they will keep that money in the trust until each one of you is twenty-one."

"Fine! That is just fine with me!" I exclaimed. "That's O.K. by you, Minnie, and you, Lizzie?" They both shook their heads "Yes". I didn't understand it and doubted that Lizzie did, but she followed Minnie's lead.

I spoke with a big important voice, "Sounds fine to us, judge. " I thought to myself, "Now who sounds like Uncle Nate?"

The judge chuckled and continued with his other documents. "Now, I have an offer for your Mama's and Papa's place. I think it is a fair offer. Mr. Schmitt has offered two dollars per acre. Your Papa owned almost two thousand acres, so that comes to four thousand dollars."

"I didn't know he had that much land!" exclaimed Minnie.

"Well, I imagine that you only looked at what he could plow, as the place. That was not over about one hundred sixty acres. You can handle just so much with a team of mules. The rest was in ranchland. That ranchland, with it's cattle, is the bulk of the offer. He offered four dollars a head for the herd of cattle. We will have to round them up in the spring and get a head count. I expect that your Papa had near a hundred head. Mr. Schmitt will pay an extra one dollar for each calf if we will wait until the calves drop in the spring. That amounts to another four hundred dollars, plus the calf count. He also said, he would like to buy all the farm equipment. He has offered another five hundred for the equipment. That comes to a total of four thousand nine hundred dollars, plus the calves."

"Children, I think that is a fair offer. I'm going on some of the deals my husband made," said Aunt Bess.

"I have to agree," the judge added.

"Minnie, you are the oldest, you decide," I added.

"Aunt Bess, if you and the judge think it is fair, that is fine with us. That sounds like a lot of money." She was, as was I, taken aback. We had no idea how much money that was. It sure sounded like a lot.

"Child, you haven't heard the rest of the good news." injected the judge. Then he reached for another document, the bank draft for Grandpa's and Grandma's place. "I told you the farm had been auctioned off, and that you would receive a fifth. That place had over ten thousand acres and eight hundred head of cattle plus all the equipment. We started the bidding at two dollars per acre and got four dollars. Then the bid on the herd started at two dollars and fifty cents, and we got five dollars per head. Finally, the bid on all equipment and other animals started at five hundred dollars and we got five thousand. That came to a total of forty-nine thousand dollars. Then we were ready to auction off the house and it's contents, and the high bidder on all the rest just up and said, 'I'll give a thousand dollars for the lot.' So I told the auctioneer that the bidding was over. The buyer had made it a round fifty thousand dollars for everything."

Sheriff Burton added, "Now, of course your aunts are going over and remove the personal things from the house. Oh, by the way, you will be glad to know that we have had a guard on the place since that scene with your Uncle Nate."

We all began to laugh and Minnie said, "Sheriff, Uncle Nate has been stuck out on our place for almost three weeks. That guard has probably put a damper on Uncle Nate's activities. Uncle Nate had not planned on that happening."

"Well, we didn't know if he would be at your place or at your Grandpa's and Grandma's place, so I put the guard out at yours. The sheriff over in that county where your grandparents lived put a guard on, their place."

Man, oh, man. Did they put a lid on Uncle Nate! If he had tried anything at either place he would be in trouble. His own words got him stuck out at our place and with a guard.

When we had quit laughing, Minnie smiled and said, "I speak for Robert, Lizzie and me. We appreciate the looking after Grandpa's and Grandma's place. We can't thank you enough for all you have done." The sheriff smiled and just nodded his head.

Then the judge continued, "Now I will show you the bank draft for their place. Well, here it is, and one fifth of it is going into that trust. One fifth is ten thousand dollars, plus the offer from Mr. Schmitt brings the total to fourteen thousand nine hundred dollars, plus the calves."

We all just looked at each other in absolute astonishment. That was a lot of money.

The judge proclaimed, "That is a long speech for even me. I think I need another cup of coffee."

"I'll take one," chimed in the sheriff.

While the women were getting another round of coffee, I tried to start talking to the judge, but they interrupted before I could even explain. The judge just looked at me and frowned.

"Now if we were to auction your Mama's and Papa's place, we might get a little more money. But, this soil is not quite as good, and the water is not as plentiful, so I think we should just accept the offer if you are all in agreement."

Aunt Bess asked, "Have you heard anything from Uncle John?"

"No."

"As soon as we get through with the sale and these matters settled, the sheriff can try to send a telegraph again."

"Oh, we would appreciate that, Judge," responded Aunt Bess.

"We know Uncle Nate was writing to him, but we thought you might have heard from him."

Minnie spoke up, "We should have let the sheriff, as he suggested, try to send a telegraph to Uncle John. We might have had an answer by now."

"I agree, Minnie, and we will." The judge looked at Aunt Bess, "I'm going on out to where Uncle Nate is tomorrow. The sheriff is going with me, and we can check on the letter. Also, we want to look the place over. We thought that he was out there and are sorry to say, that we feel we need to check everything out. We will make an inventory of the equipment and all stock, with the exception of the four mules and two wagons. You are going to need them to move your belongings to the New Mexico Territory."

He dug in his case and brought out a Bible. "Minnie, I believe this belongs to you. Your Grandma wanted you to have it. Lizzie, we found a doll all wrapped up in a box. Didn't know what it was until we opened it. Figured it was for you on your birthday. I'm sorry that we didn't get to deliver it to you sooner. Now the other doll won't be so lonesome."

Lizzie hugged the doll to her breast and looked into the eyes of the judge saying softly, "Thank you, Mr. Judge." That was the first real clear statement of words she had uttered since our parents had died. The doll was dressed in a pink dress just like the dress Lizzie had worn at the Christmas program.

"My pleasure, young lady. And for you Mr. Robert, we found this set of three knives, and just thought that your Grandpa would have liked for you to have one of them. I will give the other two, to your cousins. One for each."

"Gosh, Judge. Thanks!"

"Robert, you are not supposed to use that word! Papa would blister your backside," corrected Minnie frowning.

"Oops, I forgot, Minnie."

The judge and Aunt Bess laughed and declared that under the circumstances all was forgiven.

The judge rose from his chair and looked at his pocketwatch, "Oh, my goodness, look at the time! I must get over to the mercantile store for a meeting. I'm running late!"

"You don't have time for a meal?" asked Aunt Bess.

"And some checkers?" I added.

"No, not this time. I must run." The judge gathered his hat, cane and case to depart.

I followed the judge out of the house as everyone else called their byes from the door. "Judge, I need to talk to you real bad, I have got a problem."

"Sorry, Robert, I have to rush," he responded as he climbed into his buggy. "We will sit down and talk the next time." With that admonition, he slapped the reins on the rumps of his team and drove away.

I turned and looked for the sheriff. He was just mounting his horse. "Sheriff?" I called.

He touched the horse's flank's and called back, "See you next trip, Robert." The sheriff caught up with the judge, and they rode off side by side.

The sheriff and judge found Uncle Nate trying to run the place and do the chores, but he was falling far short of succeeding. The house was a mess. All of the animals needed water and some needed feed.

The judge jumped Uncle Nate out, "Why haven't you taken care of the stock and animals?" The judge stormed around and asked, "Why have you neglected the place? It's a mess!"

Uncle Nate replied, "There was so much to do that I could not keep it straight."

Sheriff Burton looked Uncle Nate in the eye, "This place has sold. The new owner will be here tomorrow. You be gone!"

Uncle Nate whimpered, "I should have had a say in the sale, as it is my brother that is dead."

The sheriff allowed, "You'd best try to tend to the animals and let the judge handle the transactions for the heirs."

Uncle Nate really got upset when the sheriff, the judge and the guard started a complete inventory of the equipment and all of the animals.

Uncle Nate allowed, "No one trusts me."

The sheriff and the judge didn't say one word, they just looked at each other and continued their inventory. Uncle Nate was informed the guard would continue to stay until the new owner arrived.

When the sheriff and the judge came back to town it was very late, and the judge did not come by Aunt Bess's place, so I did not get to talk to him. The sheriff went to see the new owner and would not be along for awhile. Time was running out on me, and I still had not told my story.

When the sheriff came to the house the next day, I figured that I could talk to him. Boy, everything was working against me. He just stood on the porch and told Aunt Bess that he had notified Mr. Schmitt that the price was agreeable and that we would give him possession tomorrow.

How it turned out was another kick in the pants! When the sheriff delivered the inventory and told Mr. Schmitt that Uncle Nate was there, he almost busted his suspenders.

"What can I do to get him off the place and how soon?"

"Why, go over there tomorrow and take possession. The judge has your draft, the place is yours. The aunts and the children will go out and remove all the personal items. They will not remove anything that is on the inventory list."

"I'll go over, and I will have a hand there tomorrow."

"That is fine, Mr. Schmitt. I'll go back by Aunt Bess's and tell her, that weather permitting, they will need to go out tomorrow and not hold up everything."

"Sheriff, tell Aunt Bess there is no rush. But, what are you going to do about Uncle Nate if he is not gone?"

"If he is not gone, the aunts can tell him he needs to go on home. You and your man can go over tomorrow afternoon and assume responsibility for the stock and the other animals. Aunt Bess will be there early."

"Fine! Just as long as he is gone!"

Well, I was kicked in the pants again! I was asleep when the sheriff came by and told Aunt Bess that Mr. Schmitt had paid for the land, and that on the next day she, Aunt Marjie, Minnie, Lizzie and I should go out and remove all of the personal items. He also told her that she should tell Uncle Nate that he could go on home, if he was not already gone, until we heard from the Territory of New Mexico.

The next morning, all five of us were loaded in the two wagons and headed out to our place, correction Mr. Schmitt's place. I drove the little wagon that Mama and Papa had taken to town when Aunt Pearl was sick. Aunt Bess drove the big wagon. That is the one we had used to take Mama and Papa to town for the burial. It was, or so it seemed, a long hard ride. This would probably be the last time we would see the homeplace.

When we drove up in the yard, we were met by the dogs. Ol' Bullet wagged his tail and jumped all over me when I jumped down to greet him. He licked and barked enough to drive you crazy. Uncle Nate came to the door.

"Where have you been? I've been looking for you for hours. Robert, can't you hush those dogs? What a noise!"

Everyone climbed down and went in the house.

Minnie let out a yell, "Uncle Nate, what are you doing here and what have you done to this place? It's a pig pen!" Then her voice really went up in volume, "You have gone thorough every drawer in this house and emptied them out! Haven't you?"

Uncle Nate retreated out the door, "Well, I was just….."

"You were trying to see what you could find to steal! I wonder what we will find missing . Oh, how could you go though other people's possessions?"

Aunt Bess spoke up, "Uncle Nate, the sheriff said you could go on home until we hear from Uncle John. So, I think that it is best for you to get your wagon and team and head home, NOW!!!"

"Well, I never…."

"That's right, Uncle Nate", chimed in Aunt Marjie, "Get your stuff, get on the wagon before I let Robert sic' the dogs on you. NOW MOVE!!!"

Boy, were those three women in a fury! Uncle Nate moved as fast as his fat body would let him. He threw all of his things in his wagon. By the time it was loaded, I had his team hooked up. When he turned around and headed out of the yard, with all the dogs barking and raising cane, he shouted, "You will regret this day and the way you have treated me. I stayed out here for over two weeks and looked after things, and this is the thanks I get."

Just then the sheriff and the guard rode into the yard. "Having trouble, ladies?"

Aunt Bess shot back, "No, just getting rid of a lousy varmint!"

"Have you checked the house to see if any personal items are missing?"

"No, we haven't. We were so mad to find such a mess, and that everything had been gone through, we were just running him off the place."

"That's why I thought I would come out for the move. You need to check for any missing items. Robert, you help them look the place over. You need to check your father's guns and his personal things. O.K.? We will check the inventory that we did the other day. Everything had better be in it's place. Right Uncle Nate?"

Uncle Nate just sputtered.

I answered, "Yes, sir, I'll check." Another chance to talk to the sheriff or somebody was ruined. Maybe, a little later I would get a chance. Minnie had told me to not say anything to our aunts. Then later she said she was sure I had had a bad dream, and I needed to keep my mouth shut.

The sheriff swung down off his horse and walked over by Uncle Nate's wagon. "I think that you had best just sit right there until the ladies have had a chance to go through the house and see if everything is in place. GOT ME?"

"Yes," replied Uncle Nate. "But do I have to sit here in the cold?"

"I guess not, you can go over and get in the smokehouse. That is some protection, and you can build a fire to keep warm."

You could hear the women in the house going from room to room, counting items and looking to see if any item was missing.

Aunt Marjie was the loudest, "What a mess, if that was my brother I would beat him within an inch of his life."

"Minnie, have you found any single item missing?"

"No, Aunt Marjie, just a big mess! Making it harder to load and move."

"Well, don't worry, honey, we will all lend a hand and have it straightened and ready to move in a couple of hours."

You know something, they had it all straightened in just a little over two hours. They started loading the wagons and preparing to move all household goods to town. The sheriff rode up and stated, "The livestock down by the water tank are in good shape. Did you find everything?"

"Yes, we did, Sheriff. Just in a mess."

"Fine." replied the sheriff. He yelled to Uncle Nate in the smoke-house, "Nate, get out here and get started home."

Nate came out of the smokehouse, chewing on a piece of meat. "Well, if you are going to make me sit around and be hungry, I might as well eat a bite or two."

He climbed onto his wagon.

Aunt Marjie was standing on the porch. "Now, Sheriff, I have a question for you."

"What is that, Ma'am?"

"Do I have to put up with or listen to Uncle Nate on any matter?"

"Why, no. You are your own boss."

"Thank you, Sheriff. Uncle Nate, don't ever set foot on my property. Hear!"

Uncle Nate only simmered.

Then Aunt Bess spoke up, "Uncle Nate, after this, likewise for my property. Don't ever come around. If you do I'll sic the dogs on you and then call the sheriff. CLEAR?"

Without comment, Uncle Nate slapped the reins on the horses' rumps and started down the lane. The sheriff followed right behind him.

What was I going to do? Another chance to talk to somebody had slipped away. My stomach turned over, and my head hurt with worry about what Uncle Nate might do.

We loaded the two wagons and headed back to Aunt Bess's place. It was very late when we arrived, so we just put the wagons with all of the clothes, utensils, household goods and Papa's guns in the barn for the night. It took several days to sort out what we wanted to keep and what would be given to the church for the needy. Personal items were taken in the house, while all the furniture and such was left on the wagons in the barn. We were expecting to head to the Territory of New Mexico just any time, so why unload.

Aunt Bess said, "Those things will not be in the way for a while, so just leave them in the barn. We will keep the doors closed and that will keep the weather out."

February had turned to March, and the weather continued to warm. Of course, with warm weather, the March sandstorms came. All of our possessions in the barn might be out of the weather, but they sure got covered with dust from all of the sand. The duststorms were bad, but not as bad as some years. The wind and stress was beginning to wear on everyone. I think Aunt Bess was beginning to wonder how long we were going to be under her feet. Her house was large, yet, with three more people and not really your family, things were tense at times.

The judge sent , by the sheriff, a packet for all of us. The sheriff just rode up, knocked on the door and handed the packet to Aunt Bess and rode off. I tried to catch the sheriff by cutting through the brush. But by the time I got to the road, he was already gone. Another kick in the pants.

In the packet were deposit slips for Aunt Bess and Aunt Marjie from the sale of Grandpa's and Grandma's place. A little over ten thousand dollars each sure was a tidy sum. At the same time we got documents that showed that fourteen thousand nine hundred dollars was in a trust for us. Enclosed was a letter from the judge. Aunt Bess read the letter.

Dear Aunt Bess, Aunt Marjie, Minnie, Lizzie and Robert..

Hope this letter finds you well. I will be short and to the point. Uncle Nate has, to my knowledge, not received any correspondence from your relatives in the New Mexico Territory. I will be taking this matter in my hands.

Now, enclosed you will find deposits for each of you. The children's money is in a trust, and with the signature of Aunt Marjie or Aunt Bess and me, we can draw on the account for the children. You can have money to help feed and clothe them, or whatever their needs may be.

Sincerely,

Judge Long.

Then came two kicks in the pants. First, Aunt Bess decided that now that school was open all of us should be back in classes. I think she needed to get us out of the of the house for her sanity.. We had thought for days that we would be going to New Mexico, so why start classes here and just check out in a few days. We had not been in school for over two months. But on that Monday, we all packed sack lunches, said our good-byes and loaded up in Aunt Bess's wagon to go to school.

At school the presence of all of us sure made an uproar. The teachers had a hard time controlling us. All the other kids wanted to talk, and we were out of school habits, so school was not a good thing that day. Poor teachers.

We had a great time riding to school and back to Aunt Bess's in the wagon. There were five of us, and we made the trip a picnic. We sang and talked and were almost happy for one day. One day only.

The second kick in the pants came that very afternoon. As we came into sight of Aunt Bess's farm we could see the judge's buggy, the sheriff's horse and a strange wagon in the yard.

"Whose wagon is that?"

"Don't know, Minnie."

"Maybe it's just company," suggested Lizzie.

I looked at my cousins and my sisters, "None of you recognize THAT wagon?"

Suddenly there was a series of groans and moans, "Oh, No! that is Uncle Nate's wagon."

Two kicks in the pants in one day. What I didn't know was that there would be third kick before the day was over.

We pulled up in the yard and one of our cousins said, "Ya'll go on in. I'll put the team and the wagon up." He glanced at his brother and sister and said, "Ya'll come on, I imagine that all of them are here to see our cousins, so come with me and let them go on in."

With sinking hearts we climbed the steps and went in the front door. Sure enough, there sat the jury, ready to hang us from the looks on all of the faces.

The judge looked up and said, "Come in young people, we have some news for you." We scuffled our feet as we slowly moved into the room. I don't think the judge was happy.

I finally got around so I could get a look at Uncle Nate's face. All I could see was greed, glee and self importance. That look was back. Enough to make you throw up.

"Children, " Aunt Bess addressed us. "We finally got word, that is Uncle Nate got word, from the Territory of New Mexico and your Uncle John." She wiped a couple of tears from her eyes.

Uncle Nate broke in, "That's right, your Uncle John wants me to bring the three of you out to him. He just can't get away at this time." He looked very satisfied.

The judge looked at us and explained, "It is all here in this letter. Your Uncle John wants your Uncle Nate to bring you out to him. Also, he has requested that Uncle Nate bring a bank draft for his part of the sale on your Grandpa's places. And he also requested that I prepare a letter making him guardian of the three of you and sending your trust money in a bank draft with Uncle Nate. I have given Uncle Nate his draft for his part."

We just stood there, dumbfounded and shocked. We wanted to go to the Territory of New Mexico to get away from Uncle Nate, not have him take us. The fat was in the fire and getting hotter all of the time. Aunt Bess was wiping tears from her eyes. The judge looked displeased. The sheriff pulled on his mustache, adjusted his hat and looked at Uncle Nate with suspicious eyes.

The sheriff reached for the letter and said, "Let me see that postmark one more time." After a few minutes he commented, "Sure looks to be authentic and the real thing. Postmark is from Fort Sumner. That is right close to where your Uncle lives. I guess that is the closest post office to them."

"Judge," Uncle Nate spoke up. "If I could make a suggestion. I'm here, so why don't we load the children's possessions, and then they can go home with me? Aunt Bess had been gracious enough to keep them for all this time You could prepare whatever papers you feel necessary while we get ready to travel. By going back to my place, I could save another long trip. What do you think?"

The sheriff interjected, "Judge, I suggest that for once Uncle Nate makes sense. You can prepare the documents requested in this letter and have them ready by the time Aunt Bess can have things ready for the children to leave."

"I agree, Sheriff. Aunt Bess, how long would it take to have the children ready to travel?"

"Judge, I believe they can be ready by tomorrow. Shouldn't be that hard to load them and their goods."

"Good. Uncle Nate, when do you want to start?"

To hide his attitude of avarice, he benevolently answered, "Whatever is the easiest for all of you. Whenever you have the papers ready, and the children are ready, I'll be standing by. That is the least I can do for my dear deceased brother and for my brother in the New Mexico Territory."

It took us the rest of the day to locate and load our possessions. I started to leave Papa's shotgun with Aunt Bess and then decided that if we were going to the Territory, I would need the gun.

I looked at Uncle Nate and wondered if I was the only one who saw through his plan. A plan to steal all of that money! Steal every dime of the money!!!

CHAPTER THREE

I could hardly believe what was happening. We were loading the two wagons and going to Uncle Nate's? No, this could not be happening, this is a NIGHTMARE! I had to wake up. Uncle Nate is waving his arms and giving orders left and right, but he wasn't helping get anything loaded. He wanted us to be loaded by night and ready to leave early the next day. He is a pain in the neck. We loaded the big stuff by dusk. The days were warmer and longer, so we had the wagons ready to travel.

Suppertime was a very somber and silent time. Aunt Bess and Aunt Marjie kept wiping tears from their eyes. Their children seemed to want to sit real close to us and kind of hold on the us. Even Ol' Bullet knew that something was in the air. He was lying over by the door and only his eyes moved. They followed whoever got up and moved around the kitchen. He never wagged his tail and that was strange.

Uncle Nate stretched and said aloud, "I'm going to retire. Tomorrow will be a long day, and we have lots of miles to cover. We will spend one night on the road. I know a place that is good for camping and there is water. We will be at my place the next night. Good night, all." He strutted out of the room. His self importance apparent. I felt that he had won. He would have us at his place, and we would not have a way to contact anyone for help.

The silence after his exit remained until Minnie went over to Aunt Marjie and then to Aunt Bess and gave each a big hug. They hugged back, and there were some more tears from all three. Lizzie and the other kids just sat and looked blank.

"Aunt Bess, Aunt Marjie, Mama used to say that heaven would be filled with good loved ones like the two of you. You both have opened your homes in the time of your own grief and have loved us like we were your children." Minnie paused and reached for Aunt Bess's hand and then reached across the table for Aunt Marjie's hand. "With all our hearts we thank, you."

"Aunts," I asked. "Is there any way we can get hold of you if we need to?"

"No, Robert," Aunt Bess answered. "There is not a telegraph near where you going. There is mail so you could write us a letter. I'll write down the address for both of us. We do want to hear from you. When you go to town you can drop us a note, and let us know how you are doing."

The conversation continued for a little while, and then we all headed for bed. I caught Minnie in the hall before she got to the room she was sharing with the three other girls. "Minnie," I begged, "You have got to tell one of our aunts or let me tell them!"

"Robert, all saying anything would do, is get you in trouble. If what you told me is true, and Uncle Nate even got a little scent that you had overheard, there is no telling what he would do to you or to us. We have got to do what we are told. The Judge is sending us to Uncle John's. Uncle Nate can't do anything other than comply with the Judge's orders. Plus, that letter stated that he is to bring Uncle John's money and take our trust money to Uncle John, too."

"But, Minnie…"

"No, buts about it, we are going, and you have got to keep your mouth shut. You don't have any evidence that Uncle Nate is going to do anything wrong."

"But, I heard them…."

"I know you think you did, but did anyone else hear them or see anything that would make them suspicious?"

That stopped me cold. I didn't have any proof, nor would anyone believe me. They might have their own suspicions, but without something concrete, there was nothing I could do.

That next to the last day, Aunt Marjie came over as soon as she heard that we were packing. Aunt Bess sent one of her boys to tell her. It was late and she decided that she was going home, so we came back to the kitchen for a round of hugs and goodbyes. We were ready to leave. All we needed was the money drafts and the papers that the Judge was preparing. He said he would have them over early in the morning.

The next morning, we all came out of our rooms at about the same time. We stopped and started giggling. Even though we were mad, upset and bound to go with Uncle Nate, we giggled. We had put on blue and white striped overalls, faded blue shirts and our brown floppy hats. We looked like three boys........we looked like three scarecrows.

When the three of us came into the kitchen that morning the atmosphere was somber and sullen, but when everyone saw us they started laughing. Even with the somber atmosphere, we had a good laugh. Our laughter did not last long. We are going to Uncle Nate's.

Breakfast that morning was somber and sullen, although Uncle Nate was so very jolly and in good humor. He had left his fancy duds at home and now he had on some striped pants with a light gray shirt. The shirt had seen better days. He carried a buggy whip and he had popped it several times during the morning, as we got ready to go. He didn't try to hit anybody, just kept snapping the thing. The snapping whip had it's expected effect. We were all dodging and hurrying to get loaded. We had hardly finished when there was a knock at the door. The sheriff had brought the documents.

After he was in the house he explained, "Aunt Bess, I have all of the papers in this envelope."

Uncle Nate sprang to his feet like a young deer and grabbed the envelope, "I believe that is for me and not Aunt Bess." He said.

The sheriff's face clouded, but he said nothing. Uncle Nate proceeded to go through the contents. "Yes, everything seems to be here. Now, let's be sure. Here is a draft for Uncle John, a draft on the trust and papers appointing Uncle John guardian of the children."

Uncle Nate's whole personality changed in a blink. His eyes turned into slits, and he almost drooled over the envelope. Was I the only one who could see his cunning?

"All right, Robert, you go hitch those four mules to the two wagons and then hitch my horses to my wagon, and we will start."

Aunt Marjie had decided she couldn't stay away, and she had come bustling into the kitchen just about light. She remarked to Aunt Bess, "I couldn't leave you here alone with that snake in the grass to have to listen to his bragging and planning." Aunt Bess began the last little packing for us, mostly food for the trip to Uncle Nate's place. They packed enough for a week, knowing that Uncle Nate would eat far more than his share and maybe, just maybe, there would enough left over for the three of us.

It took me about an hour to hitch six animals to the three wagons. Finally done, I went in to be greeted with, "Well, it is about time. Thought you were going to be all day. All right everyone, gather your things and let's get started. Time is passing, and we will have to camp out at least one night at best."

When we gathered in the yard Uncle Nate gave still more instructions, "I'll drive my wagon, Robert, you drive the big wagon, and Minnie, you drive that small wagon. Lizzie you can ride with your sister. Why don't you just set those food hampers right up here beside me out of the way, Aunt Marjie."

Both aunts had tears in their eyes and could hardly say a word. When we started off, "Goodbye, Goodbye," floated on the morning breeze, and the breeze carried away any of the joy that had returned to our hearts while staying with Aunt Bess. We found that saying our goodbyes became very difficult. Uncle Nate huffed, "Enough of that blubbering and wailing. Let's get started!"

Each person climbed onto his assigned place, and the little caravan of three wagons moved out of the yard. I picked up Ol' Bullet and put him on the seat with me. If Minnie had Lizzie for company and Uncle Nate had the food, then I would have my dog.

"Robert, what do you think you are doing with that dog?"

With all of the calling goodbyes, noise of the animals and the barking of all of the other dogs, I just made out like I could not hear him and headed my wagon out first. That was another thing, if I had to ride alone, then I would have Ol' Bullet to talk to.

I could not do anything to stop what was happening, so I figured I would just make the best of it until we got to Uncle John's. That is if we ever got to Uncle John's.

The trip to Uncle Nate's was just what I expected. Rough. The roads were rough and the atmosphere was rough. Uncle Nate was hollering at me and Minnie as soon as we got out of earshot of our aunts. Most of the time you couldn't hear him for the noise of the wagons and the distance between them.

We had gone down the road two or three hours, and he called a halt. He got off the wagon complaining that his horses could not keep up with the mules, and we would need to hold them up some. Minnie and I were a good mile ahead of him when he whipped his team and caught up with us wanting to stop. We found a little shade under some mesquite trees. He berated us for thirty minutes, and we did not have a clue what he was talking about. He really got mad when he discovered his waterbag had not been filled, as our two had been by our cousins. I imagined that was out of meanness.

At noon we stopped under some bigger trees by a windmill and a tank. It was pleasant under the trees, and we ate from Aunt Bess's basket of food. Uncle Nate ate as much as all three of us could eat. It was an amazing feat to watch. He just kept putting food in his mouth, even while it was half full.

After lunch Uncle Nate said he thought he would stretch out under the shade trees for a few minutes. To our surprise he fell asleep almost immediately and began to snore something awful. We walked down the road to some more trees to be away from his noise.

As we sat under the trees, Minnie suddenly started crying. "Minnie," I asked as I put my arms around her. "what is the matter?"

Through her tears, she asked, "Robert, do you know what day this is?"

"No, Minnie. Do you mean what day of the month?"

"That's right, Robert. What day of the month."

I thought for a few minutes and then said, "No, Minnie, I don't have any idea. It is March is all I know."

Minnie sighed and let out her breath. "Well, guys, this is my birthday, and I am fourteen today. I almost forgot all about it."

"Gee, Minnie, I wish we could have a party for you," cried Lizzie. "I had one, but we didn't have one for you or for Robert."

"Robert, I forgot all about your birthday. When was it?" asked Minnie.

I sat very still and quite for a few minutes. "On the day we buried Mama and Papa."

That silenced the girls, so we just sat under the trees and stared off into space and thought of the events of the past few months. We sure didn't mind that Uncle Nate was asleep. We three were together and reached out and gave each other a big, long hug, among the tears.

At about two o'clock he woke up, refreshed and ready to go. He never said anything about his long nap, and we didn't care. We had had a private time for the three of us.

We took a short rest in the middle of the afternoon. Uncle Nate had found a cup in his wagon, and he poured water from one of our bags and drank from his cup. Ol' Bullet got a little too close to him, and Uncle Nate kicked at him. Ol' Bullet howled when Uncle Nate kicked him and bared his fangs. I called Ol' Bullet, and he bristled and rolled his eyes at Uncle Nate.

"Keep that mangy mutt away from me." Uncle Nate stormed.

"Come here, Ol' Bullet," called Lizzie and the dog ran to her.

"Why, do you call him, Ol' Bullet? He sure doesn't look fast!"

"You just haven't seen him move, Uncle Nate," I said in a boastful way.

"Look, boy. You keep a civil tongue in your mouth, or I'll bust you one," growled Uncle Nate.

"It's easy to be mean when you outweigh somebody by four times," I said and ducked out of the way. I thought about that buggy whip. As luck would have it, it was in the wagon.

The afternoon was long and dusty. The wagons groaned and squeaked, complaining about the rough road. The roads didn't appear to be getting any better. If anything they were deteriorating. We did not stop until almost dark. Then we really found out about the bossing.

"Robert, you unhitch. Lizzie, you find firewood. Minnie, you get supper ready." No matter how hard we tried to please the man, he would still bellyache about something. His middle name should have been gripe. He almost brought Minnie to tears over the cold meal. The food Aunt Bess had sent was cold food. You did not heat the things she had prepared.

We finally settled down for the night. We, kids slept in the wagons where Aunt Bess had fixed beds for us. We hoped it would rain. No such luck. Uncle Nate sure griped about having to sleep on the ground.

Breakfast the next morning, was a hot breakfast so Uncle Nate didn't gripe. He ate as much as the three of us. We loaded and made the total sum of seven miles the second day, according to Uncle Nate. He had two wagons, but he brought the oldest and most worn out one. First, it lost a wheel. Now, that is hard to fix with three kids and an over- stuffed whale. It took us four hours to take the wheel off and put another one on. At least Uncle Nate had an extra wheel.

He declared, "I'm smart enough to know that you should take an extra when your wagon is old."

We had lunch while we worked on the wheel. We had to unload Uncle Nate's wagon and then find a way to get it up to put a wheel on. There was not anyway we could lift the wagon. We didn't even try to lift the wagon, ourselves. We all knew that is was too heavy.

Then Lizzie said, "I bet the mules could do it!"

"Do what, Sugar?" Minnie asked.

"Just tie the mules on the other side and let them pull the wagon up off the ground." Out of the mouth of babes.

Uncle Nate almost had a seizure laughing so hard. "The mules pull it up?" He laughed some more. "Dumbest thing I have ever heard!"

I got my first back hand for the next statement. "Well, we aren't getting it done this way. Maybe her idea will work." Uncle Nate might be fat, but he sure can move like lightning. He hit me with the back of his hand.

"I told you to keep a civil tongue in your mouth!" He glared at me and raised his hand again to strike me. That was a mistake. Ol' Bullet was right there and his hackles were up. When he bared his big vicious teeth, Uncle Nate backed off in a hurry.

After another hour or so of his swearing and ranting, he said, "Oh, go ahead and try it." Uncle Nate went off and sat under some shade trees and wiped his brow. He was sweating and stinking something awful.

I unhitched the four mules and took them around on the side away from the broken wheel. I just ran the ropes over the top of the bed and tied them down on the bottom of the wagon. I had seen Papa do it. With a soft voice I began to talk to the mules. They all knew not to jerk. They just all pulled nice and easy and slowly the broken wheel came up off the ground. I kept talking to the mules, and they all held a steady strain on the wagon.

Minnie and I rolled the wheel up to the wagon. We were hollering and straining to put the thing on. No way could we get the wheel to go sidewise and go on the hub. Finally, Uncle Nate got up and came over to where all the activity was.

"Get out of my way. Do I have to do everything?" Uncle Nate might be fat looking, but he was strong as a bull. He lifted that wagon wheel and had it on in a flash. Just picked it up and slid it on the hub. Easy as pie. We, not Uncle Nate, reloaded his wagon and hitched the mules. We had made seven miles that day. Another four miles and the sun was setting. We would have to spend another night out on the road.

We pitched camp, and Minnie prepared some supper. Uncle Nate walked down the road for a piece and was coming back, when suddenly, Ol' Bullet rushed at him. Uncle Nate may be big , but he is fast. He jumped to the side, swearing and screaming at the dog. Ol' Bullet rushed in and grabbed a big rattlesnake behind the head. If Uncle Nate had taken another step or so, he would have been bitten. It probably would have killed the snake. Ol' Bullet snapped down on the snake and crushed it. Uncle Nate had to sit down on the ground when he saw the size of that snake. The snake was over five feet in length. I cut the rattlers off and threw the snake in the bushes.

After awhile Uncle Nate was back to his old self again. Back bossing and trying to throw his weight around. Lots of being bossy. He sat around while we did the chores. He just sat on his haunches and fingered the two drafts, over and over.

I'm not too good at numbers, but I figured Uncle Nate got the same amount of money that our aunts received. So, if that was right, then Uncle Nate had in his possession about thirty-five thousand dollars. I didn't know how he figured to keep all of it, but you could bet he was trying real hard to come up with a scheme. I wondered what was going though his mind. His expression seemed to indicate that his mind was way off on other matters.

At evening we camped at a windmill. Had good water, but the people and the stock were gone. Uncle Nate commented, "Mighty nice of these folks to furnish us some shelter and water." We pulled our wagons into the old dilapidated barn. With the canvas over the hoops and being in the barn we would have a fairly snug place to sleep. With the animals unhitched and a fire going, things weren't too bad. Just too much bossing from Uncle Nate. Go do this, go do that, just like we were servants.

Sure enough, even though Aunt Bess had fixed us good food for the trip, Uncle Nate complained, and sure enough even though Uncle Nate had been sampling the contents all day long, every day he ate more than the three of us. Minnie fixed us a good meal and made sure Lizzie had plenty. She was not talking much. Just played with her two dolls. Minnie managed to slip me an extra piece of pie. Sometimes sisters can be so nice.

We slept in the wagons again on the beds our aunts had made for us. Uncle Nate would have taken one, except that they were made for small people and he is too big. I wondered if Aunt Bess thought of that when she prepared them. He slept under his wagon on the ground. Lots of muttering during the night. Guess that ground is pretty hard.

Daylight found us already up and breakfast almost finished. Uncle Nate sure pushed for us to get underway and to his place by nightfall. Guess the ground was harder than I thought. Shouldn't have hurt him, him being so fat, with lots of padding.

The hitching was done in record time with a little extra help from Uncle Nate. He was suddenly in a hurry to get home. When we saw his home, that night, we wondered why the rush.

We pulled out just as the sun rose above the horizon. That day passed uneventfully, just had to listen to Uncle Nate raving and bossing all day long. By the way, he had not said another word about Ol'Bullet. Not after Ol'Bullet killed the snake. It will be some time before Uncle Nate threatens to hit him with a stick. There was going to be trouble over the dog, that was for sure.

We arrived at Uncle Nate's a little before sundown. The welcome was cool to say the least. Aunt Pettie was just as bossy and began doing a lot of it to get us in the house for supper. After supper she told us we could sleep in the wagons, as she did not have beds ready for us. What that meant was, that they did not have beds for us. Hardly had beds for their crowd.

That crowd, included two boys and two girls. I knew from being around Uncle Nate's kids just a little that I did not like them. Now, I definitely didn't like Uncle Nate's kids. The oldest boy, Glen, was almost sixteen and already shaving. He acted like he was somebody older, smarter and important, just like his father. The other boy, George is about my age. He is a sneak and a big, fat tattletale. He is only ten, but already outweighed me by thirty pounds. He is really a big, fat bully. Wonder how he got those traits? The two girls were nine, twins named Joyce and Lois. Little thin cry babies. Really gave you the creeps. Lizzie had been through a lot for an eight year old, but she didn't bawl all the time. Now these two, one of them was crying or whimpering all the time. Minnie said that I had to be a Christian about the four snooty nosed rats. But, I can only tell what I see, and they are worse now, than when they were at Aunt Bess's.

The whole family is the sorriest bunch of people that I , in my eleven years had met. Even Ol'Bullet sniffed of them and moved back. I mean he walked backward away from them, like, they were dirty. Well, they were not just dirty, they were filthy. I doubt they had, had a bath all winter. As the weather got warmer they really got to smelling. At the funeral last January, it was so cold they did not smell, but now, whew!! Enough about this tribe of leaches and scum. Mother would not be happy with my description of these people.

The next morning began the terrible ordeal of living at Uncle Nate's. To start with, the breakfast, for us, was a porridge, while the six of them finished off what was left of Aunt Bess's basket. We ate out of the basket last night and that was the last good meal the three of us saw for a long, long time. The porridge is the worst tasting mush in the world. Must have been something they fed the hogs. They all laughed, and Aunt Pettie said, "When you get hungry that will taste real good." Well, I hate to admit it, but that mush finally got to tasting better, not good.

Especially, when I was very hungry. To help with the taste, Minnie kept slipping extra sugar for us to use in the porridge.

The unloading became a nightmare. All the furniture they had, if you want to call it furniture was thrown out in the yard, and Mama's and Papa's was carried in the house.

Minnie asked, "Why are you putting our furniture in the house, when we will be taking it to New Mexico Territory in a few days?"

Uncle Nate and Aunt Pettie just began to laugh and replied, "Oh, we are just putting it in the house to protect it from the weather." They went through the trunks and took what clothes that would fit them, and just threw the rest in the floor. When I objected, I got backhanded across the face and knocked down.

"You are in my house and you will do what I say, and that is to show some respect for your elders." shouted Uncle Nate. This began the physical abuse. Minnie and Lizzie began to cry as I picked myself up and wiped the blood off my mouth.

"Now you girls stop that bawling or you will get some of the same," screamed Aunt Pettie.

"Just get out of the way and hush or I'll send you to the barn," shouted Uncle Nate, "I'll tend to the lot of you later."

We stood glued to the floor in astonishment. This was that nightmare I had, had. Clear as a bell. Minnie looked at me with big round eyes, and sudden realization dawned on her that all that I had said was probably true.

The next few hours were pure "HELL". Forgive me Mama.

The next thing brought in the house was Mama's big trunk. When the trunk was opened it revealed Grandma's Bible. "Oh, what a lovely Bible! That is something I have always wanted. Such a beautiful book," exclaimed Aunt Pettie. She started going through the book and the addresses that Aunt Bess and Aunt Marjie had given Minnie fell out.

"Well, what is this?"

Minnie started to speak, "That is…"

I hit her in the side to shut her up before Uncle Nate or Aunt Pettie noticed that she was about to speak. Aunt Pettie needed that Bible like a hog needed Sunday. Why? She couldn't read, and she sure didn't know how to live by what the book taught.

"Why, Nate would you kindly tell me what this is?"

"Why that is the address for those two cows of aunts we left bawling in the yard. Oh, so you were going to write and tell them what was going on. I'll fix that!" He tore the paper into little pieces and tossed them at Minnie, "Here are your addresses!"

After they had strewn all the contents of the trunk, they took turns sitting or lying on the furniture that had been moved in the house. Their four kids jumped on the furniture and beds with their dirty shoes and filthy clothes. They all laughed as if it was great sport. They trampled the items in the floor, and when I tried to pick up some of them, I got that second back handing for the day. Blood covered my face in a second, and my head rang like a bell. I hadn't disobeyed, I just had displeased Uncle Nate.

"Now, I told you this is my house, and you do what I tell you!" Then he took off his belt and whipped me for several minutes. I rolled on the floor to avoid his punishment, but that just made him madder, and the licks went on and on. His family laughed, pointed and sneered.

Finally he stopped and ordered all of us out of the house and to the barn, shouting, "I'll show ya'll who owns what now, and who gives the orders." We went to the barn, but I didn't cry from that beating or any of the others.

Some of our things had been unloaded in the barn and the family started going through the rest of our possessions. One of the twins found the two dolls that belonged to Lizzie.

They begin to shout, "Oh, Mama, look what we found! Look what we found!"

Lizzie jumped up in the wagon and grabbed the two dolls, "Those are mine!"

The twins started bawling, and Aunt Pettie came running and asked, "Lizzie, what have you done to my babies?" Spying the dolls, she jerked the dolls from Lizzie and gave them back to her twins as she sneered, "I'll thank you to keep your hands of off my girls' dolls."

Lizzie broke out crying, "Those dolls were given to me for Christmas and my birthday!"

Minnie finally could take no more, and she shouted, "These things are ours, and they belonged to our parents" She started toward Lizzie to assist her. Just at that moment, Glen the sixteen years old stuck out his foot and tripped her.

"Oh, I'm sorry about that." But, instead of helping her up, he hit her in the back. Well, at that moment all fury broke loose, and the biggest free for all you could imagine started. I hit Glen with a pick handle, and when he fell down, I started hitting him with all I had. Minnie jumped to her feet and was in a tug of war with the twins and Aunt Pettie over the dolls. Aunt Pettie hit Minnie in the mouth, but Minnie hung on for dear life.

Uncle Nate began dancing around shouting, "Stop this, I said stop this!" He grabbed me from the back and threw me to the ground and held me until Glen could get on top of me. Glen held me and had hit me about two licks when Ol' Bullet jumped in the melee and began to bite Glen on the arm. Ol' Bullet got Glen off me! Uncle Nate grabbed Papa's shot gun out of the wagon and fired at Ol'Bullet. Luck was, he was off balance and missed by a mile. But that broke up the fight, and Ol' Bullet ran out the barn door.

We all got a licking with a strap. My second one and the first for the girls. This was only the first of many whippings we were to receive over the next few weeks. We fought, and it had done nothing to stop them from destroying our possessions. Clothes were given to whoever they would fit, the rest were thrown on the ground. The gun Uncle Nate had grabbed and a rifle in the wagon were Papa's. Now he claimed they were his, and if I opened my mouth I would have another licking. Of course all of our things, like the two dolls, were gone. The humiliation and the destruction of property went on and on.

By the end of the first week, we were sleeping in the barn all the time. Sometimes we had enough cover and other times we huddled together to keep warm. Our diet was reduced to mush three times a day. Work became almost more than we could bear. The weather grew hot, and we suffered from the heat.

We worked mostly in the garden, gathering eggs, cleaning the barn, cutting weeds and tending livestock. One of my jobs was to take the little herd down into the pasture each morning and bring them back at night. If I could not find one at night, I had to stay down there until I found the lost one. I spent several nights down in the bush looking for a stubborn heifer. The rest of the time I cleaned the barn, hoed weeds in the garden and cleaned chicken coops. Sometimes I could brush the mules. I liked that.

Minnie and Lizzie did laundry, what was done. They helped weed in the garden and harvest the vegetables. There never seemed to be an end of chores to do. We were up at dawn and worked until sunset. Our mush was sometimes cold just because we did not do something the way Aunt Pettie wanted it done.

Their kids became our tormentors. They would break chicken eggs and say we did it. They taunted and laughed at us. A rain of corn cobs, would shower down on us and then they would run when we chased them. Of course we got blamed for whatever the incident.

I guess the biggest problem was the milking of the three cows. I am not good at milking, but that became one of my jobs. It took me a long time to milk. Then if I should set the bucket down where one of the kids could get at it, they would kick it over or put dirt in it. Anything to get me a licking. I got a licking four evenings in a row for spilling the milk. I didn't spill the milk. It was kicked over.

They picked on Lizzie constantly. The twins would do anything to make her cry. We had several fights over that, and I got more lickings.

I would say that I had a fight with one of the four at least twice a week. I would get mad and even tear into Glen. A time or two I got so mad, I, tore into Uncle Nate. I found out just how strong he was. He tossed me across the barn like I was nothing. Then he picked me up and hit me in the face several times. All the while yelling, "If I can't break you with a strap, I'll do it with my fist." I had several black eyes over my rebellion. They mostly came from Uncle Nate.

The girls got some beatings, but mostly they were screamed at and yelled at, until they cried. Lizzie cried the quickest, but she is the smallest. Minnie got to the place if some of them started picking on Lizzie, she would hit them in the face with her fist. She even decked Glen one evening for rough handling Lizzie. Minnie got a good beating, but later she said, "It was worth every lick."

The twins would take Lizzie's dolls and throw them back and forth like they were a pair of balls. They soon became very dirty and torn. This made Lizzie cry and the twins would laugh and point their fingers at her and call out, "Cry baby, cry baby!" They would find things to throw at her, that is unless Minnie or I were around.

One day Minnie really set them off. She asked, "When are we going to school?"

The entire family laughed at her and said, "School, what is school? What are you trying to do, be a miss smarty?" The taunting and cruelty went on and on.

"We need to be in school," Minnie insisted.

Uncle Nate gloated and said, "All you are going to do is what I tell you, and that is to work on this farm."

Punishment became more severe and often. Just the smallest excuse, and the strap came out. We were all black and blue from all of the beatings, and I had several places that had bled.

Things could not get much worse, I thought. Beatings came more often, the work in the fields became harder. The worse thing was the food, MUSH. It was sorry, even with lots of sugar. All of us had lost some weight. I was really blue.

After that fight in the barn, Ol' Bullet would only be seen out in the brush. Every time Uncle Nate saw him and could get the gun, he tried to shoot him. We heard Ol' Bullet yelp a few times when a buckshot found him. Usually, he was long gone into the brush any time he saw Uncle Nate. I would sneak him some scraps when I could. One thing about Ol' Bullet, he could hunt on his own and not starve. I just wondered if he would give up and run off.

We had running off on our minds all the time. To keep up hope, Minnie would ask, "When are we going to Uncle John's?" Out would come the strap.

Uncle Nate would go into a tirade, "Keep your mouth shut. I'll inform you when we might go to John's. Otherwise just do your work and keep out of my way."

Runoff. That subject was on my mind, day and night, constantly. The next turn of events, really got us planning on running away. Minnie, Lizzie and I had been given the job of weeding the garden. We had worked for a couple of hours and had come to the windmill to get a cool drink of water. We were on the east side of the barn in the shade when we heard Uncle Nate and Aunt Pettie, talking in the barn.

"Now, woman, just be calm, another week or two of this and those three will be long gone."

"I don't know. That Minnie has set her jaw. Looks just like your Ma's jaw when she had her mind made up about a matter."

Minnie smiled at me and Lizzie as she put her first finger up to her lips and signaled for us to be quiet.

"You're right about Minnie, Pettie. But, let me tell you a little secret. The other day I caught Glen looking at Minnie. You know what I mean?"

"You mean.......?"

"Yes, looking at her like she was a woman."

Minnie's eyes got big, and her jaw really set hard.

"Now, I figure if we just let nature take it's course, Minnie will take the other two and run away."

"Where do you think they would run to?"

"I don't know. All I hope is that Glen gets her, and she will be too embarrassed to go back home. If she just runs away, we can get the sheriff of this county after her for stealing. These are the only two choices she has. Let Glen have his way or get put in jail for stealing. If she is charged with stealing, because of her age, they would send her to an orphans home and those other two brats along with her."

Their steps seemed to fade as they moved about in the barn.

Minnie started to herd us away when they continued.

"How long before we get to spend some of that money, Nate? I would like to buy some clothes."

"We can't spend any until the brats are out of the way!" he explained.

"What about that part that is ours?"

"What do you mean ours?"

"The part you got from the sale of your folks place."

"Whose part did you say?"

"Why, your part, Nate."

"That's right, Pettie, it is MY part."

"We are married and part of that is mine, and I want to buy some things."

Minnie put her hand over Lizzie's mouth when Nate raised his hand at Pettie and shouted, "You think part of that money is yours, why you dumb......" He hit her with the back of his hand. "That money is mine, and if you get any of it, it will be out of the kindness of my heart. Do you understand me?"

We thought Lizzie was going to cry out when he raised his hand again and hit Aunt Pettie.

Pettie continued, "Yes, Nate. Just don't hit me again." She wiped her tears.

"Well, stop asking dumb questions." He seemed to relax a bit. "I guess there is one other possibility on these brats. I could start to New Mexico Territory and lose them about half way. They would be too far from here to come back and too far from their dear Uncle John to go on out to the Territory."

All of us nodded our heads yes, take us toward Uncle John's. If we are going to run away, just getting us closer to him would be fine. I liked that idea better than the other ones.

"Nate, I think you should take them the other way."

"What do you know. You're dumb as dirt, woman!"

She whined, "Nate, why do you talk to me that way?"

He looked at her in disgust, "Because you are dumb and dirty."

"You want I should take a bath?'

"No, I don't want you to take a bath. You could catch your death of cold, and who would help me raise these four kids of ours."

She squinted at him, "You better listen to me about Glen chasing that girl. Word of that could get all the way back to the judge, and he would send the sheriff down here. They expect you to be gone to the Territory of New Mexico by now. And for running them off, they just might go back and tell that judge and the sheriff.

"You know woman, you might be right. But, let Glen have his fun if he can, and she will be in trouble and can't go back. On the other hand we could dump them off on somebody way out West."

They moved to the open door at the north end of the barn.

Nate had one more idea, "Look, we get rid of the brats, we'll move a long ways from here, and then we can use all of the money and live like royalty."

"Nate, that is a great idea. Let's move down to the coast. Its warm there all the time, and things are green."

"Fine with me woman, I just want away from this part of the state."

Minnie took Lizzie by the hand and motioned for me to follow, and we returned to the garden.

Minnie was fuming. "Robert, you were right all the time. They never intended to take us to Uncle John's. They intend to steal any and all of the money and get rid of us. I wish I had let you talk to one of the aunts."

"I know, Minnie. What are we going to do?"

"I don't know right now. But, I will figure out something. Now you two be careful about saying anything about what we had heard." She knew that I would keep my mouth shut, but Lizzie might just let a slip.

Later, Minnie cautioned me. "Robert, we have got to get away from here. I think that I have an idea and need to work on it for a while, so I want you do me two favors."

"I'll be glad to do whatever you want."

"Fine, I want you to watch Glen. Watch him as much as possible, and if you are sent to do a chore and are going to be away from the house, let me know. The other thing is start making a list in your mind of where you find any of the things that belonged to Mama and Papa. Such as the guns. Where does Uncle Nate keep them? Anything that is supposed to be ours."

"That's odd, because I have been looking around to see just where items are kept. That will be easy."

She shook her head, yes, and we returned to our never ending chores. We worked from daylight 'till dark, six days of the week. Uncle Nate let us rest on Sunday. He tried to be "religious." The best day of the week was Saturday. Uncle Nate and all the family would load up the wagon, their wagon, and go to town. They'd leave us to work, but we didn't have all the supervision. We would work together and try to get the work list done as quick as possible, and then the rest of the time was ours. That way we could loaf a little and look for things to put on our list of belongings. Things to take with us when we ran away.

I began watching Glen like a hawk. Minnie thought I did not understand why she wanted me to watch all time, but I did. The first time I really startled him, I caught him with his back to me and his overalls down

"Hey, Glen, what are you doing?"

He jerked up his overalls and ran into the brush. Later he sidled up to me as I was cleaning the barn and said, "You had better not tell anyone what I was doing, or I'll bust you good."

"What were you doing?" I asked innocently.

"Just you keep your mouth shut!" he ordered as he walked out of the barn.

I really went on the watch. Next time I caught him doing something, it really got his goat. "He was trying to peek in the outhouse.

With a loud voice, I called out to him, "Hey Glen, what are you doing?"

He jumped about two feet, glared at me and ran off. I didn't know who was in the outhouse and didn't stay around to find out. I was getting to him, and he knew I was on to him.

Minnie said she had caught him trying to watch her if she was in the field and had to go to relieve herself. She noted he was always trying to get around her and stand real close. As the days wore on he began trying to touch her. I started staying as close to her as I could, and it paid off. Glen would find Minnie and discover that I was there, and he would leave.

Glen was real sneaky. I discovered that he would go around outside at night and try to peek under the shade of Minnie's room. I knew that he was standing just outside of her room one night. The lights were out, but he was still trying to look in. Minnie and I had a plan. She went over and raised the shade, so he could see in the room. To make the plan really work she said, "I'll just raise this window and let in some air, it is so hot in here." Glen was doing his best to see in her room. He got closer and closer to the window. Then Minnie sprang the joke on him. We had put some water in the chamber pot. She said, "I forgot to throw this pot out this morning," And with a heave she threw the water out the window and all over Glen. You could hear him for a mile, sputtering and spewing. I followed him down to the dirt tank and saw him jump in clothes and all. That put a stop to his peeping.

Later, Minnie was down in the garden hoeing weeds, when Glen showed up and began trying to hug her and touch her here and there. If you know what I mean. Well, I had been watching, so I slipped up real close and hollered real loud, "Hey Glen, what ya' doing?" Glen must have jumped three feet in the air, and he ran off just like before.

"You showed up just right. You kept him from getting one of his toes cut off with this hoe."

"Minnie you wouldn't do that would you?"

"Just try me!"

I had noticed she was wearing overalls all the time and was very careful to go use the outhouse and not the bushes.

It wasn't but two or three days later, that Glen was trying one of his stunts. I wasn't around, and Minnie chopped down on his foot with the hoe. He was barefooted, and she really cut deep. Didn't cut off any toes, but put him in the house for about three weeks. Uncle Nate was furious at Glen, because he had to take him to the horse doctor in town to get some doctoring and it cost him two dollars. Besides, Glen could not work for that three weeks.

Minnie very contritely said, "I'm sorry. Glen just got his foot in the way, where I was chopping."

We found out that Glen was scared to death of a snake. So, I found a gartersnake and kept it handy and ready. Sometimes I would keep it in my pocket for just the right moment. The snake was not very big, and he became used to being in my pocket. The right moment came within a few days after Glen was allowed out of the house and back to work.

Glen was in the barn currying one of his Papa's horses. I had a rattlesnake rattler. I had cut this rattler off the snake Ol' Bullet had killed on the way to Uncle Nate's. Glen was working away with one hand and had the other in his overalls. I was hiding behind some hay. I rattled the rattler and pitched that garter snake in between Glen's feet and hollered, "Glen, look out, SNAKE!!!"

He could not even move, he froze and wet all over his clothes. I came running with a hoe and made like I killed the snake and tossed it outside. Actually, I never touched the little snake and I picked it up later for future use. Glen finally moved very stiffly over and sat down on a bale of hay with a very red face.

"Robert, would you go in the house and get me some clean clothes?"

"Sure thing, Glen. Won't be but a minute." I started to walk by him and realized he had not just wet his clothes, he smelled awful.

I ran to the house and in a loud voice announced to all who could hear, "Glen was scared by a snake in the barn, and he has messed in his clothes. I have come to get him some clean ones and to find out what Aunt Pettie wants him to do with the messy ones?"

She wrinkled up her nose and said, "Tell him to go to the dirt tank and take a bath, and to not come to the house smelling like a horse stall."

I took my time going back to the barn, just let him suffer in his mess. I laid the clothes just inside the door, "Your Mama said to go to the dirt tank and wash and to not come back smelling like a horse stall. Hey, Glen I sure would be careful down at that dirt tank. I saw a big diamond back down there the other day, and he got away from me."

Glen was gone for a long time. Matter of fact, he missed supper. He slipped in the back door and went straight to his room so no one would see him. Just as he got to his room I called out, "Glen, did you see that big diamond back rattler down at the tank? I sure would like to kill him for the rattles."

Glen barely ate breakfast the next morning. He rushed out followed by a barrage of questions from his family. I found him down in the garden chopping weeds. I didn't get too close just in case he had figured out how I had tricked him. Didn't think he was bright enough to have caught on, but you never could tell. Sure didn't want him to figure out that the snake I had in my hand was only a garter snake. I held the snake in my right hand and the rattle in my left. Another reason for not getting too close. He might get wise.

"Glen, look what I caught on the way down here." I swung the snake back and forth and rattled the rattles.

His eyes became large and round. He turned white and was gasping for breath. I thought he might fall over in a faint if I got too close.

"Say Glen, if I ever catch you trying to touch my sister or get a peek at her, I will put one of these in your bed some night while you are asleep. Understand, Old Buddy?"

He just stood there, frozen in place. Not answering or giving any indication that he was aware of my statement and question. To make my point a little clearer, I moved a couple of steps toward him. Before I could say a word he suddenly let out a blood curdling scream and raced down the furrow. He did not come home for supper or breakfast. I didn't tell anyone what I had done. I figured if he told on me that there would be snakes all around him from now on. I was just going to let him take his medicine for running off and not doing his chores when he got home, if he ever got home.

Uncle Nate was beside himself when it became bedtime the second evening and Glen was still gone. About noon the third day Uncle Nate harnessed up his team and went to town. We learned later he had looked everywhere he thought Glen might be, but no Glen.

Minnie caught me out in the barn and asked, "Do you know where Glen is?"

I could answer her truthfully, "No I don't, he was chopping weeds in the field, but I don't know were he is now." Thank the Lord she had asked the right question, "Did I know?". Boy, if she had asked, "Did I have anything to do with him disappearing?", I would have been cooked.

Uncle Nate began to have really wild and varied moods. First he would be mean and whip us for any little provocation. Then he would try to be nice, and boy, was that out of character! For no reason at all, he would be depressed and withdrawn. I told Minnie that I thought he was dangerous. More dangerous than before. One day I found him down by the windmill and tank muttering to himself and going over and over the money drafts and the guardian papers.

Trying to be friendly, I asked, "What's going on Uncle Nate?"

He stuck all of the papers in an envelope and stood up, "What are you doing slipping up on me like that?"

"Didn't you hear me whistling as I came down the path?"

"No, and why aren't you at work?"

"You told me to feed the chickens and then to go to the watertank in that pasture and see if the cows had plenty of water. That's where I was going, when I saw you, Uncle Nate."

"Then get on with your work and stop bothering me!"

"Yes Sir," I replied and started down the path. I looked back, and Uncle Nate was staggering up the path toward the house. Also, there was something else that I had not noticed. Uncle Nate had a jug in his hand. That accounted for his staggering all over the trail.

Uncle Nate announced that he had to go on a short business trip in a few days, and that he would make a list of what each of us was to do while he was gone. He also announced that upon his return, about the first week of June, we would start to New Mexico. I knew his plan. I had been making it a habit, when I saw Uncle Nate and Aunt Pettie going to the barn during the day, to slip up and listen to their conversation.

The first revelation from listening to their conversation was the story about the letter to Uncle John. Sure, he had written to Brother John, and John had answered, but not the letter he showed the Judge and the Sheriff.

"Pettie, that was really clever sending John a letter so when he answered, we had a letter from New Mexico Territory with the post mark from Fort Summer."

"Yes, Nate, I did think that I had, had a good idea." Maybe Uncle Nate was not as smart and clever as we thought he was. It could be that our dear aunt was the slyest of the two.

"Clever, that idea of getting your brother to write that letter we put in the envelope from Uncle John. Now that is clever, different hand writing than mine."

"My brother owed us a couple of favors, and besides he did not like the way your whole family treated him that time he went with us to that family reunion. Acted like he was trash. Well, he sure showed them. Just because that I can't read or write, who would have thought that my brother was so talented. Why, I bet he could be a lawyer or judge if he set his mind to it."

"Pettie, I would not doubt it for a minute. That is why I am going on a little business trip. I will get your brother to write me another letter, from my dear brother. This letter will instruct me to deposit his check and the brats' check in a bank of my choice, and that he is afraid for me to travel that far with that much money in hand." He stroked his chin in thought, "By writing another letter to him, he will answer, and I will have a later post mark. Then I will put the letter of instructions that your brother wrote, in the last envelope. I can show both letters to any bank, and they will let me deposit the drafts. That way all of the money will be in my name in a bank, so we can travel and not need to worry about that much money on our person."

"Very good, my dear husband."

"Dear brother may require a little hush money, but that makes him involved, and if anything comes up, his neck is in the noose with us."

"So, Pettie, I have lots to do by the first of June."

When I told Minnie of this conversation she said, "Robert, this time I believe you. I wish I had earlier. Well, at least they have given us a deadline and a date when we have to be gone."

"What are you talking about, Minnie?"

"Can you keep a secret?"

"Yes, of course I can."

"Then let's go to the water tank so we are a long ways from the house and can't be heard."

We found Lizzie and went down to the tank. When we got to the tank Minnie turned to Lizzie and pointed to some beautiful flowers, "Lizzie would you pick a few of those for me?"

Lizzie started off down the path and as soon as she could not hear us, Minnie explained, "Think about this. It is almost the end of March. The weather is getting warm and the chance of a cold storm has passed. Uncle Nate said he was going to New Mexico Territory on the first of June. We have got to leave by the middle of May, just on the chance he moves his departure up a week or so. He has got to get that letter to Uncle John. That will take about three weeks. Say that Uncle John takes a week to answer, and then it takes about three weeks to get the answer back. That is a total of six to eight weeks. So we need to figure on the six week number."

"Man that is a lot to think about. Are we really going to run away?"

"Yes, we are going to Uncle John's. And, Robert, it's not too much to think about. Just think, this is the first of April, and if that letter takes six weeks, that will be the middle of May, and we need to be gone."

"Boy, Minnie, I see why you were one of the smartest in school. To figure this all out."

"Now that we have a date set in our minds, there are two things we will need to do."

"What is that, Minnie?"

"First, have you located all of Papa's things?'

"Yes, Uncle Nate keeps them in his bedroom."

"Then, those are some of the last things we will take. Second, we will need several burlap sacks. We will put the items we want to take in them and make packs out of them . We can tie two together and put up them over the backs of the mules like they do packs. Now, Robert, we have got to be careful what we take this early. If too much begins to disappear, then Uncle Nate might get suspicious. So, before you take anything to hide, talk to me first, and let's not raise suspicion."

The next day Uncle Nate left on his business trip. Minnie had learned where Aunt Pettie's brother lived and figured that it would take him an extra four or five days. That may have added time to our schedule, but we could not take a chance, so we planned for the same date, the middle of May.

Good to his word, he had made out a work list for everyone, even Aunt Pettie, the twins and George, the bully. Boy, what a list he made for me! All of this would take me two weeks.

"Uncle Nate, you expect me to do all of this in four or five days?" Mistake, I got hit in the mouth again and for the umpteenth time.

"Boy, you just don't learn. I'll break your spirit and make you mind if it's the last thing I do."

I got up and took my list and planned the work. I also looked at Minnie's and Lizzie's list. Impossible for either one of them to get that whole list completed. So, Minnie decided that we would do Lizzie's first and then hers. That way Lizzie would not get a spanking, and if we could do Minnie's, she would avoid one also. Then all three of us would work on mine and get as much done as possible, brave the outcome and take whatever punishment Uncle Nate dished out.

Two things happened to help us. First, it rained on Uncle Nate, and he lost four more days. The rain kept us in the house or the barn for one day. We had time to make our list. Lizzie wanted to know what kind of list we were making.

Minnie tried to ease around the subject, "Oh, just a list of things, Lizzie."

Lizzie screwed up her face. "That is not just any old list. You are making a list of things to take when we run away."

Our mouths dropped open. "Where did you get that idea?"

"You, said that we could go to Uncle John's, and the only way to get there is to run away, right?"

"Say, for a girl you are pretty smart!" I remarked.

Minnie had that frown on her face. "Lizzie, you can't let Uncle Nate or Aunt Pettie know."

"I know. I can keep a secret."

We stopped trying to get away from Lizzie to plan. Instead we let her be our lookout. Just like Indians, we had a lookout. Plus, we had to get to work on those work lists so we wouldn't get another busting.

We found by working together that we had all three lists completed in ten days. Two whole days before Uncle Nate planned to be back.

Aunt Pettie was not watching us like Uncle Nate did. She had her own list to do and did not want him beating her. The twins were doomed to a beating because all they did was fuss and cry. Then George the bully, when he discovered that my list was finished, started bullying me to help him. There was arguing about me helping him.

Finally, I said, "No, I am not going to help you. You saw that we were working together and would finish our list. Now you want me to help you do your list, so you won't get the strap."

George outweighed me by thirty pounds. "O.K.", he said, "You are going to get it. Either you help, or I'm going to whip you."

I figured that I would rather take a whipping from him than help him with his sorry old work. So, the fists flew and the blows landed. Let me put it this way, George was a bully. Right? Well, he hit me one time, and I hit him about six or seven times, and he went running to his mother. Lied, that I was picking on him. Boy, if there is one thing I hate worse than a bully, it is a tattletail.

Aunt Pettie came down where I was working and gave me a good tongue lashing, and told me that when Uncle Nate got back, he would thrash me good and proper. Furthermore, I was to stop bullying her little boy, and that for fighting, I could go hungry tonight. Little boy! Man, I think I will throw up!

I couldn't let this pass, so after a while I saw George down in the back pasture. If I'm going to get a strapping, then I'm going to earn it. I had to chase him down and that thirty pounds did not make it too hard. He began to cry, and I told him this was for tattling. Let me say this, his tattling days and his bully days were all over, all over! When his Mama saw him, she blew up and wanted to know what had happened to him. All he would say was he fell down.

When Uncle Nate finally got back, I got that thrashing, but it was worth every lick. His little boy had black eyes and bruises all over him. At least we didn't get a licking for not having the work done. I had pure satisfaction out of whipping George for his tattling and bullying.

Uncle Nate, in his next private conversation with his wife, revealed that he had sent a letter to Uncle John.

"Did you see my brother?"

"Yes I did, and he sends his love. Had to pay him ten dollars to do the letter, but that is well worth the price."

"Nate, why can't I have ten dollars?"

He hit her before she could even blink. Then he took down a set of traces and beat her. He beat her something awful. We could hear her cries all over the place. The twins ran down to the tank to be out of reach of the sound she made. George put his hands over his ears and shut his eyes. I don't know if he could hear her, but it was real sad and disturbing.

After she had stopped crying, he told Aunt Pettie, "Soon as it is good and warm so sleeping out will not be a problem, I am going to make like I am taking them to the Territory of New Mexico. When I get way out somewhere I'll dump them and hightail it back home. I'm thinking the first of June would be just about right. I will have the letters I need and will have put the money in the bank."

Spring plowing and planting caused Uncle Nate a great deal of agony. He just did not like to follow a pair of horses, and with Glen gone he was in a wild mood. He knew that he had to plow and get his cotton planted to make a pretense for all of his neighbors. He wanted to appear the good farmer and loving uncle. He tried to get some plowing done, but all he wanted to do was sit and look at the bank drafts and dream of going someplace and acting like the rich and genteel.

Much to my surprise Uncle Nate elected me to plow. He had, had Glen to plow, and Glen had done a fairly good job. Glen was big and strong for his age and Uncle Nate could take all the credit. With the absence of Glen, he had grandiose plans for me to take Glen's place. My snake trick, had just turned against me, and Uncle Nate didn't have a clue of what took place. So he took me to the barn and showed me how to harness his horses to pull a plow.

We went down in the cotton patch, and he attempted to instruct me in the art of following a plow. My Papa had already made a good hand out of me, and following a plow was one skill I had mastered, even at eleven years of age. But, the difference was, Papa had used a couple of the big, strong, smart mules and not these dumb, weak horses. I played dumb and let Uncle Nate show me over and over. He broke into a hard sweat with work and overweight. After a day of futile effort he was worn to a nub. All he could do was swear, sweat and make a mess of the furrows. Papa would have laughed him out of the field.

The second morning was just a repeat of the first. Uncle Nate could not plow a straight furrow if his life depended on it. He became furious and beat the horses and swore some more. By noon, he was exhausted and at his wit's end. I guess I felt sorry for him, but it was really pride. I just couldn't keep my mouth shut. My, Mama used to say, "Pride goes before a fall." I was proud of what Papa had taught me and how good the mules could work.

I just had to open my mouth. "Uncle Nate, any two of our mules could plow circles around those two sorry horses." The next thing I remembered was getting up off the ground. I had blood and dirt in my mouth.

"I told you to keep your mouth shut. You are as hard headed as all four of those mules. And another thing, those are not your mules anymore. They are mine for feed and board. Got that?"

"You mean you are stealing them just like everything else that was Papa's and Mama's!"

I almost had let the cat out of the bag, and I got another hand across the face.

"What are you talking about, boy?"

"Nothing, Uncle Nate."

He didn't buy that and really watched me for several days. At least until something else distracted him and his mind was on something else. I soon found out what that something else meant.

"Mr. Robert, you think you are so smart and that your Papa and his mules are so smart. I'll just make you a bet. If you and the mules can plow that cotton field and put the cotton in, I'll get you right to New Mexico Territory. I figure you and those fine mules could put that crop in, in two or three weeks, and then off you and your sisters go to Uncle John's. Deal?"

I may be smart about some things, but I sure am dumb about some others. This was one of those times. Minnie cautioned me, but as Mama had said, "Pride goes before a fall."

"Deal, Uncle Nate. If you will put that in writing and give it to Minnie, I'll will do the field. Also, I want the note to say that the four mules are ours."

"You harness up a pair of mules, and I'll write the note." He had me, and I did not know it. If I could plow the field, he had his field planted with no sweat on his part. He had a little note written before I could harness a pair of mules. The note stated just what I had requested. I had been had, but pride, boy, what pride will do to you! Uncle Nate gave the note to Minnie.

I had harnessed up number one and number four. They were nearer the same size, and that made a good pair out of the other two. I would use one pair each day and let the other team rest, just like Papa had always done.

By noon, I had plowed more than Uncle Nate had done in two or three days. Minnie brought me my mush, with extra sugar. She also brought a waterbag. We hung the bag in the shade, and I had cool water for the rest of the day. I had forgotten to get water in the morning and almost died of thirst, but was too "Proud" to stop and go find some water.

She also brought water for the mules. A lot of heavy carrying for her, but she said, "You are in this fix, so I will try to help you."

Was I ever in a fix. By night I was almost exhausted, and the field seemed to get bigger and bigger. But, a deal is a deal. I had to brush the mules by lantern light, while I ate my evening mush. All I could think of was going to sleep. I had just shut my eyes, when Minnie shook me awake.

"Here is your breakfast. I'll harness the other team while you eat. This way you will get a few minutes of extra rest." She was doing part of my work so I could rest, and then she would have to do her chores as well. I would have to do better tomorrow.

That day and each day after that passed in a blur. I lost all track of time. Days just ran on and on. Then one morning I realized that I had plowed that entire field. The furrows were good and straight. Papa would have been proud. They were not as good as Papa's plowing, but he would have bragged on my work. All I had to do was plant the cotton. At least I would get to ride the planter and not have to walk like I did while plowing with a single tree.`

That night, Minnie said, "Uncle Nate is watching you plow and work. He watches every day for a while. Usually from the bushes at the edge of the field, so you won't see him. He's up to something. I just feel it. Be careful of what you say."

It took me another week to plant the field. Riding the planter was easy. Carrying the cotton seed out to the planter was hard. I had to hook up the other team to the wagon and load the bags of seed. I would park the wagon at the end of the furrows and when I ran out of seed I had to fill the seed boxes. That is when I had to carry the bags of seed out to the seed boxes. Sometimes I was at the end of the furrows, but lots of the time I was out in the middle of the field. Did Uncle Nate offer to help? Not likely! Not on your life. He was in the shade somewhere, plotting his next move.

When I finished, he came down to the field. Did not compliment the work, just walked around a bit and went back to the house.

At supper I asked, "When are we going to start to New Mexico Territory with our four mules? I have finished the job. Just like we agreed."

"That's right, Robert. You have finished the job. We had an agreement, you say?"

"Yes, you gave it to Minnie."

"Well, Minnie if you will fetch this agreement we will discuss the terms."

Minnie returned in a few minutes with a look of desperation on her face, "The note is not there, it is gone!" Tears welled up in her eyes. "We have been tricked, Robert."

"Now, Minnie. Why would you think you have been tricked? Maybe you just misplaced the agreement. Perhaps the mice got this so called agreement. Well, when you find it let, me know."

He was laughing as he went out the door.

All of that work! I should have known he would trick us. His word was worthless. Aunt Pettie probably stole the note when we were off working. Minnie thought she had hidden it very well, but with these sly, sneaky, people around, you could not hide anything very long.

Our list of things to take when we ran away was very precious to us. We couldn't let them find it. So Minnie decided that she would keep it hidden in her clothes. Maybe they would not search her. They had never searched us for any reason, so she had to take the chance. She was scribbling small and it was hard to read words. Some were misspelled. Her story, if the list is found, is that she is practicing spelling and having a hard time remembering how to spell some words. They have no idea that Minnie is so smart.

May had finally arrived. We were planning the things we would take with us. We were going to go to Uncle John's. We had heard enough lies and promises. The whippings had continued. Lizzie had had two for nothing other than asking some simple question. Minnie had had several because she would just take so much and would rebel. I had had more than I could count. I had black and blue marks all over me. Some of the licks had cut my skin, and the cuts had bled. These places were especially sore and tender.

Minnie had listend to the men in the family talking about how to go to Uncle John's. It wasn't just head west and when you get to New Mexico Territory and you will find Uncle John standing there. You had to follow the Brazos river west to it's end and then go over this ridge. At that point you will find another branch of the Brazos. Follow this branch and find a fork in the river. Take the right hand and finally, you will come out near the New Mexico Territory line and you could see the mesa. Uncle John lives at the mesa. They call their community Mesa after the table shaped plateau.

A few days after the first of May a strange man came to the farm. Not many people came out this way. In almost four months we had seen about half a dozen strangers come to the place. You had to be coming there. The road did not go by the farm, it ended at the farm. We knew that something was about to happen when this stranger showed up and wanted to see the mules and the wagons. We did not learn what he was there for until I overheard Uncle Nate's and Aunt Pettie's conversation in the barn.

"Mr. Trent sure did like the four mules and the two wagons. He offered a fair price for the lot. He is going to come back about the end of the month to pick them up and pay us. That works out just fine for us. As soon as he has paid us, I will load the brats in our wagon and take them about half way to the Territory and then dump them along the way."

"How much is he going to give you for the whole lot?"

"Pettie, it's none of your business. I'll tell you this, I got more for them than we have ever made on cotton on this sorry, dry-land place."

"Are you going to put that money in the bank with all of the rest, when you get that letter back from Uncle John?"

"Yes, Pettie, if that is any of your business."

What Uncle Nate did not know was, I had overheard Aunt Pettie tell George that as soon as Uncle Nate left for the Territory of New Mexico, they would draw all of the money out of the bank and leave. They were not going to keep taking beatings from him. I always thought that she was the sly and sneaky one in the bunch.

Uncle Nate was going to town almost every day, looking for that letter from his brother. The more time that passed, the worse his disposition became. Any provocation, and somebody got a beating.

I seemed to be the main target for his wrath. He was really upset that I had been able to plant the cotton. That was another thing he complained to his wife about, "That darn brat got out there with those mules and planted that whole field . He did it in less time than you can imagine and did a good job. I wouldn't tell him that the furrows were good and straight or that the field was plowed the best I had seen." He paused and looked at his wife, "You would not tell him, would you?"

"Oh, no. Nate. If he heard that, his head would swell up, and he would be that much more of a show off."

Each Saturday, like every Saturday if it was warm weather, the family would load their wagon and go to town. They were up early and gone shortly after breakfast. Uncle Nate always had that list of jobs for us to do. He could find more things to keep us busy than you can imagine. The place should have been a showplace, but instead it always looked rundown and junky.

The first Saturday of May they were off to town, like always. We watched them drive out of sight, with the twins making faces and sticking out their tongues at us. We rushed through the work list as fast as possible. Shortly after noon we were finished and working on our list, when we heard a noise in the yard.

They had come back early! They almost caught us, and would have, if Ol' Bullet had not started barking and raising cane. This threw Uncle Nate into a frenzy. He rushed into the house, grabbed Papa's shotgun and raced back outside to shoot at Ol' Bullet. Ol' Bullet was long gone, and in his haste to get the gun, he had not noticed us in the house. We rushed out the back door and down to the garden, where we started pulling weeds and looking very busy. By the way, we never did find out why they came back early.

The next week drug by. Days were long and hot. The work never ended. The only thing that was making all of this bearable was the fact we would be leaving in TWO weeks. It was like Christmas. It just never would come. Jobs took forever, and Uncle Nate was really on us. He carried the shotgun all the time, swearing all the time he would kill that dog, if it was the last thing he ever did.

The next Saturday, they left right on schedule and stayed gone until way after dark. We learned that there had been a carnival in town and that they had a grand time. How did we find out about the carnival?

Uncle Nate had to rub it in, "Sorry you had chores to do. You would have enjoyed the carnival. We had the best time. Maybe the next time you can go with us. Ha! Ha!" He held his belly and laughed at us. All of the family joined in and made jokes at our expense. They had won some prizes. You would have thought that the prizes were made of gold the way they carried on over them. Bunch of trash, the prizes and the people.

I had been up in the loft of the barn looking for chicken eggs when I heard somebody come into the barn. It was Uncle Nate. He sat down on a bale of hay, took out a little notebook out from behind a loose board in the wall of the barn. He began entering the amounts of the drafts, calf sale, wagon and mule sales. As he entered each item he just could not refrain from saying the amount out loud. After he had entered all of the figures, he totaled that column of numbers.

He became very excited. Then he said out loud, "Thirty eight thousand dollars. I'm rich, I'm rich. Now I will dump those brats and just keep going West. I'll have the wagon and the team and most of my personal property. The rest Pettie can use for rags, that's all they are anyway. Never see Pettie or these runny nose kids, again. I'll be free and rich." He jumped up from the bale of hay and did a little jig. Before he left, he put the little notebook back behind the loose board.

As soon as he was gone I slid down from the loft and took the little notebook out of the hiding place. Later in the day I showed it to Minnie. We decided to leave the notebook in it's hiding place until we were ready to leave.

We had been counting Saturdays for a month, and today is the one we had been waiting for. We had a hard time sleeping that last night, too excited. I had their team hitched and the wagon at the door when they came out of the house.

Uncle Nate said, "Can you believe this? He is finally learning to do things without having to be told." Uncle Nate and the family loaded up and headed to town, with the usual tongues sticking out and sneers, along with cat calls. "You don't work too hard, hear?"

We went into action. I had the burlap sacks ready, eight all total. Each one of us had a list of things to put in a sack. Lizzie was responsible for clothes, shoes, hats and her two dolls. Some of our clothes had been given to the twins and to George, now she gathered it all up and put everything she could find in a sack. It was amazing that Lizzie had kept the secret for two months, and now she was working as hard as either one of us to load her list. There was a gleam in her eyes when she put the two dolls in a sack.

Her only comment was, "Mine!."

Minnie's list included food, cooking utensils, medicine, bedding for the three of us, Mama's and Papa's personal things and her Grandma's Bible. Both girls had been wearing overalls for some time. Minnie had decided that they both would only take one dress apiece. Lizzie's best

Sunday dress was included. It did not fit the twins and was in good shape. Minnie put her Christmas dress in a sack. She made sure that Papa's gold pocketwatch was in her pocket.

Besides hurrying us, we heard her for the first time in a long time singing, "I'll fly away over Jordan. I'll fly away, I'll fly away." And then she would laugh. That was the first laugh I had heard since Mama and Papa had died.

The first thing I did when I went to get the mules and bridled them, was to take the little notebook out of it's hiding place. The rest of my list was the shotgun, shells, hobbles, ropes, the two canvas covers for the wagons, filled canvas water bags, and gear for the mules. It was amazing how fast we loaded those eight sacks.

"Minnie, I can not find Papa's rifle. I have the shotgun, but the rifle is gone."

"Oh, Robert, I saw Uncle Nate put it in his wagon when they were getting ready to go to town. Don't worry about it. We have the shotgun, and we need to hurry. It is more important to be gone, than to worry about that gun."

"O.K., but, I wanted that other gun of Papa's."

I tied the tops of the sacks with some short rope I had cut and then tied two sacks together. With two tied together we put them over Number One's back and the sacks became pack saddles.

In less than two hours we were ready to go. We went back in the house for one last look. Each of us walked up to the kitchen table and laid our work list on the table. This was one Saturday that we did not do one thing on the list. Just left them there for Uncle Nate to find.

We had one last item to attend to. I pulled Uncle Nate's little note book out of my pocket and showed it to Minnie. She smiled and made a copy of the contents and I put the little note book back in my snap pocket on my overalls.

We placed the copy on the table along with a letter to Aunt Pettie. The letter just said here is a list of money from Uncle Nate's account book. Thought you might like a copy. We would take the little notebook with us to show Uncle John when we got to New Mexico.

Lizzie came up to the table and laid a handful of corn cobs on the table.

"What is this for, Lizzie?"

"I never want to see a corn cob again!"

"Sure, Honey, but what are these for?"

"They threw them at me, and I have put some where the dolls were. Now here are these!"

We weren't sure what she meant. It did not matter, she had her reasons and that was good enough for us. I think in her mind the twins would know who left the cobs and why.

We finished our tour of the house and stood at the table one more time. Minnie added a note to the bottom of the letter. "Aunt Pettie, Uncle Nate is going to run away with the money and leave you here."

"Robert, you have Uncle Nate's little note book?"

"Yes." I patted it in my overall pocket.

"Then let's go to Uncle John's and the Territory!"

CHAPTER FOUR

It was almost sundown and Nate felt very good about a number of things. One, the letter from his brother in the Territory of New Mexico had arrived. Now he had two postmarked letters. He would put the letter Pettie's brother had written in the second envelope, and with the two he believed that a bank would let him deposit John's draft and the draft from the brats' trust. With two letters, and both in the same handwriting and both post marked from Fort Sumner, his plan was almost foolproof. This week he had opened an account in a bank thirty miles from home. The weasel looking little banker, with his soft hands and grasping fingers was more than glad to have Nate's inheritance money in his bank. Nate even thought the banker would have accepted the other two drafts without a moment's hesitation.

Nate loosened his collar and took his coat off. The coat he removed was getting very threadbare and worn. He glanced at Pettie. She was snoring softly, then she would arouse and adjust her position. Her hair was a mess and her clothes were just rags. He had no feeling for her, because he had other plans for himself and "His Money." The liquor from earlier had mellowed him some and the money was making him feel very important. He had money. The jug under the wagon seat was not as full as it was when they left town. He and Pettie had been taking a pull on it now and then. They were both flush and happy.

"When can we move, Nate?" Pettie whispered, when she roused up from her catnap.

"Keep your voice down so the kids won't hear you." He belched and coughed.

The jug made the wagon a lot smoother. They drank a little and made big plans. Plans to move and plans to live good. After a few miles, Pettie was dozing on her side, and Nate was planning.

Now Nate would go back to the bank sometime next week and see if the banker was as greedy as he acted. Nate had totaled the sum in his head for all three checks so many times, he could do them automatically. His check was for ten thousand dollars, John's was ten thousand dollars and the trust check was fourteen thousand nine hundred dollars. The grand total was thirty four thousand nine hundred dollars.

He laughed to himself and thought, the total would actually be thirty four thousand eight hundred dollars. He wouldn't tell Pettie that he had kept a hundred dollars. He hadn't told Pettie that he had been to a bank and had deposited his inheritance check. She didn't need to know, because if she did, all she would do is whine to get some in her hands. Besides, what she didn't know would not hurt her. She was dumb, dirty, fat and lazy. He would dump her.

It felt good to have a hundred dollars in your pocket. He had gotten the hundred in small bills, five's and ten's. That way it was thicker and looked like more money when he took his wallet out. He just couldn't keep from bragging, oh, just a little. Then when the opportunity came to pull out his wallet, he made sure a couple of his oddball friends got a look at the contents.

He reached around and felt of the wallet and the money in it. He chuckled. Nobody knew that there was a false bottom in the wagon in which they were riding. In the false bottom there were two things of importance to him. There was a double-barrel shotgun, a ten gage. It had gotten him out of jams many a time. Then there was an oilskin wrapped package. It held about two hundred dollars. He never thought about it unless he was going out and might find a poker game. Then he would use that money. He had money he never told Pettie about and this was some of it. He never touched the packet unless there was a game. Then he thought about all of the money he would have. Sure would be nice.

He had flashed a little of the money, and his prestige, in people's eyes, went way up. You could see it in their faces and the way they started fawning over him. They took him around to the stable and shared their jug. That was something they did not do very often. They suggested that they go to the bootlegger, and he could buy a jug. He said he had some important business to attend to, but would accept their invitation at another time. But, before he left he took a good long pull on their jug and left them standing in the middle of the stable. Later, to not share with his "drinking buddies," he went by the bootlegger and got several jugs on his own. They were packed in a wooden case for safe travel in the wagon. He would have some good moonshine at home and not have to share with those "buddies".

He had almost pranced around the little town, in his shiny pants, faded shirt, worn-out boots and sweat stained hat. Dropping hints of his impending deals and that he possibly, just possibly, would be coming into some money. Oh, the looks on all the faces! Everyone was full of congratulations and hints of being his longtime friend. They were all fair weather friends and only became interested when they thought he had some money. There was a good chance that they did not believe him and were just humoring the town fool.

When it came time for lunch he found Pettie and they went to the wagon, where she had packed a meal. She had been in the stores, drooling over cloth for dresses and lace for trim. All she could talk about was how fine she was going to look. Nate laughed inwardly. She couldn't sew, so what did she need with cloth and lace? Pettie couldn't even read, much less make a dress. He chuckled to himself about how many yards of cloth it would take it make a dress for Pettie.

After lunch he spread a blanket out under a tree and had a nice long nap. Pettie's whining and pleading for some money didn't bother him at all. He had heard it all before, and it just lulled him to sleep. He was so deep in sleep he did not feel Pettie slip his wallet out of his coat pocket. The wallet was almost out of the side pocket. She just helped it a little and looked at it's contents. Her eyes became big and round, and her mouth made an "O." She glanced at Nate before she slipped a couple of dollars out of the billfold and into her bosom. Gently, she slipped the billfold back into his pocket and quietly eased away.

The children had gone to find entertainment, and she was alone. Pettie could not remember when she had been all alone. She could not remember a time when Nate was not hollering at her or one of the bawling kids was hanging on her. There was only one mercantile in town, and she headed straight there. After she got in and began to look around, she discovered that she couldn't bring herself to spend her two dollars. Just couldn't turn lose of it. She could not remember ever having two dollars in her life. Besides if she bought something Nate would see it and want to know where she got the money. She trembled at the thought of his discovering that he was two dollars short. Well, this time she would hold her ground and play innocent.

She wanted to look around, but did not want to face the owner. She had ordered that black dress for the funeral, and then Nate had her take it back. Told her to tell the store clerk that it didn't fit and to be sure and go in when the owner was not there. She thought that Nate had had her order the dress and then he charged it, she could use it and he would not have to pay for it. She knew that Nate had taken the black suit back, claiming that the pants were too small and that he just didn't need the suit after all. Probably had charged it, too. They sure did look good at the funeral. Like genteel folks.

What Pettie did not know was the owner and Nate had had quite a falling out.

"Nate Carter, you have worn this suit, and it is second hand now. You ordered the suit. I'll not take it back."

"It's on my account, I have not paid for it, I don't want it, so just take it off the account."

"The suit is yours!" shouted the store owner.

"Not on your life. When I got it home the pants did not fit."

"You had the suit for three weeks. Why didn't you come right back?' What were you doing, wearing it to some fancy funeral, where you wanted to show off?"

Nate's mouth almost dropped open. The owner was correct. He and Pettie had worn the clothes one day at the funeral. The owner didn't need to know and the clothes were not damaged, much. He had gotten a spot or two of food on the vest, so what.

"Nate Carter, your credit is no good in my store. I want you to pay up your bill and never set foot in here again wanting credit. Cash Only!"

"If that is the way you feel, I'll take my business elsewhere!"

"Good, where are you going? The nearest store is twenty miles from here and you are too lazy to go that far. But, neighbor, I sell to you only on a cash basis from now on!"

Nate had stormed out of the store. He had a very large account with the store, and he sure did not want to go twenty miles for supplies. He would work it out.

Pettie went in the store and slipped around trying to not be noticed. The clerk came up to her and said, "Mrs. Carter, I haven't seen you since you brought that dress back. Decide you wanted the dress after all?" His question was accusing. "The dress was ordered especially for you. The owner almost fired me for taking it back. And, oh, by the way, the owner said you were on cash only from now on."

Pettie did not know how to use a charge account. Nate took care of all the business. She just told Nate what they needed, and he would take care of it. That is if Nate agreed that they needed whatever she mentioned. She slipped around the store touching and feeling of the material and lace.

She almost jumped out of her shoes when the owner walked up behind her and thundered, "Something for you Mrs. Carter?"

She muttered, " Ahhhh…. I guess not. I was just looking." Her voice quivered.

"Why, any time Mrs. Carter, if you have cash." His voice clouded with anger.

She hurried out of the store to get away from the angry store owner and went down to the stables to find the children. They always went to the stables. The other kids gathered there, and there were always some horses to look at.

The children were at the stable, and they were watching two cowboys work a small herd of cows. One cowboy had red hair and a fancy saddle and clothes. Probably thought he was a big hotshot. The other cowboy was tall and wore old worn clothes and beat down boots and hat. Both wore guns tied down low.

"Mama, come see the cows. These cowboys are driving these cattle all the way from Abilene to Red Lake Ranch out west of here. I want to be a cowboy." George was excited.

One of the cowboys, the red headed one, heard him and called to him, "Sonny, if you are going to be a cowboy, you need to lose some of that weight."

"Only skinny boys can be cowboys?" George asked.

"That's right, a horse gets tired of carrying a big fat man."

"I'll lose some weight." George ran over to his mama saying, "I'm going to be a cowboy."

"I heard you. Stop jerking on my clothes." Pettie smoothed down her skirt over her ample body.

"Hey mister, are you a good Indian tracker?" George shouted.

"The best. I can track a cow on rocky ground in the middle of the night," bragged the red headed cowboy.

George looked at the other cowboy, "I bet you're a gunslinger!"

Before the cowboy could answer, Pettie had George by the ear and was hauling him screaming down the street. "You want to get shot! Did you see the look in his eye when you asked that dumb question?" They went on down the street, Pettie dragging George by the ear.

When Nate awoke from his nap he made one more circle around town. He had to be sure that everyone knew he was becoming important and good things were coming his way. After an hour of strutting and bragging, he started looking for his family. It was time to head home, and it irritated him to spend time locating them.

He didn't find the three children at the stable or the corral looking at a herd of cows. This herd was being driven out to the Red Lake Ranch.

He overheard one of the by-standers say, "That red headed cowboy said he could track cows on rocky ground in the middle of the night."

Another one of the by-standers said, "He is just pulling your leg. He can't track in the dark."

"Well, he said he could"

The red headed cowboy had overheard the conversation and called out, "Hey, Mister. I am the best tracker in these parts. I can read tracks that are a week old."

Nate laughed with the rest of the by-standers and hollered back, "Well, if I ever need tracking done I'll remember you." He commented, "Matter of fact, some day I might have a ranch like the Red Lake Ranch, and I might need a good cowboy like you." Some of the Saturday crowd snickered, but others, not to offend him, had only congratulations. As he left the corrals he heard the cowboy laughing.

He hunted Pettie and found her down the street in the shade of some trees. He glanced around to be sure all three of his off spring were there and ready to go home. George was rubbing his ear, and the twins were fighting and bawling. His eyes rolled at the sight of his children, they were sure a bunch of clods.

"Pettie, get the kids loaded in the wagon and let's head home."

It was almost sundown when Nate and his family stopped their team in front of the farmhouse. He hollered, "Robert! Robert! Where is that boy? Robert?" He paused and then called, "Minnie...Lizzie!" Only silence greeted them. Nate climbed down out of the wagon and went in the house. Again he called for the three of them. No answer. He started through the house, and met Pettie in the kitchen. She had gone around the house looking for the children and came in the back door.

She saw the papers on the kitchen table. Grabbing them she ran out the back door and began hollering , "George! George! Read these papers to me!"

Nate caught up with them and tried to grab the papers. "Give me those papers, George, or I will bust you good!"

Pettie stayed between George and his father. She had her back to Nate and her bulk kept him from reaching George. Pettie handed the papers to George. "Read them, George!" She just knew in her heart that these papers were very important.

George looked confused. "These three pages are the work list for the three brats." He looked at the letter and read. "Here is a list of the money, money I guess that Papa is holding." He shuffled the papers and continued, "This list is a column of figures and they total thirty four thousand eight hundred dollars." George was not dumb like his brother, and he had figured out the papers almost instantly. "This other sheet is a letter that says that Papa is going to take the money and leave us."

Pettie whirled on Nate and shouted at him, "You have that much money in the bank? And you plan to go off and leave us? Why, you low down, no good skunk!"

"Now, Pettie, that is John's and the Trust money, plus my inheritance. I don't have that kind of money!" he lied.

"Then what is this list?" she demanded.

"I just made a list to help keep it straight in my mind." Nate lied again. He was still trying to reach George. "And, the list is what the judge gave me when I went for the brats." He struggled to reach George. "Give me those papers, George!"

Pettie stayed in the way. "I think you are lying, and you can't change my mind. HEAR ME?" Some more of her hair had come down over her eyes. "And, what about leaving us?"

Nate's attitude changed, and he became gruff. "I don't know where that note came from, and I sure never told you that, did I? I guess one of the brats wrote it to cause trouble."

"Well...I don't think..."

"Well, think what you like. You are not going to lay your hands on one thin dime until it is all cleared up. I'm going...to..."

He whirled and ran back into the living room. Something had caught his eye. "Something is out of place." Stopping at the table in the living room, he realized that the Bible, that had belonged to his mother was not there.

Nate hollered out the door. "That Bible you took from Minnie is missing."

Sudden realization hit him like a hammer. "Pettie, get in here and see what all those brats have stolen. I just knew they were thieves."

Pettie rushed from room to room as fast as her bulk would let her move. She became breathless and flushed. She was wringing her hands. Pettie joined Nate in the living room and began rattling off a long list of items. She numbered them off on her fingers, "Clothes, cooking utensils...eating utensils...the two dolls...the shotgun...shells...shotgun...shells...bedding...flour...baking soda...beans, bacon, ...that gold watch." The list grew as she flew from room to room.

Now, they were both shouting over the wailing of the twins at the loss of the two dolls.

"Where could they have gone?" Pettie cried looking out the window.

Nate was now furious. "The thieves have stripped the house and run away!"

"But, where?" screamed Pettie.

"I don't know, woman. Let me think." Pettie now was becoming hysterical and bawling. Her wailing was louder than the squalling twins.

Nate stood all he could. Pettie wasn't looking, so he snatched the sheets of paper from her that had the column of money and the bank list and went out the back door. Heading for the barn, he cursed silently under his breath. "Thieving bunch of brats. They are going to pay for this. I'll find them and beat the hide off of all three." He was kicking up a cloud of dust. "One of them wrote that note that said I was going to leave Pettie. I wonder how they knew that? Snooty nosed brats, I'll get them."

Reaching the barn Nate came to a complete, stunned stop. "The four mules are gone!" He turned red in the face and shouted at no one in particular. "I'll have the law on those three thieves!" A quick check of the barn turned up missing ropes, wagon canvases, hobbles, cooking spit, canvas waterbags, harness and sacks. "They will all go to jail, I'll see to it!" He became even more furious when he had listed all the missing items.

Nate backed out of the barn and stood there in stunned silence.

Pettie walked up to him and shoved the three work lists in his face, "I guess you have figured it out by now. They did not do one single thing on the list, and they are gone and took whatever they wanted with them. Clothes, groceries, personal items…"

He interrupted her, "And mules, harness, rope, water bags, canvas and burlap bags."

"They have stolen from us and run away, after we gave them a place to stay," Pettie wailed again. When Pettie started to bawl, the twins joined in, and they raised a ruckus.

"Hush, your mouth woman, and let me think."

First, Glen runs off, and I bet they had something to do with that happening. Now the three of them have disappeared. Vanished out of sight.

Suddenly, another realization hit him. "I wonder just how long they have been gone and what direction did they go?" Nate exploded with shouts and curses, "Where could they be by now?" He ran here and there in a triad of anger. His face was flushed, and he was near collapsing.

"Nate, get hold of yourself, before you have a heart attack. They can't have gone far. How far could they go in a day?" She was now over her bawling and was mad. Pettie continued, "Somebody will see them and report them to the law." She was madder. "Especially if you get the word out. Go back to town, and tell everyone you see."

"Woman, it is almost dark, and by the time I could get back to town everything would be closed. I'll get up in the morning and make all of the neighboring farms and spread the word. If I can get over to the Williams' before they leave for church, I can get them to make an announcement in church. They could stop by the Baptist Church on the way to their church and leave a message there. I'll write out the details and make a copy. That way Mr. Williams will have all the information for both churches."

Nate started planning his moves, "I heard those two cowboys talking today. One of them declared he is the best tracker in this county. If I could catch them on the road tomorrow, maybe he would help me track them."

Pettie turned and started to the house. "I will fix some supper and you will think better on a full stomach." All of the glow of the jug of whiskey had faded and left a bad taste in her mouth. She needed a drink of water. What she really would like to have is some more of that moonshine. She also wanted to think about that note that said that Nate was going to leave her. She was very mad for a number of reasons.

Nate paced the floor most of the night thinking about what might happen if those three went to the sheriff at the countyseat before he could make a report. He made coffee and thought some more. They could tell all kinds of lies and make him look like the thief, and not them. "I know what I'll do, I'll write out a description of the three and the mules to be passed out at the two churches." All he had to do was catch Williams and word would be all over the county by sundown.

Nate fixed his own breakfast by lantern light. He wanted to be on the road at sunrise. He had learned that his anger was worse when he was hungry, and he was hungry a lot of the time and angry a lot more of the time. So, he fixed a meal that would have been enough for three people.

At sunrise Nate had harnessed his two horses to the wagon and was on his way to the Williams' place. He met them at their gate just as they were about to pull up on the main road. He quickly explained to them the situation. Of course, he made the kids out to be thieves and run-aways. After he had explained to them the problem, he gave Mr. Williams the descriptions.

He added, "I just don't understand, and after Pettie and I opened our home to them."

The Williams assured him that they would have an announcement made at their church and would get the word over to the Baptist Church. Mr. Williams was a big shot over at the Methodist Church. A pillar of the community. Nate noted that Mrs. Williams, in her fancy clothes and hat, could hardly wait to get to church and spread the word. She most likely was the biggest gossip in the county and would spread the word like wildfire. Nate didn't care if she was a gossip, he needed all the help he could get, and he would be appreciate her blabbing tongue.

The Williams drove off, and Nate sat in his wagon trying to decide what to do next when he heard the lowing of cattle. The herd from town came slowly into view. Nate had forgotten that he wanted to see if the cowboys would help him track the mules. The herd approached where Nate sat in the wagon under some shade trees.

"Hello, men," he called.

"Howdy, neighbor," the red headed one replied.

"Could I have a word with you?" called Nate.

"Sure, what can we do for you?" asked the other cowboy.

"My name is…well everybody calls me Uncle Nate. My brother and his wife passed away, and I was keeping their three kids. Yesterday, they ran off. After their Mama and Papa died the first of the year, we thought that the only thing for us to do was take them in."

He squinted at the red headed cowboy, "Yesterday I heard you say that you are one of the best trackers in the county. I'd like to hire you to help me for one day."

"Well, Mister, we have got to get these cows to our boss. We would be a day late if we stopped now. He sure would be put out."

Nate in desperation blurted out, "I'll pay you ten dollars to help me find those kids."

"What about your job pushing these cows, Red?" asked his partner.

'You can hold them for the day, and I'll help this gentleman. There is water right over there at that tank, and the cattle won't suffer."

The other cowboy still wanted to argue, "Red, you are going to get us both fired!"

Nate, to stop the argument, interjected, "I'll pay you ten dollars also, if your partner will help me for a day."

"Mister, you've got that settled. Ten dollars is two weeks work on any ranch and we can be one day late and take the heat from our boss." Red winked at the other cowboy. Being late or what their bosses thought was not even on their minds. They had no schedule. They had just pulled the slickest deal that has ever been pulled on a man north of Abilene. They hired out to drive his cattle to Abilene to the sale barn. He gave them twenty dollars each and left the herd with them. The owner rode off to tend business, and the two of them took the cattle and turned north, not south. Then to make the deal really work, they kept the cattle on the road. Their tracks had been mingled with the tracks of wagons, horses and other cattle. You could not find a trace of them. Most rustlers would have taken to the brush. Their tracks would have been easy to follow. Red and Mitch were not the everyday run of the mill rustlers. They were hardened rustlers and killers. They knew cattle stealing and knew it well.

Nate and Red went back to the farm, while Mitch watched the herd. Upon arriving at the farm Red began searching for tracks of the mules. "Man there are a lot of tracks. Did you bring your team up to the barn?"

"Yes, I did."

"Then let's make a bigger swing around the buildings."

After an hour and a half of searching, Red announced, "They went south down this cowtrail."

Nate said, "Let me put a saddle on a horse, and I'll follow you."

Red started slowly down the cowpath with Nate dogging his heels. The tracks disappeared and reappeared. The insects buzzed in the brush and mesquites. Hour after hour they slowly followed the tracks, all the way to the river, Nate complaining about everything under the sun. His back hurt, he would get saddle sores, it was too hot and they were moving too slow to catch up with those brats.

It was almost sundown when they got to the river, and Red noted, "They went in the river here. I don't know if they went up river or down. They could be anyplace by now. They have been gone, according to you, for at least thirty hours and maybe more. It could take days to go up and down the river and find were they came out."

He turned his horse and started to ride north.

"Where are you going? You can't just leave like this!"

Red reined his pony around and looked at Nate. "Look, mister you paid me to look for one day and that's what you got. I've got cows to push, and my partner is expecting me back."

After that little speech, he turned the horse north and trotted off, leaving Nate with his mouth hanging open. Nate kicked his horse in the flanks and tried to catch up with the cowboy, but he was too heavy, and his horse too tired. The horse had pulled a wagon to town and back yesterday. The animal had pulled the wagon up to the Williams' and back this morning without rest. The poor animal had been carrying Nate around in the hot brushy country for hours. The horse just balked and only walked, and not that fast.

Nate got to the farm well after dark, and he was saddlesore and tired. He had not taken any food with him, and he was starving. The cowboy had had some jerky, but he did not offer to share. "Sorry cow puncher!"

Nate complained. He unsaddled the horse and limped into the house. The house was dark, and no one answered his call. He stumbled around until he found a lantern. Going to the bedroom, he found Pettie sound asleep. When he went closer he smelled liquor. Pettie was drunk. She must have found his hiding place for the moonshine.

He stumbled back to the kitchen to see what he could find to eat. There was little available for him. He finally gave up and just ate some cold corn bread. He sat at the table and rubbed his head. What a day! All that riding and not one clue where the kids had disappeared. They had stolen many items and had just vanished. Well, they were around somewhere to the south. He would post a reward with the Sheriff and offer money. That might flush out some information. Tomorrow he would go over to the countyseat and see the sheriff.

The next morning, Pettie was hung over and could hardly move. She finally got some breakfast on the table and announced, "I'm going back to bed."

"Who is going to look after the kids and do the work around here?"

"If you want the kids looked after, then you do the chores around the place, and I'll look after the kids. And if I decide to go back to bed, I WILL!" she shouted. Holding her head, she stomped off to the bedroom.

Nate ate his meal and left the house without saying another word to Pettie or to the kids.

He whipped the horses and left a cloud of dust behind him. It would take most of the day to go to the countyseat. About three hours into the trip, he passed the herd of cows and the cowboys. He did not even wave, just rode by and regretted that he had spent twenty dollars on those two cowboys and for nothing.

When he got to the countyseat, he found that the sheriff was out of town for a couple of days. He fumed around and started to leave when a deputy said, "What is the problem?" The deputy was as ugly a man as Nate had ever seen. Besides he looked mean and vicious. Nate wondered if he was a good deputy or just a hard case. The deputy's gun was worn very low and tied down.

"Perhaps you can help me. I took three children into my home when their parents passed away. They stayed at our farm for about four months, and now they have run off. Further, they stole a number of items including four good mules."

"Let me fill out a report, and we will put out the word to everyone in the county to be on the lookout for them."

"I'll put up a reward of one hundred dollars for information that gets them back."

"That good a reward, should get you some information about them." The deputy wrote out a report and said he would give it to the sheriff when he returned.

There wasn't much Nate could do as the day was progressing. He climbed back into his wagon for the long ride home. Just out of town, he met the herd and the cowboys. He pulled the wagon over to the side with the idea in mind that he was going to give Red a piece of his mind. When the herd came up to him, he shouted and waved his hands and scattered the cows.

Red rode up and demanded, "What are you doing, you old fool? Scaring those cows?"

Nate bristled and shouted, "I want to tell you what I think about you for taking my money, and I got nothing."

Red said, "Calm yourself, old man, or I'll drag you out of that wagon!"

Nate blurted out a string of curse words and whipped his horses to start. The wagon started, but like lightning Red shook out his lariat and made a loop. With one smooth motion, just as the wagon got up on the road, he threw it over Nate's head and arms. Red's horse, being a work horse, set his feet like they were roping a calf. When Nate hit the end of the rope, it jerked him over the back of the seat and out on the dirt road. He hit like a ton of bricks and lay there without moving.

"Red, you could have killed him!"

"Would serve the fool right." He stepped down and untangled his rope. He looked down at the prone body of Nate and said, "Just leave him lying there. If he is dead, people will think that he fell out of the wagon." He stepped up on his horse and helped Mitch round up the cows.

When Nate came to, he was completely disoriented and confused. It was almost dark, and there was no one in sight. The cattle and the cowboys were gone. He scratched his head, while he still sat in the middle of the road, "How did I get here?" He tried to get up, but his head swam for a few minutes. He finally got to his feet and stumbled to the wagon. The horses had only gone a few feet when Nate had been jerked out of the wagon. He climbed slowly into the wagon and started the team.

It took a long time to get home. He just let the horses have their heads and walk along at their pace. He fell asleep somewhere along the way, and to his surprise, when he woke up, the team had stopped at the barn. He eased his fat, sore body down from the wagon. Each step was pure agony and pain. Unhitiching the team took three times as long as usual. In place of going to the house, he stayed in the barn. He lay down on the hay and immediately fell asleep.

He awoke the next morning with one of the dogs licking him in the face. He could barely move his limbs. He slowly sat up and moved each part of his body to see if it would work. Pain shot through every part of his body when he got up. His head swam and his eyes blurred.

With a great deal of effort he finally made the house. It was mid-morning, and everyone was still in bed asleep. The smell of liquor filled the house, and Pettie snored and grumbled in her sleep. The whole house was a bigger mess than he remembered. It did not matter. He was going to the bank tomorrow and see if he could deposit John's draft and the trust draft.

Two days later Nate was up and out of the house by light. All the day before he had rested and schemed. Schemed how he was going to leave Pettie and her dirty kids. He had bathed at the windmill and found some clean clothes. He had packed his grip for the trip the next morning. With the two checks and the two letters in his inside coat pocket, he felt in a state of euphoria. The thirty mile trip would take all day, but he was prepared to stay at a hotel. He would treat himself with a barber, a bath and a steak at the hotel restaurant. Pettie would not miss him, and he would be away from her.

When he got to his destination the day had passed, so he left his team and wagon at the local stable and livery. He found the barber shop and had that bath and shave. They cleaned and pressed his black suit and vest while he enjoyed his soak and bath. Leaving the barber shop in his almost new suit, he strolled down the street to the hotel, where he had checked in. He rested for about an hour, put the black suit back on and descended to the restaurant, where he enjoyed an inch thick steak and fine service.

As he ate, he dreamed of living someplace where he could be waited on like this every day. With almost thirty five thousand dollars he could be very comfortable. Buy a small ranch and be a man of leisure. A man of means. As he was having his coffee, the local banker came in. When he turned to hang up his hat, he spotted Nate.

"May I join you?" the banker requested. Nate could see him eye the black suit and vest. The banker was impressed.

Nate almost swooned. "By all means." A banker had never even spoken to him, much less asked to sit at the table with him. Ah, what money could do to elevate one's position in this world. They made small talk over their coffee for perhaps an hour.

The banker arose and said, "I will see you at the bank in the morning, SIR?"

"Of course, my good man."

They nodded at each other, and the banker departed, leaving Nate floating on a cloud. Good clothes and money do smooth the way.

The next morning, promptly at nine, Nate entered the bank wearing the black suit he had worn at the funeral and at dinner the night before.

The one he had cleaned at the barber shop the afternoon before. Nate chuckled to himself as to the circumstances that he had acquired the black suit.

The day Nate argued with the storeowner over the black suit, he had watched the storekeeper, in his fit of anger throw the suit out the back door into the trash. After the argument Nate left by the front door of the store and went around the side of the building and to the back. He knew that trees at the back would afford some shade to get out of the heat. Suddenly, the back door opened and the owner hurtled the suit into the trash piled at the rear of the store. Nate looked all around and slipped over to the trashpile and recovered the suit. He looked around again, rolled the clothes into a ball and hurried by a roundabout way to his wagon. He hid the suit in the false bottom of the wagon, and when he got home he hid it from Pettie.

Again the banker was most cordial and helpful. Of course, he could deposit the two checks, John's inheritance and the Trust check, with the bank. With the two letters that explained everything, there was no problem. Clothes and money will probably turn the head of any banker, and this one was not an exception.

"Will you be staying in our community, sir?"

"That is a good possibility." Nate brushed a piece of lent off his sleeve. "As soon as I take care of these family affairs, I will be looking for a place to settle."

"I would be glad to show you around at the proper time," cooed the banker. You could see greed written all over him. Greed that would match Nate's any day of the week.

"A bank in the Territory of New Mexico, or wherever my brother decides to settle, could call on your bank. Is that correct?"

"Yes, by noon I'll have your letters of credit prepared that any bank will honor. This is a much safer way to travel with money. If someone stole the letters of credit they would be worthless because they are in your name." The banker was almost bowing. Money and clothes!

At noon Nate picked up his bank deposit book and the letters of credit. He was rich, and his head was spinning. He had pulled it off, and no one was the wiser. He was really full of himself and suffered from a good case of euphoria. He returned to the hotel and changed into his old travel clothes and slipped out quietly without paying his bill.

Back at home, late that night, he made no mention of where he had been or what he had been doing for the last two days. To keep Pettie from finding his bank book and letters of credit, he would bury them in a metal box tomorrow. He knew of a good safe place to hide the box until he got ready to leave.

The next morning, while his family slept, he took a shovel to a place he had picked and buried the metal box. It would be safely hidden in a place that his family was afraid to venture near, Rattlesnake Hill. Nate was as afraid of a snake as any member of the family, but he had discovered that the snakes were cold and stiff in the mornings, and with care he was safe. With a shovel in his hand, he had little to fear from the sluggish snakes. On the way back to the house, he detoured by the cottonfield that Robert had plowed. The cotton was coming on fine for this early in the year. He would be leaving good money in that field, but if Pettie could figure out how to get it in, she could have the money. He hoped he would be long gone.

Days had passed since the brats had vamoosed. He began to think that that was the last of them, and he would never hear of them again. Then he got a surprise. The deputy sheriff, that he had talked to at the countyseat, rode up in the yard.

The deputy didn't move to get off his horse. He handed Nate a sheet of paper and said, "Here is a list of sightings of your runaways, about five or six, and they are all on the west side of the county." Without another word he turned his horse and started to ride, but he stopped, "By the way, the sheriff doesn't believe you about them stealing things. He wonders if those items belonged to their folks. And he said to tell you, if he found out different, he would put you in jail. Those leads are

all probably false, people just saw the reward and are trying to collect it."
He spurred his horse and rode off.

Nate looked at the list and pondered if any of the sighting were real.
He also thought about what the deputy had said about the stuff belonging to their folks. Well, first things first. The sheriff had to have some
proof, and the brats had whatever proof there was. The sheriff would
have to find them first. So, he would have to beat the sheriff and find
them himself.

He spent the rest of the day preparing to spend several days hunting
the runaways. With Pettie passed out from drinking, and the kids off
playing, he made his preparations without interference.

Nate was up at dawn. As he had planned this trip for some time, he
had most all of the things needed for the trip ready to go. He loaded
bedroll, some extra clothes, an extra wagon canvas, cooking equipment,
eating utensils, two canvas waterbags, a tin of matches, harness, rope,
hobbles, and food that consisted of flour, salt , baking soda, some cured
meat and most important, his money. He had gone to Rattlesnake Hill
while it was still cool and dug up his bankbook and the letters of credit.
These last items he placed in the false bottom of the wagon. As an afterthought he collected the wooden box that held the jugs of moonshine.
Would make the trip a lot easier, and Pettie did not really need the liquor.

By sunrise that morning, he was long removed from the farm. He
headed west to the countyseat, just like last Monday. The difference was,
this time he would hunt the kids if it took all summer. At a brisk walk,
the horses carried him across the Brazos by midmorning. By noon he
was almost to the countyseat. This part of the county did not have many
roads and had even fewer people. Three miles short of the countyseat,
Nate took a two-rut trail to the north through the rough country of that
county. All along the Brazos River the country was rough, and for the
most part it was impassable in a wagon. A horse or a mule could pass
through with little difficulty.

He would visit the Double OO ranch first. It was the first one on the list. By mid afternoon he found the ranch headquarters. He had never been in this part of the county and was lucky to find the ranch on the first try. The ranchhouse was built of native rock from the riverbanks. It was large with a number of fireplaces. Nate was most impressed at the size of the house and the number of out buildings. Must be a very well to do ranch. He would ask directions for the rest of the places he needed to go. The ranch foreman was coming out of a barn when Nate halted his team. After exchanging greetings, Nate explained the purpose of his trip.

"Well, some of the boys thought they saw three boys on animals down along the Brazos the other day. But, we had that awful rain north of us last night, and if anyone was in the riverbed, they would have drowned. Awful flood back in there. The water is up five or six feet in the shallow places. In the tight draws the water must be fifteen feet deep and running like mad."

"Could you draw me a map of where the boys were seen?"

"Certainly."

Nate handed him a Big Red tablet. The foreman made a rough map of the area.

"Now, you are south and west of where they were seen, but that was several days ago. The river is about a mile north of here, and they were some east of there." He pointed out the location. "If those are your runaways, they could be on up the Brazos to the west or have gone north on what we call Clear Water Branch. Or they could have drowned."

"Thanks, for the information and the map. Remember there is a reward for locating them, and if you see them, let me know. You can leave any information with the sheriff."

As Nate rode back toward the main road he thought, they must be west of that ranch by now. He pushed the horses, and shortly they were back on the two-rut trail. He circled the countyseat, not wanting to see the sheriff at this time. On the west side of the countyseat he got back on the main road. By dark, he crossed the county line and was in the next county to the west. He found a good place to spend the night and made camp. He went to sleep not knowing that he was within twenty miles of the three.

About noon of the second day, he came to another branch of the Brazos, and it was running full from bank to bank. He took another two-rut wagontrail that followed the river to the northwest. He stopped and ate his meager lunch in the shade of a mesquite bush. Resting in the shade on that hot day, he fell into a deep slumber. Perhaps two hours had passed when he jerked awake to the thunder of horses' hoofs. Nate was surprised that he was surrounded by at least a dozen cowboys.

"Well, if it's not the runaway kid hunter, in the flesh." called one of the cowboys.

"Now, how do you know that?"

"We met him on the road home, boss." replied the same cowboy, the redheaded one. "He is the one that has the reward up for the runways."

"Boy, he must be rich to put up a reward of one hundred dollars on three kids."

Nate sensed that he was in peril with this bunch of cowboys. They were rough and had little to do with dirt farmers. In fact, they would just as soon use a dirt farmer for target practice.

"Well, farmer, get down out of that wagon, and let's see what you have got!"

"What do you mean ? Are you the foreman on this ranch?"

"You don't understand, GET DOWN?"

Nate tried to bluff his way, and with a tremble in his voice he asked, "Why should I get down?"

The big man looked at him in astonishment and then reached across his horse and knocked Nate out of the wagon with his pistol. Nate hit the ground hard and was very dazed. He had not expected the blow.

Now he sat up in the dirt and heard the foreman say, "Boys, see what he has got on him, this rich reward man!" Two of the cowboys swung down off their horses and lifted Nate to his feet. Before he could resist or object, they started going through his pants and coat pockets. The foreman's voice sounded like it was at a distance with the ringing in his ears.

The man continued, "Rest of you boys go through his gear, and let's see if we can find his poke." The cowboys jumped down from their horses and started tossing Nate's belongings into the road. They went through everything and found nothing of value, except the box of moonshine.

"Why, boss, he hasn't got a dollar to his name, and the only thing of value is this box of good moonshine," said one of the cowboys as he took a deep drink.

"He had a billfold full of money the other day." commented the redhead.

"He is as poor as a churchmouse today. Even his poor old horses are about beat and not worth taking to the glue factory."

"Farmer, you had better be glad you are not rich like Red says you are. We could hold you for ransom. If you had real good horses, we would take them, but as it is you are so poor and pitiful, we are just going to let you go."

Without further word, all of the cowboys mounted their horses while passing out the jugs of liquor. They hollered and yelled like Indians and ran Nate's team off down the road. Then they turned and rode off laughing at the top of their voices. "Hey, boss, he thought you were a ranch foreman. Dumb dirt farmer. You a foreman!"

It took Nate some time to walk to where the team had stopped. Matter of fact, it was a long walk and took the better part of three hours. The team was spooked and every time he got close, they would move off. He finally was able to catch them. To be more precise, one of the reins got caught in a mesquite. He climbed into the wagon and drove back up to the spot where his possessions were scattered all over the trail. It took a long time to pick up his belongings. His head hurt, and from time to time he would have to stop and let it clear. Finally, he had his gear back in the wagon. He decided that he would find a place to camp and rest for the remainder of the day. Let his head stop hurting.

Even with the water running from bank to bank, Nate found a nice place with some shade trees for a camp. He straightened his gear some more and realized he was out of fresh meat. He looked through his grip and found his fishing line and hook. He went over to the bank and found a cool shady place and settled down to rest and to fish. He loved to fish and had not fished in years. The afternoon passed pleasantly, and the fishing was good. There was enough for a mess for supper and for breakfast.

With a small campfire in a depression, hoping he did not attract any more company, he prepared his supper. He might be a coward, but he was a schemer. His valuables were in the false bottom of the wagon. The false bottom was not over three inches deep and well concealed. Only long flat items could be put in the space. The compartment opened from the bottom of the wagon. Not an easy place to find or get to. His few dollars that he had brought with him were safe. Out in the back country, one needed to act poor and broke. Except for the blow to the head, he was no worse for the experience.

Nate hobbled his team when he stopped, and he checked the hobbles. There was plenty of grass for the team, and water was at hand. Nate made his bed under the wagon, but he sat for a long time and watched the stars. The night was beautiful, but the beauty was wasted on Nate. His mind was scheming again. He had no thought of the world around him. What's more, he didn't know he was even closer to the three runaways. They were camped only fifteen miles east of him. If only he had known.

The next morning Nate was sore all over. He scratched his head and felt of the knot from the blow. He thought how many times in the last four months that he had been sore all over. He had to end this mess and move on to the life of a man of means. He dreamed of that good life while he cleaned and cooked the second batch of fish for his breakfast. He cleaned his equipment as he watched the sun come up.

Nate spent some time that morning checking the contents of the false bottom in the wagon. After pulling the secret pin that opened the trap door in the bottom, he withdrew a blanket and oilcloth wrapped rifle that had belonged to his brother. Next, he withdrew a shotgun, also wrapped in a blanket and oil cloth. He unwrapped each and checked for any damage that might have been caused when the horses were run off yesterday afternoon. The wagon had taken some pretty hard bounces on the rutted trail. Both guns seemed to be in excellent condition. The rough ride had not caused any damage as they were well cushioned. He wrapped the guns back in their individual blankets and oilcloth and replaced them in the false bottom. Finally, he pulled out a packet wrapped in oilcloth and some old blanket. He only looked the package over and replaced it without opening the wrapping.

This package held his money, plus the letters of credit and the bank book. He had never carried a lot, just some emergency funds. The money was wrapped in oilcloth to keep it dry in the case of rain. He had been on the road too many times when a secret stash of money came in handy. Occasionally, he would sit in on a hand or two of poker. Nate schemed, never winning big. Just a few dollars and be welcomed back. Once in a while, the stakes would start to grow, and he would excuse himself and go to his stash so he could stay in the game. That extra money had allowed to him call a bluff many times.

Nate did not cheat, he wasn't that good with cards. He was a smart player and could smell out what the other man held. His shrewdness at reading men had won him a lot of money. Most players try not to show their feelings, but few can.

He recalled one game when the stakes got bigger and bigger as the night progressed. When some of the pots got to running twenty dollars to fifty dollars every hand, some of the players got out. There were four players left. Nate, just out of curiosity, had decided to stay in the game. He had won about two hundred dollars during the evening and saw that the possibility for winning more was at hand. His hands had not run hot, but by watching the players, he had managed to do some mighty good bluffing and had won some large pots.

He kept on having a fair run at the table, and as was his habit, he would keep slipping a bill now and then off of the table so his winnings did not seem quite so impressive. That night he had observed that practice by putting bills in his pocket, and once when he went for a break, he had counted his money. He was shocked to find that his winnings were now close to four hundred dollars.

The evening wore on, and finally the pot was near two hundred dollars, and he knew that the other player in the hand was bluffing. All night when he bluffed, he had started rubbing his left temple. A dead giveaway, if you are watching the players and studying them.

The other player kept raising, and Nate matched him raise for raise. Now the pot had grown to almost five hundred dollars. The other player was about to rub the skin off of his temple. His opponent raised, using the last of his money. When he called, he thought that Nate had only the money on the table, about thirty dollars. The opponent had raised fifty dollars, expecting Nate to fold. Instead, Nate reached into his pocket and pulled out enough money to add to the thirty, and raise one hundred dollars and called. The other man just sat there, dumbfounded at the sight of all that money going on a raise. He couldn't come up with any more money, and Nate's raise and call had won the pot. The man's shoulders fell in dejection and defeat.

That extra money had gone a long way that night. Nate chuckled to himself. There was one thing for sure, he never told Pettie about his winnings. He just always managed to have a few dollars in his pocket, dollars that he kept hidden out on Rattlesnake Hill or in the false bottom of the wagon.

He finished loading his gear before harnessing the team. Clucking to the team, he started his journey on north to check out the list of names he had from the sheriff. The going was really rough at times and then there would be miles of flat, smooth, grassy valleys.

At the next ranch, the "Box W", all of the men were out working cattle. The women knew nothing of a sighting of some runaways. "We have not seen any kids. But, would you like to stay for a hot meal, Mister?" Nate was one never to turn down a good meal. He was tempted to stay around for a while and visit with a widow woman working on the ranch. She was younger than Pettie and a lot prettier. Just as he started to put his plan to work to get acquainted, the woman of the house called, "Juanita, come help us at the house. We have some things to do before the men get in." He made a mental note to remember her, and when all of the problems were cleared up, he might need to come back and visit some more.

Following the directions given him by the women, he found the next ranch, or what he thought was the next ranch, to the northeast without any trouble. The ranch was a rundown, trash-littered place. Nate snorted and thought, looks just like mine. Nate had been treated very well by the people at the ranches he had visited so far, but this was the exception.

Driving up in the yard, he hollered, "Hello, the house. Anybody home?"

The next few moments were the most hair raising in his life. A rifle shot ripped by his head and a voice called, "Get down real slow and keep your hands in the air!!"

Nate slowly climbed down with his heart in his throat. His head roared, and every nerve in his body was taunt as a fiddle string. "Hello, could I talk to you?" he asked.

"You were told to get down real slow. You were not told to talk or ask any questions!"

Nate felt a trickle of sweat run down between his shoulder blades. He could not locate where the voice was coming from.

"Just you stand real easy and don't move, Mister! Keep your hands in plain sight!"

A door on an out building away from the main house slowly opened, and the dirtiest and meanest looking man on the face of the earth came out. His clothes were barely hanging on him, and he smelled of liquor. He walked toward Nate. He kept the rifle aimed right at the middle of Nate's chest. Nate's mouth turned to cotton, and there was a taste of cold fear. Nate's vision blurred a little, and he thought he was going to lose control of his bowels.

Suddenly there was a terrific pain in his head, a flash of light, and then blackness engulfed him. When consciousness returned, Nate was tied hand and foot. It was dark, or he thought it was dark. Maybe it was a building with no light or doors. Was it night or was he blind? As his brain cleared, he realized that he wasn't blind, and it wasn't night. He was blindfolded. Then he realized that he was in one of the outbuildings. What was going on? Voices from outside came through the cracks in the wall.

"Pa, we didn't find a thing of value in his wagon. Just camping equipment, and it's not in good shape. No money or guns or anything we could sell or use."

"Now, boy. I can't believe that a man is out on the trail in a wagon, without some money and something for protection or to hunt with."

"Pa, we didn't find anything."

"Anything make you think he is the law?"

"You mean that fat butterball? Why, his hands are as white and soft as a girl's, and he couldn't lift more than a fork at mealtime!"

"You sure, boy?"

"Yes, Pa"

"I just can't believe it. Keep him blindfolded, and drag him out. Let's see what kind of a creature this is."

The door swung open and rough hands drug him by his feet out of the little building. He was jerked to a sitting position and slapped several times across the face. He almost threw up. The people man-handling him stank of dirt and filth.

"Now that I have your attention, Mister, I'm going to ask you a few questions, and I had better get some straight answers or you will get your teeth kicked in. You understand, Mister?"

Nate nodded his head, very slowly. Any more motion than that, he would have passed out or thrown up.

"Fine, now what's your name?"

In a flash he decided that he would not give them his real name. "George Stafford."

"Where are you from?"

Again, he would not tell them the truth. "East Texas."

"What are you doing out here?"

The truth this time. Well, actually he had told mostly the truth. He was from East Texas, and his first name was George. The last name was a lie, but his grandma's name was Stafford, on his mother's side of the family. "Looking for three runaway kids."

"You expect me to believe that you came all the way from East Texas to chase runaways?

The truth again. "It's the truth. There is a reward, and I was hoping to collect the reward."

"What are you doing way back in the sticks?"

Truth again, this wasn't too hard, at least not yet. "There was a report of three kids on the Brazos, and I am checking it out."

"Hey, Pa, I saw a campfire over by the lake a few nights ago. Maybe it's them, and we can collect the reward. This buzzard's feathers can be plucked, and nobody would be on to us."

"Keep your mouth shut, boy." There was the sound of flesh hitting flesh.

There was a grunt and a whimper. "Yes, Pa. Haw, Pa you knocked out another tooth!"

"Now, Mister, if we was to turn you loose and help, would you split the reward?"

Careful, they might be trying to play a trick, thought Nate. "Certainly, you're trackers. You find them, and I know where to go to collect the reward."

"Say, Mister. Just how much is the reward?"

Careful, this answer could cause lots of problems. Nate's scheming mind was in full swing at this point. "If they are brought back alive there is more then if they are dead"

Light flashed through his head again. He was knocked over on the ground, and he tasted blood in his mouth.

"I said , how much? I don't want a speech."

"Yes, sir," Nate answered trying to clear his head so he could give an acceptable answer. "On the last flier I saw, it said one hundred dollars." The truth, again.

"Now, that is better. Is that dead or alive?"

"Alive."

"And dead?"

"Fifty dollars."

"Sure worth a lot more alive than dead!"

"I agree, sir." Nate sure did not want the blood of those kids on his hands. They are kin, and he drew a line at killing and especially kin.

"Put him back in the shed, and let's have supper. Maybe, we will bring you something, Mister, if you are nice."

Once more rough hands drug him back in the shed and slammed the door. He heard them leave, laughing. He heard the crashing and break-ing of wood and wondered if it was his wagon. If they were finding his guns and money, he would be in trouble. He tried to concentrate. His head was still spinning and his stomach was very uneasy. God, those people did stink!

A woman's voice called to somebody." Bring that wood in here for the cook stove, if you want a hot meal."

Nate then figured they were just breaking up some of the odd bits and pieces laying around the yard. There was enough lumber around to cook on for a year. He suddenly remembered that it looked like another house might have been a part of the structures at one time.

He relaxed for a few minutes and listened real hard and close to see if they had all gone in the main house. That raised another question. Just how many were there? He had only heard three voices, but he'd bet there was at least one or two more in the bunch. It was very quiet in the yard. He could only hear the clucking of the chickens in the yard. The thought of chicken made his mouth water.

No time for the thought of food, even if that was his favorite subject. He thought for a few minutes and decided that he would make no moves until it was dark, and they had gone to bed for the night. His scheming mind wandered to the two guns in the wagon. But, first he would need to get loose. If they fed him there might be a chance, but they probably would watch him very close.

Time moved very slow in the dark, dank shed. At sunset the door opened. He was unceremoniously pulled from the shed. More very rough handling and being kicked in the ribs. He was drug out in the open and pulled into a sitting position. . He weaved a little and gained his balance.

"Open your mouth, and you will be fed!"

"What?"

"Just do as you are told, Mister." With the instruction came the toe of another boot in his ribs. He gasped for breath and fell on his side. Someone pulled him back in a sitting position.

"Now, open your mouth!"

Nate complied, and a spoon of soup was put in his mouth. It was good. He swallowed and opened his mouth again and again. Despite the odor of the people and the place, he ate very well.

After a few minutes and several more spoons, "That's enough, we are not fattening him up for fall butchering. Now, Mister, I have one more question."

"Yes?"

"You want to live?"

"Yes, sir."

"I like that the man is straight to the point. Fine, here is the deal. We are going to help you find the kids. You get twenty five percent and we get seventy five percent. Any objection?"

Nate was in no position to argue. "No."

"Say, he is getting to the point faster and faster. We are going to take the blindfold off, but not untie your hands and feet. To keep you real honest, we will lock you in the shed for tonight. Just to insure that you are here in the morning."

Nate was hauled back into the shed and dumped on the floor. The blindfold was removed. Just before the door was closed, he got a glimpse of the bunch. He was right, there were two more. They all carried guns all the time and seemed to be watching for intruders. This bunch of drifters wore either overalls or pants that were supported by suspenders. Their clothes were many sizes too big and just hung on them. They were a pitiful looking bunch.

He pushed himself into a sitting position and looked the shed over. It was still light, and the shed was not a very strong building. Problem was, he had to get his hands and feet loose. He searched the shed for some tool that would cut the rope. In the corner was a hoehead. Of all the dumb things! To lock him up but leave a hoehead in the shed. Was it a trick to see if he would cooperate or just a fact that they had forgotten about the head?

He listened for any sound from the house before he started trying to cut his bonds. All sounds outside had ceased with the coming of dark. The inside of the shed became very dark. He had pulled himself over to the hoehead and was trying to figure out how to hold the head and cut the ropes. He was too fat to bring his arms and hands around and down his back and legs to set them free. Then it hit him! Do the feet first, so you can move better. He turned around sitting on the ground and began sawing the rope that bound his feet. The hoehead was stuck against the wall and made it possible to work on the ropes.

Suddenly his feet were free. He stopped and listened for any sound from the house. Now, his hands. He turned back around and braced with his feet and felt for the hoehead. Finding it, he had to saw very carefully, or he would cut his hands. Feeling out each step, he began to cut on the ropes. It seemed an eternity, then all of a sudden, the ropes were off. Nate stood and rubbed his hands and wrists, working circulation back into them.

After a few minutes of listening, he decided the occupants in the house were sound asleep. He eased around the wall of the shed and felt of each board for a loose one. Being very careful not to kick some object in the floor that he could not see, Nate kept working around the shed. Luck was with him. He found some boards on the side away from the house that were loose. He put his considerable weight against the wall and felt the boards give. Pushing a little at a time, the boards gave more and more. He would need to get at least two or three off to have enough room for him to crawl through. Finally, the boards gave. They swung out from the top and opened a large opening at the bottom.

With a great amount of straining and wiggling, Nate eased his rotund body out through the opening. He rested in the cool night air. For the first time, he realized he was sweating and that there was something wet and sticky on the side of his head. Blood, that's what it was. It was from that blow on the head, when one of those jackals had slipped up behind him.

The question that plagued him at this point was, should he try to harness his team and make a break for it, or get a gun and go back in the shed and wait to ambush them in the morning? He moved around the shed and looked at the house. He was standing in a shadow created by the moonlight. Moving very softly and slowly, he approached his wagon.

His team was nowhere to be seen, so that settled part of his plan. Stay and ambush them in the morning. He slipped under the wagon and pulled the well greased pin. The trap door swung down on oiled hinges. He reached inside and retrieved his shotgun and a container of extra shells. Sitting on the ground under the wagon in the dark, he unwrapped the gun. He pushed the wrapping back into the false bottom and silently closed the door. He kept the double-barrel gun loaded all times, so there was not need to check it for ammunition.

Nate had just crawled out from under the wagon when the door of the house opened, and one of the men came out. Nate froze in his tracks. The drifter walked off to the side and relieved himself. Curiosity or something made him go back into the house and come back out with a lantern. He paused outside and lit the lantern, then he proceeded over to the shed and eased the cross bar open.

When he opened the door, Nate, despite his weight, moved like a panther. He came up behind the man and hit him over the head with the gunbarrel. The man hit the ground like a sack of flour. The lantern fell inside the shed. The glass broke and oil spilled out on the straw and trash in the shed. It caught afire and spread rapidly. Nate pulled the man out of the shed, and turning just in time, he realized that the older man was raising a gun to fire.

Nate dropped to one side and rolled. He snapped back both hammers and fired both barrels at the man in the door. The man's shot went into the shed, but Nate's shotgun blast caught him full in the chest and threw him back in the house. When Nate was scared, as he was now, he could move very fast.

Running into the shadow of the shed, he reloaded and circled to the back of the house. This move put the men in the house between him and the fire and the light that was out in front. A third man ran into the yard, and another one stood in the door.

Nate said, "Lay down your gun."

Instead, the man whirled and fired his shotgun at the same time. The blast and sound from Nate's gun and the drifter's gun almost blended into one sound. Nate staggered back, he had taken some buck shot in the left leg and thigh. The man in the door had been standing over the dead man, and Nate's blast had blown him out in the yard. Also, some of Nate's shot had carried out into the front and wounded the fourth man.

Nate felt light-headed, and he leaned against the wall for a time. The outside was well lighted by the shed on fire. The light penetrated all corners of the house, and Nate could see a woman standing in a bedroom door, covering her face with both hands.

"Don't shoot me , Mister." She was wide eyed and very scared. Her hair was in straggles, and when she opened her mouth snaggled teeth showed.

"Then get in that bedroom and close the door."

Nate slowly moved forward to inspect the two men piled in the door. One look was all it took to see that both had taken the blast full in the chest and had died instantly. He reloaded and stepped over the two bodies. The wounded man was down on the ground moaning and holding his face.

"Lord, somebody help me, I'm blind.," The buckshot had caught him in the face. Some of the flesh was torn, but the bad part was he had been hit in both eyes.

Nate, felt that he was going to pass out. He had to hold on. The man out by the shed stirred and sat up. The motion caused Nate to concentrate. He pointed his gun at the man.

"Where are my horses?"

"In the corral behind the house."

"You move real slow and easy. We are going to get them. This scatter gun is cocked and has a wire trigger."

The two of them went around to the back of the house.

"Put the harness on the horses, and bring them around to my wagon."

In a few minutes the man had the horses around the house and hitched to the wagon.

"Do you have any horses?"

"There are two in the barn."

'Let's get them!"

The two men again circled the house and went to the barn.

"Neighbor, the light is not very good here, so, I'll stand to one side and hope you don't make a wrong move."

"Don't worry, Mister. I saw how you handled that gun, and what you did at the house."

Nate almost smiled, if the man knew that most of the shooting had been reflex and luck, he might not be so easy to control.

The man led the two horses out of the barn, and they went back around to the wagon.

"Tie them on the back."

"Are you going to leave us a-foot?"

"That's the idea. I don't want you following me in the dark. When I get to the countyseat, I'll send the Sheriff back out here. Now gather up those two guns your friends had and put them in the wagon." The man moved quickly to comply with the instructions.

Nate managed to get in the wagon and keep the gun on the man. Carefully he turned the wagon around and headed back down the trail. The moonlight lit the trail, and the horses kept moving. Nate faded in and out of consciousness. His leg and side burned like fire, and his head was light. He did not know how far he could go before the pain made him pass out.

This was not the trip he had planned. He dreamed of a life of luxury. He dreamed of his childhood. He dreamed, and the pain finally made him pass out.

The horses kept walking all night. At daybreak, Nate roused up and to his amazement he saw the ranch where the widow lady was working. Maybe things would work out after all. That was the last he remembered.

CHAPTER FIVE

It was about ten in the morning when we were ready to leave. No one had to hurry us. We just hoped that in our haste, we did not leave anything important. Like matches, Minnie had to run back into the house and find the tin of kitchen matches. Took her about two minutes, but seemed like forever. We had the sacks tied two together. I swung them upon Old Number One and centered the double sack knot on his back . This allowed the sacks to hang down on each side of Old Number One.

We took all four of our Papa's mules. That way, we each had one to ride and Number One to carry the sacks. I would ride Number Four, Lizzie would be on Number Three and Minnie would be on Number Two. Minnie and I discussed some of the problems we might confront. One that worried me was the fact that I could not tie the sacks to Number One. I would have to watch them constantly and keep them centered so they would not fall off.

We helped Lizzie onto Number Three, and then Minnie and I mounted. For us to mount, we jumped on the back of the animal on our stomachs, and then, twisted around straight and sat up. There was no easy way without saddles to mount the mules. The mules probably would not have stood still for a saddle. I don't think any one of the mules was saddle broken.

Minnie led the way, and Lizzie followed. I came next, leading Number One. I immediately realized that I could not easily watch the sacks on Number One with him behind me. I would have to be constantly turning around to watch the sacks. So I called Minnie to stop and explained the problem to her. We sat there for a few moments, realizing that every second counted if we were to get away.

"Why can't I lead Number One?" Lizzie asked. Out of the mouths of babies?

I said with skepticism, "Do you think you are big enough to lead Number One?"

Did I ever make a mistake! Yes, and it was worth IT! All of sudden Lizzie was talking. On and on. We did not try to stop her, we were too amazed. She was full of questions.

"Minnie, how long is it going to take to get to Uncle John's?"

"I'm not sure."

"Well. How far is it?"

"About two hundred miles, I think."

"Then, how long does it take to go two hundred miles?"

Minnie already, with only three questions, was becoming suspicious that we had opened a door that could not be closed.

"Lizzie, I don't know."

"Robert, Minnie does not know how long. Can you tell me how long?"

"No, Lizzie, I can't."

She huffed up and declared, "If the two of you don't know how far and how long, just what am I to do?" She rode silent for some distance. She was sore and had her chin stuck out. I had not seen this side of Lizzie. I guess if I was a girl of eight and lost my parents and was homeless, I would be touchy. Come to think of it, I had become fairly touchy during the last few months myself.

Before we left, Aunt Bess's, I had had two fights with my cousins, and we had never had trouble before. I guess the pot can't call the kettle black. At least that's what Mama used to say.

I knew Lizzie did not like it when she didn't get a straight answer. Just saying I don't know would not satisfy her. Lizzie rode for sometime before she was over her pout. When she got over her pout, she was full of questions, and we answered questions for hours.

Of course, that was the solution. Minnie would lead, with Lizzie next, leading Number One. That put me last, and I could watch the sacks. Old Number One really didn't need much leading, and after a few days on the trail, we found that a lead rope was not necessary. He just followed Lizzie. Number One was so smooth that I had little trouble keeping the sacks in the center. As the trip progressed I learned to balance the sacks.

What direction to go had not been discussed. I knew that Minnie knew the way, and we just had not covered that subject. When she started south and not west, I hollered at her, "Are you sure you know where we are going?"

"Sure do. Just follow me, and I'll explain later," she replied.

I started to whistle up Ol' Bullet, but then I looked around and there he stood. Tail a-wagging and a big grin on his face. He knew that Uncle Nate was gone, and there was no reason to be afraid of being shot. As we moved off, he ran circles around and around for pure joy. One thing about Ol' Bullet, he did not run in under the mule's legs. He stayed away to the side so he would not spook them. I doubted that he would bother these four gentle beasts of burden. Even they sensed that we were leaving a place of pain and misery. Their ears lifted to Minnie's calm voice singing and the pure laughter that flowed from Lizzie. I called to them gently and saw them respond one at a time. Their ears would turn toward me when I called their name.

We went down the cowpath into the bushes. All morning we kept to the cowpath. About noon, by our Papa's watch, we stopped in the shade of some trees to rest and eat lunch. We had to help Lizzie down off the mule. The mule was so tall she could not get down, except by jumping, and we did not want her to jump. The last thing we needed was for one of us to break a leg.

During lunch Minnie explained, "We will follow these cow paths all the way to the river. Uncle Nate will not think that we went south. We will ride south for another hour or so and then turn southwest. This direction is away from people and roads. The mule tracks will be covered with cow tracks by the time they get back from town. I hope! This should be the last place on earth he would look for us. We will be at the river before dark. I figure that we will have been gone from the farm about eight hours, before we stop. If we make two miles an hour, we will be sixteen miles closer to Uncle John."

After lunch and some rest, we had to put Lizzie up on her mule. She laughed and bubbled, "You are going to get tired of putting me on this mule!" Her laughter lifted our spirits. She was, for the moment, over her miff about us not answering all her questions. Our spirits were all lifted by leaving that blasted farm and the pack of dogs that lived there. We all suddenly realized that we were laughing at anything and everything. A burden was lifted off our backs, and we felt free. We heard birds for the first time in months. Butterflies caught our attention. The warm sun and soft breeze felt marvelous.

"Let's make as good time as we can and get as far from that farm today as possible," Minnie said, as she skinned up on her mule. I put the one set of sacks, that we had taken off during our lunch, back on Number One and climbed on my mule.

All afternoon we rode south and west, only stopping to rest when we could find good shade. We were not used to riding, and we all got tired pretty quick. A few swigs of cool water did wonders for our dry mouths and sore backsides. We would pour a little water in my hat and give it to the mules and to Ol' Bullet.

"Be sure and give Ol'Bullet a good drink, " called Lizzie. "He saved my life and has to look after all of us on the way to Uncle John's"

No doubt he would perform many good deeds on the road. Alert us if someone was coming and sure spot snakes on the trail. His running in circles had stopped after a few minutes, and he took the lead on the trail. He seemed to know that this was snake country, and he needed to give us ample warning if he found one on the trail. We could not afford for a mule or one of us to be bitten. We were getting further and further away from any help with each passing hour. There was some farming to the west of us, but mostly ranching. We would be out of the area soon and needed to be extra careful every minute.

The sun beat down, and it grew hotter as the day passed. Thank goodness, we all had wide brim hats to cover our faces. We all wore overalls, long sleeve shirts and lace up boots. Uncle Nate had put our boots up when it got warm and said we might need them later. Well, it was later, and we needed them. Papa would not let us go barefooted away from the house because of snakes. So one of the first items on our list was to find our boots. Then when it came time to leave, that was one of the first things we secured, and we put them on.

The buzz of flies and bees in the mesquite was a hypnotizing sound. The drone of the insects lulled us. We had to fight to stay awake, because it was very important to put as much distance between us and our dear uncle as possible. The sun began to sink slowly in the west.

Finally, Minnie turned and said to us, "Looks like we are not going to make the river today, so let's start looking for a good place to camp before it gets dark."

She had hardly finished her statement, when the mules ears pricked up, and Number One made a low snort. I knew that snort. When the day of plowing was over and Papa would start to the house, Old Number One would snort when he could smell water from the mill or tank. He snorted again, and I noticed all four of them hastened their pace.

"Minnie, I think the mules smell water. Number One did that snort thing he does when he smells water." All four mules must have smelled it, for they picked up the pace just a little.

"You're right about the pace, Robert."

Just a few minutes passed, and we could hear the water running. The river appeared around the next clump of mesquites. We had made the first day without a hitch and reached the river. Camp was set up in short order. Minnie knew all the things that needed to be done, and she kept the two of us busy doing the number of things that were necessary.

She had me unload the sacks and hobble the mules. There was ample grass along the riverbank. With water at hand and good fodder, the mules would not roam very far. Next, was collecting firewood. There was lots of driftwood along the banks of the river. I started a fire and found some rocks for Minnie to set pots and pans on. She had Lizzie unpack the bedding and place the three bedrolls next to the fire. Soon she had sourdough biscuits cooking in the little Dutch oven and some bacon frying in the skillet.

When we got further from farms and ranches, we could shoot some quail and perhaps some ducks. I had seen ducks up the river north of our camp. I might try my hand at fishing. I had a little metal box that had some hooks and string for fishing. We had brought flour, salt, baking soda, salted bacon and some cans of beans with us in an effort to have food for the entire trip.

Minnie had us a hot meal in about thirty minutes. We had hot biscuits, bacon and beans with cool water to drink. As we sat around the fire, Minnie began to explain some problems of the trip.

"Now, we have got to be on guard that someone does not find us and send us back. The further we go west, starting tomorrow, the chances of meeting people becomes less."

She motioned at the river, "We will have water all the way because we will be following one river or another most of the way. Lizzie, I have been thinking about your question. I think that we should cover the two hundred miles in about ten days."

Minnie pointed at the sacks, "We have plenty of food for that period of time."

She sat for some time and then continued, "If the weather holds, we should be able to cover about twenty miles a day. We covered about sixteen miles today, I think. We really did good today, considering that we left about ten, and we are not used to riding. We will toughen up in a day or so, and it will be easier on us."

Minnie stood and started preparing our beds, "Let's get to sleep and get all the rest we can. I would like to be on the move when the sun comes up and do most of the riding when it is cool. We can make better time and not wear us out so completely. Robert, you run down to the river and wash real quick, and then Lizzie and I will take a turn. Hurry!"

I returned to my bedroll and crawled into my bed to settle down when I saw that Minnie and Lizzie were back from the river. Minnie had taken a pair of scissors out of a sack.

"What are you going to do, Minnie?'

"Cut my hair. I need to look more like a boy than a girl."

She began trimming her hair the best she could.

"Minnie, you want me to help? I could cut it a lot shorter than you can." I got up and went around behind her. By the firelight and the moonlight I cut her beautiful blond hair. I got it as short as mine, but it sure was a butchered up job.

"I'm glad there is not a mirror, you would kill me, Minnie. I sure hated to cut your beautiful hair."

"No, that is just what I wanted. To look ragged and rough. A girl out here is in danger all the time, and this might just help us get through."

"You think we could have some trouble?'

"Yes. There is no telling what we may run into in the next two weeks. Now, go to sleep. I will let you trim on this a little more in the sunlight. Some time tomorrow I will cut yours like mine, and then I will cut Lizzie's. That will make us all look alike. Ragged and unkempt."

"Are you going to cut my hair, Minnie?"

"Yes, sweetheart. I will make you look like me and Robert. O.K.?"

Lizzie answered drowsily, "I always wanted to be a boy." And she was asleep.

Minnie and I were asleep in a few minutes. We did not worry about animals or anything. We had Ol' Bullet to guard us until morning.

Just as it began to turn light I awoke. Minnie was already up, had a fire going and breakfast started. I looked around for her and discovered she was down at the river. I joined her and we stood and listened to the voice of the river. It was soothing and pleasant. It was as hypnotizing as the sound of the insects had been yesterday. Made you just want to sit down and listen all day.

"Sure reminds me of camp meeting and the trips to the river."

Minnie looked at me and reminisced. "Seems like a long time ago, but it was less than a year ago. So much has happened in the past few months. I wonder if we will ever see good times again. If singing will ever be as much fun as it was with Mother and Aunt Pearl."

"You're right, Minnie, about lots happening in such a short time. I believe we will see some of those good times again, and you will want to sing and sing some more."

Lizzie's voice broke our reverie, "Hey, where are you guys?"

"We are down here by the river, Lizzie."

"Oh, I woke up and looked the wrong way," she said with a sheepish grin.

Minnie turned from the river and called me, "Let's eat and get started for the day."

We had breakfast, were loaded and on the way about sunrise. It seemed that everything just fell together on this second day. The loading of the mules was easier. Each one of us had our jobs and performed them in short order. I will thank the Good Lord all of my life for the four gentle mules that were so important to our success. They stood still as we loaded and crawled aboard. I wondered if they remembered the whip Uncle Nate had used on one or the other of them on occasion.

Minnie called, "We will cross the river right up there. The water is not very deep. We won't even get our boots wet."

We rode up the bank for about a hundred yards and turned into the river. She was right, the water was not deep. Suddenly Minnie pulled on her reins.

"I think we will ride up the river for awhile. The water does not seem to get any deeper, If Uncle Nate should track us this far, he will have a very hard time finding our tracks in the riverbed."

"Do you think that he will put out the energy to follow us, Minnie?'

"By all means, Robert, he will do everything he can to find us. We know too much and can cause him too much grief. The only thing that will keep him from hunting us, is if he breaks a leg."

"That is scary, Minnie! That he might chase us."

"He won't chase very far. He will go to the sheriff and claim we ran away and stole 'his' property. Remember what you heard him tell Aunt Pettie out in the barn?"

"Oh, that is right, Minnie. He said he would tell the sheriff that we were thieves."

"Now, do you see why we need to cover our tracks?"

"You, bet, Sis!"

We rode up the river for perhaps two hours. The early morning was cool and the ride was pleasant. The sky was clear and a deep blue. Insects of all kinds flew down to the water and back into the brush. I saw fish splash in the river several times. We flushed several flocks of water fowl and saw quail and dove along the bank of the river.

"If we can take the time later on, I can catch us a mess of fish, Minnie!"

"Great idea, we just need to get as far away as possible over the next few days."

"Lizzie, did you see all of the ducks?"

"Yes, Robert," she replied, with big eyes.

These birds were on the way back north from their winter roosting grounds. There were hundreds of birds on the river.

"I hope us disturbing all of these birds does not draw attention to us," commented Minnie.

"Lots of things could disturb the birds, Minnie."

Just then our first encounter with wildlife occurred. A mother coyote and a couple of pups were drinking at the water's edge. They jumped and ran into the brush when they saw us approaching. Their actions startled another large flock of ducks. Sent them streaming into the morning sky.

"See, anything could disturb them, Minnie."

"Right, and somebody might investigate and find us instead of a coyote. I think we have gone far enough in the river. By going this way for two hours, Uncle Nate would not know which way we went or how far. He won't know if we crossed the river or not."

She spotted a gentle slope out of the river. "Let's rest in the shade of those trees before we go up out of the riverbed."

We stopped our mules in the shade of some trees overhanging the bank. Sure felt good to get off the mule. They rode easy and gentle, but after a long time sitting on them, your body began to object. Especially, short legged Lizzie. She did not complain while we were moving.

When we took her off she noted, "My legs are asleep, don't drop me!"

"Why didn't you say something, Lizzie?"

"I didn't notice until I started to get down."

The cool sand made a soft place to sit, and when we stretched out, it sure felt good on our backsides. Swarms of gnats, flies and other insects filled the air along the bank. We decided that we had had enough rest when the insects discovered us and started biting. We quickly put Lizzie on her mule, and Minnie headed her mule up the incline. Lizzie followed leading Number One. I checked the sacks as we went up the bank.

We settled into a rhythm of riding about two hours and then taking a break. We also figured out that if we got off and walked along with the mules, it rested us. At each break I would check hoofs and mouths on the mules. Papa said that a mule needed all the love and attention he could get, and we humans were appointed to provide the love and attention.

Just before we took our noon break, We noticed a small waterfall and some large rocks with water running over them. Also, there was lots of shade and a good beach for us to rest on. At least, here there were not as many bugs.

"Good place to rest and eat," Minnie directed.

We unloaded the sacks, and I hobbled the mules. Why take a chance on having to catch one of them, if he wandered off. Minnie had biscuits and strips of bacon left over from supper last night. We had made breakfast on them this morning, and now they would be our lunch. This way we would only build a fire but once a day. I sure did enjoy a short swim while Minnie trimmed Lizzie's hair.

"I thought you were going to do that this morning, Minnie."

"I felt we needed to put as much distance between us and Uncle Nate as possible. If I am figuring correctly, we have traveled another eight or ten miles this morning. Maybe some further, as we were moving at sunrise, and we may have gone as much as fifteen miles. I can only guess."

She got out the scissors and said, "Robert, come trim my hair and then I will do yours."

After thirty minutes we were the sorriest looking bunch of kids in all of Texas. Trim, was not a good word to describe our hair. Butchered would be a better word! One thing about our looks, we all looked alike. Suddenly it dawned on me, if someone saw us now they would think that we were three boys. With our floppy hats, blue and white striped overalls and long sleeved blue faded shirts, we would pass as three brothers. Now, as for an explanation of what we were doing so far from any farm or ranch, that would be another matter. Best plan was to stay away from all people.

We loaded up the mules, unhobbled them and left the riverbed. The climb out was fairly easy and the travel was smooth out on the top. Shortly after we left the river we saw a cloud of dust. We slowly made our way toward the dust. It was a road. It shocked us because we did not know that there was any form of civilization anywhere near us.

"Minnie, what is that road?" I asked. "And what do I hear?"

"I have no idea." replied Minnie.

We stopped back in the brush, helped Lizzie down , tied the mules and slipped up close to the road. To our amazement, it was a herd of thirty or so cows, being driven by two cowboys.

"Where do you suppose they are going, Minnie?"

"I have no idea, Robert."

We heard one of them call out to his partner, "Do you think we can make Red Lake tonight?"

"We should be able to, by sundown."

"I sure hope so. Then one more day will put us back at the ranch. Would be nice to sleep under a roof and in a bed for a change."

"You sure are getting to be a softy, Mitch."

"I won't argue that point, Red. I sure like some comfort, like driving these heifers down a dirt road and not through the brush."

"It's pretty nice. Think the boss is going to be mad that we are a day late?" asked Mitch.

Red circled and herded a stray back into the bunch. "Nah, he will just be glad we're back with a whole bunch of free cows."

We all looked at each other in puzzlement. Free cows, how do you get free cows?

The herd was almost past us when Mitch said, "We would be home tonight if you had not stopped and got mixed up with that old crazy fool yesterday."

"Boy, he sure is a character!" laughed Red.

"You can say that again!" exclaimed Mitch.

"Man, he sure was in a boil over those kids running off and stealing all of the stuff."

"What I want to know is, why you had to spend a day helping him look for those kids?"

"Beats, me. The ten dollars I guess. Just thought they could not be very far away, and I could track them. They went into the river and I had no idea which way they went. Not a trace of them." replied Red.

"I hope he never finds them," declared Mitch.

"Why? They stole stuff and ran away."

Mitch said, "I look at it like this, Red. I had an old man that was a drinker, just like that old skunk. Drinking and blaming the world for all of his problems. No wonder those kids ran away!"

"Maybe so, Mitch, but we are late getting back from selling that last bunch of 'free' cows."

Mitch rolled a cigarette and asked, "Say, where did you put the money from those cows?"

"It's here in my saddle bag."

"Good. The boys would be very unhappy if they didn't get their cut from the sale of those critters."

"How much is our cut?"

"Well, the boss gets half and that is almost three hundred. Then if you divided the other three hundred by the nine boys...I think that is about...Thirty or thirty five dollars each."

The herd and the cowboys were down the road some distance. We could just hear their voices, over the bawling cows.

Red called out, "Say Mitch, isn't this the best deal we have ever worked?"

"Yeah, Red. The boss sure has things worked out. Running cows to Abilene, and some up on the Llano, sure is smart. One thing that I like is, after we deliver a herd to Abilene, the crew breaks up. The law will be looking for a gang of riders, and we go back in twos and threes."

"If we had been a big gang that old man with these cows would not have made the deal for us to drive them to Abilene."

Both cowboys laughed, "He sure was a dumb one!"

"Yeah, I know, we're not over five miles from that old geezer's place, the one that was looking for the kids. And we have only come about ten or twelve miles from that little town. So, let's push them and get out of this country. Somebody just might remember us."

With open mouths we crept back to the mules, "Minnie those men are rustlers, and they were talking about Uncle Nate!"

Minnie muttered, "We've got bigger troubles than seeing two rustlers. They are going down the road, and they are not looking for us." She was frowning and looking worried. " Do you realize that we only have gone about five miles from Uncle Nate's?" Her frown was deeper on her brow, as she continued, "I don't understand. How could we travel this long and only have gone about five miles?"

"Minnie, I know what has happened."

"What, Robert?" she was almost angry.

"Yesterday we followed all of those cow paths and they wind in and out and around bushes. You go five miles and have only moved two miles forward. Understand? All morning we have been winding around following the river and through the brush, and it just takes a long time."

All she could say was, "Oh."

"Besides that , Minnie, we rode south yesterday and today we have been going northwest along the river. We have, today just gone…," I paused looking for a word to describe our efforts. "We've gone in a sort of a circle." I stooped to the ground and drew a crude map.

Minnie's eyes squinted and she declared, "We may not be far away, but we sure fooled Uncle Nate. Robert, Lizzie, you stay put, and I'll see if the herd is out of sight." Minnie slipped through the brush, and in a few minutes she returned and said, "Mount up and let's get across the road and out of this country."

It didn't take a second order. We "pitched" Lizzie on her mule and mounted in a beat. We eased up to the road for one more look and then hurried the mules across and into the brush on the other side. I stopped Minnie back in the brush a short distance.

"Why, do you want to stop, Robert." asked Minnie.

"Let me get a branch and rub out our tracks where we crossed the road."

I grabbed an old mesquite branch and returned to the road. I looked both ways and then ran to the other side. With a few quick sweeps with the branch all of our tracks were gone. You would have to look close to notice that tracks had been rubbed out. I hoped you would have to look close!

I ran back to the others and mounted again and said, "Let's get out of here!!! Suddenly we heard the rattle of a wagon and a team. We were far enough back in the bushes to not be seen. The wagon and the team went by in a cloud of dust. I was still afoot, so I ran back to the road and watched the wagon receding out of sight.

I ran back to the girls, "You won't believe who that was. UNCLE NATE! He was whipping those poor old horses."

Minnie sputtered, "Uncle Nate? Where in the world is he going?"

"I know. I bet that road goes to the countyseat, and he is going to see the sheriff. Now for the second time, let's get out of here!"

Riding remained fairly easy the rest of the day. We made good time all afternoon, with only two short stops. The idea that we were that close to our starting point prodded us to keep riding. We rode until the sun set behind the horizon. There had been no complaining and little conversation all afternoon. Guess we were a little blue and down in the mouth after a good start yesterday and such a nice cool morning traveling in the river and along it's banks.

We found a good camping place down in the river bed where another stream joined the one we were following. Unloading was done with a minimum of effort. Again I hobbled the mules and built a fire. Lizzie laid out our beds and helped Minnie around the camp fire. There had been other campers here in the past. There were rocks already in a circle.

"Wonder who camped here one time?" quizzed Lizzie.

I answered, "No telling, Lizzie. Maybe, cowboys, Indians or travelers, just like us."

"Are there Indians out in the bushes, Robert?"

"Nah, Papa said that the soldiers had chased the Indians out of Texas, and they are all on the reservations."

"What's a reservation?" Lizzie asked.

"That is the name they use, for where the Indians have been taken."

Minnie shortly had supper ready, and it was the same fare as last night. She sure did know how to make beans and bacon taste good. I guess it could have been that I was starved. After our supper, we swam in the river. That got rid of all the hair that was down our backs.

"Minnie, I am going to put a hook with a grasshopper in the water, and see if I can catch us some fish for breakfast." I had my fishing line in the water only about two minutes when a catfish hit the line. I drug him up on the shore and put him on a line to keep while I fished some more. This fish probably weighed about two pounds, and one more would be enough for breakfast. In a few minutes I had a second fish, just a little smaller than the first, but plenty for us.

"Minnie, I wonder what the name of that stream is, the one over yonder?"

"I don't know, Robert. The one we are following is called the Brazos. There're lots of tributaries on the Brazos, at least that is what Papa used to say. He also said to go to Uncle John's from our old place, you ride west until you cross the Brazos and stay on the left side until the river runs out. From Uncle Nate's I figured that if you ride west you will hit the Brazos, but by going south we would throw him off the trail. If I remember Papa right, he said that even from Uncle Nate's, you cross the river and stay on the left side. Then go west until you cross over a hill. On the other side, about two miles west is another branch of the Brazos. That is the one we will follow to the New Mexico Territory. He said that the two branches are only about five miles apart."

"Then, that ought to be easy to follow and even a girl would not get lost." I piped, with a grin on my face.

"You want to be the guide on this trip, Mr. Smart Pants?"

"YOU, are doing just fine, Minnie."

The second surprise for the day suddenly announced himself. A diamond back rattlesnake about five feet long suddenly started buzzing. Everyone was on their feet in a flash. Before we could say a word Ol' Bullet was on the job. He rushed in and snapped at the snake. When the snake struck at Ol' Bullet, Ol' Bullet would dodge away. This went on for perhaps ten minutes. You could tell the snake was getting tired and tried several times to slither away. Ol' Bullet was not going to let that happen. The snake coiled once more and struck out. He was too slow that time, and Ol' Bullet had him behind the head. They thrashed around for a few moments. Then Ol' Bullet dropped the snake on the ground and stepped back to see if it was dead.

"I need to go to the bushes," I declared and darted away. That big snake had been within two or three feet of me. If I had moved the wrong way.........my knees got weak. I returned from the brush in a few minutes.

"You are the guy that is always doing something with a snake, now get rid of that thing!!!"

"But, Minnie he would make a good belt and beside we can skin and dress him out for breakfast and let the fish go."

"ROBERT!!!"

"Yes. Ma'am! He is gone." I picked the snake up by the tail and carried him away up on the bank and out of sight. What I did not tell the girls, was that I cut the rattler off. That rattler had fourteen rattles and a button. Just about the biggest one I had seen!

"Lizzie are you all right?" I heard Minnie ask as I returned.

The yes was slow and drawn out, "Yeeeeeees, I guess. That snake was a lot bigger than the one in the garden. And Ol' Bullet killed them both. Come here Bullet, and let me hug you!"

The dog trotted over and sat down beside her for his petting. He had been there before and liked her petting on him. I claimed Ol' Bullet as my dog, but if there was a bet, I bet that Ol' Bullet would choose Lizzie over me.

"We need to get to bed. We are only about ten miles as the crow flies from Uncle Nate's, and that is too close for comfort. Ol' Bullet will guard us all night." She removed her boots and tied the laces together and hung them over one of the branches of a tree. "Give me your boots, and let me hang them up so varmints want get in them. I forgot to do this last night."

We took our boots off and passed them to her."

"Now, to sleep. Bullet, you lay down by Lizzie!"

Darn old dog went over and curled up right beside Lizzie. His tail thumped against Lizzie, and soon she was asleep. I watched the stars overhead. There were millions, and they twinkled and twinkled. The last thing I remember about that night is hearing Minnie softly humming and me trying to count stars.

Dawn found us up and starting breakfast. The circle of rocks had kept hot coals burning, and we did not have to start a new fire. I cleaned the two fish with my knife and put them in the skillet. Minnie heated the biscuits and cooked the fish for us. Nice change from the mush that we were given for the last three or four months. We cleaned our utensils in the river and broke camp. We were getting into a routine, and loading the gear was getting easier. By sunrise we were up out of the river bed and on our way. No snakes and no varmints in our boots. Mules seemed glad to be on the road again. They moved at a brisk pace, and the miles seemed to just roll by. Of course, we now knew with all of the winding around the bushes, we were not making near the miles we wanted.

In a matter of an hour, we were in rough country and traveling became very slow. Trails wound around and around, coming back in on the same trail. We were lost in the maze of brush and trails for hours on end. We rested and tried again, trying to follow the river. The river was very crooked and hard to follow. Banks were steep in places and covered with loose dangerous rocks in others. By noon we had covered about two miles. We were exhausted and out of sorts.

When we stopped in the shade of some trees for lunch and rested I asked, "Minnie, what would happen if we did not follow the river so close. Go out on the flat and just keep the green trees in sight?"

"It's worth a try, Robert. We are loosing time this way."

We had plenty of water with the river at hand. This time we were not down in the river-bed, so I watered the mules out of my hat and gave Ol' Bullet a good drink.

Lizzie was lying on one of the wagon canvasses after her lunch. When I looked around, Bullet had joined her, and they both were asleep.

"Minnie, this heat is going to be hard on us, much less Lizzie. Let's rest until she wakens and then see how much ground we can cover by sunset."

"Robert, we have got to cover more miles than we are. We have been gone two and half days, and we are not over twenty miles from our starting point, if we are that far. At this rate, about six miles a day, it will take us over a month to reach Uncle John, and we don't have enough food. We could not have carried that much on the mules along with us. We have got to find a better way."

"Minnie, do you remember Papa talking about going out to Uncle John's?"

"Yes, that is how I know about the rivers."

That's not what I mean, Minnie. Do you remember anything about the land. Is it rough , flat, mountains or valleys? "

"Oh! I see what you mean. Let me think."

She studied for a while and finally said, "Robert, I don't remember much about the land. Something about prairie is all I can recall now."

"What I am thinking is, that not all of the way will be rough. That some of the land will be like we had around home. Then we can make good time. See?"

"Well, maybe you are right. Let's hope so."

Another hour passed, and Lizzie finally roused up. "Have I been asleep long?"

"Just a while, sweetheart," Minnie answered.

We loaded all of our gear and mounted the mules. The rest seem to help us and the animals. We had been out only two and half days, and we all seemed to be drained. We pulled back from the crooked river and found some better passage. The surrounding country was still very rough, and we had to pick our way around ravines and gullies. Some of them were very steep, and it took lots of time to find a way through. After a long and hard afternoon, we decided to make our way back to the river to camp for the night.

"I'll tell you one thing, Minnie. If somebody was following us through this country, they would be lost forever. If we weren't going west, or trying to, we would be lost."

The river was a welcome sight. There were some trees along the banks, and again we pitched camp under them. "What if tomorrow we try just going up the river bed? It's flat, and the water is not very deep"

"I think it is worth a try, Robert."

"Now, you take Lizzie and play in the river, while I prepare us some supper. How does bacon and beans sound, favorite brother?"

"Well, my favorite sister, it sure beats MUSH, even with a ton of sugar."

We all laughed, and Lizzie and I started to the river. The water was not over two feet deep in the middle, and we had a lot of fun splashing and falling down. By playing in the water, we washed our clothes and took a bath at the same time. It was so hot, that when we came out of the water we were dry all the way though in a matter of minutes.

"Supper is ready," Minnie called.

It was only sour dough biscuits and bacon, no beans tonight, and it tasted great. NO MUSH!

After we ate, Lizzie and I cleaned up while Minnie went down and splashed in the river for awhile. She returned, and we all sat on the wagon canvas and just enjoyed each other's company. We were pretty well hidden, and Ol' Bullet would hear if somebody was coming along.

After a period of time, I took the mules, one at a time down to the stream and let them roll in the water and the mud. The water cooled them off, and the mud protected them from flies and insects. As I brought them back to the campsite I re-hobbled each and brushed out their tails and manes. Of course we would have to sit on a dirty back the next morning. But that was fine, the mules needed the water and the mud.

As it became dark, we put the fire out. We did not want some lone rider to see the light from the fire. We just sat quietly under the starlight until Minnie spoke softly, "Sometimes when it is very still, like now, I think I can hear Mama's voice."

"I sure do miss Mama and Papa," Lizzie said in a murmur.

"We all do, Lizzie."

"Lizzie," I said. "Mama and Papa and Grandpa and Grandma are all in heaven and looking down on us. All of our family is watching us along with the angels in heaven."

"Can they see us and hear us?" Lizzie asked?

"I think so," replied Minnie. "They are looking out for us each day."

"Would you please sing us a song , Minnie?"

"All right, here is one of my favorites. She began to sing, "*Sweet Hour of Prayer.*"

Before she had sung two verses, Lizzie was sound asleep. She continued to sing some of her beloved songs. I slipped into my bed and again started counting stars and meteors.

Like the other days, when dawn came, we were up and had a cold breakfast. The packing of gear was a routine. Today I kept the shotgun out of the bedroll in hopes of shooting some fowls for our meal. Lots of birds along the banks, but they were too far away or flying too high to shoot.

Riding in the river bed did prove to be a faster way of travel. We did a lot of winding back and forth, so westward progress was slower. The only other problem, was the mules kept kicking the shallow water in the air and all over us. At our first stop, I put the shotgun in the bedding in one of the burlap sacks to keep it dry. Our clothes were soaked, for the most part, by that first stop. Not that it mattered, as it just made us cool.

The river became even more winding. Lots of the time you could see where we had left hoof prints along the river on the turn behind us. We worried about leaving the hoof prints for fear we would be trailed and taken back or worse.

By noon we were ready to get out of the water for a time. We had some cold biscuits and bacon once again and rested for a short period. Our clothes dried, and we were ready to find a way out of the river bed.

The mules had been having a little trouble bogging down in the mud of the river. Every once in awhile one of them would seem to sink. I worried that if they sank very far and began to pitch to get out of the mud, that one of us would be thrown off. If Number One bucked, all of the sacks would go into the water and all of our gear would be soaked.

The mules kept struggling in the mud. Suddenly Minnie screamed, "Number Two is stuck and is sinking in the sand."

I shouted, "Lizzie STOP! Minnie don't fight him. Give him his head."

Lizzie had reined up and was watching the mule and Minnie with big round eyes. Her face had turned white. Minnie let the reins drop slack, and the mule stopped struggling.

"Robert, what are you going to do?" Minnie questioned me.

"Get a rope to help Number Two out of the mud." I was afraid to use the word quick-sand. Papa, one time at the river at camp meeting had pointed out quicksand and told me to not fight the sand. If an animal was caught, just put a rope on them and give a gentle pull. Usually it will start trying to move and, with another animal pulling, it will come free.

"Lizzie don't get down off Number Three. Just sit still and let me help Minnie. O.K.?"

She just nodded, but did not move. Number Three seemed to be on good footing.

I eased Number Four forward, beside Number One and pulled a rope from one of the sacks.

"Now, Minnie, I will come alongside Number Two and pitch you the loop. Put it over his head. I don't want to rope him, it might cause him to start bucking or struggling again. O.K.?"

She nodded and didn't say anything. I could tell that she was scared.

I brought Number Four up close to Minnie and the mule. I tossed her the loop, and she eased it over Number Two's head. Not having a saddle, I had to loop the other end of the rope around Number Four's neck. Next, with a little coaching, Number Four moved to the left and onto good solid ground. The slack came out of the rope, and Minnie's Number Two began to move forward. Very slow we moved up on good solid ground. Number Two got his feet on good ground and gave a lurch forward, spilling Minnie in the water. He jumped up on dry ground and stopped. He stood very still as if he was uncertain as what to do.

"Minnie, are you O.K.?"

"Yes, just toss me the rope and pull me ashore."

Soon she was on dry land and holding the bridle of Number Two. I went back out into the water and slowly led Lizzie and Number Three to high ground. Old Number One just followed real easy and did not lose a sack. We all got down and rested for a while and let Minnie dry off. She reached into the bib pocket of her overalls and took out Papa's watch. Lifting it to her ear, she breathed a sigh of relief.

"It's still ticking, so I guess it is going to keep running. Robert, if I can be dumped into the river, so can you. You still have that little notebook in your overall pocket?"

I felt in my snapped pocket and replied, "Yes, it is right here."

"Well, let me have it and put it in the oil cloth with the Bible. It will be in a water tight sack and wrapped in oil cloth."

I unsnapped the pocket on my overalls and handed Minnie the notebook. "Sure don't want to lose the only information we have that Uncle Nate was trying something."

"Right," Minnie responded as she put the notebook in with her Bible. "Well, let's get going."

We stayed up on the dry river bed for an hour or so. About the time we decided to stop and rest, we found a cut in the bank so we could go up on top and out of the river bed. "Let's get upon high ground and see what is around." We climbed out of the river bed and stopped on top. The landscape had not changed much. Looking to the west, I thought I could see a ridge and higher ground. Probably not anything of importance.

Mounting back up, we rode till noon without further incident. Just a lot of weaving and winding around to get across gullies. Finding another cut in the bank, we went back down in the riverbed where there was shade for our noon break.

"Boy, I sure would hate to get caught down in this riverbed in a flash flood!"

"Robert, you worry too much. There is not a cloud in the sky. The water is very shallow. Why borrow trouble?"

"Yeah, Robert, you worry too much," piped up Lizzie.

"All I said is I would hate to get......"

"We heard, so come eat and let's rest for a while."

The terrain had leveled out some and travel on top was much easier. We made good time all afternoon and again went down into the riverbed for the night.

Making camp was an easy task, when we each did our part. I unloaded the mules and then gathered wood for a fire. There always seemed to be lots of driftwood along the banks. It was dry, so it burned smokeless. A good idea when you are running from the law, your mad Uncle and anyone who might spot you. By the time I had watered and hobbled the mules, supper was ready. More biscuits, bacon and beans.

"Minnie, tomorrow I am going to shoot or catch something, so we can have something besides bacon."

"I just hope no one hears that gunshot and comes to check who is here."

"We must be at least twenty miles, as the crow flies, from the farm. If they can hear a gun-shot they sure have good ears."

"I was thinking of somebody who lives out in here or someone who is traveling through."

"There is always that chance. We will have to take that chance if we want something else to eat beside bacon. That slab of bacon is dwindling pretty fast."

We went through our nightly routine, and soon we were bedded down for the night. I had kicked out the fire. Ol' Bullet curled up next to Lizzie. As it had become a habit, Minnie started singing a few verses of hymns and soon, under the millions of stars we were asleep.

The next morning passed quickly. Breakfast over, I loaded up and unhobbled the mules and we were on our way. The river turned southwest for a few miles. The traveling had become easier on flatter land.

By noon we had reached a place were the river turned back northwest. In the bend was a great place for our lunch. Big overhanging trees and cool water. Ol' bullet played in the water with Lizzie. We rested and filled our water bags, as we had done at every stop. This kept them full all the time, just in case of an emergency.

We followed the river fairly straight to the northwest for the rest of the day. Travel had become much easier. We made two stops during the afternoon, and still covered more ground in that half day than we had covered in any full day.

Riding out on a high point, we could see the ridge that I had seen earlier. It wasn't a mountain, just a barrier that ran from north to south without a break. Made you wonder if you could get up it and on top. Looked to be two days ride on fairly level ground. Might be some surprises hidden between us and the barrier.

We started down the slope and almost immediately found a cut in the bank, so we could go down in the riverbed. Much to our surprise, we were at a fork in the river. We stopped and studied the two branches for sometime. The one to the left was a much smaller stream. The one on the right carried a much larger body of water.

As we made camp and cooked our supper we discussed the fork. We decided that we should follow the main branch of the Brazos. The other one must just be a creek. While we talked I cleaned the shotgun. I had carried it all day long and did not get one shot.

I remarked, "If we are going to have fresh meat, I will have to hunt and not just ride on the back of Old Number One all day."

"I guess it will be all right to hunt. We will camp early and let you hunt and see if you can get us some fresh meat."

"Hurrah! We must be at least twenty five miles from that old farm and ten miles from anything else."

"Food is ready, and I want to take a splash in the river, so come on and eat," admonished Minnie.

After supper I brushed out the knots and tangles in the manes and tails of the mules. Before hobbling them, I took them down to the water and let them roll in the mud. Soon it was pitch dark except for the stars.

"Minnie, did you see flashes of lightning on the horizon?"

She stood up and watched for a few minutes and then said, "Yes, I see some a way off in the north. Doubt it is coming this way. Most clouds in this country move to the northeast."

We all settled down for the night. I noticed a few thin clouds over some of the stars, but I was asleep in a few minutes, and the clouds were forgotten in my dreams of Uncle John's.

A thick fog had rolled in during the night. We could hardly see the other bank of the river. There was no real concern about the fog. We finished our breakfast in record time and broke camp. We crossed the river to the east side and climbed the steep cut out of the river bed. The fog was even thicker out on top. We couldn't see much, and we discussed the dangers of riding off into a gully. I took the lead, with Ol' Bullet to keep a lookout, and we made reasonably good time.

By mid-morning and our first rest stop, a breeze had come up. It cleared the fog away by the time we started again. The sky was really

blue and clear, and there was a fresh smell in the air. The fog had damp-
ened all of the foliage and everything was dripping wet.

Minnie traded places with me when we resumed our trip. We made
very good time and covered mile after mile without much detour. At
lunch we just sat on some rocks overlooking the river and noticed that
the river was running faster.

"Must be from the rain in the north last night."

"Maybe we should get on the other side, Minnie."

"Oh, that water is not even two feet deep, let's eat and then go some
further and perhaps cross later in the day. There is no danger now."

"I guess not." I answered.

Lizzie, who usually was quite, pointed to the west and said, "Look,
aren't the clouds beautiful?'

Those clouds rolled in, and it turned out they were more fog. When
the fog cleared again, about noon, the sky was overcast and dark.

We ate our lunch of biscuits, dipped in bacon grease, and watched
the river from the cliff. "See, the water has already gone down and
slower, so we are doing fine on this side. Anyway this branch is going to
run out, and we will have to go over a hill to see the next branch. Can't
be much further. We should turn west shortly and head uphill."

The day wore on, and the river did not turn west. We figured it must
be just farther than we anticipated. We made our usual stops to rest. We
walked some of the way to stretch our legs, and still the river did not
turn west. By evening we were uneasy about the direction of the river.
Surely we had covered ten or so miles. Our directions indicated that the
river would end, and we would go about five miles west to another river.
None of that was happening.

The sun began to set and we were looking for a camping place, when
Lizzie said, "Is that a lake? See, over there?" In the distance we could see
the lake. We discussed the lake for a few minutes and decided to ride
down to it for the night. The lake was about two miles away, but it was
easy riding, and we covered the distance in good time.

It was a great camping place. Trees were plentiful. There was an abundance of grass for the mules and fish in the lake. I caught a mess in about thirty minutes. I had them cleaned before you could say, "Jack Robinson," and gave them to Minnie for cooking. That was one fine meal, fresh fish with hot biscuits and hot beans for a change. NO MUSH! Minnie is a good cook, and we are eating very well.

We had kicked out the campfire and gone to bed before we noticed the lightning in the west. By the time we were settled, we could hear thunder.

"Robert, how much are we above the water line of the lake?"

"Two or three feet, Minnie."

"Could it rain enough to fill the lake and get to us?"

"Sure would be a lot of water to do that."

"Minnie, I'm scared," whispered Lizzie.

"Robert, I hate to suggest this. But, let's break camp and move to higher ground while we have moonlight to work by."

I got out of my bedding and watched the approaching storm.

"It is coming this way and is getting bigger. O.K. Let's move."

We were packed when the first wind hit out of the west. Not strong, but a prelude of what was to come. I removed the hobbles from the mules, and we started walking up the slope to higher ground. I was leading Number One and Number Four. Lizzie was leading Number Three, and Minnie was leading Number Two.

Just as we got up on the bluff we had noticed earlier in the evening, the wind hit. We got out one of the wagon canvasses and put our gear under it to keep it dry. I threw some big rocks on the west edge of the canvas and told Lizzie and Minnie to get under the canvas.

I was hobbling the mules when the first real flash of lightning hit and thunder clapped and rumbled. I tried to get the hobbles on all four, but Number Two bolted at the thunder and pulled the reins out of my hands. He only ran a little way, but the next flash and ground jarring thunder sent him up the hill. I hung on to the other three and the rain hit. It rained hard for better than an hour. I managed to hobble the other three mules. I got under the edge of the canvas and held onto the reins for dear life.

Then a lull came in the storm, and the rain stopped. I crawled out to see if I could see Number Two, but in the darkness, it was no use. Minnie and Lizzie were a little wet and some scared. The rain started again, and I crawled back under the cover. I tied the reins to my leg in case I went to sleep. That was a wishful thought. The thunder kept it up most of the night. Wave after wave rolled through the valley. It seemed to never stop.

Finally, the clouds broke and the moon came out. We tried to sleep on the cold wet ground under our canvas. The next morning we were all wet, stiff and sleepy. Most of our gear had been soaked during the night. With daylight, I worked and worked to build a fire. When I had a fire going, we piled lots of wood on and begin drying our clothes.

Minnie managed to feed us some breakfast, but she did not have much to work with. The flour was wet and ruined. As we tried to put our gear back in order, Lizzie pointed at the lake. It was more than full, it was running over and down the valley in a wide muddy torrent. It was up over the spot were we had first camped. Boy, was I glad that Minnie wanted to move.

Minnie finally asked, "Robert, do you think that we took the wrong fork on the river?"

"I'm afraid so, Minnie."

"If this river is running at the fork like it is running here we are trapped and can't get across to the other side."

"Minnie, we have one more problem."

"What, Robert?'

"Number Two bolted during the storm. I had taken the hobbles off to move to higher ground. When the lightning and thunder kept up, he got away."

"Robert, we have three mules and we may find Number Two later. Don't worry. Right now we are trapped until the river goes down, so let's get to work and put our time to the best effort. Lizzie and I will spread out the wagon canvases, that are not wet. Then we can spread out our bedding and extra clothes to dry. Robert, you hobble two of the mules and take Number One and see if you can find Number Two."

By the end of the day, the bedding and our few clothes were dry. Minnie had thrown away all of the ruined food stuff. I hated to tell the girls that I couldn't find Number Two.

Minnie took the news in her usual calm fashion. "Papa used to say, 'We can't do anything about water under the bridge.'"

"I guess that we can't do anything about water down in the river. Robert, is it too muddy to go back to the fork?"

"Not if we stay up on the top of the banks. That is mostly hard ground and rock."

"This day is gone. Let's have some supper and get some sleep. In the morning we will go back to the fork"

CHAPTER SIX

Light was filtering through the tree branches. His vision was blurred, and he was completely disoriented. Sounds from outside were strange and distant. He tried to turn his head, but the pain almost made him pass out. He struggled up through haze and cobwebs. Fighting nausea, he made a second effort to turn his head. Pain flashed, and he sank back into the darkness.

Nate had no recollection of the time, nor did he know where he was. The bed was soft, and he seemed to float on a cloud. Hands moved him, and his bandages were changed. Bandages? It all came rushing back. His encounter with that bunch of polecats.

But, where was he now? Every time he was conscious, he tried to piece the puzzle together. When he moved his head, a blinding pain made him pass out again. Time had no meaning, and as he drifted in and out of consciousness, he became even more confused.

He heard a woman's voice, "How is he doing, Doctor?" He strained to hear the answer, for he was sure it had to do with him.

"Considering all the damage and the loss of blood, very well."

Another voice, this time a man. "When will he come around enough for me to talk to him?"

"Hard to tell." I know that voice, now let me think. But he could not grasp and hold on long enough to put a name to the voice.

"He sure took a beating."

The woman's voice, "I have been on ranches all of my life, and I don't recollect seeing anybody this badly wounded and live."

"He had been hit in the head, from the looks of that gash down the left side of his head, real hard. I had to stitch up four inches. His wrist had rope burns, and then he had taken a shotgun blast. From the look of the wounds, it only raked him on the left side from head to thigh. If that blast had been a foot further to his right, you would have been digging a grave."

"Any idea where he came from, miss?" the second voice asked.

The woman answered, "We think from the north. When the dogs alerted us, the team pulling the wagon was headed south."

"Well, I think I will take a ride out that way and see if I can make some sense out all of this."

I know that voice, that is the sheriff. I had started to town to find him, but now....he drifted off in darkness for a few moments, and then he heard the woman.

"By the way, Sheriff, he had a team, and there were two more horses tied to the tailgate of the wagon. They may have been his second team, but we think they are saddle horses from the looks of them. All four horses are in the corral."

"Thanks, ma'am. I know he was hunting those kids that were staying with him. But, what in the world happened? That he got beat up and shot up is sure a mystery. I'll look at the horses now if you will show me the direction."

If I could just get awake, I could tell them what happened. I need to tell the sheriff. I'm not a violent person, and I did not start that gunfight. Nor, did I start the fire.

"Sheriff, I'm going to give him another dose of pain killer and by the time the sun comes up again, he may be able to talk."

"Fine, Doctor, I'll look at the four horses and then ride up the road to the north and see if there is any evidence of what might have occurred."

More time passed, and he was given medicine and soft food. Mostly hot broth to drink. The day passed, and he was aware that someone washed him and changed the bedding again. He became aware that the sun was going down from the angle of the light on the wall.

With daylight the next day, something startled him awake. May have been a dream or pain from one of the wounds. When he opened his eyes, his vision was clear, and a woman was leaning over his bed.

"Good morning".

He tried to speak, but his jaw would not move or his mouth work.

"Don't try to talk, your head is bandaged. Just lie still, and I'll get the sheriff and the doctor."

He blinked at her and tried to smile. She smiled back and left the room. In a few moments the sheriff and the doctor returned to the room.

"Good, you're awake," said the doctor, as he began to examine Nate and his wounds.

The sheriff spoke, "Well, Nate, you have had yourself quite a little experience."

Nate tried to lift a hand, but couldn't, so he just nodded.

The doctor cautioned, "Now don't try to move just yet or talk. I think you have a concussion from that blow on the head. I do know you lost a lot of blood and took almost a full load of buckshot. If that shot had been any closer or just a little to the right…..well you are a lucky man."

"Nate," the sheriff was looking at him. "I think I figured out what happened. You nod or shake your head, and we will see if I have this right. You rode up to the house and were taken at gun point or wrestled down and tied up. That would account for the rope burns?"

Nate nodded.

"Somehow you got loose, got a gun and there was a fight?"

A nod.

"You came out on top and managed to come to this ranch in your wagon?"

Another nod.

"That's what I thought. You can fill me in on the details later. I found two dead men at the house. There were three other people there, scared half out of their wits. Nate, you must have been a terror. Doctor, the woman is so scared she can't talk. One man is blind and his face is a mess from buckshot, and the other man just won't talk. He has a gash down the top of his head. Doctor, I really hate to ask you, but I think that you need to take a look at these poor folks. Nate really left a mess out there."

The door opened, and the woman came in and stood close to the bed. "Are you hungry?"

Nate nodded.

The doctor spoke, "You can have broth today. Tomorrow I will take the bandages off, and you can open you mouth enough to eat. O.K.?"

Nate just looked at the doctor this time, but everyone heard the sigh.

The next day when the bandages around Nate's head came off, he told the full story to the sheriff. "Sheriff, I was only looking for the three kids, and those skunks jumped me. Tied me in the shack that burned. I cut my ropes on a hoe head and got out. I went to the wagon and got my shotgun. The first man, I hit on the head. The second was fixing to shoot me when I shot him. I circled the house and came in the back. There were two others. One was outside, and the other one was in the doorway. The one in the doorway turned and fired. He hit me, and when I shot, I hit him and killed him. Some of the shot went by him and hit the man in the yard. He is the one with the shot up face.

The sheriff added to their conversation, "Nate, you are a weasel and skunk, but I know you didn't kill in cold blood, and you probably were defending yourself. The doctor and two of my deputies went out there to get those poor people and to doctor them, and they were gone. Their footprints went to the east and south. Guess they are headed for Clear River and the lake. Not much over that way. I think somebody will find them dead out there in some gully, Either starved, snake bit or fell off of a cliff."

Nate closed his eyes and tried to block out the events of that night. The medicine the doctor gave him helped him sleep, but the doctor had cut down the medicine, and now he was having nightmares.

"One more thing, Nate."

Nate opened his eyes.

"The two men you shot, both of them had single barrel guns. You must have hit them with a blast from that double-barrel gun. I think that was the difference in the outcome. If either one of them had had a double-barrel, you would not have faired so well. Did you use both barrels on both men?"

Nate closed his eyes again. He had never killed a person in his life. He might have cheated a little at cards. And he might even steal, but not kill. He only nodded to the Sheriff.

More than a week had passed, and Nate was able to move about the room and go out his door in the cool mornings and evenings.

The Doctor had teased Nate. "Nate if you didn't have all that fat around your waist, that shot might have killed you. You got most of the buckshot in the middle. Some all the way up and down. You are one lucky bird."

All Nate could do was come up with a thin smile.

"Nate, may I call you Nate?"

Nate looked at the lovely widow woman who had been taking care of him. "Yes, ma'am."

"I will bring your supper to you out on the little porch this evening. You need lots of fresh air. Your wounds are healing fine, according to the doctor. You may have some dizziness from time to time."

The afternoon in the shade of the ranchhouse was great. This was the best he had felt since arriving back at the ranch headquarters. The owner of the ranch, Mr. Wilson, had looked in on him several times, but said he would visit when Nate was up and around.

Nate was surprised when Mr. Wilson came around the corner and pulled up a chair beside him.

"I want to thank you for cleaning out that nest of varmints that had occupied our north line cabin."

He whirled one of his spurs, and continued, "They had wrecked the place and killed our rider. You probably did not know that, and we only found him two days ago, when we went to clean the place up. Our rider was in a draw about two hundred yards from the cabin. We didn't find his horse."

He paused again and then pondered, "How those folks traveled is beyond me. They only had, best we can tell, those two horses you brought in. They had only been at the cabin for a few days at the most. Our supply wagon had been to the line cabin just a day or so before all the commotion happened."

Mr. Wilson continued after a few minutes, "I want you to know you can stay here until you are well."

A callused, rough right hand extended toward Nate, "Partner, thanks and get to feeling well real soon." The men shook hands and the rancher returned to his work.

Not long afterward the widow woman brought Nate his supper on a tray. She sat and made small talk while he ate. Then as she was preparing to leave, Nate said, "Could you stay a little longer and visit? I don't get to visit with such a lovely lady very often."

She blushed slightly and set the food tray back on the table. Then she said, "Thank you, we don't get visitors here at the ranch very often."

"You are alone, I take it?"

"Yes, my husband worked for the ranch and was killed when a horse fell with him."

"My sympathy."

"Thank you, besides not getting visitors out here, we don't see anybody with your good manners."

"Just trying to be polite. May I ask a question?"

"Of course."

"How long has your husband been….I don't mean to be nosy…..or offend."

She cut him off, "Mr.Nate."

"Call me, Nate."

Again she blushed slightly. "Thank you, Nate. My husband passed on two years ago this round-up"

"How terrible."

"Thank you, Nate."

Things were progressing better than he had hoped. She was smiling all the time and cutting her eyes at him every few seconds.

"Must be hard on you living out here with all these men and all alone and everything."

"It is hard some of the time. But, the owner told me I had a job here on the ranch as long as I wanted to stay. I have no training and could not get a job in town, so I think that I am fortunate."

"But, don't you get lonesome ?"

"Oh, there is plenty to do, and I stay busy."

"That is not what I meant. I mean do you get lonesome for……"

"You mean for a man?"

It was Nate's turn to blush and not slightly, "Well…….Yes!"

She laughed and slapped her hand on the table, "You mean that way…?"

Nate had turned a bright red. He was not expecting the conversation to go that way and that fast. He swallowed, "If I'm not being too personal."

She rose and looked at him with a smile, "Why don't I come back late this evening after the sun goes down, and we can sit on the porch and discuss the matter in more detail."

Nate could hardly get his breath. "I would love that."

She picked up the tray and said, "I best be getting back to work, or I will be missed."

"Till this evening, then."

Her smile of promise was all the reward and answer he needed that she would see him later.

She turned to go and then turned back, "The other day, while you were resting in your room, a boy about ten years old, with blond hair came to the back door of the ranchhouse. He said his family had been caught in that awful rain and all of their flour and salt had gotten wet. Could we spare them some. I gave him about ten pounds of flour and perhaps a pound of salt. Do you suppose that he is a member of the gang you cleaned out?"

Nate's mouth had dropped open. "Could you describe that boy a little better?"

"Well, he has blond hair, cut very short. He was wearing striped overalls, laced boots, a faded blue shirt and a brown floppy hat."

Nate's brow wrinkled and he frowned. "Was he, by any chance riding a mule?"

"Why, yes, I believe he was."

Nate's whole character changed in a flash, "Dear lady, did you see which way he rode off?" She thought for a few moments and added, "He went around the north side of the house and, I believe he rode off west. I can't be for sure. The barns got in the way, but he went out toward the barns."

Nate sat and studied the situation for a few moments. The description fit Robert, but it could have been any traveler's kid. Send the kid to the door begging and you will come out with a whole lot better chance of getting a handout. "One more thing. Did he have a dog with him?"

"Yes he did."

That did it, Robert had been at this ranch house while he lay only a few feet from him. All thought of a little flirting with the widow lady vanished. He had to get on his feet and go after those brats.

All of his attention was now on the subject at hand, "Did you see anybody else with him?'

"No, just him and the dog."

"Did the doctor say how long I had to stay in the bed or resting?"

"Not to my knowledge."

Nate's sudden interest in a kid and the lack of paying her attention, as he had been, cooled her, and she left without a word. Just a toss of her head.

"Women!" Nate exclaimed.

He was in a state of agitation. Those kids had been right here in the last few days. Then all kinds of questions entered his head. Had they heard about the shooting? Did they see his wagon? Did they see his horses? The questions just kept popping in his head.

He arose from the chair and began to move around the room. He flexed his arms and legs to see if they were functioning properly. They seemed as good as new, even his left arm that had taken a few buckshot. He stretched and bent over, very slowly, to see if he became dizzy. There was a little dizziness, but not anything that he could not handle. He still had stitches in the side of his head. He couldn't remember when the doctor said that they would come out. Except for the stitches, he was ready to go and right now.

He went outside his room, but saw no one. He wanted to know where his horses and wagons were kept. Just then a ranchhand came around the building, "Pardon me, could you tell me where I could find the owner?"

"He is in the barn,"

"Which way is that?"

"Just go around the corner, and it's is in plain sight."

"Thank you!"

Nate walked around the side of the house and toward the barn. He spied his wagon and horses in the corral. He walked on down to the barn.

Then Mr. Wilson looked up from the hoof he was filing, "My God! Man, are you supposed to be up and about?' "Just had to get out of that room . The walls were closing in on me. I'm outside most of the time. You know, animals to tend and workers to oversee."

"Good, a man laid up too long could get sick, is my doctoring." He put the file on a bench.

"That's right. Say, I'm thinking about getting on my way soon, and I wondered when that doctor was going to be back to take these stitches out?"

"He should be back tomorrow or the next day." Mr. Wilson rubbed the horse's leg.

"Good, as soon as he gets them out, I'll be moving along."

"Sorry to see you go." Mr. Wilson continued to examine the leg of the horse.

"Thanks, I don't want to wear out my welcome." Nate turned and walked back to the house. He did not want the man to see that he was getting weak and shaky. Back in his room he lay down. Now that he knew the location of his wagon and horses, he could be ready to go on short notice. He was a little sorry that he had upset the widow lady. Could have been a nice evening. She'd calm down, and when he was through with his business he could always come back.

About noon the next day the doctor arrived. He gave Nate a good physical and took out the stitches. Nate commented, "I hope you don't have to take any more stitches out of me anytime soon."

"Well sir, you are just about healed up and good as new," said the doctor as he was putting his instruments in his bag.

"Doctor, is there any reason that I could not leave tomorrow?"

"If you feel like going, have at it. I don't have any reason to keep you."

"Say, Doctor, how much do I owe you?"

"Oh, I guess five dollars would cover it." Nate's pants where hanging on a chair and he dug into the pockets. He found his wallet and handed the doctor the five dollars.

Snapping the bag closed, he nodded to Nate and started toward the door saying, "Thanks, Nate."

As he was opened the door, Nate called to him, "Thanks, Doctor. I'll probably be on my way tomorrow."

Nate had his last evening meal at the ranch in the dining room with the owner and his wife. They were very good host and hostess. The meal was second to none. Nate had his appetite back, and he did the meal justice.

"I want to thank you both for all of your hospitality."

"You are welcome in our house anytime, Nate." replied Mrs Wilson

Some folks sure do live high on the hog. The ranchhouse was five times bigger than Nate's home. There were all kinds of help on the place. Cowboys, blacksmith, carpenter, cook and laundress and on and on.

To make conversation Nate asked, "How many hands do you have on the ranch?"

"Counting the wife and myself, about twenty five. Some of them are out on the range in lineshacks, and we don't see them too much. Then, when it is round-up, all of the hands are involved." responded Mr. Wilson.

"How often do you go to the countyseat?"

"We try to not go over twice a month. Takes too much time from the ranch, and we grow almost everything we need here on the place." Mr. Wilson lighted a cigar and offered Nate one.

"I noticed the garden and the orchard." Nate declined the cigar. That was one habit he had not picked up.

"You know raising crops?"

"My Papa was a farmer, and we kids got lots of opportunity to learn about farming." He smiled and shifted his round body in the chair.

Puffing some smoke into the air, Mr. Wilson squinted through it and asked Nate, "How would you like to run a farming operation for me?"

In a jovial way Nate remarked, " I thought this was a ranch."

"It is, Nate, but to grow and have all the feed and supplies for a big operation, we need to grow as much as we possibly can. We need corn, hay, maize, grass and a lot of other things, including food stuff."

"I hadn't thought of it that way. Just thought you grow cows." Nate's interest was up. What kind of deal would the rancher make him? It might be worth coming back and exploring the idea.

As the meal came to an end, Nate complimented the widow lady on the fine dinner. She had served the table without a look or a word spoken to Nate. Cold iceberg.

Nate said his goodnights. "I again want to thank you for your hospitality." He arose and returned to his room. He passed through the room to the little porch to just see if the cold widow lady showed up. He thought he caught a glimpse, or a flash of a skirt, going around the corner and out of sight. Oh, well, another time.

When breakfast was finished Nate said his goodbyes. His wagon had been loaded with all kinds of food. Enough to supply him for a month. He hitched his team and climbed aboard. The rancher handed Nate his double-barrel shotgun and said, "Been keeping it safe for you."

"Thanks," Nate said, as he whipped up the team and started down the road to the south. He wanted them to think he was going home. The rancher had insisted that he take the two extra horses. Said Nate had earned them, and if he could break them to the harness, he would have a relief team. Nate never turned down a gift.

After driving south for about an hour, Nate turned west and continued until he came to the Brazos river. The river had gone down considerable and soon he found a secluded place to camp. Nate wanted to go through all of his gear and sort everything out. The polecats he had the shootout with had thrown everything out on the ground searching for valuables, and then they threw it all back in the wagon. The ranch hands had just piled supplies on top of the mess, and now it was a bigger mess.

He found a slope down into the riverbed and drove along it for some distance. The spot he picked had some shade trees, and the water ran gently and slow. Good fishing spot and an excellent camping location. He was down behind the riverbank and concealed on the other side by some islands in the riverbed. He hobbled the four horses and made a fire. It would be hot today, but a campfire was a pleasant companion. He thought for a moment about what a fine companion that widow woman would make, but he had other things to take care of first.

Nate worked slowly as his strength was not back to it's normal level. Finally, all of the supplies and gear were stacked on the ground. Before he did anything else, he made sure that the double-barrel shotgun was loaded, and that he had shells close at hand. The next time some cowboys tried to have fun with him, there would be another story to tell. He suddenly realized that if he had to shoot again, it would not bother him.

He tied an extra canvas to the wagon and then stretched it to a mesquite to make a shade. He enjoyed going through all of the new supplies. Sometimes Nate was like a little boy at Christmas. He was filled with glee and good humor as he went through all of the supplies. Why, he could stay out hunting those kids for two months with this much food.

He would work for a while and then sit in the shade for a spell. His strength was, in this hot weather, far below norm, and he sure had to take it easy. His cooking was not always the best, but for his meal he had beans, potatoes and sliced onions with some bits of bacon thrown in for flavor. The cast-iron Dutch oven made excellent sourdough biscuits, and he had a feast.

With a full stomach, the next thing to do was to take a nice nap. Nate had always enjoyed a good nap. In late afternoon he awoke and began to go through more of the supplies. When everything was sorted, he decided to take a break and set a line and see how the fish were biting. He spent the rest of the afternoon fishing and sitting in the shade.

Finally, his mind turned to the problem of the three runaways and how to get his hands on them. If his instincts were right, the three were trying to go to the Territory of New Mexico. He had to keep them from getting out there at whatever cost. That brought him to a halt. Whatever the cost?

Nate spent the next two days resting and eating like he was starving. His horses were hobbled, there was plenty of grass and they were getting fat. So he started sampling everything in the supply stack and eating fish at almost every meal. If gluttony was a sin, Nate would go straight to

Hades on greased skids. He ate like a horse, and his strength returned almost overnight.

Now he was ready to chase those kids all the way to breakfast and back. With deliberate planning he reloaded the wagon. Hitching his team to the wagon and tying the spare team to the rear, he was ready to start again.

Just as he cleared the slope out of the riverbed, he saw dust to the south. No matter to him, he stayed close to the river and moved to the northwest. He had gone less than a mile when he found a two-rut trail that paralleled the river. Perfect, it was going the same direction he wanted to go and the traveling was much smoother.

To his amazement, right at noon there was a good slope down to the river and a good place for lunch and rest. He was doing better, but he found that the heat hurt him. He should be just about due west of the ranchhouse and all of the outbuildings. Hobbling the team he gathered firewood and built a fire. He enjoyed a good lunch and then crawled under the wagon and took a good nap.

Suddenly he was awake. The thunder of hooves and the bawling of cattle had awaken him. He was confused for a few minutes, and then he had his bearings.

He grabbed his shotgun and shells and climbed the riverbank. The noise came from a half mile to the north. He slid back down the slope and trotted down the river bottom . He trotted the best his fat body would let him. Suddenly he was at the crossing the cowboys intended to use. There were about one hundred cows in the herd and about eight or nine cowboys pushing them toward the river.

He heard a the cowboy call out, "Hold them here and let me see if the water is down enough and that there is no one down on the river."

There was milling of cattle and shouting by the cowboys as they turned and held the herd. A cowboy suddenly appeared. Spurring his horse, he rode down into the river-bed and across and up the other side. Just as quickly he made a return trip. He waved his hat and the other cowboys pushed the herd toward the river. They came streaming off the bank down into the riverbed and up the other side. The cowboys did not give the cattle time to drink or stop. Strange. Just as quickly as the herd had appeared, they vanished to the west. They became just a cloud of dust. Nate climbed the west bank and watched them disappear out of sight.

What was all of that about? Only, rustlers pushed cows that hard. They were in a hurry, a big hurry. He felt that everything was wrong about this situation. First, he could well be in the wrong place. If those cowboys or other rustlers came back and found him, he was in big trouble. He "trotted" back to the wagon and whipped the horses up. He got out of the riverbed and tried to make as good time as possible to the northwest. He had to cross the cattle trail, but he had no choice if he was going west to find those brats. He had to go this way to get away from, he believed, the rustlers.

Pushing the team hard for a couple hours should have put ample distance between him and the scene at the river crossing. This time he moved away from the river to make camp. Down in a gully out of sight he felt that he had some protection. He had made a cold camp, and there was food left from his last meal. No fire to guide unwanted visitors to the campsite. The sun sank behind dark thunderclouds in the west. Just his luck, it would come another storm and flood the whole country. If the roads became impassable, he could be stuck in one spot for days.

When it became total dark Nate waddled up an incline to the top of a knoll. From the top, even in the moonlight, any campfire within miles could be seen. Nate sat on the hill for near two hours, searching the terrain all across the south horizon. Total darkness greeted him and filled the night, with the exception of the faint moonlight. He returned to his camp and rolled into his bedroll. Sleep came quickly and he, because of the late hour, slept beyond sunrise.

His camp was well concealed, or so he thought. He heard horses' hooves and jerked awake. He grabbed his shotgun and ran into a clump of trees just to the rear of the wagon. He was about twenty yards from the rear of the wagon. He could now hear voices and hooves as they approached the camp.

The riders burst into sight up above his campsite. One of them pointed at the wagon and shouted, "There he is!" The riders, five of them, turned to the left and found the best decline down into the gully. Dust swirled all around the wagon, and, for a moment, Nate could not see it. As the dust settled, he could see one of the cowboys was up in the wagon. The cowboy turned and said to the leader, "He's not here!" "Spread out and find that skunk," the leader shouted.

Riders began to fan out in all directions.

"He can't have gone far on foot, not as fat as that toad is!"

There was lots of shouting and dust raising, before one of the riders spotted Nate in the brush.

"Here he is , boss!" shouted the rider.

"Shoot him! Shoot him! Don't let him get away! He has seen too much!" shouted the leader.

Due to all of the terrain and the dust from the horses kicking and stomping, only the one rider could see Nate. That rider pulled his hand gun and fired at Nate.

Nate was in shock. They were trying to kill him. What for? What had he done to them? His hands shook something awful, but the bullet whizzing by his head made him react. In one upward motion, Nate cocked the double-barrel shotgun and pulled the triggers. To his horror and amazement the cowboy flopped over backward out of the saddle. The horse screamed and began to buck and run every which way.

As Nate reloaded, another rider came into view.

"Here he is!"

There was pistol fire from all directions. The cowboys were shooting at shadows and figments of their imaginations. The cowboy in front of Nate rode back and forth shooting into the brush. Nate did not hesitate one moment, he cocked the hammers and fired. That double-barrel blast covered a big pattern at ten to fifteen yards, yet was deadly.

Both cowboy and horse went down in the dust. They completely disappeared when they fell. There were bullets flying all around, but none came close to Nate. Gun blasts, screaming of horses and shouts of men blended into a constant roar. Nate had dropped onto his big belly and kept his head down. When he looked up one time a lone horseman rode up out of a gully and out of sight. Then all was still and quiet, except for the cries and moans of wounded riders and horses.

"Boss, help me, help me. I'm gutshot!"

The boss did not answer....no one answered.

When the dust settled and only one cowboy was crying for help, Nate finally ventured out from his hiding place. Two horses were dead. The others had run off. In front of the brush where Nate was hiding there were two dead cowboys and one more near his wagon. The wounded one lay off to the side where they had ridden in.

"Please, Mister, help me. I've got to have a doctor. I'm gutshot!"

Nate stood mesmerized by the carnage. He had killed again, in self defense both times, but......his legs gave out, and he sat on the ground.

The rider's calls were weaker. "Please, Mister, can I have a drink of water?"

Nate wobbled to his feet and took a canteen of water to the downed rider.

"Here, have a drink."

"Thanks, Mister."

He drank several swallows over a few minutes. Handing the canteen back to Nate, he said, "Who are you? Some lawman?"

"No, I'm not a lawman."

"Then how come you keep nipping at our heels?"

"What do you mean, nipping at your heels?"

The cowboy was getting weaker, and Nate had to lean closer to hear.

"Why, you met us on the road the other day, and the boss knocked you out of the wagon. You didn't do anything, and the boss figured you were a Pinkerton Man undercover. Then, we found your wagontracks crossing our trail yesterday. And here you are again. Why are you trailing us?"

"Young man, I am not trailing you, and I certainly am not interested in what you are doing!"

The rider rested for a few minutes and muttered, "Then what are you doing out here?"

"Chasing three runaway kids."

"Oh!" and the cowboy died right in front of Nate's eyes.

Now, it was quiet. Very quiet. Nate looked all around at the destruction and death.

Nate had hobbled his horses last night, so even though they shied and snorted, they could not go very far. Nate harnessed his team and tied the relief team on the rear of the wagon. Then he stopped, looked around at four dead men and two dead horses. He could not bury all of these men. He doubted that they would be found in this gully. Buzzards might give the location away. Also, the other rider might come back. Those were just chances that had to be taken when you were an outlaw. The coyotes and such would clean the bones in short order.

Avarice and greed surfaced in a twinkle. Nate looked all around. The two saddles were worth..... then their four hand guns and two rifles, still in the scabbard on the saddles.

Without another thought, he started collecting guns. Then he took the two saddles off the dead horses and put them in the wagon. It took a lot of struggling to get the saddles off, but he was sure it would be worth the trouble.

Turning back to the dead men, he commented, "The price of the life of crime," and began going through their pockets. Much to his surprise he found a little over two hundred dollars, one pocket watch, several pictures, and pocket knives. Upon closer search of the bodies, he found two hide-away guns, one in a vest pocket and one on the inside of a boot. Plus, he found a knife with an eight blade hidden in the boot of the third cowboy. The reason Nate found that gun and knife, he was taking the boots off those two riders. The other two pair of boots were not worth having.

Nate opened the trap door to the false bottom in his wagon. He wrapped the guns and knives in the cowboy's slickers. Then he put all of his loot in the false bottom. He chuckled as he recounted his loot. There were four handguns, two rifles, one eight inch knife, several pocket-knives, one watch, two pair of boots and over two hundred dollars that had gone into the false bottom. The two hundred dollars and the pocket-watch, he added to his oil cloth and blanket packet. He figured that he might now have as much as four hundred dollars in the false bottom. The way he had wrapped all of the items, they would stay dry in rain or if he ran over water and it splashed up on the bottom of the wagon. The blanket solved the other problem, the guns would not rattle and give away the fact that something was in the floor of the wagon. The two sad-dles, he tossed into the back of the wagon. If someone asked about them, he could just say he found the two dead horses and nobody around.

This had been a very profitable morning after all. He was alive and not wounded and had just picked up two hundred dollars in hard cash and three hundred dollars worth of equipment. What a good day! He sure would need to use a relief team to pull the wagon. Especially with the increase in the load of supplies and all of this equipment.

Now back to chasing those brats. Where could they be by now? East of him or west of him? They were at that ranch where Robert was beg-ging supplies. That ranch was south and east of his present location. But the kids could have come from anyplace and could have gone any direc-tion. Well, maybe not any direction. What were their options? There were only two. They could have gone back to the river to the east or to the west on this branch of the Brazos.

He decided to go east to the high ridge. He was already east of the west branch of the Brazos. By getting on a high point and watching for movement, he might get a break. Also, he could see any campfire for miles around. Before starting that part of his trek, he released one horse from the harness and replaced him with one of the horses tied to the rear of the wagon. Harnessing the saddle-horse with his best horse would give him a chance to harness break the animal. Tying the released horse to the tailboard, he proceeded up the ridge. The saddle-horse wanted to act up a little, but with one swift kick from his team member and a snap or two of the whip on his rear, the saddle-horse accepted the load of the wagon. They made fair headway, and in an hour or two, the new horse was behaving very well.

Reaching the top of the ridge, Nate realized the wagon was very visible. Moving down the east slope, he found a sheltered place that would make a fair campsite. There was no water, but he had plenty in a small barrel for the horses, and he had two canvas waterbags. After hobbling the horses, Nate took one quick look both directions from the top of the ridge. As nothing was moving, he returned to the wagon for a cold camp meal. All during the day he would go back up on the ridge and look east and west for any movement. He wished he had a pair of binoculars. They would really help see long distances on this ridge.

All day he watched and waited. Luck always was on his side. Proof was all around him. Extra horses, loot from the shoot-out and lots of supplies from the ranch. He smiled and said to himself, "And did not spend one dime for any of it."

During his evening meal, at dusk, he was sitting on the tail of the wagon. Luck smiled on him as always. Across the distance to the east, a flicker of fire came through the dusk of the evening. He almost laughed out loud. Luck was with him. There they are, just a few miles away. It was dangerous to travel at night in this rough country, but come morning he would head that way.

Sunrise found Nate loaded, horses harnessed, his meal over and he was a mile east from his camp site. Going was not too bad, and by lunch he could see a lake at the bottom of the long slope. That must be the location of the fire he had seen last night. Fortune was smiling on him once more.

He had used the relief team that morning, his horse and the other saddle-horse. That combination had worked even better than the team the day before. The second horse must have had harness training and had pulled a wagon or a plow. He had pushed the team hard all morning. To keep up the pace, he changed teams and even ate his meal sitting on the seat of the wagon as the animals moved on east toward the lake.

Dusk found him near the lake. He did not make a fire or a real camp. He stopped in some brush and waited for night. Soon he saw a fire to his right. The fire was not over a half mile from his location. He started to go the distance in the wagon, but decided that the wagon would make too much noise and alert the kids to his presence. He tied and hobbled his team, even though they were still harnessed. He double checked the hobbles on the two extra horses.

Taking his shotgun and plenty of ammunition, he moved to the edge of the lake and then turned to his right and proceeded toward the campfire. He had to go slow in the dark. Too easy to stumble and give his position away. He silently covered the half mile to the fire. Creeping up outside the ring of light, he got a real surprise.

Someone jumped him from the back and rode him to the ground. He struggled and rolled back and forth trying his best to shake his attacker off. The attacker had the strength of three or four. Nate couldn't budge him off his back, nor could he break the hand hold.

"I've got him! I've got Him!" shouted the attacker in Nate's ear. "Come help me! Come help me!"

A figure from the fire ran to the struggle. "What do you want me to do?" asked a woman.

"Get his shotgun!" shouted the attacker. They were rolling all around the campsite. They rolled up close to the fire at one point.

The woman picked up the shotgun.

"Pull back the hammers!"

The woman struggled with the heavy gun.

"I've got them cocked!"

Just as quick as he had been grabbed from the rear, the attacker shoved him away and sprang to his feet. He grabbed the gun from the woman.

"All right you varmint night stalker! Get to your feet and make peace with your maker. I'm going to blow your head off."

He stuck the gun in Nate's ribs.

"I thought that was you out there in the dark. I had gone out in the dark for a nature call and heard your wagon."

Nate could taste fear.

The attacker pushed Nate toward the fire with the end of the gunbarrel. He pushed very hard and Nate fell.

"You killed my Pa and my brother, and now it's your turn."

In the firelight the looks of the attacker was even more frightening. The speaker's eyes were wild, and he drooled at the mouth. His breath came in heaves, and his hands trembled. That was the worst part, the trembling hands. He could accidentally fire that shotgun at any moment.

"Come up here in the firelight, so I can see your face real clear when I let you have it."

Nate moved forward. His heart was pounding from the fighting on the ground and from terror. The man was the one he had hit over the head with the shotgun barrel. The sheriff had said one of the people at the line-shack was crazy in the head from a blow. This was the man.

The attacker began to babble about justice and killing this varmint would help balance the scales.

Nate tried to swallow, but his mouth was too dry.

Without warning the crazy man hit Nate on the right side of the head and laughed.

"Now that ought to balance the scales. I hit you on the left side of the head, you hit me on the head and now I hit you on the right."

When Nate was hit, he tumbled over on the ground. His head was spinning. and blood was running down the side of his head. As luck would have it, the attacker did not hit him as hard as he had at the line-shack.

The woman spoke up, "Don't kill him yet."

"Why, not?"

She was in control of her faculties, or so he thought.

"Because, we need to punish this sinner some, and we need to know where his wagon is?"

The wild man drooled some more and tried to think. Nate could see only violence and a wildness in his eyes. His babbling was frightening.

He spoke, "Then can I kill him?"

"Yes, when I'm through with him. Now, Mister, I heard him say you have a wagon. And, I want to know where it is."

Nate's head was still swimming, and he could not clear his eyesight.

"Mister, I'm asking you one more time. Where is the wagon?"

When Nate did not answer her, she went to the stack of supplies lying on the ground and pulled out a hunting knife.

"Now, let's see if I can get your attention and some answers."

She stuck the knife in Nate's left nostril and pushed just a little.

"Now talk!"

The pain was horrible, and blood trickled down his face and chin.

Nate, trying to buy time and clear his head said, "It's out there in the dark."

The knife brought more blood, and the pain cleared his mind. Blood was dripping off his chin and tears were running down his cheeks.

"How far out in the dark?"

Nate answered, "I don't know. A long ways, I guess."

She pushed the knife a little deeper, and Nate almost passed out from the pain.

She motioned to the babbler, and said, "He heard your wagon, so it must not be very far, is that right?"

Nate was trying to focus and come up with an answer that would please the hag, "I walked a long way and sound carries very far in the still of the night."

"BULL!!!" she shouted in his ear.

"I just don't know how far I walked. I saw your campfire a long way off."

"This knife's not getting me the results and answers I want. Give me one of those hot sticks out of the fire."

The babbler was standing close to the fire, and he picked up a hot, burning branch.

"Can I hurt him?"

"Yes, but we can't kill him just yet," said the wild haired old woman.

"Want me to go look for his wagon?"

"Not yet, we can do that in daylight and not listen to his lies. Now we have to punish him for his sins. Mister, do you know how to pray?"

Nate never made a sound. His tongue was tied. He could only nod, "Yes."

"Good, you get up on your knees and pray until it is sunup, and then just like they crucified Jesus, we will offer you for sins, yours and ours. We may have to offer you as a burnt offering."

Nate could not believe his ears, she was as crazy as the babbling one. Her attention was on sin and punishment of the sinner by fire.

She grabbed the hot poker and shouted, "Get on your knees, SIN-NER!"

Nate got down on his knees. His hands trembled, and his heart was pounding.

She put the hot poker up to Nate's eye, and he could feel the heat on his face.

"Now let's see if the pig will scream, cry, beg or just lose his bladder."

The babbler walked around the fire, talking to himself. Occasionally he would point the gun at Nate and mutter some more. Several times Nate thought that he was going to pull the trigger. The hammers were still back. Nate had to do something.

He started moving his lips as if in prayer, that was all that saved him from a lot of pain.

"He does know how to pray. A man of God. Let's not disturb the man when he is praying," she said, as she laid down the hot poker.

The mood of both the babbler and the wild woman could change in a heartbeat. Nate's scheming mind searched for the ploy that would keep him alive. Then it dawned on him. Praying!

The old woman was quoting bits and pieces of scripture and would holler some religious phrase.

Nate would move his lips and then shout, "Praise the Lord."

"Give praise," retorted the straggled old woman.

He watched the woman to be sure that she saw his lips moving like he was 'praying'. Actually, he was going over the events that had led up to this situation. It was the only thing he could think of to say for he sure did not know how to pray.

Once in a while he would lift his face to heaven and seem to employ the maker's attention, and to be sure he had everyone's attention, he would shout again, "Praise the Lord".

The babbler came close and pointed the gun right between Nate's eyes. "You want it here, or here?" He moved the gun down to Nate's crotch. Then he stumbled off, laughing.

Nate spoke for the first time and came out with probably the biggest lie of his life, "Lady, would you let your brother be shot before he has made peace with the his maker, the Lord?"

She paused, as if thinking of what to say, then, "No, my brother. Make your peace. I'll pray for you."

"Before you pray, I'm concerned about the gentleman with the gun. The hammers are still back, and if he should make a mistake before I am finished......"

"You're quite right." She walked over to the crazy one and gently took the gun from him.

"Let me hold the gun for awhile." He made no objection to her. She tried to uncock the gun, but she did not have that much strength. She had had trouble cocking it in the first place. She just laid the gun against a big stone and walked over to Nate.

"Now, brother, continue your praying," she admonished.

The night drug on and on. Nate even dozed some, there on his knees. When his knees began to hurt, he asked the woman, " May I, get down on my face to my maker?"

"Hallelujah, a real man of God. He wants to get down on his face and pray!" She turned her face to heaven and held up both hands.

The babbler had sat down close to the fire and had dozed off. The blind one had never moved anything but his head. He moved it to the right and then left. It was as if he was trying to hear better. One side and then the other. This was the chance he had been waiting for. Fortune was smiling again.

The woman was still holding her hands to heaven and had her face turned upward at the same time. The crazy one was dozing, at least Nate hoped so, and the blind man was very still. Nate crouched on his hands and knees and took one more look at the three. Then while he had the nerve, he sprang for the shotgun.

The blind man shouted, "He's tricking us!!!"

The woman screamed at the top of her lungs. As Nate remembered, scream and cry was all she could do at the line-shack. The babbler came awake and lunged for the gun. He and Nate collided, but Nate's weight, for once, was to his advantage. His momentum knocked the babbler to the side, and Nate grabbed the shotgun. What Nate did not realize was that the force of the two bodies colliding had knocked the babbler into the fire.

Now the babbler screamed from burns to his hands. His effort to get out of the fire only stirred the flames. Suddenly the campfire flamed up and the man's clothes were aflame. He lunged one way and another. In his crazed state he ran into Nate and knocked Nate to the ground. The gun fired.

At close range the blast hit the babbler full in the chest. The blast carried him backward ten to twelve feet. He hit the ground dead. The gun blast echoed off the surrounding hills and valley walls. Silence followed.

Nate slowly got to his feet and stood in stunned silence. Everywhere Nate had gone, death had followed. Now the death count was six. Not that he had killed all of those, but six had died due to his presence. He picked up his shotgun and unconsciously reloaded.

The gun blast had silenced the woman. The blind man turned his head trying to find Nate. He heard the shotgun snap closed.

"Are you going to finish what you started? Are you going to kill both of us?"

"No, I am not going to kill you. I'm going to leave you here. I think leaving you alone, out here, is a far worst fate than my shooting you. By shooting you, I would be getting you out of your misery." Nate turned and walked off into the darkness. No sounds followed him.

At sunrise Nate moved his wagon north around the edge of the lake and made camp. After hobbling the horses, he brushed them and then let them graze. Like many places he had camped in the last few weeks, there was ample water and plenty of grass.

He was sore, bruised, and his head hurt. Besides he was suffering from very low morale. Instead of finding the kids, he had found more trouble. Death was waiting for him at every turn. No matter how hard he tried to shake off the forbidding feeling, it grew in his belly.

He estimated that by now he was so far from the kids, it was hopeless to find them. The day passed slowly. Fishing did little to lift his spirits. He ate very well, as always, from the supplies. For entertainment, and to pass time, he took out all of the loot from the cowboys and examined it very thoroughly.

By night he was feeling better and decided to take a dip in the lake. First water he had seen that was deep enough to cover his rotund body.

The water was cool and refreshing. He splashed and enjoyed the water. When he came out to dry, he noticed that the stars and moon were hidden behind a layer of clouds. Finding his bedroll, he put it under the wagon in case of rain. He stood looking all around at the clouds and stretched to ease more of the pains in his body.

He moved slowly the next day. His head was hurting from the lick the babbler had given him He needed someone to look at it, but that was out of the question. Letting the horses set their own pace, he kept them headed west. The ground sloped gently up and toward the ridge that lay between two branches of the Brazos. This passage would bring him back to the road, or rather the trail, that would either take him back to the "Box W" or take him west and north after the brats.

Reaching the top of the ridge, he paused for a long look west. Those brats could be anywhere out there. The line of mountains that rose in the west, extended all the way from the north to the south. He wondered how far it was to those mountains and if there was an easy pass through. If his path was blocked, then the brats were blocked as well. One thing that was strange about the mountains was, there were not peaks, just a long flat barrier.

Heading down the long slope toward the west branch of the Brazos, he determined not to give up on finding those snooty brats. They held his future in their hands and needed to be stopped. The sheriff would take care of that problem. They were thieves and runaways. He would show them. The farther he went west, the more he resolved to find them. Despite the leisurely pace, Nate reached the west branch of the Brazos by the end of the day. He found the trail that paralleled the river and turned to the right and northwest to pursue the brats.

He smelled wood smoke from somewhere up ahead. Excitement suddenly filled him. Was the smoke going to lead him to the campsite of the kids? Could he be that lucky? He reined the team to a halt in a draw and tied them to a mesquite. Checking the load in the shotgun, he started forward hunting the source of the smoke. Following the riverbank, he wound along, checking the river bed for a wood fire. His expectations rose as the smoke became stronger and stronger.

"Just hold it right there, Mister." A voice came out of a stand of trees.

Nate froze with his heart sinking into his boots.

"Put the gun on the ground and move away real slow."

Nate lowered the gun to the ground and voluntarily raised his hands.

"Now turn around real slow and face me."

Nate turned very slowly. He did not want to provoke someone into shooting him.

"What's the idea of trying to slip up on me and my camp?" the voice continued from the trees.

In the failing daylight Nate could not see into the trees or detect the source of the voice.

"I asked you a question, Mister."

Nate finally found his voice, "Just being careful. I've been jumped before and was trying to be sure that this was a friendly camp."

"What do you mean jumped?"

Nate cleared his throat, "I stopped at a line camp the other day and a bunch of varmints jumped me and put this gash in my head."

The trees separated, and a man came out. He was lowering his rifle as he came, "Are you the one that had the shoot-out up at the "Box W" ranch's line shack?"

All Nate could muster was a weak, "Yes." For some reason relief was flooding his body. This would-be bush-wacker was friendly.

The stranger was only a few feet from Nate, "Turn your head, and let me see that gash."

Nate turned his head showing the man the left side and then showed him the gash on the right side. The wound on the left had had stitches and was doing very well. The new wound was red and enflamed. It was giving Nate headaches and lots of pain.

"My God Almighty, they sure put a pair of gashes in your noodle!"

He stuck out his hand and continued, "Glad to shake your hand, Mister. They call me Curly. Used to have some hair. You did me and my buddies a real favor. If you had not shot up that bunch and run off the rest, we would have. That line-rider they killed was my best friend. We had rode together for fifteen years."

As they shook hands, Nate said , "They call me, Nate."

Then the stranger filled in a blank, "I work for the "Box W", and I'm the northwest line rider. My cabin is on up north a-ways. I just camp here on occasions to see if any cows have been rustled and run off to the west. Come on up to the camp, and we will jaw for awhile. Will be nice to have company."

Nate said, "I'll go back and get my wagon."

"Fine, I guess that is what set my dog off. His ears sure came up in a hurry. He is lots of company, and in all of the years out here on the range, he has never let somebody sneak up on us."

Nate returned to his wagon and drove along the bank looking for a cut down into the riverbed. Just when he thought that there wasn't one, he saw the "Box W" rider standing on the bank up ahead.

"I figured it would be hard to see the cut in the darkness and dusk. Turn right past those trees." he pointed to a clump of trees.

The cut led down to the riverbed and the best campsite that Nate had seen. Besides good grass and plenty of water in the river, there was a natural spring.

"Mighty good campsite."

"Yes, sir, I've been using this place for the last ten years. Old Jim, the line-rider that got killed, and I rode for the OO for a while and then came to work for the "Box W."

Nate unharnessed his team and put hobbles on them, "What you got on the fire?"

Curley replied, "Beans and coffee."

Nate said, "Let me see what is in the wagon that will go with that. Your boss provided me with lots of supplies, so let me share them with you."

After digging around in the wagon. Nate came back with an arm full of items, "I think that we can have some biscuits, potatoes and some cured beef. Then some peaches for dessert."

"Lord, man, you are living good!" exclaimed the cowboy when he saw all of the food.

"Compliments of your boss, Curley."

Soon they had biscuits cooking in the Dutch oven while potatoes and some onions fried together in a skillet. The beef roasted over the open fire.

After a good meal the two settled down over coffee and a low fire. "Mighty fine meal, Nate."

"Well, as you can see, I do like to eat well," Nate patted his big round belly.

Then Curley took a twig from the fire and lighted his pipe, "I noticed it. Is that why you travel by wagon and not a horse?"

"Partly. Mostly I need a lot of supplies, as I'll be out for I don't know how long, hunting three runaways. They stole four mules and lot of personal possessions. There is a reward of a hundred dollars for them. I've been on their trail for almost two weeks. Have had some reports of sightings of them in this area. Have you seen any strangers around here?"

"Matter of fact I did. I saw three young boys on the west branch of the Brazos about…." He paused and thought. "Must have been three days ago."

"Were they wearing striped overalls, blue shirts and floppy hats?"

"That description fits them to a T", replied Curley.

"They are not three boys."

"I saw them. There were three boys!" exclaimed Curley.

"I think they are trying to disguise themselves. Two of them are girls. The oldest is thirteen and youngest girl is eight. The third is a boy, of about ten."

"That sure fits them."

"Which way were they going?" asked Nate.

"They were heading west, well northwest, I think they were looking for the road up on the caprock."

"What's the caprock?"

Curley chuckled and said, "Lots of people think that it is a mountain. Have you seen that ridge west of you? It stretches from north to south."

"I thought it was a mountain in the distance."

"It's not a mountain. We call it the caprock. That's where you go up on the Llano Estacado."

"What does that mean?"

"I don't know, that's Spanish. All I know is that it is a great big plain that most people stay off of."

"They were headed that way?"

"I think so."

"You said that there is a road that goes up on top?"

"Right. The trail that runs along by the river is the road that goes up on top."

"That is good news, neighbor. Say, I may have some information for you about rustlers."

"What is that?"

"I was camped down on the river, south of here, oh about ten miles. Ten or so cowboys ran a herd of about one hundred cows across the Brazos. I mean they ran them across the river."

The cowboy's attention focused, "We had a bunch run off a few day ago."

Nat nodded and shifted positions on the ground, "Then later some of them jumped me, thought I was some kind of law man, and they tried to kill me."

"Man, you do have the darndest luck!" said Curley with a grin.

"I was off to the east of the river, and they trailed me to my camp."

"You saw them run the cows off?" asked Curley

"Not run them off, just run them across the river, Curley."

Curley scratched his head and pondered, "I bet that is the bunch that has been running cows off."

"Well, they trailed me, and we had a shoot-out. By some fate of luck, I shot two and the others, in their panic, confusion and the dust, shot two of their own. When the dust settled, there were four dead cowboys. The fifth rode off toward the river."

"Man, you ought to be the law. The real law has been chasing that bunch you found at the line cabin for months. The others, are a gang of rustlers that the law has not been able to lay a hand on. They come and do what they want and then ride west and disappear. Badlands out that way and the prairie. Not many people travel that direction."

"Well, let's get some shut eye. I need to go to the ranch headquarters and tell the boss that you have at least cleaned out some of the rustlers."

They turned in, and the following morning, after a generous breakfast, they bade each other "Adios."

The "Box W" man rode south, and Nate turned north in pursuit of the brats.

CHAPTER 7

The sun rose, on the second morning after the storm and rain, to a beautiful day. The beauty of the morning was lost on Minnie, Lizzie and me. Blue skies gave us little to rejoice about. Mud caked most of our possessions. We had managed to dry out our bedding and clothes the day before. We had spread one of the wagon canvases on the ground and that gave us a dry place to sit and to sleep during the day. Then, we stretched the second canvas between some mesquites and had some shade. Our clothes and bedding were spread on the bushes and left to dry. The mud was shaken off of items as it dried.

Minnie said, "I will wash out everything when we get back to the fork." We took turns sleeping and watching for any movement on the horizon. We did not see any movement, nor did we build a fire that would give us away.

Minnie tried to cheer us up, but we were tired and scared. "Robert, what is wrong?"

"I just let the mule get away!"

"Don't worry Robert, we have three."

"I know, but these are Papa's mules."

She looked at me for some time. "What would Papa do?" I was sort of down in the mouth for letting the mule get away. I sure was disappointed that I couldn't find number two or any tracks that led to the animal. I spent a good portion of the day looking for the mule.

"He will make the best of it, I guess."

"Right. Now don't worry. It will be all right."

In between rides, I kept firewood carried up to the campsite and cleaned the gun and other non- cooking items. "Here is some more firewood, Minnie. I found some dry caught up high in that ravine, it shouldn't smoke."

I did sleep for a long time in the afternoon. Lizzie slept most of that day and had to be forced to eat. After sleeping for several hours, she perked up and began to help Minnie. Minnie felt that riding on the mule all day for several days had tired her out. Then the storm had kept us up most of the night. Lizzie was just worn out.

Minnie spent some time that day cleaning our cooking and eating utensils. She had me find more dry wood and keep the fire going. The pot of water on the fire came to a boil and then she began to wash and boil, all the eating utensils. The cooking utensils were used for washing and boiling other items, so they were cleaned at the same time.

"Why, are you boiling everything, Minnie?" ask Lizzie.

"For a good reason, Lizzie. The sack that had all of these things in it was washed full of mud and water. I don't know what was in that water. Mama used to say, 'If the water does not come from a well, then it needs to be boiled.' Also, you need to boil and wash all of your dishes. It will keep you from getting sick."

By the end of the day, we had put our gear back in fairly good order. Of the eight burlap sacks with contents, all had suffered some damage. The three with bedding were soaked through and through. The one with clothing had faired some better. Only part of our clothes were soaked. The Bible that Minnie had wrapped in a piece of oil cloth and canvas had not suffered any damage. The food sack had suffered the worst damage. Our food source was reduced to fish that I could catch. All of the flour and salt was wet and ruined, therefore, we could not have biscuits. Minnie was afraid to cook the bacon as it had been wet and muddy. Hunger could become a real problem and could cause us to turn back.

We slept on one canvas and kept the other one stretched over us that night. The stars were bright and the sky clear. The Milky Way shown brilliant and clear from the northeast horizon to the southwest horizon. Night birds and small animal sounds filled the night air. We listened to the sounds of the night and were thankful that we had only gotten wet and that we had only lost one mule.

The morning dawned beautiful and clear, even more beautiful than the day before. Grass was greener and flowers were beginning, only one day after the rain, to open and show their colorful beauty. Now it was time to start back to the fork. We redistributed our gear in the eight sacks and placed them back on Number One. I would still ride Number Four, and the girls would ride Number Three. If they felt Number Three was getting tired carrying double, then Lizzie could ride with me.

The journey back to the fork in the Brazos was hard and treacherous . Most of the ground was muddy and very slippery. We traveled for short distances on good firm ground and then tried to cross an area of wet red clay. The mules slipped and slid trying to find good footing. When going down a slope, the mule would slide down on his haunches. Going up a slope might require several attempts, and on a number of occasions the rider or the gear was dumped on the ground and into mud.

Minnie promised us that when we got back to the fork we would spend time and let the ground dry out. She also promised that she would wash our clothes and get out all of the mud.

All day we slipped in the slimy red clay. When we were just about exhausted, something triggered in us, and we began to laugh at every little thing that happened. Even the lack of much to eat at lunch brought on the first round of humor. We only had a couple of small pieces of fish for lunch, and our stomachs were growling. That was left over from breakfast and last night's supper.

"Minnie, if you don't quit eating so much, you are going to burst those overalls!" I teased. The overalls were already two sizes too big for Minnie, and they just hung on her. For some reason that statement struck us as funny, and as the day wore on, and we were worn out, everything would cause peals of laughter.

With mud all over our clothes and in our hair, we could not hold back those peals of laughter. When one of us fell on our bottom, that brought on more laughter. By the time we reached the fork late in the afternoon, we were caked in red mud from head to toe. We would fall off and get back on the mule, covering him in red mud also. The effort to stay on was compounded by the fact that there was mud on the mules and on our bottoms. Two muddy things put together just caused more sliding, and back into the mud we went.

When we reached the riverbank and looked down, we found the river was almost back to normal. As we were finding a way down, we were trying to decide what should be done first. Take a bath, wash clothes, go fishing, build a fire, or just go to sleep. We were exhausted from all the work of walking in the mud or climbing back on a mule's back. Minnie and I had reloaded the sacks on Number One at least ten times. Number One would start up a slope, and the sacks would slide off his back. Then we would get down and drag the sacks up the slope, slipping, sliding, and falling down with each effort. When we got down to the riverbed, we just slid off the mules and sat on the ground.

Minnie finally decided. "Robert, go fishing. We are in need of fresh meat." I started fishing so we could have something to eat, as we had not had any other food. Minnie and Lizzie gathered wood from along the riverbank and started a fire. One piece of luck was with us, our matches were dry. We even laughed with relief about the fact that Minnie had almost forgotten the watertight tin box that held matches.

Then out of the blue I said, "Oh, I bet Uncle Nate would have a fit if he could see us now.

"He would say, you kids have been playing again and not working. I'll just have to give you a good busting for this. Now all three of you are going to get it!"

I had practiced at mocking and imitating Uncle Nate to the point that I could give a very good imitation. With my last statement and imitation of him, we laughed until we cried.

"Robert, quit! You are making me split my sides!" cried Minnie.

"See, I can walk like Uncle Nate," chimed in Lizzie. That bought more laughter from us, three dirty and bedraggled runaways.

"I can just hear some of the stories Uncle Nate is telling on us!" exclaimed Minnie. "Why, they ran away and stole all kinds of 'MY' possessions. They took four prime mules. I gave them a home, and this is the thanks I get!"

"You know," I said sobering. "I bet that is just what he has told the sheriff. That we are thieves and runaways."

"Who cares what he told the sheriff?" asked Minnie.

"They've got to find us, to take us back, and we would just do it all over again!" I blurted out.

"I don't want to go back!" shouted Lizzie.

"And we are not going to go back!" Minnie shook her fist in the air. "We are not going back!"

"I'll get the hooks set, and then let's go for a swim, just to make Uncle Nate madder!" I hollered.

That was just the right incentive to get us up and moving. In a matter of minutes I had several hooks in the river and was hobbling the mules. Minnie and Lizzie had a fire going where Minnie had set up our camp. She took the pocketwatch out of her pocket and put it in the toe of one of her boots, stuffing the sock on top. We shed our boots and socks and then paused. We stopped and looked at each other, and with squeals of glee and shouts of joy, we ran to the river and jumped in, clothes and all.

In a flash we had plunged into the river and begun to splash water into the air and on each other. We flopped and jumped in the shallow water until exhaustion overcame us. We returned to the bank, and Minnie said, "Robert, you check the fish lines, and I'll get us some clean, dry clothes out of the sack, if there are any."

I returned in a few minutes with two good sized fish. I put them on a line and returned them to the water. "These big grasshoppers sure make good bait. We will have all we can eat tonight, and then I can check the lines and I bet we can have fish for breakfast. We can clean and cook some for in the morning and to have as we travel."

Minnie brought me my clothes and directed, "Now, you can go down around the bend, strip, take a bath and put on these clean dry clothes. Lizzie and I will go right over by those big rocks."

"Just watch for snakes around those rocks. Take Ol' Bullet with you, and you will be safe. He needs to swim and take a bath. He's muddy all over, I think he likes the mud, but he likes water best. I'll go up the river a little ways 'cause I saw a good place for me when I set my fish lines. It has a good beach."

We separated and went to wash and change clothes. We were still dressing in overalls, faded blue shirts and our old brown floppy hats. The girls were finished and were back a long time before I was. Minnie pulled out the two fish on the line. She set about cleaning the fish while they waited on me.

Shortly I came trotting up the bank. I was struggling to carry a big turtle. "I had to leave my clothes to carry this big guy back. Do you think we could make a meal out of him, Minnie?"

"Sure we can. I watched Grandma and Grandpa prepare turtle from the river several times. Just lay him on his back and go back and get your clothes. The fish you caught will be ready in a few minutes," She gestured to the fire and the roasting fish.

Just fish with no salt is not the best, but if you were hungry, it tasted mighty good. Tasted a lot better than MUSH! We ate both of the those fish and left Ol' Bullet very little to naw on.

After going for my clothes, I fished until dark and then reset my lines. I had caught three more little fish, and we had the turtle. Minnie, to my surprise, killed and cleaned the turtle and started cooking it over the open fire. "We can warm him up and have turtle soup for breakfast."

Lizzie said, "Huh!"

Minnie turned to us and pointed out, "We have lost some time, but I don't think we need to stay here another day. I have washed our clothes, and they will be dry in the morning. So, what say we go west and to Uncle John's in New Mexico Territory?"

"What are we going to do for food?"

"I don't know, Robert." But as Mama used to say, "The Lord will provide."

We spread out our canvas and prepared our dry bedding and turned in for the night. We left the little fire burning, and the coals winked at us in the dark. Ol' Bullet came around and licked my hand, and then went over and curled up with Lizzie, just like he had done every night. In the storm he got as close to Lizzie as he could. She put her arms around him, and they even slept that way.

At dawn I went up river and took one more good swim. We had discussed that this branch of the river was much smaller and would run out of water up at the head waters. This must be the fork we had missed.

Checking my fish lines, I had four good sized fish. I returned to camp with my catch and my lines to find Minnie had a fire going and the turtle soup almost ready to eat. While the turtle heated, I cleaned the four fish and gave them to Minnie to cook.

We sat around the fire and spooned the turtle soup right out of this pot into our mouths. I want to say I liked it, but I have had better tasting breakfast. Fish cooked and gear loaded, we started up the left fork of that branch of the Brazos River. We made good time as the river narrowed, and the bed was smooth and easy on the mules and us. We had to find a cut and leave the river as it got narrower and narrower. The water was running swift and from bank to bank at this point, and we found a good cut and left the riverbed. To the west we could see a rise, and farther on we could see what appeared to be a mountain range. It ran from the north to the south. To our left there was another ridge of mountains. They ran parallel to the river.

"Wonder how far it is to those mountains, Minnie?" I asked.

"Looks like a long way, Robert. I don't remember Papa talking about any mountains between home and Uncle John's."

"Minnie, if there are mountains, how do we get over them?"

"There will be a pass. There always is a pass. I studied that in geography."

"Minnie, didn't Papa say we would come to the end of this stream, if this is the branch?"

"Yes."

"I believe that this must be the right one. That ridge ahead looks like it would block any river from going to the west, and this water is running east."

"That is strange logic, Robert, but you may be right."

The ridge was a lot farther away than it looked. We followed our usual routine and rode about two hours at a time, and then we would rest for awhile. By noon, the ridge looked no closer. If anything it was moving away from us. And that mountain was really a long way off. The stream bed had not changed much. All morning, there was the same volume of water. The only changes would be the width of the riverbed. Sometimes the banks were close to each other, and at another junction they would be a mile apart. This portion of the river ran fairly straight, and riding on the bank became easier and easier. We crossed several small streams feeding into the main branch and even found a couple of springs.

We made cold camp at one of the springs and had our cold fish. There was fresh, cool spring water, and we filled our water bags. After some rest, we decided to see how far we could go that day.

"Minnie, I bet we are getting close to the headwaters of this river. We are seeing springs that feed it, and we are climbing all the time. That ridge is not moving away like it was!"

"Robert, ridges don't move away. That is just an optical illusion."

"What's an opt...optic...what did you call it?"

"Optical illusion. You have seen water mirage on the horizon?"

"Yes."

"That is an optical illusion. That mountain, may not be a mountain. There are no peaks, just a long flat and unbroken line. That mountain has no peaks and is one straight line. Also, I don't think it is as far as it appeared in the early morning light. The light has changed it's appearance. Another illusion."

"Boy, Minnie, you sure are smart."

"I'm smart too," piped up Lizzie. She had not said two words all morning.

"You sure are Lizzie. You are an excellent student in school. When we get to Uncle John's, and you go to school, we will all be proud of you." Minnie looked at me, "You are smart, Robert. For your age you are very smart, and you really learned a lot from Papa. You know lots that I don't know, and you sure are a help."

All of these compliments from a sister can get to be too much. I knew it was time to change the subject. "Is that smoke?" I asked, pointing almost due north.

"Looks like smoke, maybe from a smokestack."

"Wonder who lives over there. Sure is a long way off and a lonely place."

The day wore on, and we were tired, so well before sunset we began to look for a campsite. We came to a sharp bend in the much smaller river, and there was more water and a sandy beach below. We stopped and sat on the mules for a moment. The ridge looked like it was just right out there, and we would be there anytime. The "mountain" had changed it's appearance some more. It looked less and less like a mountain. Just a bigger ridge. Much bigger.

Off to our left there was another series of ridges and flat mountains that ran parallel to the river. These ridges ran to the west and disappeared in the distance. The entire area was cut with deep ravines and gullies. The mountains were imposing, but these on our left, did not stand between us and Uncle John.

"Let's find a way down to the river. There is not a cloud in the sky, so we shouldn't worry about rain tonight."

We made camp on a smooth sandbar in the riverbed. I had to hobble the mules on top, because there was no grass in the bottom. I took my bedding up to sleep near the mules. Felt that I needed to be close. We had always been able to camp closer to them. They were good watch dogs. That left Ol' Bullet with the girls.

Supper consisted of more fish. Boy, fish alone is difficult to eat.

Turning to Minnie I said, "I think I'll walk along the banks of the river and see if I can find some eggs."

"What kind of eggs would you find, Robert?"

"I don't know, but some fresh eggs and fish would not be so bad. Now would it?" Lizzie and Minnie looked at each other and then at me.

Lizzie spoke, "You, want me to eat eggs from out in the….?"

Minnie's nose had wrinkled up, and she expressed herself this way, "NOT ON YOUR LIFE!"

I got up from the campfire and wandered down the riverbank and then up on top, when I found a cut. I had not gone far when I came upon a bird's nest. Two big blue quail ran away. I took off my hat and put near a dozen eggs in it. I walked a little further and another pair of quail ran. This time there were only ten, but that made close to two dozen. They were big eggs for quail eggs. If you divided that by three, we could have almost eight each. I returned to the camp and showed the girls the eggs, and they almost died. After some tall arguing, they finally agreed to try them.

The clincher to get them to try was, "They are just eggs. If I broke them in the skillet and stirred them up, you would think they were chicken eggs."

We were sitting around the campfire, not talking, just watching the blaze and enjoying the starlight night.

"Let's take Ol' Bullet and climb up on the bank so we can see the stars."

We climbed up the slope and walked out to where the mules were grazing. The night was very still and sound carried a long way. We heard a coyote in the distance and tried to guess how far away he was when he howled. Night birds cheeped in the bushes. Some quail called in the distance.

Suddenly, the night stillness was split wide open with the blast of a shotgun. The sound came from the north. We all jumped at the sound. It wasn't real close, but it was very clear and very loud. The sound echoed from the surrounding low hills and river banks.

"That was a double-barrel," I said.

Minnie pointed to the north, "There is a fire!"

All was quite for a few minutes, and then there was a different sounding shotgun blast, and it was answered by the double-barrel gun. Again, the sound reverberated over the countryside. With the double blast, the sound echoed for several seconds and slowly died out. Then silence returned to the still night. All birds and animals had gone silent with the guns blasting. Slowly they began to sing, and the coyote called to his mate.

The fire grew and the light filled the night to the north and made a glow.

"Listen, do I hear a wagon moving over rough ground?"

Faintly, if the breeze was just right, you could hear a wagon, or what sounded like a wagon. The fire grew and grew. It blazed bright for perhaps an hour, and then it began to diminish. Soon it burned out, and the night was completely dark again.

"Wonder what that was about?" I asked.

"None of our business, Mr. Robert."

The next morning the sky was covered with heavy dark clouds. We almost panicked, being down in the riverbed and afraid of another heavy rain. We had our breakfast of scrambled eggs and fish as quickly as we could and cleaned up camp. I had the mules unhobbled and ready to pack by the time Minnie had her pots and pans cleaned and packed. Lizzie had rolled up the bedding and put all three in the burlap sack. A big job for a little girl. I took charge of rolling up the canvases and stuffing them into burlap bags.

Minnie and I put the four double sack arrangements on the back of Number One. We helped Lizzie up on the mule, and then Minnie and I mounted our animals.

When we came out of the riverbed, we got a faint whiff of something burnt. As the breeze was from the north, we surmised that the smell came from the fire we had seen last night. The clouds hung heavy all day long. The temperature was at least twenty degrees cooler than it had been the day before. No rain fell during the morning, but the wind started to blow harder. We had made good time until the weather began to turn bad, and the wind had gone to the west.

The riverbed narrowed more every mile, and a number of small tributaries branched off the main stream. When we left the campsite, we came out on the north or the right side of the river. We were headed west, and one side seemed as good as the other. The cut, up out of the riverbed, was easier to traverse, so we were riding down the north side.

The ridge we had watched for two days was directly ahead. Unexpectedly, the main branch of the river came to an abrupt halt. Several tributaries flared out in a fan shape from where the river seemed to end. Water ran in three of the lesser tributaries. When I tested the water it was cold, like from a spring.

Minnie spoke, "I remember Papa said when you get to the end of the left branch of the river, the branches off of the main body will look like a fan." Sitting on a slight rise above the "fan", it was very apparent that this must be what he was talking about.

Minnie spoke again, "He also said that the ridge top would be two or three miles further west, and that from the top you could see the other branch of the Brazos River." She squinted at the horizon against the west wind. "We are almost to the top of the ridge. I can't see the big ridge. It's covered with….it looks like rain or haze. We had better find a place to make a camp and get ready for some bad weather."

I rode out several of the tributaries and found one that was going to give us the protection from the weather. As it was noon, the spending of some extra time locating a tributary with good shelter and water was time well spent. The one we chose was on the north side of the river. It had a spring and not much watershed for runoff. The camp could be pitched down among the rocks and out of the wind.

One wagon canvas was made into a tent among the rocks. We had good protection on the west, as the tent was pitched up against the west wall of the ravine. This ravine had an almost solid rock wall all the way around the spring. There was evidence that this spot had been a campsite before. A ring of rocks with ashes was already in place and in a fairly sheltered spot.

I gathered firewood from around the ravine as there was none on the ravine floor. I had to hobble the mules down the ravine a few yards. As the clouds were approaching, and remembering the experience from the last storm, I also put lead ropes on the mules and tied them securely to the base of a tree. I sure didn't want a mule bolting in this storm, like what happened to me the last time. At least there was water, some grass and shelter.

We had fish for lunch, and then we were out of food. Even with the weather threatening, I got the shotgun and left the camp to see if I could kill our supper.

Mama's admonition kept holding true, "The Lord will provide."

I had not been out hunting for more than thirty minutes when I shot a cottontail. Then more luck came my way. I spotted a covey of quail huddled under a clump of bushes. They were trying to stay out of the wind. What I did next was not very sportsmanlike….but…. we needed food. I shot into the covey sitting on the ground and got the whole covey. Nine birds with one shot. Sure saves ammunition that way. Papa would have busted my tail, for sure. While I was putting the quail in my hunting bag, a "chicken" ran out of another clump of bushes. It startled me at first. A "chicken"? I didn't stay startled for long. The bird had run into a bigger clump of bushes. I just eased up and waited for a few minutes, and sure enough, the "chicken" ran out of the bush and bang, I had a "chicken" to go with my rabbit and nine quail. The thunder and rumble of the approaching storm covered the sound of my gun. Supper and breakfast were "In the bag." I laughed all the way back to camp.

It began to rain, and then it poured. I was soaked by the time I got back into camp. I had seen the rain coming from the west, and it came in torrents. I almost missed the basin where our camp was located. The rain was so blinding that I nearly passed to the north of the site. A lightning flash revealed that the basin was only a few feet to my left. I slid down the bank and was greeted, not only by a tail wagging dog, but by two very worried sisters.

"What happened, Robert?" asked Lizzie.

"I almost got lost, I came within about ten feet of missing this basin."

Minnie inquired, "Did you get anything? We heard the gun. We thought three shots, but with the thunder, we were not sure."

"Yes, I did! Wait until you see what I bagged!" I reached into the bag and brought out the rabbit.

Minnie clapped her hands, "Roasted rabbit is one of my favorites!"
"Wait, there's more."

I reached in and brought out my "chicken".

Minnie's and Lizzie's eyes got big, and there was a flood of squeals.

"I don't believe it, "exclaimed Minnie. "A chicken, way out here!"

I then pulled out the nine quail and laid them on a rock.

Minnie was beside herself, "Let's get busy and clean this game and have supper!"

Lizzie pleaded that we clean the chicken first, as that was one of her favorites.

We cleaned the game as fast as possible, doing the chicken first, and put it on to roast. One of the items we had taken when we left Uncle Nate's was Papa's spit. It consisted of two metal rods that you could push into the earth and then a third rod that went across the top to make the spit. We placed the chicken on the top rod, and Lizzie was assigned the task of turning it.

Beside the roaster, when we had loaded for our trip, we had taken a small Dutch oven, a skillet, a pair of lightweight pots and our eating utensils. Our eating utensils for each of us consisted of, a tin plate, a tin cup, knife, fork, and spoon.

We cleaned the animals into the largest of the lightweight pots, and despite the rain, I carried the entrails and skins of the cleaned game away from the camp. Entrails and such might draw some animals we did not want, so I had to go quite a distance. But, that was no problem, we would have a good meal tonight and breakfast tomorrow. Plus, with the rain, I would not need to take a bath.

By the time the animals were cleaned, and I had dried off, the chicken was roasted. We were under our wagon canvas tent and enjoying a hot meal, a dry camp and a warm fire. We had the chicken, and Minnie cooked the rabbit and the quail for tomorrow.

She commented that there would be enough for breakfast and for lunch. Then I would need to hunt, or if we were at the river, I could fish some more.

The rain pounded the earth and the canvas until way in the night. Water ran off the tent and made a rivulet that joined the stream that ran near at hand. Water ran off the banks, and there were a number of other rivulets that poured into the stream, but we were dry. Then as quick as it started, it stopped, and within another hour the sky was clear, and the moon was shining bright. The rain had refreshed the earth, and the air was sweet with the fragrance from plants and the damp soil.

We let our campfire burn down and crawled into our beds, hoping for a good night's rest.

"Minnie, do you think we can reach the other branch of the Brazos tomorrow?"

"Robert, if I remember Papa's directions, we are only about five miles from that branch. Of course the rain will have made the ground slippery again, but we should be able to cover that distance."

Sleep came quickly. I had drifted off when Ol' Bullet began to growl. This was the first time since we left Uncle Nate's that he had growled during the night. My eyes were adjusted to the dark, and I could see his ears perk up.

"What is it ,boy?"

Ol' Bullet came to his feet, and he growled again. Another low growl rumbled in his throat, and he took a step or two toward the south.

I got to my feet and heard Minnie ask, "What is it?"

"Shhhh!" I said as I pulled on my overalls and boots.

A faint sound filtered through the night. I went down the ravine toward the three mules, with Ol' Bullet trotting at my heels. The mules had turned to the south, facing down the draw. Their ears were perked up and turning one way and then another. They were like Ol' Bullet, hearing sounds I could not hear. Their ears kept twitching from side to side.

I went back to the camp and told the girls, "You stay put and I'll see what is going on. Ol' Bullet is going with me. His eyes and ears are better than mine."

The moon and the stars made the night almost like day. I could see objects at some distance. I went very carefully down the sandy bottom of the ravine. Ol' Bullet trotted at my side. His head was held high, and I could see he was testing the air and listening. We progressed down the gully to the intersection of several ravines.

As we got closer to the intersection, the sound that had been so faint grew louder and louder. I got down on my hands and knees and put my ear to the ground, one of Papa's tricks, and listened. The ground vibrated from the pounding of hooves. The sound that we heard was cattle on the move. I crept from gully to gully, listening to the ground at the mouth of each, in an effort to determine which direction I needed to go. When I got to the correct one, I didn't need to drop down and listen. The sound of cattle was clearly coming from this gully.

Ol' Bullet and I crept forward, being very cautious. If these cattle were about to stampede or just were milling, they could run over me and Ol' Bullet in a flash.

I knew that Ol' Bullet was a smart dog, and at that moment he proved it beyond a doubt. He went down on his belly and kind of whined, a very low and soft whine. I dropped to one knee and placed a hand on his back and looked down at him. He was looking past me up at the top of the ravine wall. I could feel him tremble under my hand. Before I could look around, I heard a voice in the dark.

"Get those critters bunched! We've got to move them out!"

My heart stopped, and I was filled with terror. The rider that had called out was right above us on top of the ravine wall. He was silhouetted by the moon. I nearly passed out. If he looked down, he could not miss us. We were in trouble and in a bad place. If they ran the cattle down the ravine, Ol' Bullet and I were trapped and would be trampled. I thought if he looks this way, we will run. Dumb plan! If he just sits there, we will move, because he was looking to the south and toward the sound of the cattle. We were about to run when the rider wheeled his pony and rode away.

My heart slowed a bit, and I found I could breathe. I reached for Ol' Bullet's back to motion him to follow me, and we ran back down the ravine. Then the earth began to shake and tremble. The cattle were on the move and coming down the ravine toward us. We ran faster and faster, but there was no way we could outrun them. A notch in the bank of the ravine loomed ahead. I ducked into the pocket of the notch and pressed my back against the wall. Ol' Bullet was at my feet, with his tail tucked between his legs. Smart dog!

Cattle streamed by, with cowboys on top of the ravine and some down in the ravine. Wet and smelly cattle came bawling down the ravine, filling the air with their sounds. The earth shook so bad I thought I could not stand on my feet. The sound of the cattle faded into the night, but some of the riders just trotted along down the ravine.

I heard one of them say, "Best bunch we have taken in a good while."

"Yep, there must be at least two hundred in this bunch."

"If we had not hit the ravine when the storm hit, we would have lost the whole lot."

"We had better catch up!" With that comment the two riders, spurred their horses and chased after the herd and their partners.

Rustlers! They are rustlers! You don't run cattle in the dark, unless you are in a hurry to get away. Only rustlers are in that kind of hurry. Even a farm boy like me knows that you don't run cattle in the dark. They might stumble, stick their legs in holes or just gore each other. Regardless, you could lose a bunch, but if you are a rustler you don't care much. You just run and take your chances.

I raced down the gully behind the herd and cowboys, praying with all my might that they did not turn up the ravine toward Minnie and Lizzie. I didn't think that they would, as that ravine was a dead-end.

Sound still hung in the air but was diminishing rapidly. In a few minutes I was back to Minnie and Lizzie. I fell on my knees in the sand in an effort to catch my breath.

"What was all of that?" asked Minnie.

"Are you O.K.?" chirped Lizzie.

"What did you see?" inquired Minnie.

"Where is Ol' Bullet?" cried Lizzie.

I held up my hand for them to stop until I had caught my breath. Ol' Bullet came racing into camp, with his tongue hanging out. He flung himself at Lizzie and almost knocked her down with joy. Apparently he had chased after the herd. Lizzie hugged and hugged the dog.

Finally, I could talk. "They are rustlers, and they were running off a herd of cattle!"

"How do you know that ?"

"I heard one of them say, 'This is the best bunch we have taken in a while.'"

"That doesn't mean that they are rustlers!"

"That by itself might not, but who runs cattle in the middle of the night in the dark?..." I answered my own question. "RUSTLERS! You don't run your cattle in the dark. You will get a bunch hurt!"

That sobered Minnie and Lizzie to silence.

"We are lucky that they didn't turn them up this ravine, girls."

That sobered them even more. They were silent for a long time. Then level headed Minnie broke the silence.

"This has been enough excitement for one night. Now let's get some sleep, because we have a big day tomorrow. We should get to the other branch of the Brazos." Sounded just like Mama.

Sleep was not on my mind. I could still hear the thunder of the hooves. If that notch had been any further, Ol' Bullet and I would have been trampled. The night was now still, and you could hear the night creatures. The moon was brilliant, and the stars twinkled in the black blanket of the sky.

The next thing I remember was Minnie singing softly and the sound of her preparing breakfast. By the time I was fully awake the sun was peeping over the horizon, and Minnie was calling, "Come on you sleepy heads, breakfast is ready."

I had not overslept since we had started our trip. Back home, Mama always had to drag me out of bed, unless there was something happening that I wanted to do or see. A real sleepy head. I splashed water over my face and said, "Boy, that water is cold. I'll refill our water bags before we leave, and we will have cool water all day." I pulled on my overalls and shirt. "I think that I will go barefooted today. Sure would feel good."

"And, what about rattlesnakes, little brother?"

"We have only seen that one that Ol' Bullet killed."

"Correct, but today could be the day of a snake."

I knew that Minnie was right. In this rough country I was surprised that we had not seen snakes, lots of snakes. I had no idea why we had not seen any. Just luck I guess, and I hoped our luck would hold.

I joined the girls at the campfire, and we enjoyed three quail apiece. What an excellent breakfast! Sure wish we had some flour, salt and baking soda. Minnie could make biscuits, gravy and season the meat. I'm supposed to be the hunter and provider, but just where could I find those items?

I fetched the mules for loading. They were clean and shiny in the morning sunlight. We packed the burlap bags and loaded them on Old Number One. We rode out of the ravine, looking west for the top of the ridge. We reached the top in just under an hour. With anticipation we approached the ridge. It was higher than you would have believed. On top we could look back and see for miles.

"Robert, there is the lake where we camped and got caught in that bad storm," pointed Minnie.

"Sure is, and you can see that branch of the Brazos winding on for miles." The early sunlight reflected off the water for miles and miles. The river wound and snaked all the way to the horizon.

"I wonder how far we can see that direction?" I asked.

Minnie laughed, "All the way back to Uncle Nate's."

"You mean that is as far as we have come?"

"No, I'm just teasing. I think we have come farther than that."

I turned my mule back to the west. "Minnie, a rider!"

"Where?"

"Right over there." I pointed. "See him?"

"Yes, he is riding pretty fast….. he is going north…… toward that ranchhouse." And it was her turn to point. From the top of the ridge we could see the rider very clearly. The ranchhouse and the out buildings were clear with the morning sun shining on them. They were all white-washed and stood out sharp against the background of earth tones and the greens of the vegetation.

"Wonder what his rush is?"

"Probably going to report those rustled cattle."

Lizzie broke one of her long silences, "Do you suppose they would give us some flour, so we could have biscuits?" Out of the mouth of babies.

Minnie and I looked at each other. "Do you suppose that we could get some from them?" I asked.

"I don't know. Let's get off this ridge. If we can see that rider, I'll bet he could sure see us against the sky line."

We rode down the west slope of the ridge. The west slope was smooth going for a couple of miles. Then there appeared ravines everywhere, cutting into the west slope and making a runoff for water down to the west branch of the Brazos.

"Minnie, let's ride north along this smooth ground and not go down in all of those ravines yet.. Maybe we can figure a way to get some flour, and this way we will be closer to the ranch."

"That might be a good idea, and it looks like there is an easier way across all of those ravines over that direction." Again, she pointed at a long smooth slope that ran from the ridge down toward the riverbed.

"Sure might make going down better."

We turned north and rode in silence for about three miles. The horseman arrived at the ranch headquarters at about the time we arrived at a point due east of the ranchhouse.

Minnie broke the silence, "Look, here is what I saw. Not a smooth ridge, but the side of a deep ravine. We were high enough that we were looking over into the ravine. I saw the north wall of this ravine in the sunlight." The ravine had a sandy bottom that ran all the way out of sight.

Minnie spoke again, " I'll bet that ravine goes all the way to the river. Looks like it goes just north of the ranchhouse. That will give us cover to get by the ranchhouse and to the river."

Lizzie pointed and asked. "Cowboys?"

A large group of mounted men rode away from the ranchhouse, headed south. They were riding hard. I wondered how long a horse would run at that pace.

"Minnie, this is a good time to get past that ranch house, with all of the men gone."

"You're right , Robert. Let's use this draw and see if it will carry us past the ranch."

All the way down the ravine I kept thinking of how I could get some flour and salt. When we stopped to rest, I crawled out on the ravine's bank to see how far we were from the ranchhouse. It was due south of us and only, maybe a half mile. Then the idea hit me.

"Minnie, you may not like this idea, but hear me out. Most of the men are gone, so that leaves only women. Let me go over to the ranchhouse and try a little begging. I'm not too proud. I think I can pull it off. I'll be begging for my family that got caught in that rain the other night, and all of our supplies got wet. Women might take mercy on a kid in old torn clothes. Give me my worst looking overalls, and I'll give it a try. What do you say?"

"I say, for a ten year old, you sure can talk a lot."

"Minnie, I'm not ten. I'm eleven! And I don't talk a lot!"

"O.K...O.K...Simmer down. I forgot that you are eleven." She frowned, squinted at me and continued, "And, it is hard to believe that you are nearly as tall as me." She paused and then said, "Bur, you sure do talk a lot." Minnie gazed at the ranchhouse. "Oh, Robert, what if you run into trouble? They may want to see your family or just hold you!"

"We have taken a lot of chances to get this far, and I think that this is just a chance we will have to take."

"What would Lizzie and I do if they hold you?"

"Go on down to the river and hide. They won't believe that a kid would disobey, and I'll run away from the ranchhouse. I will slip away and meet you down on the river. What have we got to lose?"

"O.K. but you be careful, and you go to the back door. Women would answer the back door most likely."

I changed my overalls to the worst pair I had, just had three pair. Put some dirt on my face and hands and tried to look forlorn as possible. Poor little old me!

I mounted Number Four, motioned for Ol'Bullet to come, and we rode out of the ravine and to the house. I went to the back door and knocked. A woman came to the door, just like Minnie said.

"Ma'am," I said in a humble voice. "Could you help me, please?" I had tears in my eyes. "My family got caught in that storm, and all of our supplies got wet and ruined. Pa would have come to the door, but he is too proud to beg."

"What do you need, young man?"

"Well, if you could, let me have some flour and salt. We sure would be grateful."

The woman said, "Just a moment, and I'll be right back."

She was back in probably ten minutes, but it seemed like ten years. She handed me three sacks.

"Here, boy. This is ten pounds of flour and a pound of salt. Also, I have put in a pound of baking soda. You can't cook much without baking soda. Will that get your family to their destination?"

"I think so. My family and I sure do thank you."

"Well, if we can't help a stranger in need, then what is this world coming to. You are the second stranger that we have helped or taken in recently." She smiled and said, "You are not as tall or as fat as he is. He is almost as wide as he is tall. He was all shot up and hurt when we found him."

I took a chance, "We heard gunfire to the north of us. Was he hurt in that gunfight?"

"Yes, he was. Appears he is looking for three runaways and rode into a den of skunks and had to shoot his way out. They tied him up and beat him. He is in a bad way. He sure is a brave man, that Mr. Nate!"

I almost fell off the mule when she said, "Three runaways," but when she said, "Mr.Nate" it was all I could do to stay on Old Number Four. I tucked the sacks closer to me and said, "Thanks a lot. I got to get back to my family." I sort of waved and kicked, Number Four in the ribs.

My heart was beating faster than when the cattle chased me and Ol' Bullet in the ravine. I rode around behind the barn and then turned to the northwest. I was trying to stay out of sight of the back door. I reached the ravine some west of Minnie's and Lizzie's position, but they saw me coming and had moved that direction.

I rode down into the ravine and shouted, "GET ON THAT MULE, AND LET'S GET OUT OF HERE!!!" That startled them into action. They climbed on Number Three, and we headed west down the ravine. I kept hollering, "HURRY, LET'S GET OUT OF HERE!!! LET'S GET OUT OF HERE!!!" We pushed the mules hard, and to my surprise Number One kept up and the sacks hadn't fallen off with him running.

We ran the mules for a couple of miles before I slowed to a walk.

"What in the world is wrong, Robert?"

My face must have looked wild, "You are not going to believe this! Uncle Nate is in that ranchhouse."

"What did you say?'

"Uncle Nate is at that ranchhouse!" I was almost hysterical. I continued, "The woman that gave me the supplies said he was looking for three runaways, and she gave a description that fit him to the letter. And, he was involved in that gunfire we heard the other night, the night we saw the fire." I was breathless.

Now Minnie and Lizzie were upset. You could see what was going through their minds just by looking at their faces.

We rode on without lunch. There was no mention of stopping and eating our rabbit. There was no stopping for another four hours. We came to the river and followed it northwest until sundown. We had covered more distance that day than any other. We also, realized we were following, not only the river, but a faint two rut trail. The trail ran parallel to the river. This was the river that would lead us to New Mexico Territory and Uncle John's, but that just might not happen with Uncle Nate hot on our heels.

Our hearts finally slowed back to normal, and we could talk about our situation. We found a spot on the river that we felt was secure and protected. We were all jumpy and had a hard time doing things we had done easily.

Finally Minnie broke the silence, "I think we have panicked for nothing. Look, if he was in a fight two nights ago and is as bad as the woman says, he's not going anyplace soon. Stop and think, Robert, just what did the woman say"

I thought for a long time and answered, "He rode into a den of skunks, and they tied him and beat him." I paused, then continued, "He shot his way out, and that he was in a bad way." Again I paused and then added, "She said he was a brave man."

"That's what I wanted to hear."

"What? That he is a brave man?"

"He is in a bad way. If he is laid up and can't travel, we will get the jump on him. And then for another thing, she did not know that you are one of the runaways. Right? So, we can just clear out, and Uncle Nate will not be any wiser."

That all sounded reasonable, but your mind sure will play games on you. Minnie took control and got us to work. That took our minds off the events of the day.

She took the flour, salt, and baking soda from me and said, "Robert set your fish lines. You catch us some fish. Lizzie and I will tend to the camp and get a fire going. We can have biscuits and gravy with our fish. Give the rabbit to Ol'Bullet. We will eat fresh meat."

After the lines were set, I returned to camp and helped unload Number One. I hobbled the mules and put lead ropes on them. There was very good grass, and I would let them graze until we went to bed, then bring them to the camp. I was still jumpy and wanted the mules close to us.

I had caught four good size fish by the time I had returned to the fish lines. I cleaned them away from the camp and then took them to Minnie. She cooked the best meal of the whole trip. She rolled the fish in flour to cook. We had not had lunch , so the four fish with biscuits and gravy were just about right to fill us up, and they were delicious.

After supper Minnie kept us busy. First, we went our separate ways and had baths. We put on clean clothes so Lizzie and Minnie could wash our dirty ones. The washing of clothes entailed taking them to a flat rock and beating them while they were wet. Afterward they hung them over bushes to dry. I brushed the mules and worked the tangles and burrs out of their tails and manes. All of this kept us busy right up to full dark. By the campfire, we sat and talked for awhile. For the first time Minnie took out Grandma's Bible and read to us a few scriptures. Just like at home with Mama.

Minnie sang softly a few hymns and a couple of other songs. Like I said, "Just like home with Mama." I remembered the mules were still out grazing, but that was my last thought until daybreak.

I had left my fishing lines out all night and had five fair size ones the next morning. These I took to Minnie and declared, "If you will clean these, I will see if there are any eggs around here." I climbed out of the river bottom and started searching for eggs. Minnie told me to not be gone for over thirty minutes.

Suddenly a "chicken" ran out of a bush. I just stopped and gaped. Where in the world were these "chickens" coming from? Then a thought struck me, I bet there are eggs in that bush. There were only four, but I kicked up another "chicken" after a few minutes and found three eggs in that nest.

I returned to the campsite and presented Minnie with the "chicken" eggs for our breakfast. These eggs were a little smaller than our chickens' eggs at home, but that didn't matter. We had biscuits, eggs, gravy and fish for breakfast. You can't beat that.

The good food and uninterrupted sleep gave us a better outlook on things the next morning. After breakfast we hurried to get packed and loaded.

I went up to get the mules and saw dust to the northeast of us. I took the mules down into the river bed and called Minnie and Lizzie up on the bank to look at the dust. We decided that it was miles away and that the herd was going west. Our trails might cross, but we were doubtful that that would happen.

We loaded and took the faint two-rut trail to the northwest. The dust from the herd did not seem to be getting closer, just was out there. It was very hard to tell what direction the herd was going. The two ruts really made traveling easier. We stayed out on the rutted trail all day. At rest time we would swing over to the river and find shade.

At lunch, we went down into the riverbed. For the first time in a long time, we found a good resting place and even built a fire. Minnie warmed up the leftovers from breakfast. We did not rush, for we had decided to ride until sunset. We would rest a little more, but go as far as we could. The faint road and smoother ground helped us make excellent time

I had seen lots of rabbits during the morning and took the shotgun out of the bag with the hope of shooting some for supper. Now I couldn't find one single hare.

"Robert, you should know that the rabbits are only out when it is cool. You will be able to find us a couple later this afternoon."

"I think that we may be too close to the herd by sunset for me to hunt."

Minnie took notice of the herd by the river for the first time since early this morning. "We are getting closer to them each hour. There may be cowboys with them so I can't shoot my gun. Maybe we will just have fish."

Sunset found us back down on the riverbed. This site was as good or better than any we had occupied. No clouds on the horizon and another good meal of fish lifted our spirits even more. We believed that we were far ahead of Uncle Nate, if he was even coming this way.

The bluff, that we had thought was a mountain, was just over to the west. The river was almost running parallel to the bluff at this point. The two ruts continued to follow the river and afford us a good path to follow.

We discussed the possibility that the river did not go up on the bluff, just followed along down the front edge. On the other hand Papa had said, "Just follow the river all the way to the Territory of New Mexico." Then the river must come from up on top. We felt that the trail we were on probably followed the river up on the top of the bluff.

Good traveling encouraged us, and we made lots of miles the next day. Guess we were getting used to riding on the mules. Even Lizzie said she is not tired like she was when we started. The trip started out with our having to stop every few miles to rest. Now, we just kept going for miles and miles. I believed if we had to, we could go half a day without stopping.

The next morning there was no dust on the horizon or anywhere to be found. Minnie turned to me. "Robert, you are the smartest about things like this. What happened to the herd?"

"Gee, Minnie, I don't really have a clue. They could be stopped. I don't think they pushed all night, but, after what happened the other night in the ravines, I don't know."

"Well, let's just keep riding and see how much trail we can cover today. The last three days we covered more ground than all the rest put together. If I have kept the days straight, we have been on the trail thirteen days. I had planned for us to be at Uncle John's by now. I don't know how much further it is, but we can't turn back. I thought we could cover about twenty miles a day. But, I forgot about all the turns and twists in the river. I never thought about the weather, and what it could do to us."

We rode and climbed all day with no sight of the herd. To our surprise, the river and the trail both turned straight toward the bluff. We could see for miles behind us. When we would rest we would find some shade, and there was always water. The river was at hand, and we crossed or saw lots of springs, but, no herd. They had vanished.

"Minnie, I think the herd stopped." I pointed to the northeast, "I think they are out there somewhere, and when we get up higher we will be able to see them."

At noon we stopped by a clear spring with good shade. It was becoming hotter each day, and the shade was more important. I climbed some rocks and had a good clear view of the flat land to the east. Really it wasn't flat, just lots of rolling hills and gullies. The country was rough and broken, draws and creeks running ever which direction.

That was when I saw the herd. They were just about where I had pointed, and they were stopped. What caught my attention was a swirl of dust. The dust kept coming from one spot. It was rising from milling cattle. The cattle were not moving. They were bunched and something was happening to them, but they were too far away for me to tell.

"Minnie, I see the herd. I can make out that it is a herd. There is lots of commotion and a some dust."

"Could they overtake us if they come this way?"

"I don't know. Possible."

Minnie came up on the rocks with me. She shielded her eyes and studied the herd in the distance. "You are right, no telling what they are doing?"

Lizzie called, "Could we get on top of the bluff today?"

"If we don't make it today, we will tomorrow, if the road keeps going this direction."

We mounted again and returned to the trail. The bluff was still farther than it looked. Evening came, and camp was pitched, in a small grove of trees near a small brook, off of the trail perhaps a half mile. The river was reduced to a narrow bed without sandy places to camp or trees for shelter.

We tied the canvas to two trees and truly had a tent for the first time. With a canvas floor and a roof over our heads, camp was very comfortable. The fire was down behind rocks so the light could not be seen from a distance. There was grass for the mules and ample water. Everything was fine, that is until Minnie mentioned food. We had none!

I got the shotgun and started down the slope away from the camp. There were lots of rocks and could be lots of snakes in the crevices. Ol' Bullet trailed along, and true to form, he found a snake that could have struck me. The one-sided fight was over in a blink.

We came out on a flat grassy area. I wasn't paying much attention until Ol' Bullet gave a little bark. There, not twenty feet from me, stood a small animal. It looked something like a deer that I had seen in a book at school. The difference was that it only had two short horns and different markings. It wasn't much bigger than Ol' Bullet. I didn't hesitate. The gun came up, and in one shot we had supper. I had to take the chance of someone hearing the gunshot. We needed food.

When I came into camp, Minnie recognized the kill as an antelope. Then I remembered reading about them. We dressed the kill some distance from our camp. Minnie cut the meat into strips that would roast over the fire. She salted the meat some as it cooked and made her biscuits and gravy. What a meal! She continued to cook meat well after supper.

"We should have meat enough for all of tomorrow. It is great having flour and salt again."

The moon was full that night and the air very clear. The sky was really bright and clear. We had put out the fire. We sat for a little while listening to the night creatures and watching the moon and stars. Lizzie gave out first and went to sleep. Minnie made sure she was covered. We talked of small things for a time. Of Mama and Papa and home. We could talk about them without crying. It had taken some time to come to that place. It was good now to talk about them and all they had tried to teach us. This way we would remember those things and not forget the lessons. We slipped into our bedrolls for the night.

It must have been almost midnight when the ground began to shake and tremble. Ol" Bullet was on his feet and growling when I awoke. I had never felt anything like this. The earth was shaking! Ol' Bullet took a few steps toward the trail and did a low cough. The mules' ears were up, and then it dawned on me.

Cattle were on the move. Minnie and Lizzie stood beside me now, and we all listened. Then the sound came out of the night, lots of hooves.

"Robert, are we safe here?"

"Yes, I believe that we are. There are rocks between us and the trail and we are a long ways from it."

The noise increased, then out of the dark came lowing and bawling cows. They came abreast of us and then they poured by, a river of cattle. We heard cowboys calling and whistling as they pushed the cows up the trail.

We could only stand there and watch. Then the tail of the herd came by and more cowboys. Just for a moment I saw the cowboy that had been silhouetted against the moon back in the ravine. These were the same cowboys, and they were rustling cattle.

I turned to Minnie and Lizzie, "It's them again, it's the rustlers!"

CHAPTER EIGHT

What a break! Just when he thought the brats had slipped through his fingers, up pops his old luck. That cowboy had drawn him a rough map that showed right where the brats were camping. The tables had tilted in his favor, and he would capitalize on this tip. He didn't really expect to find them at that location. It was just the fact that he had a lead and knew that he was close.

The two rut trail was hard going and the ground was very rough for a wagon. The rocks and cuts in the trail made his wagon jar and tilt one way and then another. He realized by mid-morning that he would have to change teams at noon. The pulling was too hard for a pair of horses, and the wagon was heavy. Probably the wagons that had gone over this terrain had been pulled by a team of four and not by a team of two. His wagon was loaded with supplies, bedding, loot and two saddles. All the equipment and supplies had overloaded it, and the team was struggling.

He stopped and rested the animals after every hard pull. At this rate it would take him all day and perhaps two, to make the top of the bluff that was just off to his left. A barrier to going west.

The cowboy had said, "Getting up the cap will be really hard in that wagon. It can be done, but you will have to work at it and take your time."

"It doesn't look all that high."

"Looks are deceiving, and that bluff is deceiving! From here to there is full of ravines, cuts, gullies and more gullies."

Nate stopped on top of the rocky spine and surveyed the road ahead. It appeared to become worse with every yard. As he started down the incline into the next ravine, his luck changed. The ground sloped down at a steep angle. The road went down sidewise to the slope and not straight down. The wagon began to tip to the right, and Nate had to jump. The wagon slowly rolled over on it's side and all the contents spilled out on the ground.

Nate hit the ground and rolled down the slope. The horses broke lose from the wagon and ran down the embankment and out of harm. The team tied on the back jerked their heads when the wagon rolled and broke their reins. He sat up and inspected his situation. He had not been on the road more than two or three hours and now this. Not even a half day and of all the cursed luck! All he could do for several minutes was curse his luck and the brats.

He finally got to his feet and dusted off his clothes. Feeling around, he found no broken bones that he could tell. Taking a waterbag from the wreck, he went over and sat in the shade under a tree. It took some time for his head to stop spinning and his eyes to refocus. "Guess I hit my head, when I jumped."

The few supplies left in the wagon had not been very hard to unload. With all of the supplies and equipment piled to one side, Nate turned his attention to retrieving the horses. On this hard uneven ground that took some time. The horses did not run from him. It was just difficult getting down to the team and back up the incline. Also the two single horses were some distance from the wagon. It took a lot of slipping and sliding on the rocks to get to them. Then it took even more effort to work back up the hill to the wagon. As the horses were brought back to the wagon, he hobbled them. At least he would not have to chase them down again, he hoped.

His feet slipped on the gravel and sandstone with every step. By the time he had the four horses back to the wagon, it was noon. He looked down at his hands and saw that they were cut and bleeding from catching himself when he fell, or when he grabbed some brush or rock outcropping in an effort to pull his fat body up the grade.

Scratching through his supplies, he found a couple of cold biscuits and a can of beans. He opened the beans, took the biscuits and found some shade. Despite that his lunch was only cold biscuits and beans, he found he had a good appetite, and the fare tasted very good. He finished his meal with a can of peaches. When he finished the peaches, he tipped his hat in salute to Mr. Wilson, the ranch owner, who gave him the peaches. Then he leaned back in the shade to take a well deserved nap, or so he thought.

When he awoke, he tackled the task of setting his wagon upright. He tied the two harnessed horses to the side of the empty wagon. He took ropes and tied the two single horses to the same side. Getting all four to pull at once might be difficult, but he needed that much power to upright the wagon.

With some hollering and a little use of his whip, the horses did in fact pull together, and the wagon was pulled back on it's wheels. When it dropped back into an upright position, the impact with the ground knocked dirt and dust out of the wooden structure. Nate stood observing the situation. "Well," he sighed, "It could be worse." With another sigh he started reloading the wagon.

By the time all of the supplies and equipment were reloaded, he needed to find a campsite. He hitched the team and found a couple of short ropes to tie the other horses behind the wagon. When all was ready, he walked down the ravine a little distance and observed that a fairly good campsite was right at hand. The campsite was about half way between the river and the trail, yet out of sight and very well concealed. It was close enough that he could lead the horses to water two at a time.

Making camp was a pleasant diversion. It took his mind off the misfortune of the morning. He had experienced wagon rollovers before. He had not liked them in the past and did not like this one any better. But making camp, and preparing a "good" meal, took his mind off those difficulties. He kept the fire small and had no smoke. He knew that he was on a trail traveled by settlers, cowboys, rustlers and pilgrims of all sorts. Some were good honest folks, but others were of a very questionable type.

Night soon came, and he let his fire burn out. No need to set a beacon for some unsavory character. With his horses hobbled on good grass near the wagon, and his world put back together, he rolled into his bedroll. As he lay there, he realized he was only a good walk from where Curley had said the brats were camped. Curley said there was a good winding game trail along the river. Horses could follow the trail without much effort. That trail would not do him any good, but he would be on guard for any unwanted visitors coming down that trail. With that thought he rolled over and went to sleep.

Nate's eyes popped open. What was that sound? There it was again! Horses! Riders in the middle of the night only meant one thing. Rustlers or outlaws! Those riders were on the wagon trail. Their voices carried over the sound of hooves and the occasional snort of horses.

"Red, let's cut to the right at that next trail. Let's go to the river and make camp there," called one rider.

"Sure, we have come far enough to have outrun that ranch bunch. We have been to the top and back and they are still down on the flat country looking for us. We have been up the trail delivering those doggies, while those ranch hands just mill around, and we are almost back to our hideout."

"That was one of the best raids we ever made, Red!"

"Sure was, and we now know where there are cattle for the taking!"

Nate suddenly recognized that name and voice. That was the Red that helped him look for the brats. Then a jolt went through Nate. That herd of thirty cows that Red and his partner were driving was probably stolen. He had seen them twice on the road with that herd. No wonder they thought he was a lawman, after all of that. His story of looking for runaways, they thought, was a cover to hunt rustlers. Someone shouted, "Here's the turn-off trail!"

"Boy, I'll be glad to get off this nag!"

"Do you realize we have been in the saddle for near fifteen hours?"

"Yeah, but it was worth it. If you think otherwise, just reach down and check your poke and feel that money." commented Red.

"More money than I have ever had!" exclaimed another rider.

"And more to come, just like you got that!"

The riders rode within twenty-five yards of Nate's camp. He just knew that one of his horses would neigh, and they would know that there was another camper near at hand. They went by him and on down to the river.

"We just crossed that game trail. Could be the ranch bunch will come that way, looking for us."

"I doubt that they are still on the trail. When we went up the caprock yesterday, we probably lost them. They don't go up there. Guess they are scared." Several of the outlaws laughed.

"A lot of people are scared of the plains. No landmarks and if you don't know where you're going, you will get lost and most likely starve."

"Here's our campsite. Let's get bedded down and catch some shuteye."

There was some creaking of saddles as the men dismounted and unsaddled their horses. A small fire was built and bedrolls spread out.

"Hey, why the fire? You want someone to see it?"

The fire was kicked out, and someone said, "We can build one in the morning and have coffee."

A reply came, "Sure will taste good."

Then there was silence as the men bedded down and went to sleep.

Nate didn't know what to do. If he tried to hitch up and leave, they would hear him. If one of his horses neighed they would be on to him. He finally crept from his bedding. Then one at a time he led his horses back away from the cowboys. He covered their noses as he led them to a new grassy glade. There he hobbled the horses. Then he put lead ropes on each, before tying the rope to a tree base.

He crept back to his wagon and got out his shotgun and plenty of ammunition. Picking up his bedroll, he moved into a clump of trees. He had a good line of vision to the wagon, but was concealed. He just couldn't hide that wagon or move it, for fear of the noise.

Daybreak came, and to Nate's surprise he had slept. The smell of coffee filled his nostrils. He heard the cowboys moving about their camp. He rolled his bedroll up and checked his shotgun. He just felt in his bones that there was going to be trouble.

"How much do you think our cut will be this time?" asked a gruff voice.

"We drove about four hundred head up the trail. At three dollars a head that would be….. will somebody help me figure out our cut?"

There was murmuring among the riders.

"Red, you are good with figuring, help us figure this out."

Nate heard Red's voice. "You dumb bunch of hard heads. I could tell you anything, and you would think it was right. I could tell you forty dollars or one hundred dollars and you would not know the difference. Bunch of rock heads."

The gruff voce broke in, "Ah, Red, you are honest with us. You would not cheat your riding partners."

"No, but somebody else might do so. Here, give me that paper and let me figure what you are going to get, so you won't get cheated. I'll take it away from you gambling."

"Red, you beat all. At least you tell us when you are going to cheat us. And you playing cards is one way." There was a murmur of agreement, some chuckling, and then silence as Red did his numbers.

"Boy, this coffee is good," one commented. There were several grunts and comments of agreement.

Red interrupted them. "Best I can figure, the boss gets six hundred dollars, and we each get about seventy five to eighty dollars."

"That sure beats working for a living. Those cowpokes for the 'Box W' only get a dollar a week and found. Seventy five dollars is more than they will make in one year."

"The boss sure makes a lot. "

Red was on his feet. "Do I hear somebody complaining? This is the best you bone headed cowboys will ever have it. The boss has to pay other people out of his share. He is the one who figured out how to drive the cattle up on the caprock and then turn south and circle around to the place they call Big Spring. Those buyers from Abilene take the cattle off our hands, and we have no risk."

"Red, we are not complaining. This is a good set-up, and we like the deal."

"O.K. just keep your mouths shut and do your job."

"Pour me some more of that coffee."

"Sure be glad when we get back to the hideout and have a some good cooking. Not just coffee and beef jerky."

"Ahhh…quit your belly aching. You might get fat, if you had three squares a day."

"Yeah, I just might. I might get as fat as that toad we caught on the road."

"Now that is fat."

"That fellow still bothers me."

"How's that?"

"He's just been around a little too much. And acting like he is hunting kids. I still bet he is some kind of a lawman."

"Well, if that is the way you feel, the next time we see him, we'll just fill that fat body full of lead."

"Good idea!"

The cowboys began to break camp. There was the sound of horses being saddled and cursed. Nate could hear the men move off into the brush and back. One cowboy's horse broke away and ran up the draw, almost colliding with Nate's wagon. The horse veered around the wagon and plunged on up the draw. The rider came trotting along behind cursing with every step. He suddenly stopped at the sight of Nate's wagon.

"Hey, boss. Come see what I have found." called the rider.

"Well, I hope it's your horse, you knothead. Letting that horse get away was not smart. Now we will have to find him."

Red broke out of the trees and pulled his horse to a sliding stop. He called back to the camp. "I'll be…. boys, that fat lawman is around here some place. Here is his wagon! Let's spread out and find him. Shoot to kill, and we don't stop until he is dead. GOT IT?"

The camp bustled with activity as men mounted and others started running out into the brush to look for Nate.

There was a lot of shouting and yelling. "You look over there, and I'll check that draw."

Nate had little time to think about what was going to happen. They were going to search until they flushed him out and then shoot him. He cocked both barrels and stepped from the trees.

"HEY, YOU!!!" Red and the man on foot both turned together. Neither man had drawn his gun. When they saw Nate they both started trying to get their guns out. Their eyes turned big and white when they saw the double-barrel shotgun. They were not quick draw gun fighters. They got their guns out, but that was all. Nate brought the double-barrel up and fired one barrel at Red and the other barrel at the man on foot. The result was devastating, At that close range Red was blown out of the saddle and the rider on the ground was dead before he fell.

Then Red's horse screamed and ran back toward the camp. The shots brought several cowboys riding, hell bent for leather. They had their guns out and were ready to fire. When they rode up to the wagon, all they found was their two dead companions. Nate had faded into the brush and was circling the wagon.

He called from the other side of the wagon, "Fat toad am I?" The two riders on that side of the wagon wheeled their horses, looking for the source of the voice. All they could see was brush. They forced their horses closer to the trees, and Nate stepped into the open. Again, before either of the rustlers could aim their guns, the double-barrel roared twice. The two thieves were blown from their horses, one dead and the other mortally wounded.

Nate again stepped back into the cover of the brush. He had always been a good fisherman and a better hunter and marksman. But, this was like shooting ducks in a rainbarrel. This time he retreated some distance. This action would make them come to him and he could pick them off one or two at a time. "Call me a fat toad, will they?" He heard the other horsemen thrashing around in the brush looking for him.

Nate was a coward by heart and sure not a killer. But, when his life and his goods in the wagon were threatened, his personality changed. He crouched behind a boulder and waited. That was one of his best defenses against this many guns. He could wait.

He didn't have to wait long. A lone rider came up the ravine toward Nate. When the cowboy was only ten or twelve feet from him, Nate stepped from behind the rock and said, "You looking for me?"

The cowboy had a startled look on his face just before the double-barrel gun cut him half into. The blast knocked down the horse and threw the rider back into some foliage. The horse struggled to his feet, blood running down his shoulder. Looking at the horse's wounds, Nate whispered to the horse as he patted the trembling animal, "Sorry you got some of the buck shot."

Nate moved to his left, keeping boulders and brush between him and the riders. He could hear every movement they made, while they could not hear or see him. As he moved further to his left, he also moved closer to the wagon. Close to the wagon would be one of the last places for the rustlers to look for him. They thought of him as a fat, plump and soft- handed pushover. The outlaws did not realize that in the last few weeks, Nate had been involved in the deaths of seven people. That was before today. He had changed with all of the killing, and now he had killed five more and was ready to kill again.

There was shouting and confusion at the rustler's camp. Nate had moved closer to them. He was within fifteen feet of one of the rustlers when the man saw him. When the rustler saw Nate, he had already pulled the trigger on the double-barrel. The man screamed as he was blown from his horse. This caused more shouting and confusion among the outlaws, and they broke and rode south.

The adrenaline slowed and Nate sank to the ground. He couldn't believe what had just happened. Certainly he had taken them by surprise, but to kill six of them and not get a scratch was unbelievable. He sat on the ground for a long time. All of this time he felt sick and weak. What was he doing killing men? The realization that they wanted to kill him had driven him to be ready, but so many dead.

When Nate returned to his wagon, he took a long drink from a waterbag and then just leaned against the wagon. His body was still shaky. It took some time to bring the horses in and hitch up a team. Tying the spares to the rear of the wagon, he climbed up on the seat to start. A thought flashed through his head. He had found money and guns on the men after that other shooting. Could there be enough money to make it worth his while to search these rustlers. He climbed down and began to go through pockets and saddle bags. To his disgust, all he found was about forty dollars. Nate gathered the pistols from the men and found them all worn and in bad need of repair. He noted that there was not one rifle among the riders. A very poor and sorry lot of rustlers. He pitched the guns into the brush and turned back to his wagon. Climbing aboard he headed back up the draw to the two rutted trail.

He and the horses struggled all day long. The heat became unbearable, and the horses suffered from all of the hard work. Swapping the teams several times did little to increase their progress. It was just a hard climb over such rough terrain. They made about five miles that day, even with lots of stops. After a long day of straining, they seemed no closer to the top.

Nate turned the team toward the river late in the afternoon. He and the horses were exhausted. He doubted that the horses could put in two days in a row working this hard. Grass was plentiful and finding a good camping place was not difficult. A bubbling stream and shade always made a good place. When the horses were hobbled, Nate sat down in the shade of the wagon, leaned back against the wheel and was soon asleep.

Just as the sun was going down, Nate awoke. He checked the horses and set about fixing a hot meal. He had eaten cold food for breakfast and lunch. This time he prepared cured beef with chopped up potato and onion. He cut the beef in little chunks and added the chopped potato and onion. He made sourdough biscuits and coffee. Feast for a king he thought, as he cleaned the last morsel of food.

He was awake and on the move early the next morning. He had just finished breakfast, when he heard a voice say, "Mister don't even think about moving." Lord, what now? Nate just sat on the ground and did not move. He heard a whistle and soon three cowboys rode into his camp. One came in leading his pony.

"Put your hands in the air!"

Nate did as he was told. Without warning rough hands grabbed him and threw him to the ground. One rolled him over on his stomach, and a second tied him hand and foot. He had a flashback to the line-cabin.

"All right 'mister mastermind', we finally caught you!"

Another cowboy spoke, "That's right. We have been trying for months to figure out who was masterminding these rustlings, and now we got him."

Nate could hardly believe his ears. He looked at them and began to laugh as he said, "You think I'm a mastermind behind the rustling?"

"We heard the big shooting down yonder about five miles, and we found what remains of your gang."

"You found my gang?"

"That's right. We're going to hold you until Mr. Wilson gets here, and we can turn you over to him."

One of the cowboys straddled his pony and rode out shouting, "I'll be back by dark with the boss."

The men settled down around Nate's fire. When eating time came they helped themselves to Nate's supplies, but they did not offer Nate a single bite.

"Say, that old fat boy sure does eat well. We don't have near as good food at the ranch as he has out here on the trail." The day wore on, and along around mid-afternoon Nate had rolled under the wagon and gone to sleep. He had always been one that could sleep in the face of all kinds of adversity.

Nate was jarred out of his sleep by the roar of six guns. He did not move for fear of being shot. Bullets were flying all directions. One grazed his head and for a few minutes he was out. There was a good deal of blood on the ground where he bled. Then it was silent. He closed his eyes and kept very still. Boots moved over loose gravel as quietly as possible.

"Did we get all of them?"

"These three are dead, and the one under the wagon isn't moving at all. Looks like he got shot in the head. That one under the wagon is the lawman! This is how he managed to kill all of our partners. They had four guns, and they ambushed them. Ol' Bert said that they had a trap set for them and gunned them down."

"You mean that these men were part of his posse? Why is he tied up?"

"I don't know, unless maybe they had a falling out. And I don't know if this is all of his posse, but Red...I mean Mitch, I forgot that Red is dead, will be happy that we plugged these. Sure serves them right for shooting all of our partners down at the camp."

"Do we wait for Mitch? What should we do with this wagon and the horses?"

"I say that we go find Mitch and leave the wagon and horses right where they are. They aren't going anywhere, and we can move a lot faster on horseback."

Nate was shocked at the name he heard, Mitch! That was the other cowboy who was driving cattle when he got Red to help him. That proved to him that the cattle were stolen. Who would have thought about looking for stolen cattle in towns and on the main road.

Nate listened to them argue some more as they mounted their horses and rode away. He waited for some time before rolling over and looking around. The three cowboys, that had "captured" him and tied him up, lay on the ground dead. The shooters thought they had killed lawmen and instead had killed innocent ranch hands. Now Nate had to figure out how to get untied and get out of there.

Nate finally worked his way over to one of the dead cowboys. One of the cowboy's spurs was turned up at an angle. The angle was just right so that Nate could saw on the ropes around his wrist. The good cowboys had tied his hands in front of him. Not like at the line-shack. He managed to cut the ropes and then untie his feet. He could not believe his good fortune. Neither the ranch-hands who "captured" him first, nor the outlaws who had killed his captors, had looked in the wagon for weapons. His shotgun was out of sight, but a good search would have found it. He checked the gun and shook his head and muttered to himself, "Time to get out of here".

In record time he had retrieved his stock and had them hitched to the wagon. He was on his way, even if it was late in the day to be starting. He had to get some distance away from those three innocent cowboys. He pushed hard all the rest of the afternoon. He thought about those poor cowboys who had died over a mistake. They thought he was a rustler, and the rustlers thought he was a lawman. Regardless of what anyone thought of him, he could not forget the words that one of the rustlers said, "We have heard all about you and your double-barrel shotgun!"

Nate and the horses struggled 'till almost sundown to make as much headway as possible. That wasn't much. They had moved a couple of miles in the rough terrain and needed a good shelter for the night. He could not afford any more trouble with rustlers or cowboys. His time was precious, and the brats were getting further and further ahead of him.

He found an ideal spot off the trail some hundred yards. He had seen the trees off to the side and worked his way over to them. He was only a couple of hundred yards from the top of the caprock. He started to go up on top, but he did not want to be in the open tonight.

Camp was made and a hot meal cooking when he heard a voice call, "Hello, the camp. Hello, the camp" He had not heard horses or hooves, yet someone had sneaked up close enough to call to him. Casually he moved over to stand in the shadow of the wagon and out of the fire-light. "Hello, out there. Who are you?"

"I'm from the "Box W" Ranch. Mr. Wilson, sent me to find you."

"How do I know that you are from the ranch?" Nate asked, as he slowly picked up his shotgun. It had been leaning against the front of the wagon. He didn't think that the caller could see him pick it up in the dark. "Come on in, with your hands out to your sides."

"I'm unarmed." A figure came out of the dark. He had his hands out to the side and did not have a gun.

"Come on in closer, stranger." Nate had the shotgun aimed at the man's chest.

"Thanks, your coffee sure smells good."

Nate reached in the wagon and brought out an extra cup. He pitched it to the man. The man almost missed the cup, as Nate had pitched it out of the shadow. "Pour the coffee and you can explain what is going on, and why you are here."

"Sure been a lot of shooting back down the trail," commented the stranger.

Nate said nothing, just kept the shotgun on the man.

"Mind if I squat on the ground?" The rider asked. He eased himself down.

Nate did not have time to answer before the cowboy continued.

"Mr. Wilson and a bunch of his riders came back to where you were camped. You were gone, and three of our hands were dead. We knew you didn't do the shooting. All three of our boys had been shot with hand guns, not that cannon you are holding. We figured that maybe, just maybe, the rustlers had come back, and there was a gunfight. Or, maybe you had gotten away, and then there was a still a gunfight. Whichever, you were gone, and the boys were dead. Mr. Wilson is taking them back to the ranchhouse."

Nate continued to stand in the dark and listen to the "Box W" rider.

"Mr. Wilson sent me to find you and let you know what is happening. I would like to spend the night with you, and then Mr. Wilson and his crew will be here sometime in the morning."

Nate spoke for the first time, "Can you give me some information that will make me believe you?"

The stranger rubbed his jaw, "Well, a couple of things that the rustlers would not know. You spent some time at the ranch. You were shot and beaten by some varmints at a line shack. Then, you spent one night with a cowboy called Curley, and he told you about the runaways. Then you told him about the shootout that you had with the rustlers. Am I correct so far?"

Nate studied him for a few minutes and then said, "Go back out there and get your horse and bring him in. Be sure your gunbelt and gun are hanging off the saddlehorn. Understand?"

The rider nodded his head and answered, "Right" and retreated into the dark. Nate changed positions from in the shadow of the wagon to standing in the shadow of some rocks. Shortly the man came walking back in with his hands in the air, his gunbelt was over the saddlehorn and the gun in the holster.

"Satisfied?"

"Maybe, move away from the horse." Nate waited until the rider was several steps back. Then he moved into the firelight, took the holster from the saddle and put it in the wagon.

"Sit, pour some more coffee, and you can convince me some more that you are on the level."

"Well, what if I told you that Mr. Wilson almost busted his gut when the rider told him that they had captured you? Mr. Wilson allowed that they were fools, and that they were holding Mr. Nate"

That was the clincher. The only people that had called him Mr. Nate were the ranch owner, Mr. Wilson, the doctor and the widow woman. There was one other possibility, that this man worked for both the rustlers and the "Box W" , and there probably wasn't a way to know until the ranch owner showed.

Nate, for the first time, asked a question, "How long have you worked for the 'Box W'?"

"I've been with the ranch since it first started. The owner, Mr. Wilson, is my-brother-in-law. His wife is my sister, and I'm the ramrod on the spread."

Nate had to work to keep his mouth from falling open. This was the next in command at the ranch. When he spoke, he spoke for the owner.

The ramrod spoke again, "Actually, the ranch is owned by my brother-in-law, my sister and by me. It is a three way split. For the benefit of the riders and hands, my brother-in-law is the man."

Nate walked over to the wagon and placed the double-barrel over behind the dash board. Then Nate picked up the ramrod's gun and handed it to him.

"Guess that removed any doubt in my mind. Sorry about the shotgun." "Look, out here you can't be too careful. You have been through a heap of trouble since you hit this country."

"You can say that again!"

"Mr. Nate, can I call you Mr. Nate?"

"Yes."

"How many men have died, not of your actions, but where you were involved?"

"I haven't counted them. I don't want to remember the deaths!"

"That's the difference in you and a killer. Most killers will cut notches in the gun handle or carve numbers on a board. Some nonsense about keeping a score. These men are very dangerous."

The fire had burned down until it was almost gone. The stars were out, and a full moon was shining. The caprock was large and dark just to the west of them. The camp was pitched right against the cliff.

"Much farther to the top by the road?" Nate asked motioning at the cliff.

"About two hundred yards up the road, that is after you get back to the trail."

"With the bright moon, could we walk up there?"

"Sure, would be a pleasant walk. Except that I have on cowboy boots, and they are not made for walking."

"Many snakes in these bluffs and cliffs?"

"Many, many, but they don't want to be around a human. You can smell their dens if you get close. If they are given any chance, they will crawl away. The only dangerous ones are the ones cornered or mad."

Nate shivered. The snakes at home scared him. The only time he went to Snake Hill was early in the morning when it was cool, and the snakes were sluggish. He had killed a lot, but he was horrified of them. Guess Glen got that from him. He remembered Glen getting scared by a snake in the barn and messing his clothes. Glen was almost a grown man. Wonder what happened to him?

He stopped his reverie and looked at the ramrod, "Been snake bit?"

"Not in all of these years. But, I'm real careful. Usually, keep a dog with me. Rode off this morning without him. Dumb stunt, 'cause in this country there are plenty of rattlers."

The horses heads came up, and their ears turned toward the trail.

"Riders!" exclaimed the ramrod. He kicked out the rest of the fire.

He and Nate were on their feet and listening to the horses. The ramrod spoke, "They are going up the road to the top. Sounds like about five horses. They aren't pushing hard, but will cover a lot of ground by morning, or until the moon goes down." He pointed into the moonlight, "There they go. They will be up on the prairie in a few minutes." Both men moved toward the trail.

The horse's hooves made a lot of noise on the rocky trail. You could hear them in the quiet night for a mile or more. When they went over the top and hit soil, their hoofbeats completely disappeared. They listened for a few minutes and then returned to the camp.

"Mr. Nate, I need to ask you a question. I know you said that you didn't like counting, but help me get a count on the dead rustlers. Could you do that?"

Nate sucked in his breath and let it out real slow. "Let me see, there were four the first time. And then, I believe that there were six and then five at the last mess." Nate hung his head and said, "I really don't know, it's all run into a blur, rustlers, squatters and all."

"Well I'll be..... they are pulling out. You broke their backs. We thought that there had to be about twenty in the gang. That was a guess, from the horse tracks and how they were hitting us. Hitting us in two or three places in a night. That group was the last of them. There were only about five, and with what you have killed, that would make about twenty."

Nate didn't have any comment to make on the matter. He sat down rather heavily and then said, "Ramrod, how would you like to build another fire, and I'll make another pot of coffee. I believe that I have some whiskey in the wagon, if it did not get broken when the wagon turned over. We can doctor our coffee and celebrate the passing of outlaws."

"A great idea, Mr. Nate."

The ramrod had a fire going in a few minutes, and Nate put the coffee on. Nate then hunted the bottle of whiskey and poured some in the tin coffee cups. "Might as well be enjoying the whiskey, while we wait on the coffee."

The fire went out, but the two men did not notice. They consumed the bottle of whiskey and forgot the coffee. By the time the bottle was empty, they both were very drunk.

They laughed and saluted all dead rustlers. "May all dead rustlers rest in a fire of brimstone." Then they saluted the live ones, with the hope of them soon joining their partners in the grave. "Here is to the rest of the rustlers. Hit the fast rail to Hades to be with your partners."

"Mr. Nate, you are better than all the law in the county. Why, they had been, or so they said, trying to catch that gang for two or three years. Let me tell you, that gang would work us awhile and then move to one of the other ranches and so on. But the sheriff, bless his little heart, could not catch them. His problem was, he stays in the countyseat and only sees you when he comes around at election time." The ramrod's words were slurred, but Nate did not notice, because he sounded just like the ramrod. DRUNK.

"I think I met your sheriff. Seemed a bit on the lazy side." Nate was having a hard time sitting up straight, much less standing.

"Lazy did you say? Why he can hardly get up the energy to swat a fly." The ramrod made a swatting motion with his hand.

Nate remembered something he wanted to tell the ramrod. "Ramrod, I know how the cattle here are disappearing."

"The blazes you do!"

"Mr. Ramrod, they were driving them up on the caprock, as you call it, and then they would go south. They went down to a place called the......now let's see what was that place..... oh, I remember, it was the Bid Spring.... No I mean the Big Spring..!" With that declaration he fell over on the ground and passed out.

The ramrod looked at Nate and shook his head, "Some folks just can't hold their liquor." He tried to get up, but instead he fell back down, looked all around and passed out. The two never saw or knew that a mother skunk and a whole string of baby skunks came into the camp.... sniffed around and left.

When the sun came up the next morning both men paid no attention to it. They slept until almost noon. They both had slept on the ground and were sore and bruised. They slowly came to life and barely moved.

"Oh, my, head, " groaned Nate. "My head is splitting!"

The ramrod said, "I haven't done that in years. I'm not used to the hard stuff. I'm going to be sick." He jumped up, ran in the brush, and Nate could hear him.

Nate did not get sick. He figured that he had more body to soak up the whiskey, so it didn't hurt him quite so bad. He finally made coffee, and it was ready when the ramrod came back. In fact Nate had had two cups before the ramrod got back. They sat on the ground and sipped coffee till past noon. On about the third pot, and a number of trips to the brush for various reasons, they began to feel better.

Nate suggested that a swim would do them both good. The ramrod agreed, and they went down to the little pond, made by the spring, for that dip. They walked up to the pond, shed their boots and just walked in. "Might as well wash my clothes," commented the ramrod. Later they shed their clothes and soaked in the water. The ramrod could lay on his back, and the water would cover him, but Nate was just too big around. The water washed away the dirt and restored them to normal.

While their clothes dried on some bushes and they had a long soak, they talked some more about this and that. Finally, the conversation got around to women.

"You married , Mr. Nate?"

"Yes. How about you, ramrod?"

"Nope, but I got my eye on a real pretty widow at the ranch, and I believe she will agree to marriage by the Fourth of July celebration."

Nate almost drowned in that shallow pond. That pretty little woman was the ramrod's woman. Nate had been making eyes at her, and she had been making eyes back at him. Oh, Lordy!

When they returned to the wagon, they prepared a meal fit for a king. There was no liquor for a celebration, so they just enjoyed the good food.

The ramrod stood up and listened, "Horses." Then he pointed, "There on the trail." The riders came into sight, and disappeared down in a ravine and then reappeared. They drew closer, and the ramrod noted, "That's the men from the ranch." He and Nate hastily put on their clothes.

The ramrod threw his saddle on his pony and rode out to meet the cowboys. In a few minutes he returned with the crew from the ranch. They arrived in a cloud of dust and snorting horses.

Mr. Wilson stepped down off his pony and said, "Well, Mr. Nate, we meet again." He extended his hand to Nate. "Put her there!"

Nate shook hands with Mr. Wilson and then all of the cowboys. After the introductions were over the ramrod said, "Nate, would you make a fresh pot of coffee, and let me tell these boys what has happened?" Nate started the coffee, and all of the hands got their cups from their saddle-bags. As soon as the coffee was ready, and they had a cup, the ramrod said, "Now boys, I want you to hold on to your hats. The rustlers are gone from this range. Mr. Nate has driven them out. Single handed he drove them out! Not only are they all gone, but Mr. Nate found out how they were getting rid of the stolen cattle. Boss, you and I should look into that little piece of information."

They all looked at him in astonishment and with mouths hanging open. "Ramrod, how do you know this?" asked, Mr. Wilson.

"Last night, must have been mid-night or later, four or five riders went up the trail to the top of the caprock. Now, no one rides open range at night unless it is an emergency, and you sure don't ride that trail at night. That is, unless you are a rustler and want to get out of the country without being seen."

"That did not wipe them out or mean that they are leaving the range. Four or five of those rustlers going someplace is just a sign they are up to no good."

"But, that's not all. Mr. Nate and that double-barrel shotgun have put about fourteen or fifteen of those rustlers out of their misery. Plus, you must take into consideration that we know of at least ten we have buried. And those were not cowboys, at least we did not know them. Right?"

Silence only followed that statement. You could see the bewilderment on the faces of all the riders. Finally Mr. Wilson spoke up, "Mr. Nate, I would like to shake your hand again." So did all of the hands.

"I can't believe that we might not lose hands and cattle in the future."

"Well, for the near future, the rustlers are gone. At least sure thinned out," replied the ramrod.

"Mr. Nate, are you set on going out on the Llano Estacado tomorrow?"

"Yes, I am."

"Do you really think you will find those kids?"

"I need to try."

"Then, let me tell you what little we know about the Llano Estacado. It means fence, I believe, and it is as flat as a table top for hundreds of miles . We have been told that at high noon , you could ride in a circle, and loose all sense of direction. You would not know what had happened until the sun started to settle. Also, we have been told that there are no landmarks to go by. You are just out on a sea of grass with not one object to take a bearing on. Then there are Indians. Some are friendly, but it will only take one bunch of renegades to make it a bad day. We hear that there are outlaws, not rustlers, out there. Outlaws are a different breed. I don't like rustlers, but I would put up with them a lot quicker than I would an outlaw. A rustler has some code of honor, but not an outlaw. One more thing, I think that this river, or it's tributaries, goes all the way to the New Mexico Territory. You just have to find the right branches and take the right turns. I haven't talked that much in the last two months, but I needed to tell you what you're getting into. The bad part is, if those kids have gone out on the Llano, they are probably dead by now or worse."

Mr. Wilson stood, and without further ceremony or speech he mounted his horse. "O.K. if my two line riders stay here with you, Mr. Nate? The rest of us will ride for the headquarters, and we can be there by dark. I am indebted to you, Mr. Nate. If you decide that you want to come back and help with this place, that offer I made the other day stands." With a salute to his hat brim, he wheeled his horse and led the riders of the "Box W" south.

The ramrod remained for a few moments more. "If you come through this country again, you have always got a bunk at the ranch." He mounted his horse and was gone in a cloud of dust.

Evening settled over the badlands east of the caprock. The shadows stretched across the hills and ravines. It would get dark at the camp sooner than on the flats, since they had camped up against the bluff. Nate did the cooking, and the two line riders hardly said a word. Just ate and tended to their horses. As it became totally dark, Nate told the two line riders, "I'm going to walk down to the trail and then up on the caprock. I have on walking boots and would like to see where I am going tomorrow." The cowboys just nodded and squatted at the campfire with their coffee.

It took Nate the better part of an hour to walk back to the trail and then to climb the last two hundred yards up to the top of the caprock. One thing became very clear, that it was flat. He could not really believe it was as flat as was pictured, but it appeared that way.

There was lightning down on the western horizon. It was angry and mean looking. As he watched the lightning increased, and he could tell that the clouds were coming closer and closer. The clouds and the storm appeared to be miles away, but it was hard to tell in the dark with no conception of distance. He knew that they were in for a blow and rain.

It took another hour in the dark to returned to the camp. Nate was going to tell the two cowboys about the storm, but they were asleep and dead to the world. He lighted a lantern and rearranged the wagon so he could sleep inside. No need to get wet when you can sleep in the dry. He double checked the hobbles on the horses. He had tied two to the front of the wagon and two at the rear.

By the time he had done these few chores, and picked up his coffee pot, poured out the contents and tossed it into the wagon, the storm was close enough that he could hear the thunder.

He was asleep when the wind finally hit. It rocked the wagon and jerked on the canvas. He heard the cowboys move under the wagon to take shelter. The weather deteriorated rapidly and rain began to hit the canvas top. If there had been room in the wagon, he would have called the two cowboys. There was barely room for fat Nate and his supplies. The rain came harder and harder. He had never heard rain and wind like this. It came in torrents and sheets.

When Nate got up the courage to look out of the rear of the wagon, water was running under the wagon a foot deep. The wagon was on a flat, level area and not in a ravine. The sound of the rain and the wind drowned out his voice when he called the two line-riders. Either they could not hear him, or they had moved and taken shelter against the bluffs. The rain came so hard, that he could not see the two cowboy's horses tied to some trees, only ten yards away.

Just when Nate thought the storm must be at it's peak, all hell broke loose. The wind screeched and the rain became horizontal. Rain turned to hail. The hail turned from pea size to marble size and then to quarter size. Holes started to come in the canvas cover on the wagon. Nate pulled the two saddles over him and then his extra wagon canvas, for protection. He could feel the beating of the hailstones. The storm went on and on, with the wind increasing. The roar and the pitch of the wind went up another pitch, and then Nate knew that he was in, or on the edge of, a tornado.

The canvas top ripped apart and was gone. If it had stayed on, the wagon would have turned over. Rain poured into the wagon, soaking Nate and some of his supplies. Water was the last thing he was worried about. If that tornado touched down there, he was a goner, wagon and all.

Then, there was a great roar from over toward the bluff. Just one roar, and then only the storm and it's fury. The flashing lightning did not reveal what had happened or the cause of the roar. The lightning did show that water was standing under the wagon more than a foot and a half deep. The next flash of lightning revealed that the horses were still tied to the wagon.

Nate started to get out of the wagon, then decided that he had more protection under the two saddles and the other canvas than he would have out of the wagon. Hail filled parts of the wagon and began to melt. The first thought that crossed Nate's mind was, "Is all of the loot water-proofed and protected?" There was nothing he could do but ride the storm out and hope for the best.

Just as suddenly as the storm had roared in, it quit. The only sound was running water. Nate called to the two line riders to no avail. That really puzzled him. Where had they gone? He thought about getting out of the wagon, but all he was going to do was step into two feet of water. He just sat in the wagon, wet, bruised by hail stones and getting cold. The temperature had dropped with the hail, and now he was freezing. No way to build a fire with the ground covered solid with hail stones and water.

The water ran off very fast. Up against the bluff, the land fell away rapidly and the water receded in an hour. Nate considered getting out again, and then came to the conclusion that until the sun came up, he would stay put. He could not even light his lantern. The lantern had turned over, and what little oil he had spilled out and was washed away by the rain. The lantern was useless and much of his supplies were probably ruined and soaked.

Little by little the sky lightened, and a new day was heralded. Birds were singing in the vegetation, and other animals called and moved about. Nate had dozed and awakened with a start. It was light, and he could see to get out of the wagon. He stood up and stretched to relieve his aches and pains. What was that sound, that…buzzing? He thought he had heard that sound before, but that buzzing. His heart lurched and beat faster! RATTLESNAKES! There were RATTLESNAKES out there! That was what was making that buzzing!

Fear gripped him, and panic almost caused him to jump from the wagon and run. Just as he was about to get out of the wagon, he looked down. The ground was covered with snakes. Not just a few, but dozens and dozens. He was horrified. He was trapped. He couldn't get out of the wagon. They were all over the ground.

He realized that the two horses at the rear of the wagon were down. They had been bitten by no telling how many snakes. He cut their tie ropes and moved to the front of the wagon. Looking down he found he could get out of the front of the wagon. Why weren't there snakes at the front? The question whirled in his head. It didn't matter, he could get out of the wagon. The two horses on the front had pulled back as far as their ropes would allow, and they were stomping the ground. Their eyes were wild and crazy, but no snakes were close to them, yet. They were the reason that there were no snakes under the front of the wagon. They were pulling the wagon, a little at a time away from the snakes. They would jerk together, and the wagon would roll just a little ways. They had probably saved Nate's life.

Nate got out of the wagon and hooked the two horses up short. He tied the tie ropes to the end tongue and pulled the wagon down the slope. They went half-way to the trail, and then he stopped to hitch the animals properly. While he was hitching the team, he kept looking for the line riders. Then an object up at the base of the cliff caught his eye. It was a horse's head, sticking out from under tons of rock and dirt. He stood very still and solemn.

The two cowboys and their horses were buried under tons of rock and dirt. They had sought shelter from the rain, and the cliffs had collapsed on them. They had been buried alive. Nate paused. That is where the snakes had come from, out of the cliffs. There had been snake dens in the rock and crevasses, and with the collapse of the face, the dens had been opened up.

He turned away and moved his team and wagon toward the river. He would find a place and dry out his bedding, clothes and supplies. He hoped that his supplies were not too badly damaged. The other things would dry, but supplies, if ruined, would need to be thrown away.

His heart was heavy. He had seen five cowboys, innocent cowboys, die because of him. The dead rustlers and squatters did not bother him, but this….. just for nothing. This range was hard and men died, but to have seen two dozen die in the past few weeks had changed Nate. To see outlaws and murderers die was one thing, but innocent people. That was something else. He knew that when he left home he could not have killed even a rustler and now he had the blood of several men on his hands.

By noon most all of his belongings were dry, and he had the second canvas over the hoops of the wagon. He started reloading his supplies. To his surprise very little was destroyed. Most items were in waterproof bags or containers, and he was still in good condition. All of his loot in the false bottom was completely dry. The oilskin wrappers had protected the guns and the money. The boots had gotten some water on them, and he might have to throw them away, but at a later date. The only thing that got wet was the shotgun. It had been wrapped in just a blanket, and the water had soaked through. He cleaned the shotgun very carefully. His gun had saved his hide several times.

He had a hot meal of just biscuits and gravy. It was easy to fix, and he was not in the mood to spend much time on a meal. He wanted to get to the top of the caprock. When he got underway, he found himself at a fork in the trail. He was on a crest below the caprock. The left trail went, or so it appeared, up on the cap. The right trail went down a slope and back to the riverbed. The two paths were very dim. Which way to go? To the left looked really hard for a team and a wagon to climb. To the right, it seemed to be just some more of the same terrain he had been crossing. He chose the left trail. It would put him on top and maybe ahead of the brats.

The two horses struggled and strained in an attempt to pull the wagon to the top of the caprock. Two horses were not enough to pull the heavy wagon and it's load to the top. He finally unloaded half of the equipment and supplies and then went to the top. Even with half a load, it was difficult and took hours. He returned to the stash of supplies and loaded the other half. After hours more of hard work, the horses topped the caprock and the balance of his belongings were secure at the top. No wonder, he had to unload half of his equipment. That trail was rugged and steep. Now he knew why the rustlers liked that trail. Few people on horseback would follow them and none, but a fool like him, with a wagon.

He hobbled the horses and used a long tie rope on each. He had stopped the wagon about one hundred yards off the trail. There was lots of grass, and he had water for them. He was too tired to think of much. Supper consisted of two cold biscuits and a can of fruit.

Night approached, and the night creatures were coming out. Nat had his cold supper, and watched the stars and the moon. He looked west and saw only open space. He wondered what lay ahead on this sea of grass. For the first time in days he thought about the near thirty-five thousand dollars in the bank at home. He thought of how he could keep it all. He never thought about Pettie and the kids.

He rolled into his bedroll and started planning how he would invest that money. Investments enough to keep him in the style he desired. To live the life of leisure and comfort. But, first he had to get those BRATS!

CHAPTER NINE

During breakfast the next morning, Minnie, Lizzie and I discussed what we would find on top of the bluff. We did not have any options. We had to go up the trail to get to the top of the bluff, and that's where the rustlers and the herd had gone.

We broke camp and loaded Old Number One. Mounting the other two mules, we started up the last part of the trail before reaching the top. With our eyes pealed for any unusual activities along the trail or off to the side, we rode toward the bluff.

After about two hours of winding trail going over ridges and down into ravines, we were perhaps a couple hundred yards from the top. Off to the right was a stand of trees.

"Minnie, let's ride over to that clump of trees. I think we will find water there, and we can rest for a few minutes before going out on top."

"Good idea, Robert. That will give us a chance to watch and see if anybody is following us or just coming up the trail."

We rode over to the clump and found that not only was there a grove of trees, but there was a spring and a small pond of water. This morning with the sun against the bluff, we had seen several bright and glistening wet streaks running down the face of the cliffs. Water and springs were in abundance all along the face of the cliffs. Dismounting, we scouted out the area. This spot had been used by campers many times. There was evidence of several campfires. I found an empty whiskey bottle.

"Hey, Minnie look, somebody was drinking here. Or they threw out this bottle when they came by. Probably have been lots of people come this way."

"Good campsite and a real good place to watch the country down below," commented Minnie.

You could see for miles to the east. This morning nothing moved or caught our attention in the vast area we could observe. A few hawks circled high in the sky and caught updrafts, when they could find one. This afternoon, when it is hot, the hawks could soar and soar, using the updrafts from the hot badlands below us.

I turned and looked up at the last little distance we had to go to reach the top. "Minnie, I think that I should walk up the trail to the top and see what is up there."

She turned and looked up the face of the cliff, "Sure doesn't look very hard from here to the top."

As we searched the trail together, she frowned and said, "You found that bottle, and this is a bottleneck for travel from all over this place. This is not much of a road, but it may be about the only way for a wagon. There may be other trails for horses, but no road of any kind."

"That's why I think I should take a look and see if there is anything coming our way. If there is, I could hide in the rocks and brush. Let's not fall into some strange hands."

"All right, Robert. You go take a look. If you don't see anything you wave, and Lizzie and I will come and join you. We want to see also."

"If I don't see anything, I'll wave, and you can come up with the mules. You could be on top in half an hour at most. No need for all of us to walk up there and then have to walk back to get the mules."

"O.K., but Robert, I can't impress on you or tell you how important it is to be careful. Don't let anybody see you."

I turned, whistled for Ol' Bullet and trotted off, calling back, "Sure!"

It did not take me long to reach the top. Climbing the last few yards, I got a surprise. It was not the top of the bluff. It was just a crest set against the bluff and looked like the top. We had followed the trail, thinking that it went up and over the top. Instead the trail sloped back down to the river and ran off in the distance. Standing there I could see miles to the northwest. There wasn't a thing to see, not a moving thing. My shoulders dropped in disappointment. We thought we were at the top of the bluff.

I turned and waved at the girls. I saw Minnie lead a mule around to a rock so Lizzie could mount. Then Minnie handed Lizzie a lead rope for Number One. Minnie mounted and led the extra mule. I watched the trail and their progress as they wound their way up the last yards.

"My, goodness, Robert, there is nothing up here. This is not the top of the bluff. There is nothing but more hills and ravines!" Minnie exclaimed, upon arriving at the top.

"You're right, Minnie. You can't see anything but more of the same."

"You mean we are not at the top of the bluff?" Minnie inquired.

I pointed up and said, "The bluff rises another hundred yards above us here. There may be a way up there, but I can't see any real trail. No, we just have topped this crest. The trail followed the bluff and came up to this point. From down below it looked like it went right on up on top. We are not there yet."

When they came to a stop at the crest, I mounted Number Four and took the lead rope for Number One, not that he needed one.

"Robert, it looks like this trail divides." She pointed at the ground. "This looks like a trail does go to the left, and it may go up to the top"

"But Minnie, the worn trail goes to the right and along with the river. Don't you think we had better stay with the river?"

"Yes, we'd best go that way."

We turned the mules to look at what we had covered. Our view stretched out over the bad lands It was hard to believe that we had crossed such bad country. There were some little plumes of dust here and there, but we could not tell what caused them. Other than the dust, we could not see any movement.

"Sure looks peaceful," commented Minnie, shielding her eyes against the sun in the east.

"It does now, but we know that at times there is trouble out there. For example, I wonder what all the shooting we heard the other day was all about?"

"That is none of our business and best left alone." said Minnie. Sounded just like Mama.

"Minnie, look right down there. Down the face of the bluff. Can you see the head of a horse sticking out from under the dirt?"

"Oh, how horrible!"

I shouted at Lizzie, "Don't look, just keep looking up the trail." Of course she didn't mind.

She squealed, "Oh, that poor horse!"

Minnie called to her, "He didn't suffer. The cliff caved off and killed him instantly."

"Let's get started and get away from this place and, what did you call it….a bottle neck?" The girls murmured their ascent.

We rode down the slope and back toward the riverbed. Travel was some easier. The ravines were not cut quite so deep, and the razorback ridges were disappearing. The sun rode high in the sky when we stopped for our noon meal. The temperature right against the rock bluffs was making us suffer. We had not taken any rest stop since leaving the crest by the bluff. Going down into the riverbed and finding some good shade was the best thing that happened to us that day.

Minnie spread out a canvas in the shade of some overhanging trees. The sandy riverbed was soft, and the gurgling water made the site very pleasant. We had cold biscuits and antelope meat for lunch and then rested in the shade for some time.

"Robert," spoke up Minnie, "Do you think if we rest a little longer at noon and then ride until sunset, we will cover more miles?"

"Minnie, we should take our long rest in the hottest part of the day. Let me explain. We ride until noon, stop and take a short rest. Then ride until about three o'clock, by your watch, and then find shade and rest until the heat breaks. We could eat a little and get a good rest at that time. Mount back up at about six or so and ride until sunset. We would have plenty of light from sunset until dark to make camp and get a hot meal."

"You know, Robert," said Minnie, with her hands on her hips. "Sometimes you talk a blue streak. But I will give you credit, you sometimes have got a good idea."

She got up and started clearing the camp. "Well, what are you two doing? Going to sit there all day? Let's move and see how far we can go!"

The trail was easy to pick back up. By following the game trail, the going was easier. Up ravines and down washes was the order of the day, just like so many before. After a while the up and down almost put you to sleep. The buzzing of the insects in the bushes lulled us more. I found myself dosing and nodding. Lucky I didn't fall off the mule.

The day progressed without event, other than the long break at about three and back on the mules at about six. We rode until the sun set behind the bluff. Returning to the riverbed, we found a campsite that had been visited many times. We worried about camping there, but with Ol" Bullet to do the warning, we felt fairly safe.

Minnie ordered me to go fishing. I first hobbled the mules and tied them out on the grass. I had started tying them every night after losing Number Two. The river had narrowed down to a stream and was about three feet deep. To my surprise the fishing was even better in the clear running water.

She had a fire going and was making biscuits and gravy to go with the fish. I cleaned them and then set lines to catch breakfast. Like always, Minnie sure could turn nothing into a good meal. Of course, having flour, baking soda and salt did not hurt the cooking.

We were up at daylight, and sunup we would be on the move. By the time Minnie had breakfast ready, I had packed all the other gear and had brought the mules up to the campsite. We finished our meal, and Minnie packed up quick. She had cooked extra, and we would have that for lunch. Shortly after breakfast, we rode up out of the riverbed to continue our trek northwest.

The sun broke over the eastern horizon, and sunlight filled the valley. All around us, birds were singing and doves cooing. You could hear the quail calling from down the river. This was always the best part of the day. It was cool and fresh smelling.

"Girls, look," I pointed to the north. "Is that the bluff over there?"

They both looked in the direction I was pointing. "That looks like the bluff is in front of us as well as on our left. Do you suppose we will have to go to the east and around that bluff?"

Minnie chimed up, "Maybe that is something else, just a rise back in there."

As we rode, we all kept looking at the ridge in the distance. The ridge began to stretch from the east to the west.

"Robert, that is looking more like the bluff on our left. Do you think that they are connected somewhere up ahead?"

"We should be able to tell by evening."

We took a short rest at lunch and then continued toward the barrier that lay in front of us to the north. Three o'clock came, and we returned to the riverbed to find shade. The weather was getting hotter and there was no breeze. The two bluffs were closing in on us and the heat was stifling. We continued to parallel the one on the left, but the north one was beginning to crowd us in, on the right. We felt that we were in between the two bluffs.

At six o'clock we were back on the trail. We were getting closer to the bluffs with every hour. The mystery of our situation would soon be resolved, one way or another. The discovery was made at noon that the river had narrowed some. At the afternoon break, we noticed that the river had narrowed some more. It became apparent that we were in a valley between the two bluffs. The only question in our minds was, "Are the two bluffs connected?"

By sundown the valley walls were not more than two or three miles on each side of us, and they were closing in.

"I guess, we just keep going on up the valley. This river comes from that direction. It must come off the top off the bluffs. If it does, maybe we can find a way up to the top of the bluff," I observed.

Minnie replied, "Look, this trail is very visible now, and there must a way up to the top. Lots of animals and people have used this trail."

"Yeah, and I hope we don't meet some animal on the trail, two legged or four legged!"

The sun was almost to the western horizon when we heard the ringing of a bell. We got off the trail and found a place to hide. Presently an old man came down the trail leading a burro. There was a rope going from the burro to a big billy goat. The goat had a bell around it's neck that rang with every motion of the goat's head. A small herd of goats followed behind.

Just when we thought he was going to pass us, his dog began to bark and ran up toward our hiding place. The little old man turned and called, "If there is someone hiding in the rocks, please come out. I can't hurt you. I do not have a gun or a rifle, so I'm harmless. Please come out."

We rode forward and approached him.

"Why you are a bunch of children!" he exclaimed, his eyes wide open. "What are you doing way out here in the wilderness?"

He approached us and then exclaimed, "A boy and two girls! My eyes deceive me! Bless my soul. What are you children doing out here?"

When we got to him, he smiled and said, "Please, don't be afraid. Some people think I am crazy, wandering around out here with some goats and a burro. But, what they don't know is that I go all the way to the mountains, and sometimes I find gold."

The two dogs ran up to each other and circled, smelling. And then with tails wagging they trotted off down the trail. The old man said, "There is a good camping place right back up there. Let's all go there, and you can tell me your story. I'm sure you have one."

We finally found our tongues, and had the courtesy to say, "Hello".

He smiled and said, "See, I knew you were girls, but from a distance you sure looked like boys. That is a good disguise!" He helped with the pitching of camp and added some seasoning to the stew Minnie made from the antelope meat.

While Minnie was fixing dinner, Ol' Bullet took it upon himself to go hunting with the other dog. The two dogs came trotting back with a "Chicken" each. I jumped up and went over to Ol' Bullet, and he gave me the "Chicken". The other dog trotted up to the old man a laid the "Chicken" at his feet.

"Good, I see you have trained your dog to hunt prairie chickens."

"What kind of chicken?" I asked.

"Prairie chickens. They are smaller than a barn yard bird, but they taste just like them to me."

"We have had them several times and thought that they were chickens that had runaway from somebody's farm."

"Oh, no. they are all over this rough country and up on the caprock. You will also see a big bird up on the caprock that is called a pheasant. Really good eating. I have only had one a few times. With no gun, I only get to eat one when I am invited to a meal. But, my old dog and I have prairie chicken very regular."

I was elected to clean the two birds. After dinner Minnie cooked them on the spit. We would share our antelope with the old man, and he would have one bird.

After the evening meal he asked, "What are you doing here?"

We finally told him our story, all the way back to Mama's and Papa's deaths. He listen intently and with a sympathetic ear. We even told him we were going to New Mexico Territory.

His eyes got big, and he sputtered, "Territory of New Mexico?"

"Yes, we have an uncle there who will take us in and give us a home." replied Minnie.

"But, all the way to New Mexico Territory across the Llano Estacado?"

"What's that?" I said, full of curiosity.

"That is the prairie that you are about to come to."

"When will we get to this Llano Estacado?" I asked.

"Why, tomorrow. It is only about three or four miles up the trail. It is also on the top of the caprock that surrounds you. This trail will take you up on the caprock."

"What is a caprock?" asked Lizzie.

"Well, my young lady, that is the rock that is the top of these hills. The only thing is that all of the hills are the same height, and there is a flat rock resting on all of those hills."

Minnie spoke up again, "Will you tell us about this Llano Estacado?"

"The Llano Estacado is huge. It goes for hundreds of miles north and south and a couple of hundred miles east and west. It is covered in grass. People get lost all the time on the prairie and starve to death. They just wander around and around. The words mean picket fence. I don't know why they call it that, but they do."

"Do you know the way to New Mexico, Mister?" asked Lizzie.

"No, little lady I don't. I've never been very far out on the grassland. I stay here along the east side and travel north and south. I go all the way from the mountains in Colorado to the mountains in Mexico. If I follow the cap to the north, it will bring me to a place where I can see the mountains of northern New Mexico Territory. Then I go through them to Colorado."

"Our Papa told us we could follow this river all the way to the Territory of New Mexico," I inserted.

"It might go all the way. I just don't know. I hope your Papa is right, because if it doesn't you can get lost out there."

"Papa told us to keep to the left-hand forks, and that it would eventually take us to New Mexico."

"That could work, I just can't help you." replied the old man, with a shake of his head.

"We have come this far, we can make the rest," I said with pride.

Minnie broke in and said, "We have come, I would guess a hundred miles, with all of the wandering around and getting lost."

"Well if there are three kids in this world that make it, you are the three!"

I spoke, "Thanks. Mister. We appreciate you thinking that we can make it."

"There is one thing I do know. You are about a day from a fork in the river. That fork is five or six miles after you come out on the prairie. At the fork, the left one goes west, and the other one goes to the north. Where the two forks go I can't tell."

"Thanks for that much help, Mister."

"You're welcome. Let me tell you what else I know about the prairie. It's not much, but maybe it will help you. Stay close to the river, and you will have water. Watch the horizon for riders. There are Indians and out-laws on the Llano. Keep your dog close, he will be of great value. Keep your mules close, the Indians like mule meat. That's about all I know."

Lizzie spoke up and said, "I wish you could go with us to the Territory of New Mexico. Our dogs like each other."

"Little one, I would love to go, I'm headed to Fort Concho at San Angelo. My daughter is married to a soldier boy at the fort. I promised her I would be there by the Fourth of July. If my reckoning is correct, I have about a month to walk two hundred miles. With my bum leg it will take me that long. Sorry."

"That's O.K., Mister. " replied Lizzie.

We kicked out the fire and found our beds. This would be the only night on our trip that we would all sleep with no fear of harm. The next morning with lots of good-byes and see you again, we parted company. The little old man was out of shouting range when it dawned on me; we did not ask him his name. For that matter we had told him a lot, but not our names.

The trail started sloping up, and the valley walls closed in on us. The left bluff or caprock still ran north until it turned to the northwest. The north caprock ran from east to west and then curved to the northwest. The two caprocks were running parallel when we made camp for our lunch.

We traveled on up the climbing trail, headed to the top of the caprock. We didn't tell the old man that we had prepared and eaten all of our prepared food last night and this morning. The antelope was almost gone, after we divided with him, and we had only the one chicken. One small chicken did not go very far with three hungry kids. That bird was gone after we had lunch. We had no meat for supper. There was only one way to have some fresh meat, I would have to use the shotgun and go hunting.

I left Ol'Bullet to guard the girls, and I went hunting. Dumb. I don't know why I didn't use Ol' Bullet. I just got the gun and told Ol' Bullet to stay. Maybe I thought it was better for him to be in camp. I went a good half mile off the trail and shot two "chickens" with two shots. I didn't tell the girls I shot them on the ground. Minnie cleaned the two chickens and started roasting one for dinner. She would roast the other one before we got back on the trail. We would have good hot meals of chicken, biscuits and gravy. I'm starting to not like biscuits and gravy, but it beats going hungry and sure beats MUSH.

While the other bird roasted on the fire, we spread a canvas on the riverbed in the shade of some trees, just like we had done for two weeks now. We took turns sleeping and turning the roasting bird. With the "Chicken" roasted, we packed up and with new energy made our way toward the Llano Estacado.

I estimated that, from the old man's directions, we should be up on the prairie by our three o'clock rest time, but we were not up on the prairie until almost five. We took our rest in the hottest part of the day and then started the last climb to the Llano. We could spend the night at the fork in the river, if everything went according to plan.

We really didn't realize that the valley between the caprock had come to an end. We just rode out onto the prairie and that ended the rough and tumble country. We stopped and looked back down the long valley. We could see all the way back to the crest that we thought was the top of the bluff. With the light slanting against the north caprock, it was very visible. The east wall of the west caprock was in the shadows and was not clear to our vision.

We turned our horses to the west. "Minnie, can you see the trail?"

"Not really. There are two ruts here, but they fade in the tall grass."

"Are we going to have to follow the river bed?"

"No, I think we can ride along out here on the prairie. We will be able to keep the trees and brush along the river in sight."

We nudged our mules and started west. The prairie was endless. The grass waved in great waves, stirred by the breeze.

Minnie pointed toward the river, "See, we can keep the green foliage of the river in sight. When we want to rest or camp, we can go over to the river."

The riding was pleasant and smooth. No hills or ravines, just flat land for miles and miles. The grass stretched so far into the distance, it was hard to determine the horizon. The miles slipped by, and we were covering more every hour than we had ever dreamed of in the bad lands.

Occasionally, some wildlife would catch our attention. We saw rabbits, quail, dove and "chickens" all the time. The mules would kick them out of the grass, and off they would go.

I noted , "This will be good hunting."

Minnie spoiled that idea. "And just who would hear your gunshot and come to investigate? That hunting you did when we stopped could have attracted somebody we don't want to meet."

"Boy, you sure know how to pour water on an idea," I complained.

Not long after we left the rim of the bluff, we saw our first herd of antelope. They were standing right in our path, and when we got close the herd broke and ran. Fleet footed does not do them justice.

"Bet there is not a horse that can keep up with them!"

"They are fast," declared Minnie.

By sunset we were so far out on the prairie that there was grass in all directions. There was no break in the sea of grass or object to be seen. We turned toward the river and found a bend in it. As we descended into the river we found that this was also the fork in the river. It had shade and a campsite, and that was all that mattered at this time of day. The shade was made by a different type tree than we had seen all along the river below. We spread a canvas in the shade on the grass. We had cold "chicken" meat and hot biscuits and gravy for supper.

"We could use some fish. Robert, do you think that there are any in the river?"

I had been looking the river over. The river had changed from a wide meandering, sometimes deep, sometimes shallow river, to a narrow defined stream cutting though the prairie. The grass went all the way down to the water's edge. The banks were sloping, and water ran from bank to bank.

I laughed and said, "I guess there are fish in the river, if they can climb up that bluff and then swim up to here. Papa used to say that there were fish in every river. So, I guess fish are in this one." With those words of wisdom, I added, "But, I think I will go egg hunting." It was better than a Easter Egg hunt. There were "chicken" eggs all over the place. Breakfast would be great tomorrow. Better than great! Fish, eggs, biscuits and gravy.

Dawn found us up and excited about heading west toward Uncle John's. We had no concept of the distance or what lay ahead. Our goal seemed to be near at hand. For one thing the ground was flat, and you could see for miles and miles. Breakfast was all that I had dreamed it would be. We were packed before sunrise and headed west on the west fork.

Travel was a luxury for the first time. No gullies or ravines to negotiate. No hard climbs to get to the top of the next rise. The prairie just rolled on and on, out of sight, tall grass waving in the breeze. We would be to Uncle John's in no time at this rate.

We kept the riverbed in sight by watching for the green vegetation sticking above the banks. The stream wandered some, but we could ride in a fairly straight line, by making some slight turns as the stream meandered around. We were not going due west, we were going northwest all day. At our first rest time, we turned north to the river and found little shade. There was not much of a place to get down to the water. The banks were grassy and sloped too steep. A ten foot stream was running very cold and clear. No mud or sand in the water. I could clearly see fish.

Back on the trail we made exceedingly good time 'till lunch. The terrain was rolling in some places and flat in others. The grass came almost to the belly of the mules. Again we turned north to the river, looking for a clear spot to rest and eat. There was no shade, and the only place to camp was in a bend of the stream on a sand bar. We kept the mules right with us and sat in the shade they made.

All the way up to our afternoon break, we just rode. No break in the horizon or object to see. We understood what the little old man meant about getting lost and turned around. If we had not been following the streambed, we would not have had a sense of direction. In the afternoon we got a break. In the bend of the river a fairly deep cut had been made. The walls had been cut by the water. They were twelve to fifteen feet high and made a shade. The bottom was sandy. Plus, there was a trail down to the water. Good location for a long hot afternoon. A breeze blew though the cut, and with the water, it was cool.

The last ride of the day was hot facing the west sun. We were hurting from the heat and glad to find a campsite. We were in luck! We found a place almost like the afternoon location. Camp was organized and supper was started. We had "chicken" left over, and with the standard fare of biscuits and gravy, it wasn't bad.

I had no idea how far we had traveled that day, but felt that we might have made twenty to twenty-five miles. At this rate, we should be in New Mexico Territory in a few days. Boy, was I wrong!

After our evening meal I went egg hunting. Ol' Bullet trotted along with me and scared up some various birds in the grass. It was amazing how quickly I had enough eggs for our breakfast. Returning to the camp, we all did some chores that had to be done regularly, if at all possible. Minnie and Lizzie not only cooked and washed the utensils, they had to wash our clothes. I had to comb the mules' tails and manes almost very day. I checked hooves and mouths on the mules, then inspected hobbles and tied ropes. Made sure we had cool water in the water bags. Then, I guess my biggest contribution to the trip was providing fresh meat.

Next morning we saw antelope again. They ran off into the distance as we pushed to the northwest and then turned back to the west. This encouraged us and made riding a little easier. We discovered that there were numerous tributaries on the stream. I took time to explore a couple, and found that we could find better camping places out on the tributaries than on the main stream. Some of the tributaries had more trees and were more accessible. Trails led down into them and back out further on. Also, these trails usually let the rider cross the tributary without riding long distances out of route.

We were delighted that the day had gone so well. We found a good place for our noon meal and an even better place for our afternoon break. Hunting for eggs and prairie chickens was easy and the fishing was excellent. We were eating very well to be in the middle of nowhere.

We were getting ready to depart for the last ride for the day when a sound of horses came from the west. With the experiences of the past weeks, we were very cautions and suspicious. The girls moved back down in the streambed and held the mules while I scouted to see what was happening. I crawled up the bank and keeping low in the grass, I crept forward.

Our resting place had been within a half mile of another camp. A camp of rough looking men and a few women. They were camped on a small lake with lots of trees and shelter. We would have to go around these campers. I kept low and circled for a better look. There were a least ten men in the camp and three or four women. They appeared rough and dirty.

As I crept closer, I noticed a boy about my age. He was tied to a tree with a long piece of rope, like you would stake a mule to graze. When one of the campers would pass, they would hit or kick him. He made no sounds and hardly looked up. I had to get closer to be able to hear them. I lowered down in the grass and moved forward.

Something touched my back when I stopped the next time. I almost jumped out of my skin! Turning, I found Ol" Bullet was right behind me and had bumped me when I stopped. He had been following me all this time. I heard some of the campers talking. I listened and hoped there were no dogs in the camp. They would probably have barked by now it there had been any.

"What are you going to do with the boy?" a big ugly man asked a bigger and uglier man.

"I may roast him on an open fire, why?" growled the giant man.

"Do you think his Pa will come looking for him?" asked the other man, grinning.

"I hope so. That thieving Indian cheated us on the last horse and cow trade. Not only did he cheat us he had twice as many guns, so he could make it stick."

"Boy, that is a smart deal you have worked out as the middle man. Buy stolen cattle from rustlers and trade the Indians for ponies. Then turn right around and trade the rustler's cattle to the Indians for ponies and the Indians' ponies to the rustlers for cattle."

"Yeah, but trade so we have a few ponies and some cattle left over to sell, and there is our profit. This deal is better than stealing or killing for hire. We have a lot less risk and are making money off both sides. We could not make the deal work if we weren't holding this lake. Which reminds me, has Slim come back?"

"Naw, he should be back any time."

"Well, all he had to do was ride out to the headwaters of the lake and see if the springs are running or not. The lake is down some, and if it goes dry, we are out of business. It shouldn't go dry as it is spring fed."

While they spoke, a rider came from the west.

"There he comes now, Big'en."

The horseman rode up to the two men and swung down from the saddle. The rider was dressed like the rest of the camp. Worn out clothes, beat down sweat stained hat and boots that needed to be replaced.

"About time you were getting back, Slim."

"Yeah, if you don't like the time I take, next time you can go yourself," Slim replied with a snarl in his voice.

"Cool your potato, Slim. We were worried about you," said Big'n with sarcasm.

"Yeah, I bet. You could see me all the time on this flat table."

"What about the springs?"

Slim cut off a chew of tobacco and said, "Could be a problem. Maybe not, but two of the springs are not flowing like they were last year. The rest are O.K., but if the others fall off, we've got trouble."

"Even if this lake goes way down, it is the only water for miles and miles, so the rustlers and the Indians have to deal with us. That is, if they want to trade."

"Could the Indians be messing with the springs?"

"Naw, they know where they are, and they use them some, but there is not enough water in either one to water all of their ponies," Slim responded.

"And the springs are so close that we could see them out there on the prairie."

I slipped back away from the camp and returned to the girls. I briefly told them what I had seen and heard. I told them all about the Indian boy.

I looked at Minnie. "The most important piece of information I learned is that in fact, this lake is spring fed."

I continued, "Minnie, that means that this stream is the wrong one. This lake, with the springs, is the headwater for this tributary." My words were slowly sinking in on her.

"Minnie we are on the wrong fork. Staying with the left fork was not the correct information." Minnie's shoulders dropped, and she was near tears.

"I have led us up the wrong fork twice now. We are never going to get to Uncle John's if we keep going in the wrong directions."

"Look, Minnie, I lost a mule, and you lost the directions." I tried to make a joke of the fact. "So we are even. You ask me what would Papa do? Now I am asking you that question."

"I didn't lose anything!" blurted out Lizzie.

"I guess you are right, Robert. We'll just make the best of it. We go back to the fork, take the right fork and see where it goes. We don't have any other choice. We can't go back, not now." She shook her head and added, "We have lost two days coming up to this point and it will take us two days to go back."

"Look on the bright side, Minnie. We should be at least half way. The weather is fine, and we will eventually get there."

"You would think so, wouldn't you, Robert."

Lizzie asked, "Are those bad men at the other camp?"

"Yes, they are, Lizzie."

"Then I don't guess we can ask them how to get there?"

"No, we can't," Minnie cautioned. "We need to get away from their camp, and a long way from it. Let's go Robert!"

"There is more. These men are trading with the rustlers and the Indians. They are a bad bunch, and we have to get away tonight. We can't move during the day. They could see us very plainly on this prairie. I'm surprised they didn't see or hear us coming up to this campsite. We can't have a fire, they might smell the smoke. So, we keep down in the riverbed until dark. We need to sleep some because we are going to ride back to the east by moonlight." Thank goodness there was a full moon.

Then I really sent Minnie and Lizzie into a state of shock. "Last, and this is dangerous and I know it, I'm going to get that Indian boy out of that camp. We can't just leave him for them to torture and beat."

Minnie finally found her voice. "Robert, are you out of your mind! Why, if they catch you, we are all caught. You just can't go in there and get that boy!"

"Listen, Minnie. My plan is simple. I will wait until it is dark and the camp is asleep. Then I'll crawl in and cut the boy loose. If he wants to come with us fine, or he can do whatever he wants. If he comes with us, we can redistribute the sacks and let him ride my mule. I will ride Number One."

"Robert, you are crazy!"

"I may be girls, but I can't let him stay. If you had seen how they are treating him, you would not want to leave him either. Bunch of grown men slapping and kicking a boy. He is tied up like an animal." My bravado was all talk. I have let my mouth get me into trouble any number of times in the past.

It was a long time until dark, so we spread the canvas back out and got out our bedding and tried to sleep. We had leftover cold biscuits and some fish. Beat not having anything. Especially since we could not have a fire to cook.

Time passed very slow, but we all slept some. I led the mules to some grass in the riverbed and let them graze. They had had plenty of water and were in good shape. We might have to swing out from the river in our run back to the east, so I wanted them well watered and fed.

The sun settled in the west and finally dark came. We had repacked our burlap sacks, and I put them on the mules just as if the Indian boy was going to come with us. We put two sets of sacks on Number One and two sets on Number Four. I would ride Number One and let the Indian boy ride Number Four. Number Three had been carrying double for days and did not show any problems.

I slipped out of the ravine and back through the grass to the outlaw camp. I was glad Ol' Bullet was at my side. His ears and eyes could keep me out of trouble. I crept closer and closer, stopping to listen for voices in the camp. When I got to the camp, all was quiet. There was only one man up walking about, and he was staggering around. He was drinking. I wondered if the others had already passed out from drinking.

The moon was starting to come up in the east. I had to move soon, so the light was not so bright that I would be seen if somebody was awake. I crept slowly, right into the middle of the camp. Not a person stirred. I could hear some snoring and mumbling.

When I got close to the Indian boy, I could see he was watching me and Ol' Bullet. He did not move one muscle. He just watched. I slid up to him and took out my pocket knife. This had been Papa's and was as sharp as a razor. With just a few saws with the knife, the rope was cut and the Indian boy was free. I placed my finger over my lips and made the sign to be quiet. I guessed that that is the sign in Indian, too. Next, I motioned for him to follow me. I started sliding back through the grass with the Indian boy right behind me.

My heart jumped into my throat. One of the outlaws was up and staggering toward us. He was drunk, and he was going to step right on us. He stumbled and almost fell. Then he saw us, but in his drunken state he was very slow.

He said, "What the….."

Those were the last words he ever uttered. Out of the dark Ol" Bullet leaped and caught the man by the throat. The man struggled, but could not cry out. He fell to the ground thrashing about, trying to get Ol' Bullet off of him. Ol' Bullet had cut off the air and then bitten the man's throat out. The man made no sound when he opened his mouth. He was bleeding very bad, and in a few moments he lay still.

The Indian boy and I crept back to the girls through the grass. Ol' Bullet ran ahead of us and went to the water. He stuck his face in the water and splashed about, then he drank. The Indian boy showed the first emotion when he saw Minnie and Lizzie. His eyes opened a little wider, and his mouth formed an O.

We hastily mounted and rode down the ravine for some distance and then entered the main stream. We continued on for a mile or two. At the first slope out of the river bottom, we reined the mules up the slope and out onto the prairie.

The moon was climbing high, and the prairie was lighted almost like day. We pushed the mules, and on the good level ground, we made good time. Minnie had looked at her watch when we started.

"Ten o'clock. We will stop in two hours and rest for a few minutes." As she started to put the watch back in her pocket, the Indian boy reached out and caught her hand. Minnie sucked in her breath, she did not know what the boy was going to do. He only turned her hand over, looked at the watch and shrugged his shoulders.

Minnie would look at her watch in the moonlight ever so often. We took our first short break at midnight. Then back up on the mules. I didn't know how bad the Indian boy was bruised or hurt. Didn't know if the ride was killing him or what , we just had to ride. He never made a sound.

At two we took another break. Lizzie was having a hard time staying awake. When we mounted this time, I heard Minnie say to Lizzie, "If you get sleepy, it's O.K. Just lay back against me, and you can sleep."

Four o'clock came and after another short rest, we were mounted and moving. By now all of us were becoming sleepy, all but the Indian boy. I awoke with a jerk. The Indian boy was leading Minnie's mule and my mule, and we had been asleep. He put his finger to his lips in the sign to be quiet and smiled. Hey, that was the sign in Indian to be quiet. And I smiled back at him.

Dawn found us all awake. The Indian boy led us down into a ravine and turned to his right. That would be south I figured. We made several turns and I became confused in the maze of ravines. He knew where he was going. It suddenly hit me, this was his home and country. He knew his way. Around the next bend, we came out into a bigger open ravine. There was water and trees for shelter, and there were Indians. Lots of Indians!

It was the camp of the Indian boy's tribe. There was a lot of confusion and commotion when he led us into the camp. Then some of the men became hostile. One of the men spoke and all of the others got quiet. He and the boy embraced, and they spoke for some time, with a lot of hand motions and head shaking.

The chief, I guess he was the chief, motioned and called for someone to come to him. A woman with long gray hair approached. She did not look the chief in the eyes and kept her head bowed. I wondered what was going on. There was more talking and arm waving, but the woman did little moving. Then she walked over to us.

"My name is Gray Fox."

Our mouths dropped open.

"The chief wants to know why you save his boy?"

I replied and asked a question. "He was hurt and tied up. Are you Indian or are you white?" I had heard of white women being held captive.

She did not answer me, instead she turned and spoke to the chief, still keeping her eyes downcast.

The chief walked over to us and looked us over. Then he spoke to the woman.

The grayheaded woman turned back to us and said, "The chief wants to know what are white children doing on the Llano?"

Minnie spoke, "We are trying to cross the Llano to a relative who lives on the other side."

The woman looked at us in disbelief, "You want to cross the Llano?"
"Yes."

"Crazy. Only whole tribes cross the Llano." Then she turned to the chief, and there was a LOT of talking and arm waving.

Again, she turned back to us, "Chief thanks you for what you did for his son. You are to come to my tent. I am called Gray Fox."

In her tent we were given food. We didn't ask what it was, and while we ate, she told us her story.

"I was captured forty changes of the seasons ago. I was captured when I was very small and made a member of the tribe. I forgot the white words, but as white men came onto the Llano I listened, practiced and remembered the words. I was the chief's second wife for many years. But, now I am a shaman, a medicine woman."

She spread food in front of us. "You are to eat and rest, and I will be back soon. Now I must see about the chief's son."

Later Gray Fox returned to the tent. "Tell me your story and why you were on the Llano."

We started slowly and finally had the whole story out. We even explained how we were following the rivers and forks. She did not ask one question the whole time. When we finished, she stood for a long time looking into the eyes of each of us, as if she was looking into our souls.

She went over to Lizzie and knelt, "You have the spirit of your mother."

She turned to me and said, "You will be your father's image."

Then to Minnie, "You have the strength of the horse, the wisdom and cunning of the fox and the love of all the mothers on the Llano."

The flap on the dwelling opened, and the chief stepped in. He spoke to the woman for a few minutes, looked at each of us and went out.

"The chief says for you to rest today and tonight. Then his men will take you back to the fork of the two rivers. Some of them will escort you for two or three days on the north branch. This river, is called Yellow House and the other is called Blackwater."

We rested all day. Sleep did not come easy, being in the camp of Indians. Uncle Nate would have a heart attack. Matter of fact, anyone in the family would. Why, Aunt Marjie would faint dead away. Aunt Bess would like to make a deal with them, some kind of deal. She was always cooking up a deal for her husband.

The Indian boy came, and Gray Fox introduced him as Young Eagle. She translated some for us and then the Indian Boy gave each of us a woven necklace. We did not have anything to give him, as Gray Fox instructed us to do. Then an idea hit me.

"Minnie, Lizzie, I want to give Young Eagle Number Four." For a moment they both stared at me and then they both nodded. I motioned for Young Eagle to follow me outside. We went over to the mules, and I handed Young Eagle the reins. His eyes lit up, and a grin spread over his face. He said something to Gray Fox, and she smiled.

"He says you have honored him by giving him one of your animals, when you only have three."

By night we slept very sound, in the middle of an Indian camp. In the middle of a hostile Indian camp, we had been treated with dignity and honor, the best I could tell. We were not afraid anymore.

The next day we were escorted back on our way, by a large number of the tribe. Gray Fox stood by her dwelling and waved goodbye to us as we left.

That morning she had asked, "Please, tell no one that a white woman dwells with Kiowa. That person died long ago. Now I am shaman and am important in the tribe." We asked her to not let them eat Number Four.

The escort took us back to the fork in the two rivers. Young Eagle went that far. The main body of Indians, about twenty, rode off to the west, and another five took us north on the Blackwater. We traveled three days up the Blackwater with our Indian escort. They hunted and shared their meals with us. We did not do anything but ride and enjoy the company. Then they, too, left us to our own devices.

The day they left, they were gone when we woke at daylight. That night they were there, but next morning they were gone. We had not exchanged one single word with them in three days. Yet, they hunted and shared with us. The day seemed very quiet without our escort.

We returned to our own routine, and the time passed without event. On the second day all the quiet and being alone changed. We were riding north, parallel to Blackwater River.

I happened to look over my shoulder and YELLED. "It's those outlaws and they are after us!" With us and our eight sacks of goods, the mules just could not outrun the outlaws on horses. We knew that we could not outrun them and sure couldn't fight them, but you just can't lay down and die.

"Ride for that ravine," I yelled.

We pushed the mules as hard as we could, and in desperation, I began to toss our burlap sacks off my mule. I yelled to Minnie to do the same. The mules did some better without the bags hitting their sides. With just the three of us on the two mules, they ran faster than before.

"Down in the ravine, get down!" I was frantic.

We charged down the embankment into the ravine. As we hurtled over the edge of the ravine, I saw, or at least I thought I saw Indians. When we skidded to a halt in the bottom of the ravine, and I looked back, I did see Indians. Lots of Indians! They did not have guns, just lots of lances and arrows They were hiding just behind the side of the ravine we had just come over.

The outlaws came charging and hollering. They figured they had us cornered and trapped. Their horses were carrying them at top speed toward the ravine and the Indians. As we sat there stupefied, a familiar figure appeared. The Indian boy reached for our reins and led us down the ravine to the north and out of harm. He held his finger to his lips and grinned. We grinned back and put our first finger to our lips.

It didn't last long, at least not the shooting. There was a lot of commotion after the shooting, then everything was quiet. As we sat on our mules, another familiar figure appeared. Gray Fox smiled and motioned for us to follow her. We rode farther north down the ravine to an Indian camp. We were in shock. Just out of nowhere, here comes young Eagle, Gray Fox and the whole Kiowa tribe.

Gray Fox spoke, "Please, won't you get down and rest? This has been a little strange to you. Yes?"

All we could do is smile weakly and shake our heads.

I asked, "What has happened?"

"The outlaws are dead and will bother no one again."

Suddenly the camp was full of riding and yelling Kiowa warriors. They rode their ponies and shook their new guns, lances and spears. Gray Fox spoke, "They are celebrating a victory over a foe."

A huge fire was built, and one band of riders with fresh game thundered into the camp. There was more riding and yelling.

After a big meal, and lots of bragging on the part of the warriors, the chief stepped to the center of the encampment. He held up his hands and spoke.

Gray Fox translated, "Many of our enemies have been killed today. They steal from us, they violate our women and then they steal my son. Brave warriors fought the battle today and defeated these thieves. But, the real warriors are the white eyes. They took great risk to save my son. They may be children, but they are very brave. Especially the white-eyed boy. He went into the camp of the snakes and brought out my son. He took his companion dog and fought one of the thieves and killed him. He leads my son to safety, all the while not knowing what might happen to him or his white-eyed sisters. I say he is as brave as any man in Kiowa nation." There was lots of shouting, yelling and dancing around the camp. Many men danced by us and tapped me on the shoulder with a lance or bow.

Gray Fox stopped and looked at us, "That was a long speech for Young Eagle's father."

"Gray Fox, why do the men tap me on the shoulder with a lance or a bow?" I asked.

"They are paying you great honor. This is their way of saying that the chief is right and that you are very brave. For a white eye." She smiled with a twinkle in her eyes.

At sunset a huge fire was built up, and the eating and dancing began. The Indians danced 'till dawn, but we three braves were asleep long before light filled the eastern sky.

When we awoke, Gray Fox had some breakfast for us and told us the rest of the story. " The chief was furious at the outlaws for taking his son and beating him. He went to the their camp to brag how three white eyes had snatched Young Eagle right out of their hands. And that the three white eyes had returned his son to him. He bragged that he would never do business with the outlaws again, and that he would spread the word to all the Kiowa tribes of what snakes they were to steal children. He deliberately told them the white eyes were riding shod mules, and then he told them that the three white eyes were three children."

As we sat with our eyes wide open she continued, "The braves watched the outlaws and trailed them. The outlaws found your mule tracks and followed them. The chief has been clever. He had you taken right back out the way you came in so your tracks seemed to continue to the forks of the rivers. He even sent Young Eagle with you so there would be three sets of tracks. The outlaws tracked you and followed you just as the chief thought they would."

Gray Fox looked at us and said, "You know the rest. The chief set a trap for the outlaws, and you led them right into it. Now if you will come with me, I have something to show you."

Gray Fox led us outside and around the dwelling where our eight burlap sacks were stacked. Our two mules were staked out on good grass, and someone watched them day and night.

"Indians like mule meat, you know. The chief has banned the eating of mule meat forever, because you gave his son a mule."

The next day we loaded our two mules with our eight sacks and rode out of an Indian camp again in less than a week. Boy, Aunt Marjie would just die!

By the end of the day, we could see the first of two small abutments. The Indians had told us what to look for on our way west. There would be two abutments and then almost flat land all the way. They had loaded us with cured meat, so we would not need to hunt for several days. We had to travel slow, because of the load of three kids, eight sacks and pounds and pounds of meat. It was a big load for the mules.

The Kiowas were more impressed that we were going to cross the Llano than they were about the run-in with the outlaws. The Indians did not fear the Llano as did the white man, but they respected it. They knew their way across the Llano. The Kiowas only traveled in tribes to cross the Llano, not just small groups. They could not believe that three children were going out on the Llano alone.

"Minnie, would you have started this trip if you had known what was going to happen?"

"I don't know. Probably not."

"Boy, I would have. Just think! We have seen rustlers, outlaws and Indians. All we need now is the U.S. Army to make the trip complete."

"I liked the little Indian girls that played with me." chimed in Lizzie. "I would come again."

"Now, Lizzie, weren't you scared just a little when we rode into that Indian camp?" asked Minnie.

"No, I had Ol' Bullet to look after me, like always!"

What can you say to that? One sister is spirit, one is love and strength and I will be my Father. And we have a dog that loves all three of us.

We rode toward the first abutment and started looking for a campsite. We found an excellent location for the night, like many of the places we have stopped. We rode up into one of the ravines that lined the face of the abutment. We had protection from searching eyes. To our pleasure and delight, we found water and grass in there. The walls of the ravine were about ten feet high and sheer. It wound around, and we came to the spring that fed a good sized pool I unloaded and hobbled the two mules for the night. They had water and good grass and were close to us. Minnie got busy preparing the meal and soon had it ready. As we ate the sun sank behind some clouds and the western horizon..

My fondest memory of the Kiowas will always be an Indian boy named Young Eagle, sitting on a mule, waving good bye, holding the first finger of his right hand over his lips and of course, his face in one big grin.

"Robert, what are you day dreaming about?"

"That is what Papa would always say. What are you dreaming about?"

"Go take a dip in the stream, and Lizzie and I will go a little later. Be sure to put on clean clothes."

Sounded just like Mama, but I'm glad. The water was terrific, and a bath was not bad. I went back by the mules and checked the hobbles and lead ropes. That was when I noticed the storm clouds in the west.

"Hey, Minnie, come up here and look at this cloud."

Off to the west a storm was brewing. Lightning was crossing the night sky dozens of ways and bouncing off the ground.

"Minnie, do you think that that storm is headed toward us?"

"Can't tell, sure looks bad. I'm glad we are down in the ravine."

The storm grew and became enormous. Lightning filled the cloud and was striking the ground. We kept an eye on the cloud as it approached. It had not rained as of yet. We could see in under the cloud and see all the lightning and fury of Mother Nature.

We all stood watching the monster build and build. There was rumbling and thunder that shook the ground. Suddenly a long black tail dropped out of the cloud.

"MINNIE, THERE IS A TORNADO!", I screamed, and we ran for the ravine!

CHAPTER TEN

Every muscle in his body ached. Moving all of his equipment to the top of the caprock had been pure pain. To help the horses, he had walked beside the wagon all day. Loading and unloading gear repeatedly had not helped his bruised body. He would have preferred to stay in his bedroll and rested all day. He had made his bed under the wagon last night. To make a sleeping place, he had put down two old saddle blankets on the tall grass. Then he had unrolled his bedroll on top of the two saddle blankets. He thought, I almost left the two blankets with those dead rustlers. The two blankets on the tall grass and his bedroll had made the best bed he had slept on in days.

He slowly crawled out of the bedroll. Oh, how his body ached! What he really wanted was a hotel. They had hot baths, soft beds and a restaurant. He would give one hundred dollars to spend a few days in a comfortable hotel. A good hot steak with all the trimmings would be worth another hundred dollars.

Pain shot through his body with every move. No amount of stretching and slow bending was helping his pains. Pulling on his boots, he took a few tentative steps. Those few steps set off shooting pains all over his body. Now, enough is enough, he had to get started after those brats. But, first he had to get his body to working.

With some effort he pulled his bedding out from under the wagon. He tossed the bedroll into the wagon and spread the blankets out on the grass. Lowering his body down on the blankets he turned his back to the warm sun. This had worked before, just let the hot sun warm his body, and it would loosen him up so he could move without pain.

The sun's rays got hotter and hotter. Nate turned around and let the rays hit the other side. Then he chuckled, for he was like a chunk of meat on a spit. Turning real slow and basking all the way around. The warmth was helping, and the pains were seeping away.

He got a fire to going and made coffee. The warm liquid helped his aches and pains from the inside and the warm sun helped on the outside. After a couple of hours he made breakfast. Just biscuits and gravy with his coffee. Later he brought the horses to the wagon. He examined them carefully, checking their feet and deciding if they were rested enough to pull the wagon. They seemed fairly rested. Perhaps they could pull for short periods and then rest and make some mileage today. Best way to test the horses was to hitch them up and give it a try.

To his surprise, they covered about ten miles that day. It took near fifteen hours to cover that amount. Lots of stops to let the horses rest and time to hunt the trail. The trail was very dim, and he had trouble following it. Several times he had gotten down off the wagon and had walked around hunting the trail. This could prove to be a problem, if he lost the trail. Nate felt that the trail should have been plainer to the eye. Herds of cattle should have left a better trail.

A few miles farther out on the prairie he found a game trail, and there were lots of cow tracks along the way. Following that trail was much easier, and they made up lost time. By night he was far out on the Llano Estacado. During the day he had found several waterholes for the horses to drink. The puddles were probably made during the storm two nights ago. There had been heavy rain, and every little hole was full of water.

Evening came and with it a cool and gentle breeze. The day had been hot and muggy from the rain. He had perspired hard for most of the day. A dip in a pool of water would be delightful, but there were no pools, just puddles. Enough for the horses to drink, but he could not drink that muddy water. He had a fair supply of water for his use, and as long as there were puddles the horses would be well watered.

Nate took time to cook some of the cured meat and heat a can of beans. That with some sour dough biscuits dipped in the meat grease made a good meal. He looked for a can of fruit, but it was all gone. Watching the sunset and the approaching night, Nate drank coffee and schemed about the money.

Unlatching the false bottom in the wagon, Nate removed the package with his extra money, the bank book and the letters of credit. Carefully he read and reread the documents and counted the money. Besides the thirty four thousand dollars in the bank, he had accumulated another thousand from gambling and from the dead rustlers. He had a total of thirteen hundred dollars in the packet, counting the money he had when he left home. If this was what being rich felt like, he sure did like the warm glow that money brought. He returned the packet to the hiding place under the wagon.

The next day was uneventful. Just lots of grass and not a landmark to navigate by. On the second day Nate realized that the game trail faded out, and he had nothing to guide him. He thought that he was miles from the east edge of the caprock and any sense of direction was difficult. He knew he was going northwest and making remarkably good mileage. The land was flat and easy on the horses. No ravines or hills to pull. Only miles of grass. Occasionally he would find a shallow gully that filled when it rained. Some that he found had small ponds still standing from the storm.

The third and fourth days on the Llano Estacado were just repeats of the first two. He estimated that he had covered at least fifty miles in the last four days. Nate did not know he was actually moving parallel to the caprock during the first few days of travel. As he progressed he moved farther away from the caprock. He was nearing the junction of Yellow House and Blackwater, but he had no knowledge of the two streams.

His path was a few miles to the west of the junction, and he was headed straight for the Yellow House.

His water supply was very low, and he needed to find fresh water. Four days of eating out of his supplies had made a dent in them. He was becoming concerned about the restocking of goods. For four days he not seen a moving object. A few birds had flown up out of the grass indicating that they might be nesting nearby. He did see some wings of ducks or geese high in the sky. Once he thought he saw something running away from him in the tall grass. But, he only got a glimpse of the backs of whatever he saw, if he saw something.

On the fifth and sixth day he was very concerned about water and direction. He had discovered that the only way he could keep going north or northwest was to move in the early part of the day and late in the evening. When the sun was overhead there was no feel for direction. He also discovered that moving in the early and late hours was easier on the animals and him. A long rest from noon until late in the afternoon was good for both him and the horses. Then they would make some distance 'till sundown. With plenty of grass and water for the animals he did not need to worry about them. But, his situation was becoming very precarious.

If he was having this much trouble with water and direction, what about those brats. He began to think that maybe mother nature might do his dirty work. The heat, no water and no food might drive them to some other destination, or they would die. He wondered where they were. What trail did they take? If they had come up the way he did, he should have run across them. The rancher had indicated that the trail he took was the only one. What if there had been another, and they found it. Perhaps it was an easier trail, and they were out ahead of him.

On the seventh day he hit the Yellow House River. The cool water was delicious. After his evening meal he stripped and took a swim. Well, he got in the water and splashed and rolled. The stream was not deep enough at this juncture to cover his rotund body.

He rested at the stream all the next day, debating on the direction to take. East would take him back to the caprock. To the west was the way to the territory of New Mexico. Yellow House flowed from the west. Was there any chance that it went all the way to New Mexico? He decided to go west, as that at least was the direction he wanted to go. If the stream ran out, he would go further north and find another one. Also, he might find other travelers on the Llano and just might find the three brats. Looking for them was like looking for a needle in a haystack.

The next morning he turned the team to the west and followed Yellow House stream. The travel was not difficult, but he had to go way out of the way to get around some of the tributaries of Yellow House. His westward progress was not much, although he traveled a lot of miles. The stream first went west and then turned to the southwest. This did not bother Nate. He knew that if the general direction was west all would be well.

At the end of the day Nate found a good tributary for his camp. To his amazement he could drive the team and wagon down into the streambed. He walked his team back down to Yellow House and watered them. They had grazed off and on all day, so they were well fed and only needed water. He built a fire and prepared his meager meal. He would have to hunt in a day or so, and he really needed to find a place to restock the wagon. He rolled into his bedroll in the wagon, just in case it rained. No reason to be sleeping on the ground and getting wet.

Next morning as he finished his coffee, he thought he heard horses' hooves. But, by the time he got up on the level so he could see, there was nothing around. Whatever it was really disappeared fast on this flat table.

Hitched and on the way, his spirits lifted some when he saw a flock of ducks off to the northwest. He just might shoot a duck or two and have some fresh meat. He had been reluctant to shoot his shotgun. The sound would carry for miles and might bring some unsavory person to see just who was shooting. About the middle of the evening he saw dust to the west. This caused him some concern. He decided that he would wait and see what was ahead. By late afternoon he had seen some riders to the north. They were not Indians and looked like cowboys, so he thought, "I'll take my chances."

When he was a half mile from the camp by the lake, five riders rode out to meet him. They came with guns drawn and ready for trouble. Nate held up his hands and said, "Afternoon."

The riders hauled up on the reins, and one them asked, "What are you doing here?"

"Well, neighbor, I'm lost as you can see."

"Where you from and where you headed, stranger?" asked a fellow with a long dirty beard.

"I came up on the caprock some fifty miles back to the south. Thought that was the trail I should be on. I'm trying to go to New Mexico Territory to find a brother."

"You sure are lost, stranger. There's no way across the Llano Estacado. No road or trail. The Indians know how to cross it, but white men stay out of the middle." commented the first rider.

"How does a man get to New Mexico Territory?" I inquired.

"Most folks go around the north end of the Llano. That's about two hundred miles from here." spoke up a thin frail cowboy. "You can call me Slim. I'm the ramrod with this bunch. Come on up to the camp and have supper. That's the least we can do." Yeah, Nate thought, besides cutting my throat.

When they were settled around the campfire and eating, Slim asked, "Been on the road long....say what do they call you?"

"To answer both of your questions. I've been on the road for almost a month, and they call me Nate."

"Mr. Nate which way did you come up on the caprock?" asked Slim.

"I don't know that the trail had a name. Some cowboys showed me where I could go up. Well, I need to rephrase that. They showed me a trail, but it wasn't for a wagon. It was for horses. I like to have never got that blasted wagon and the horses up on top."

"Do you know what ranch this trail was on?" Slim inquired.

"I believe it was the 'Box W'." replied Nate.

"Hey, we have got some good friends that work down around the "Box W".

"What're their names, maybe I met some of them?"

"Well, one of the bosses is called Red."

Nate almost passed out. These men were connected to the rustlers and knew Red. Rather the dead Red. "Don't believe I recognize that name." Not only were they connected to the rustlers, it appeared that Red worked for the "Box W" and ran with the rustlers. The man had called Red one of the bosses. What would they do if they found out he had killed Red?

"Thought you might have run across him. Good old boy."

Nate was almost having a heart attack. Dead old boy was more like it. For once in his life Nate kept his mouth closed. "You been at this location long?' asked Nate.

"Pretty long time, but we are moving in a day to two. The Kiowa are getting restless, and we have had one run-in with them lately. So, we think we will move northeast a-ways. We have another camp over there. This Kiowa that we had the run in with thinks this little piece of ground is his, and he wants us gone."

Nate just nodded his head in agreement.

"Ever seen an Indian?" ask the bearded man.

"No, don't believe I have." replied Nate.

"Dirty savages. Did you know that they will eat horse meat and mule meat?"

"Now Slim, I'm a stranger, but are you pulling my leg?"

"NO! And they will eat dog. Just like you would eat chicken."

"When did you have this run-in with the Indians?"

Slim rubbed his nose and replied, "Been two, three days ago. We had ten men in our camp and ten from the north camp came down, and we sure got shot up."

Nate's curiosity was whetted, "What happened?"

"Pilgrim, it's a long story. I'll tell you later when it's not so late."

The camp turned in, and Nate retreated to his wagon. He could not sleep. If they knew that he had killed Red, they would shoot him, or worse, at the blink of an eye. Sleep came late in the night. When he awoke, he was staring into the muzzle of a forty-four.

"Just come out of the wagon nice and easy, Mr. Nate. Nice and easy."

"What is wrong? What is going on?" asked Nate.

"You're the one that shot up Red's camp."

They knew! But, how did they know?

"You don't use a hand gun like a man, you use a double-barrel shotgun. Like this one," Slim had Nate's gun in his hand.

Nate crawled out of the wagon. How was he going to get out of this?

Then a thought came to him. "Slim, you got me dead to rights. I shot up Red's camp. I caught him cheating at cards. I called him out, and he said I could pick the weapon. I guess that he thought I would chose a hand gun, but I chose shotguns. He just died laughing and went to the packs and came back with a single barrel twenty gauge. I got my double-barrel out, and he laughed again. I know he did not know shotguns, so I told him I would give him first shot at twenty paces. Red was almost crying he was laughing so hard. He stepped off twenty paces, turned and fired. That twenty gauge at twenty paces only hit me two buck shots. I did not give him time to think. I pulled up the barrel of this TEN gauge and blew Red to hell."

Slim stood with his hand gun down at his side, "You caught him cheating?"

"That's right, but you can't ask him unless you plan on visiting Hell."

Slim sputtered and fumbled around and finally said, "Come to the fire and have some coffee." He handed Nate his shotgun and walked back to the fire. "We were just making sure who you were. We had heard that the camp was shot up. But, no talk about Red cheating at cards. I knew that Red sure did like to play poker. The only description we had was the gunman used a double-barrel shotgun."

"Thanks," said Nate in a friendly voice.

The camp was stirring, and coffee smell filled the air. Nate sipped the coffee and watched the outlaws move about the camp. There were three women. They didn't appear to belong to one certain cowboy. Just were there. Breakfast was some kind of mush. Nate thought of the brats, and the mush they had been given.

"Here, Pilgrim, put some of this in your food. Makes it taste better."

The man had handed Nate a bottle with some little green...what do you suppose these little green...beans are?

Nate put his finger to the top of the bottle and tilted it so some would run on his finger. He then tasted his finger. His eyebrows went up, and he exclaimed, "Man do you eat this stuff?"

"Sure, they're called chili peppers. Comes from Mexico. Sure makes things taste better."

Nate handed the bottle back to the man and said, "I'll just pass for now, thanks."

The day wore on in the camp. There was a lot of sleeping, some drinking, and some card playing.

Nate just watched. He felt that it might not be a good thing to get in the card game with the outlaws. If they cheated, Nate could not very well call one of them out. That was a big fat lie about Red. He worked on some of his gear and watched. These were the outlaws who were trading and buying the cows from the rustlers. He had talked his way out of one scrape, so best kinda hang back and not be too visible.

Just as the sun was going down, a couple of cowboys rode in from the north. They were even harder looking than those in the camp. There was a long discussion between Slim and the two riders. After the discussion was over Slim pulled out a bottle, and all three had a drink. Then the two riders swung into the saddle and headed back to the northeast.

Slim walked over to where Nate sat in the shade of his wagon. He sat down by Nate and said, "We are moving camp tomorrow. You are welcome to come along. I know that you are trying to go to the Territory of New Mexico, but this sure is not the trail you want. The New Mexico Territory line is out to the west somewhere, but I don't know where. Never been further west than this lake and the springs that feed it. The springs are only three miles west of here."

Nate thought for a moment. Being with them was dangerous, but if there were Kiowas running around, he was safer with the outlaws. "I think I'll tag along, being you invited me."

"Good, we can always use another good gun, and that cannon is mighty impressive."

Nate went to eat when one of the women rang a bell. Any food would be better than the mush they had this morning. Supper was beef that had been cut into small bits and pitched into a stew pot. The women had added something that Nate did not recognize. As he had eaten from his meager stock at noon, this really began to taste pretty good.

Then it hit him! His mouth was on fire and his eyes were watering. What in the world had he put into his mouth? He thought he would die. He sputtered and coughed trying to get his breath. Looking around, everyone was eating the meal with no difficulty. They all went to laughing and pointing. Must be some kind of a joke they played on all newcomers to the camp. He kept trying to eat the food. Take a bite and then drink some water. His fat body began to sweat, and tears ran from his eyes. He gradually ate one plate, while the others consumed two or more plates and bragged on the good cooking.

"What in the world is this stuff, Slim?"

"It's called chili, Mr. Nate."

After dark the men gathered around the campfire and talked. Nate let some time pass, and after he had been included in some of the conversation he asked, "You said that the run-in with the Indians was a long story. Do we have the time to hear it now?"

"Sure, Mr. Nate."

Nate shifted his big round body to get comfortable and to listen to Slim's story.

"We had been trading with the Indians. They are really sneaks and cutthroats. We had a pony trade going, and they put it to us. Our boss then, he got killed, got the chance, and he had kidnapped the Chief's son. He was going to hold him until the Indians brought us the rest of the ponies that were due in the deal. We had the kid tied to that tree right over there. Then one night this kid, a white kid, slips into our camp and cuts the Indian boy lose."

Nate was about to lose interest in this story of Indians and crooked deals. The information about a little white kid got his attention There were not many white kids on the Llano.

"The chief comes riding in here a day or so later, bragging about his deal on the horses and how this little white kid got his son out of the camp. We would have had a showdown right then, but he had thirty braves to our ten men. We were outnumbered three to one. He actually said that the white kid and his two white sisters are braver than all of us put together."

Nate sat straight up and asked, "Did you say a white boy and his two white sisters?"

"That is right! He said that the three were so brave that they rode shod mules. Not unshod ponies, so no one will know if the rider is white or Indian."

Nate jumped up and exclaimed, "Those three are worth some money. I saw a poster, and there is a one hundred dollar reward for capturing them. They are runaways and have stolen some valuable items."

Nate gave no indication that he was after the three, or that he had put up the reward. He just wanted to know where the brats were, NOW!

"Do you have any idea where they are?"

"No, Nate, we don't. They were in good with the Indians for cutting the little Indian boy lose, and they got clean away."

"What do you mean, clean away?" Nate inquired.

"We rode out the next day and found their shod tracks. We followed them to some ravines and lost them. We camped over there for the night and then the next day we picked up the tracks. We followed them and finally got close enough to see that the three had an Indian escort. We kept below the horizon and kept checking on what direction they were going. The Indians took them back to where Yellow House and Blackwater join.

"You mean the Indians are going along with these three?"

"That's right. But, at the fork, the main group of Indians rode off, and only a few went with the white kids. We watched and those few Indians only went north with them for two or three days. We thought that we would catch the kids and hold them and maybe if the chief thinks so much of them, he would give us our ponies."

"Did you get them?"

"No, we saw them, and they started running. Guess we scared them. Anyway we chased them, and ran into an Indian ambush. The Indians killed nine of our men, and we did not kill one of them. The rest of our men skedaddled out of there!"

"You men have really had some hard luck," lamented Nate to get their sympathy.

"Well, maybe our luck will change. We are joining forces with the crew over at another camp. Those two you saw ride in here this afternoon are from that camp. We made a truce and drank on it. Should be a good arrangement for all of us. We pack and leave in the morning."

Nate had a hard time going to sleep. All he could think about was that the three brats were close at hand. Maybe in two day's ride. Now if he could work it around that the outlaws helped him to capture them, he could split the reward with them or even give it all to them. Sleep finally came, but Nate dreamed all night about catching those brats.

With morning, the camp prepared to travel. Breakfast was coffee, chicken eggs and some Mexican bread called tortillas. The bread was tasteless and dry. Nate soaked his in his coffee, and that gave the bread some taste. He had his team hitched and his gear ready to go long before the others were ready. About mid-morning the camp broke and began to stream out across the grass covered plain. They traveled on horses and in wagons. Some of the wagons looked like they would not make it to the next hilltop. Nate came along last so he could watch the crew of outlaws and their women. The travel was slow, and the only stop all day was at noon. They stopped long enough to make coffee to go with some more of those tortillas.

Sunset was on them just as they arrived at the northeast camp. The occupants had been expecting them and had a big fire going, and a party in progress. There was a lot of hand shaking and hugs for the three woman. The northeast camp had two women, so the men from each camp were real friendly to the women from the other camp and so on. The second camp had a big meal of antelope, beans and lots of whiskey.

There was one man who thought he was a fiddle player, and he played. Sounded like a cat scratching to Nate. The crowd loved it, and they danced and drank until they passed out. Some were still trying to dance come dawn. Nate left the party early and crawled into his bedroll. He had moved his wagon a good ways from the camp when he saw that a celebration was going to happen. Sleep came hours later. The howling and so called music went on and on.

Sometime during the night there was a fist fight. A lot of loud hollering and cursing. Then you could hear the fist hit flesh and the grunts and swearing of the two men. Just as suddenly as the fight started, it stopped. Next day Nate would learn that Slim had hit both men with a piece of wood, knocking them both out and giving them mighty sore heads.

All day the next day there were people sick and complaining that they would never do that again. But, the next night there was more of the same, and they added card playing. Nate again retreated to his wagon early and fell asleep, despite the noise and carousing of the camp. He was jerked awake by a gunshot and then a second. He crawled out of the wagon, pulling on his boots and pants. He grabbed his shotgun and headed to the center of the camp. More gunfire rang out. There were flashes of pistols on the left and on the right. Nate stopped and crouched on the ground trying to determine what was going on. There were two more gunshots, and a man screamed, and then it was silent.

A voice called out, "Somebody help me I'm shot."

Slim's voice carried across the campsite, "Everybody hold your fire. Let's don't kill each other in the dark."

The stillness stretched, and Slim spoke again, "Everybody just stay calmed. Ya'll calm down now? Let's see who is shot."

Dim shadowy forms crept out from behind tents and wagons. One woman was crying and another cursing. The fight had been over one of the women, or so it seemed. The other woman was mad that her "man" had been trifling around with someone else. Nate could not figure out who went with who, so he returned to bed.

The next morning Slim appointed a burial detail. The shot man had died later in the night, all over some cheap whiskey and a camp follower. The camp was somber for the rest of the day. That night there was little drinking, and the women stayed out at their tents. Some of the men played some card games, but there was no gambling.

Nate overheard plans to raid the Indian camp and steal back their horses. Slim had sent scouts out each day to see if the Indians could be located. There were reports that the bunch that had shot up the first camp was moving north. The scouting of the Indians by the white men did not seem to bother the Indians or upset them. One report was that the scout sat on a ridge and watched about a dozen Indians ride within a quarter mile of him, and the Indians did nothing. There seemed to be a truce between the two factions.

One rider had already been gone two days, and the camp had begun to worry that the truce was at an end. Late the third day the rider came in. He had followed a band of Indians north to the Blackwater. This band had driven a fairly large herd of ponies to the Blackwater stream.

Leaving the herd with old men, boys and the women, they rode north to the Running Water. The scout said that there were at least fifty ponies at the Running Water. Just as he was about to turn south and come back to camp, a band came in from the north with more ponies. These were added to the ones at the Running Water, and all of them had been driven to the Blackwater. He estimated that there were near one hundred ponies at the Blackwater and near fifty braves.

The number of horses was attractive, but the number of braves was a concern. The outlaws had more weapons and better weapons, but the odds of three to one made them hesitate. With two gangs together, they felt they might handle that many Indians. Slim and the other leader, Nate did not get his name, decided that this many ponies was too good an opportunity to pass. To be real sure of success, what they needed was still more guns. Nate did not know if they were counting on him and his shotgun or not. The only way to get him to help them was for them to help him find the brats.

The need for more guns was the problem, the big problem. Riders were sent to three other outlaw groups working up and down the Llano. With their combined strength, they could easily handle the Indians and have the ponies. Two days later riders started arriving in two's and three's. Slim was counting on a combined force of close to thirty riders. The odds were more than even. The only problem was, when you get that many outlaws together, there is bound to be trouble. Big trouble!

Slim and his partner in this deal had taken all of the liquor out on the prairie in one of the wagons and hidden the whiskey. At least there was no drinking, but there were card games. There were several fist fights over the games. No gambling, just card games. On the second day, while waiting for the other riders, the gambling game finally started, and trouble began to brew.

Nate had stayed mostly to himself during the move and the wait on the other riders. But, when the gambling game began, he just had to watch. He got up close, and finally he just could not stand the temptation, and had to sit in for a few hands. He would play a while and then leave. He claimed that his legs hurt if he sat on the ground too long at one time. Actually he was checking out each player. Looking for the dangerous ones, dumb one, the sharks and the bluffers. There were always these categories in a game. Sometimes there was a real good player. One that did not cheat, do dumb things or bluff. He was the one you had to watch.

Nate would get in and out of the game as the pots dictated. If his cards were running good, he would stay in. But, if they turned bad he got out. This way he was always some ahead. The game ran all day and into the evening. Some men lost all they had and some won. That is poker.

Nate, the night before in the dark, had opened his trap door and gotten some extra money out of the packet. He put the packet back and put the extra in an empty tin can. A can that had had peaches in it. Nate had cut the top completely out and washed the can. He put the money in the can and turned it upside down in a box of canned goods. He even sat a can on top of the empty money can. This was his bluff money. He knew he would eventually need it. He had always needed it.

The game wore on. Nate was winning some and losing some. Not enough winnings to make anybody mad or get a fight started. The pots came and went. More men dropped out because they had lost their poke. The game was not stopped for a meal or a nature call. You just sat out a few hands and then got back in. Nate and three others were the only ones left by midnight. Nate estimated he was at least fifty dollars ahead.

The pots were getting bigger and bigger. With only four players, and they were the winners of all the money in the camp, there was a lot of money in the game. Nate had sat and counted the piles of money each player brought to the game. Also, he had counted the winnings of each player. He had a very good mind for that sort of thing. Numbers were one of his best talents.

He had watched the three other men play all afternoon and night. The one on his left was a smooth, sharp player. He was not aggressive or stupid. He was good. The man on his right was lucky. He had drawn cards all day that were above average. He had won a lot. The man across from Nate was the bluffer. Nate could feel that moment coming. The man on his right and left knew when to stay and when to fold. But, the man in front of him was going to bluff at the wrong time and very soon.

The cards were hot for the man to Nate's right. Some things never change, do they? Like always luck runs out, and the smart player got the now unlucky one. Cleaned him out in one hot hand. Now it was Nate, the smart one and the bluffer. The very next hand was the one Nate was waiting on. He had seen it coming for an hour. The bluffer was trying too hard to win.

This was the hand. Nate had gone to the bushes after the last hand. While he was out in the dark he reached in his wagon, got out the extra money and put it in his pocket. The pot was big and finally the smart one folded. That left Nate and the bluffer. Nate had been counting the bluffer's money and knew that he was down to around one hundred dollars. The bluffer bet twenty and raised ten. Nate called the thirty to him and raised another ten. That was ten to the bluffer. He looked at his money, and he bet the ten and raised another thirty. Nate, called the thirty and raised another thirty dollars. That was thirty to the bluffer, who, one more time called and raised another twenty dollars, all he had. Nate only had ten showing on the blanket. The bet was twenty dollars to Nate. He reached into his pocket and pulled out some money. Nate very carefully counted out a hundred dollars.

Nate said, " I call and raise you another twenty." He had seventy dollars laying on the blanket.

It was quiet at the card game on the blanket. The bluffer's eyes popped, and he said in a low voice, "Where did you get that money?"

"Why, out of my pocket. You saw me get it out."

"You can't bring extra money to the game if you run out in the game."

"That is true, but you saw me take the money out of my pocket, right?"

"I think I saw you cheat. Mister, you are a liar and a cheat."

The other men tried to argue him out of calling Nate a liar and a cheat. Nate calmly reached over and picked up the money, "If you can't raise or call, you lose."

The bluffer jumped to his feet and drew his gun. Before he could shoot, two of the men grabbed him and held him.

Nate putting the money in his pocked said, "Sir, are you calling me out?"

"Yes, you sorry….."

"Now, now my good man. As you can see I don't carry a gun."

" 'Cause you are a coward!"

"Now, don't be insulting. I'll tell you what let's do. Will you agree that if you are calling me out, I can pick the weapon?"

By then the bluffer was so mad that he would have agreed to anything, "Yes, you…."

Again, Nate stopped him, "No need to be nasty.

"Choose, you double-crossing varmint!"

"I think that I will sleep on the choice of weapons until in the morning."

With that Nate turned and walked away while the other men held the bluffer.

Nate had hoped that the bluffer would have changed his mind by morning, but no such luck. He was madder than ever. Nate refused to talk about the expected fight or the choice of weapons. Slim came around to him and asked, "You going to fight that idiot?"

"Sure. Why, not!"

"He may be a lousy card player, but he is one of the best gunman in the camp."

"We'll see," was Nate's only comment. He counted winnings, and to his surprise, he had won over three hundred dollars. Good wages, better than punching cows or dirt farming.

After breakfast and some real stalling, the bluffer was becoming more uncontrollable. He ranted and called Nate everything under the sun. The shouting and ranting had the entire camp standing around. Some drank coffee, and others just watched. Finally, Nate stood and looked at the red faced gunslinger.

"You ready to die?" That question really hit the bluffer below the belt, and he went absolutely frantic to get a gun and shoot Nate. The other men had restrained him and had taken his gun away, trying to make it a fair fight. If a gunfight can be fair.

Nate got up from his breakfast and looked at the red-faced opponent. "I believe I have the choice of weapons?"

"Just get on with it." shouted the bluffer.

"Let's see, we could use…knives…guns…course…clubs…no…how about shotguns?"

"Shotguns?" asked the bluffer with disbelief.

"Why yes, shotguns. You find yourself a shotgun."

Nate calmly walked to his wagon and returned. The bluffer had found a shotgun and was waving it about. Nate looked real close and saw that the gun was sixteen gauge with a light barrel. That meant that the gun was a bird hunting gun.

Nate lifted his hand for silence, "Now, let's pace off about…say seventy-five feet, twenty-five yards, and I'll give you the first shot. How's that?"

Everybody started talking at once, and the so called gunman was laughing, "First shot?"

Nate checked his gun to see if it was loaded, but of course he knew it was loaded. He walked up to the sputtering fool and grinned, "Ready?" His cold stance took the bluffer back a bit, but he was so mad that he had lost all control of his senses.

The challenger turned his back and began to step off the twenty-five strides. At the end of twenty-five strides, he turned and shouted, "Go to Hell, Mister." People scattered to get out of range and the line of fire.

The cowboy raised his gun and fired. The pattern was all around Nate, but at that distance only a few of the bird shot hit him.

To safeguard his eyes, just as the man fired Nate raised his arm, gun in hand as if he was preparing to fire back. One buck shot hit the back of his arm, but did no damage due to the heavy coat that Nate was wearing. Nate had put on the heavy coat before coming to breakfast. He knew that it would absorb most bird shot at seventy-five feet.

Nate had the gun pointed at the shooter. He lowered the gun and held it in both hands at his waist, calmly looked at the man and said, "Go to Hell." And fired. He fired both barrels of the ten gauge loaded with buckshot. That gun was good enough to kill a deer at one hundred yards. The blast hit the man full in the chest and knocked him on his back about ten feet from where he was standing. He never moved. He was dead.

The camp was in complete silence. The sound of the gun blast echoed even on the flat prairie. The entire camp stood in stunned silence and made no moves.

The only sound was Nate slowly reloading his gun. He brought it to a firing position and turned around the circle with the gun at the ready. "Anybody want some of this?" Not a sound or a movement came from any of the outlaws.

Nate moved away from the camp and back to his wagon. He took off the coat and examined to see if any of the bird shot had drawn blood. Only one shot had broken the skin and was just under the surface. He took out his pocket knife and dug the shot out. His coat had not fared so well, there were a number of shot holes in it. Nate said to himself, "I've got to be back another ten strides to stop this bull."

Last night after the card game Nate had gone back to the wagon, lighted a candle from his supplies and privately counted his money. To his surprise he had picked up about three hundred dollars. He knew that he had won several times and that the last pot was large, but he did not realize just how much he had won. He recounted the money and started to take the package in the false bottom out to put all the money away for safe keeping, when he remembered the rustlers boot with a gun hide-out. He dug through his equipment and found the pair of boots. He place the three hundred dollars in the secret pocket on the inside of the boot. He put the pair of boots in the false bottom with the money packet. There was no need to carry any money now, nobody would play cards with him.

He approached Slim and asked, "Have you thought about how we could pick up that hundred dollar reward on those kids?"

"I thought about it some. None of our scouts have seen hide nor hair of them. It's just like they fell off the face of the earth."

"Well, could you tell the scouts again to be on the outlook for them. And to remember they are riding shod animals."

"Sure thing. Say what is my cut?"

"How about half? Half for you and the boys, and I get half for getting them back. It's a long journey."

"How are you going to get me the reward money, if you have to take them back?"

"That's easy. I'll give you fifty from my money and then when I collect the hundred I'll have my money back. Right?"

"How do I know that the reward is only a hundred?"

"Well, Slim, you will just have to trust me on that."

Nate turned and walked away, smiling to himself. If they found the brats, he would only be out fifty dollars. Sometimes the cards do fall right.

Later in the day Nate was asleep under the wagon when a commotion broke out in the camp. He rolled out from under the wagon to witness the arrival of the largest group of riders he had seen. They rode up shouting and yelling at the camp, and the camp was just as loud in response. There was a lot of back slapping and hand shaking. They all seemed to be close friends.

But from what Slim had said, they were enemies to the end. Now here they were, or so it seemed, laying aside their differences to steal ponies.

The truce was short lived, at least among some of the men. You could see the men circling each other, glaring and sneering. Just like a bunch of cur dogs. All during the evening this continued. Finally it happened. There were two men, one from each group that had a real grudge against each other.

"So if it's not the dirtiest cow stealing, low down skunk in Texas," snarled one of the men. This man had a pistol on each hip and a large knife in a scabbard on his belt.

"Well, it takes one to know one, you sorry excuse of a man." replied the other fellow. He was armed with only one gun, that Nate could see. There was a knife much like the first man's stuck in a scabbard on the side of a boot. They were both mean looking and spoiling for a fight.

The two leaders tried to keep things from boiling over, but that was not to happen. The two men continued to hurl insults at one another. The more they shouted the worse the insults became. Then it happened. The first man had a hide away knife. It came out of nowhere, and he hurled it at the second man. The knife missed and hit a man standing to the side. The third man looked bewildered and slowly sank to the ground.

Like lightning the second man drew his big knife and shouted, "You sorry……. you killed my partner!" The first man drew his eight inch hunting knife. Nate saw the light flash of the sharpened edge. It looked just like a razor.

They lunged at each other trying to find an opening. They faked and feinted, sometimes just cutting a sleeve or a vest, and other times drawing blood. Soon their clothes were hanging in shreds, and still no one had the upper hand.

Nate stood to one side and watched in fascination at the duel. More blood was running, but neither one could get the advantage. They started slugging and wrestling, along with swings and cutting with their knives. Then the balance tilted to the man from Slim's gang. The other man slipped on the slick grass and fell forward. His opponent's knife cut down and glanced off of the belt buckle going into his groin. The cut laid open a gash six inches long and blood gushed out all over the ground. He grabbed his groin and screamed with pain while drawing his pistol.

The pistol shot went wide and missed, not only the other fighter, but everyone in the camp. The next shot came, not from the two fighters, but from a partner of the wounded man. This shot too, went wide of it's mark. The shot tugged at the sleeve of Nate's shirt and made a small cut in his arm.

The shooter shouted, "I'll get you for cutting him!" He cocked his gun to shoot again. Before he could fire, Nate pointed his shotgun at the ground and pulled on the trigger. The roar deafened the outlaws at that close range, and the blast threw grass and dirt all over them. Everyone froze, including the two fighters.

Nate calmly said, "The next shot is for you stranger. Drop the gun!" The barrel was aiming at the second shooter. "Let's keep this fight between these two and not kill each other."

"Why, you,..." The second shooter shouted and turned his gun toward Nate. Nate did not hesitate. The blast hit the man dead center and blew him some ten feet to the rear. Some of the shot hit some by-standers, and they scattered.

Nate reloaded his shotgun and calmly looked around at the crowd. "Who wants the next load?" All was still and quiet for a few seconds.

"You shot one of our gang!" yelled another man as drew his pistol to shoot Nate. That was a mistake he would not make twice. Before he could aim, as he was not a shooter, Nate had fired again. This man was hurled to the rear and hit the ground dead.

"Gentlemen," Nate shouted over the noise. "This shotgun has twice the range of any pistol in the camp and is more accurate. I will kill any man who moves. I can reload and fire more rapidly than you can cock your hand guns. Now, who wants to die?" His voice was filled with anger and determination. The little round man was not a soft toad like many of the men in the camp believed, He would and did kill.

The camp became very still. The two fighters had stopped, and one of them was lying on the ground. He died while the gunfight was going on. The man from Slim's gang was holding his arm where he had been cut. Blood dripped from his finger tips, and he was wobbly on his feet.

Slim's voice broke the silence, "Let's just all cool down. We need every man to fight the Indians. If you have to fight, we will make a ring, and you can lay down your knives and guns and fight with your fist only. Anybody else want to fight?"

Peace settled over the camp, an uneasy peace. Slim moved over close to Nate, "Nate, thanks, you probably saved an all out shoot out. We would have lost half of the men and would not have had enough to attack the Indians."

The other gang leader eased up close and remarked. "You are sure deadly with that scatter-gun."

"It is called, in some places, 'a peace maker,' and in others 'a widow maker'. Either way, I guess that it is correctly named."

Calm returned to the camp and soon the evening meal was in progress. Nate was not welcome at any of the campfires, but he was not turned away from them either. There was fear in some of the eyes. Respect in others. His presence was soon forgotten, and the men began to talk horses and the raid. Nate had heard the outlaws talking about how much money they would make on this raid. Something about a hundred ponies that would bring fifty dollars a head at the fort.

At the next conversation with Slim, Nate asked, "If I might ask, what fort do you deliver the ponies to?"

"We don't have to go to a fort. A buyer comes around with a cavalry detachment. We meet them up on the Tulie. That is about a two or three day's drive. There is a trading post there. They have some corrals, and we can hold the ponies until the buyer comes. He's usually there about once a month. That's where we can trade ponies and cattle. We buy all of our goods there, and sometimes there are some new women around."

"Not a bad deal, cattle from the south and ponies from the Kiowa's in the north."

"You have got that right. These gangs range south down to the sandhills and to the north to the Kiowa homelands. We don't push too far into their home territory. The army is about to put them on the reservation, and then all of that range will be open to the takers. And that's us. Great cattle country!"

"Man what an operation! When you get this cattle country, you will need some backers to stock the range, won't you?" Nate was scheming. This might be the investment he was looking for. He furnishes the money and lets these cowboys do the work for half. Of course, he would keep the books, and that would give him control.

Nate continued, "I have some contacts that could put up the money to get the operation on it's feet."

Slim true to form asked, "What's our cut?"

"I think I can get them to go for an even split. Sound O.K.?"

"I'll have to talk to the boys."

Nate knew that it was already settled. He would furnish the money, and they could do all the work. But, more important, he would keep the books and control the money. He would have a license to steal, a little here and a little there.

The camp was in preparation for the raid. Men were cleaning weapons and checking their mounts. Harness and saddles were double checked. Plans were gone over several times. Scouts rotated from the encampment to the Indian camp. They kept an eye on the movement of the Indians. The Indians acted like they didn't know the outlaws were around. Slim alluded that the Indians knew when somebody went to the brush.

One scout claimed to have seen tracks of shod animals. He claimed that the tracks were over to the northeast. Over on the Blackwater. Nate got really excited about maybe they had found the brats. That was the only report, and the cowboy could not remember right where he saw the tracks. A scout went back out to cover that area, but no tracks.

Slim had become much friendlier after Nate mentioned a partnership in the cattle business. They had discussed all facets of the cattle operation. Slim might be an outlaw, but he sure knew cow business.

Nate was sitting in on the discussions of the raid. He didn't offer advice, he just kept his mouth closed, for once. They were in such a meeting when another report of tracks came in.

This rider reported seeing tracks of shod animals down south. This was confusing. Tracks in the north and now in the south. Little did Nate know that both reports were correct. The north tracks were from the mule the three were riding. The south tracks were Young Eagle's mule.

Nate was in a turmoil because of these conflicting reports. There was no way that the kids could be in two places at once. One of the reports was false. He would bet that they were to the north. Somewhere on the Blackwater. The outlaws, when he had asked about going out hunting the kids, had said a flat, "No." They thought he might upset their plans. Well, he a had couple of plans of his own. Nate was a schemer.

Nate would take his horses out and exercise them every day. He periodically would move his wagon. Claimed he was in the smoke from the campfires, or some reason to be moving around. Actually he was moving his wagon further and further from the camp. By the time the raiders were ready to strike the Indian camp, Nate had left the camp.

He had brought his team up to the wagon before dark. Actually he was about a quarter of a mile from the camp. He was downwind, so sound would not reach the camp. With a near full moon, Nate had hitched the team and driven off into the dark. He knew he would be missed in the morning, but that was the way it would have to be.

The lake where the camp was pitched was surrounded on three sides by some low bluffs. The outlaws said they were called stairsteps up on the Llano. Nate followed the bluff in the moonlight to the east and then to the northeast. There were not ravines or tributaries of streams to impede his progress. With a fresh team he made good time all night.

By daylight he looked back and could not see his wagontracks in the grass. He stopped and got out of the wagon and walked back over the way he had just come. If you got down and looked real close you might see some broken grass stems here and there. But, he doubted that the outlaws were going to look for his tracks. At the camp there were so many tracks that his would be lost in all of the others.

Nate had heard the riders talking about how hard it was to see tracks in the tall grass. The most tracks were found around the waterholes and along streambeds. No tracks for miles, and then tracks at a water hole. The tracks would lead away from the water and disappear in the sea of grass. It took time, and a good tracker, to follow a set of tracks, if they were fresh. The outlaws would give up real quick.

Nate climbed a knoll and scanned the terrain that he had just crossed. There was no dust or signs of anyone following him. They probably just couldn't figure which way he went or that he was worth following. "Good," he thought, as he climbed back on the wagon and continued his journey. By letting the team rest some every hour or so, he figured that he could keep moving all day. He might hit the Blackwater by sunset.

Sunset found him at a stream. He surmised it was the Blackwater. The outlaws had said that the Blackwater was the next stream north. Actually, they had drawn a rough map on the ground showing the Yellow House and the Blackwater. The two had forked some distance to the southeast of the outlaw camp. The Yellow House ran west, south of the outlaw camp, to the springs. Then the Blackwater ran north for a ways and then turned northwest. The campers had said that they were only about fifteen miles from the Blackwater. Slim's map had shown that the Blackwater made a circle around the present location of the Indian camp. Riders had indicated that the Blackwater finally turned west, but they did not know how far west it went. They sure did not know if it went to New Mexico Territory.

Nate had to take some chances. Chances that he would find the brats. The outlaws were not interested in finding runaways, they were interested in one hundred ponies. Moving the wagon up one of the ravines in the face of the bluff, he made camp. The ravine had run back into the bluff and then made a turn to the left. It continued on for perhaps fifty yards. There it dead ended, but it made a perfect shelter. A small spring ran out of the face of the rocks, and a little grass grew around the water.

After building a small fire, Nate walked back down the ravine. When he made the turn to his right, the campsite was completely out of sight. His fire could not be seen unless you came up the ravine, or you rode up on the bank looking down. You had to take some chances.

Because of his meager supplies, Nate wandered out into the grass and found chicken eggs. He had seen the women from the camp hunt eggs, and they had had them for breakfast several times. He soon found enough for his supper and for his breakfast. He made a pan of hot biscuits and gravy with the eggs which was better than any of the meals he had taken at the outlaw camp.

Nate's biggest worry was that he would drive right into the Indian camp. They were camped with their ponies somewhere on the Blackwater. If the kids were ahead of him, they would find the Indians. If they were behind him, he would lead them to the Indians. They would not know he was out there, but, he would not know where they were. You had to take some chances.

During the evening he watched a vicious storm to the southeast. The clouds rolled and boiled with thunder and lighting. The lighting struck the ground repeatedly, and he could hear the roar of the storm. Realization came in a flash. That cloud had spawned a tornado. He watched it move from the southwest to the northeast. The storm moved off, and slowly the roar of the cloud diminished. He remembered the one on the caprock and those poor cowboys who had died. He also remembered the snakes, and his flesh crawled.

Daylight woke Nate, and he spent little time getting ready to move. Breakfast, loading and hitching the team did not take an hour, and he was on the trail before sunup. He saw some tracks in a clear place, but then they disappeared. No shod tracks appeared at any place where other tracks showed. This seemed a dead end.

The streambed had steep banks in some places and very shallow banks in others. The water was not deep in anyplace and was not over ten or so feet wide. This stream could run out anytime. Nate had no idea how close to New Mexico Territory he was or where he was on the Llano Estacado.

The stream ran northwest for a couple of miles and climbed up a step onto the abutment. Then the stream turned due north. As he came up on the top of the abutment, he heard the sounds of a battle. The outlaws, as they had planned, had attacked the Indian's camp at daybreak. The din of battle sounds came across the prairie on the gentle northwest breeze. The roar of the guns was audible and clear. The battle only continued for a half hour, and then it was very quiet. Only the sound of the breeze filled Nate's ears.

About mid-afternoon Nate topped a small hill and saw the aftermath of the battle. Indians lay all over the low marsh lands of the Blackwater stream. The outlaws had described this place very vividly. A flat wide area with lots of water and vegetation growing in some marshes. As Nate approached, his team shied and wanted to balk. It was the smell of blood from the dead horses and men. Nate felt ill and wished he had never seen so much death in one place.

The ponies were gone and so were the outlaws. Not one Indian moved. The stillness was eerie and frightening. Nate took the team around the carnage and staked them upwind from the battlesite. Taking his shotgun he slowly walked back through the battle area. Not only were the Indians dead, but most had been shot several times. Nate looked at the bodies and then saw that every Indian had been shot in the forehead. That meant that after the battle the outlaws had walked through the bodies and shot them, in the head, one at a time.

The number of dead horses was surprising. The outlaws wanted horses but had killed the Indian's ponies. There were at least twenty dead ponies and one........Nate stood still. That is one of the mules the kids were riding. Nate moved over the area another time. This time looking for evidence that the kids had been there. He found nothing, other than the one dead mule.

CHAPTER ELEVEN

The tornado roared toward us.

"Get in the ravine!" The wind became furious, and the rain and hail began to fall.

"Robert, this is not going to protect us from the storm!" The elements were beating us with rain, hail and trash.

"Get down on your knees and cover your head." We got down and crawled up against the west wall of the ravine for what little protection it could give us.

"Minnie our stuff!" I had to yell over the roar of the storm. "Our belongings are being scattered and blown away." Clothes were sucked out of the bag that they were in. Utensils were hurled with the force of bullets up against the ravine walls. Bedding that was laid out was sucked into the air and vanished in the dark of the storm. Soon all of our belongings and supplies were gone. The wind had whipped them down the ravine and out of sight.

I yelled to Minnie, "Use your body to protect Lizzie!" Trash and dirt in the air was pelting us and cutting the skin.

Lizzie cried, "I can't breathe." The force of the storm was sucking the breath from our bodies.

Minnie screamed over the ear splitting noise, "Lay down on your stomach. Get low!" Suddenly there was a greater roar, and the tornado was on us.

"Minnie!" Lizzie screamed. She was being lifted up, and I grabbed for her. We felt light and then we were floating above the ground. We were off our feet and being sucked out of the ravine.

I screamed, "Minnie! Lizzie!" But the girls were picked up and pitched over on the grass at the top of the ravine. I was up off the ground for fifty to sixty feet and then dropped. We were not blown far, but we were dazed, soaked and covered in mud, grass and trash.

Lizzie looked down at her clothes and cried, "Straw from the prairie is stuck in my clothes and in my hair."

After the first tornado had gone by, the wind subsided a little. I sat up and looked to the west and there was another tail trailing along behind the first. It was perhaps a mile south of us, but the wind was again terrifying.

I shouted to the girls, "Get back in the ravine, there is another tornado coming." We crawled back into the ravine to get out of the force of the wind from the second tornado.

I watched and was horrified that the second tornado was coming straight at the ravine. Suddenly it swerved to the east and moved off. It missed us by about a quarter of a mile. It threw sand, dirt and grass into the ravine and covered us up.

The clouds were moving rapidly and in thirty minutes the sky was clear and blue.

"Robert, where are you?" called Minnie.

"I'm over here," I replied, as I stood up.

"Where, Robert?"

"Over here, behind you, Minnie."

She was so confused that she could hear me, but could not locate me. She turned and said, "Now I see you." Like it was dark or something.

"Minnie, get the straw and dirt out of your face, and maybe you can see me better."

She pushed her hair out of her face, along with the mud and grass. "Oh, there you are. Robert, why are you so black and dirty?" She was still dazed.

I did not reply. I just limped over to the girls and put an arm around each one. We stood there for several minutes, holding each other. We were covered with mud and grass. It was in our clothes and hair. We had some small cuts and lots of bruises.

Minnie asked, "What happened?"

"A tornado came over us, or near us, and sucked us out of the ravine. It blew me out there and dropped the two of you here on the bank of the ravine."

"Oh, my goodness, where are our belongings?"

"Minnie, they are scattered all over the ravine and the plains."

I held Lizzie close and said to her, "Don't cry, Sis. The storm is over, and we are all right."

She sobbed and sobbed.

"Robert, we have got to see what we can find and bring it back to camp before it gets dark."

"O.K. but, everything is wet and dirty. We will have to wear, and maybe sleep in, our wet clothes until they dry. They should dry out before dark. But, we will have to sleep on the wet ground."

To get Lizzie to stop crying, Minnie took her to help pick up the items scattered all over the ravine and the plains. Actually, we had rounded up a large portion of our meager belongings before dark. But, I could not find dry wood to build a fire, and when the sun went down it really became cool.

I told the girls, "I am going to take Number One and ride farther up the ravine and see if there are any more of our belongings there."

I could not believe my eyes. I had hobbled the mules down the ravine from us. Actually, they were just out of sight from our original campsite. When I got to the mules I was stunned. Number One was covered in mud and dirt, but he seemed to be all right. Number Four was down on the ground. I went up to him and saw that a small tree trunk was driven through his neck. I guess it killed him instantly, but he may have bled to death. There was a lot of dark dirt under him and along with the wet ground it was hard to tell. We were down to one mule.

I just sat down on the ground and cried. Number Four had worked so hard on the farm. Now, after all his effort and carrying us for miles he had been killed by a little tree. The tree was not over three inches in diameter and seven feet long. Minnie and Lizzie heard me and came to see why I was crying. They, too stopped in disbelief. Then all three of us had a good cry. I guess we needed to get some stuff out of our systems. Lizzie had already had one cry, so she stopped first and went over and sat by Number Four. She stroked and petted him.

"Poor Number Four. We loved you and are sorry you are dead. I bet, you have gone to mule heaven."

That was one of the worst days of my life. The saddest was when we lost Mama and Papa. Today was the worst. I had been responsible for the loss of Number Two in a storm. I had been a big shot and had given away Number Three to Young Eagle. And now when we needed a mule so bad, I had let my sisters down. I had not found good protection for our animals, and I had not protected my sisters.

"Robert, " Minnie called.

"Yes." I replied through my tears.

"I know you feel responsible for the bad things that have happened on our trip. Robert, you are not to blame for any of it. Number Two would have gotten away regardless. He was scared in the storm. If he had not gotten away, he probably would have hurt himself real bad. You gave Number Three to Young Eagle, and that showed your big heart. Now this storm was not your doing, and Number Four just was at the wrong place at the wrong time. You feel this way, right?"

"Yes , Minnie." I sobbed.

"Just be thankful that we had Number Four this far. We might lose Number One to any number of happenings. Let's go check our belongings before it gets dark. Once it's dark and the moon is up, you can take Number One and look for other items. O.K.?"

We trudged back to the camp. I led Number One back with us. Even Ol' Bullet was covered with dirt.

Lizzie said, " Bullet, I'll give you a bath when we find water." The girls started going through our gear. It looked pretty bad.

The moon came up, and I mounted Number One. In the moonlight I could see bedding and clothes scattered all over. It took me close to three hours to gather it up. Guess I should be happy it didn't take longer. I also guess the tornado just went over us. If that is correct, I can understand why it did not scatter our stuff worse. It just sucked up all of our things as it passed over. Then both tornadoes had covered us up with grass and mud.

The girls washed down at the pool of water and Lizzie, good to her promise, gave Ol' Bullet a bath. Lizzie finally went to sleep on one of the wagon canvasses by the pool, while Minnie tried to wash some of our clothes by moonlight. I kept bringing in what I could carry and would go back for more.

Minnie said, "I think our stuff just got caught up, like in a big whirlwind. If we had been in the full force of a tornado, no telling what might have been the outcome."

"If this is the results of a whirlwind, then I'm sure glad that we weren't in a real tornado."

We finally stopped. Minnie said to me, "Go down to the pool and wash best you can in the dark. Then come and let's get some rest if we can." After a bath and washing my clothes best I could, I came back and stretched out on the canvas by Lizzie and Minnie. Minnie covered us with the second canvas and we fell asleep very quick. I did not stir until I woke up cold. I put my clothes on and went back to sleep.

The dawn was beautiful. I even noticed that the earth smelled fresh, and the birds were singing. When we arose, we found we were sore all over and sure stiff. We had taken a beating and a half. Our joints slowly loosened, and we began to move.

I gathered up our cooking and eating utensils. They were not scattered as bad as I thought they would be, but some of them sure were dented. We finally got a fire going, and I thanked the Lord for watertight tins for matches. I found the sack with Minnie's other cooking items over a small hill. Two of the burlap sacks were oilcloth lined to keep out moisture on seed. These two sacks, with our food, had kept our flour, salt and baking soda dry. We had learned to keep our flour and such in a water proof bag. I found more old dead wood for the fire and Minnie cooked up some biscuits and gravy. We sure put the food away.

With the new day, we had to make an inventory of our belongings. Out of the eight sacks, I found them all. I was very surprised that they were just scattered about. Some that had heavy items did not blow very far. We had three sacks with bedrolls. We recovered all of the bedding and spread it out on the grass to dry. We had one sack with the two wagon canvases. To my amazement, I had found the two wagon covers better than a mile from our campsite. In the moonlight they had shown like two white birds on the grass of the plains. Minnie had her two sacks, one with food and one with utensils. Our clothes were in the worst shape of anything. They had been sucked out of the sacks and scattered all over the prairie. Also, they were full of mud.

The last sack, with our odds and ends in it, had not even moved. It had the gun and shells in it, Lizzie's two dolls and Minnie's Bible and Uncle Nate's bank book. Lizzie had not played with the dolls on the trail. She did not want to get them dirtier, and she wanted to show them to Uncle John and Aunt Mary. She wanted her New Mexico Territory Uncle and Aunt to see what her Texas Uncle and Aunt had let those two twin brats do to her presents from Grandpa and Grandma and Papa and Mama. She was very emphatic.

Minnie, spent the day trying to wash out bedding and clothes. Washing by hand in a pool of water, it is a real chore. She did the best she could and then laid everything out on the grass to dry. We had more biscuits and gravy for lunch. I never thought we would have a different meal again. I just knew that every blasted thing we owned was blown out of the country.

After a long day, we took stock of our situation. As we checked though our belongings, I cleaned the shotgun the best I could. I did not want Papa's four-ten shotgun to rust. We had all of our belongings, and they had been washed the best Minnie could. We were clean and dry again, and best of all, we still had one mule.

Minnie's suggestion was the one we decided to use. We could hang all of the sacks on Number One, just like we had been doing. Number One would have to carry the eight sacks and Lizzie.

She said, "That's not fair. If I ride Number One, where will the two of you ride?"

I, the big mouth said, "Why, Lizzie, Minnie and I are going to just walk like pioneers of old."

Minnie turned to Lizzie, "Sugar, we will walk, but if we get tired we will ride, too."

"Well," Lizzie allowed, "If you can walk, I can walk, too."

The day was almost gone, and we were back together to some degree. One thing I did learn that day was that Ol'Bullet was a great hunter. He usually stayed in the camp to be with the girls. Today, as I was going out to look for eggs in the middle of the afternoon, for some reason, I took Ol'Bullet with me. We had been out on the grass for only a little while when a "chicken" ran out of the grass. Without thinking I hollered to Ol'Bullet, "Get'em."

Ol' Bullet ran that chicken down before the bird got up good speed. Then to add to my amazement, he came trotting back with the bird in his jaws. As I patted him, his tail beat a steady left to right rhythm. Then to add to this miracle of a dog, he ran me another "chicken" down and brought it to me without any command. A hunter and a retriever in one dog. Would you believe? We had roasted "chicken" for supper. With salt and our old standby of biscuits, the food was fine.

We enjoyed sitting by the fire, and just being alive and well was very fine.

Minnie looked at the moon and commented, "This time last night I didn't know if we would see the dawn of today."

We only had scratches and bruises. How lucky could you get? Sleep in our bedrolls that night was pure joy. We woke to the smell of breakfast cooking. Eggs and making our usual fare of biscuits and gravy. As we were rested and ready to get back on the trail, the routine that morning was done with joy in our hearts. We were alive and not seriously hurt. As I had only Number One to get ready, I could spend more time helping the girls get ready to move.

Minnie walked on one side of the mule, and I walked on the other. For a change, we were closer together than being strung out on the mules in single file. Conversation was easy, and we began to enjoy the arrangement.

The day was beautiful and as we came up an abutment, we could see for miles. We looked back, and we could imagine where the two rivers had forked.

"Minnie, do you suppose that Young Eagle is O.K.?" I asked.

"Sure, with him back with his family, he's fine."

Lizzie spoke, "Do you think of Mama and Papa much?"

I replied, "Sis, every day and sometimes several times a day."

"Me too, Sugar." added Minnie.

Lizzie's bottom lip hung out just a little, and her head dropped, "I have a hard time remembering what they look like."

Minnie and I both were quiet for several minutes.

I looked up at Lizzie and said, "Lizzie, I did not want to admit it, but I do too."

We walked on in silence and watched Ol' Bullet flushing birds out of the grass.

"Bullet sure has been a good dog!" exclaimed Lizzie. "He has slept with me almost every night."

Far to the northwest we could see a low bank of clouds.

"Hope we don't see another cloud like the one we were in." I remarked.

We followed the river, walking through grass that stretched forever.

"What did the little old man call this, …….. a sea of grass?" asked Minnie.

I pointed out across the grass, "See how it sways and waves just like water."

"Minnie, how long do you think we have been going west?" I asked.

"If I haven't lost my count, we have been on the trail about three weeks, about twenty days."

"What is the date? Got any idea, Minnie?"

"Well we left about the middle of May, so it should be the end of the first week of June."

"We sure need to get to Uncle John's before much longer, because it is going to be hot in late June and July."

"Maybe it has been the rain or that we are some further north, but the days don't seem so hot."

"Well, you are not riding on a mule now, walking may make it hotter."

"Say, look at the birds way up in the sky." I said pointing.

Minnie observed, "Those are ducks or geese."

"Minnie, did my dolls get wet?"

"No, Lizzie they did not."

"Good, I want to show them to Uncle John and Aunt Mary."

"Say, I wonder how Aunt Bess and Aunt Marjie are doing?"

"Like always, Aunt Bess has a deal, and Aunt Marjie is about to faint," Minnie said with smile.

We walked until ten o'clock by Minnie's watch, and then we took a break. We moved down to the stream and found some shade. The water in the stream was cool and refreshing to us, Ol' Bullet and Number One. They both rolled and rolled in the water.

Noon came without our having seen one moving thing, other than some birds. The grass had changed in height. Along the stream it was four and five feet tall. Out on the prairie it was at least three feet tall. This was making it hard to walk. We decided to stay in the streambed, and see if we could do better. There was a sandy strip along the side of the water, and it looked easier to walk on than the tall grass.

After a lunch of cold biscuits and chicken, we sat in the shade of some short trees and listened to the buzzing of the insects. The still warm air made us sleepy, so we dozed and rested. When aroused we started up the streambed. The walking was easier, and as the stream ran fairly straight, we made better headway. At three o'clock we found some shade for our long afternoon rest. We spread a canvas and lay down. We did not worry about falling asleep. Ol' Bullet would be on guard and would give a warning.

We were moving again at five and had planned to walk until sunset, if we weren't too tired. We had been walking for some time when I said, "The only thing bad about walking down here is we can't see if anything is around."

"True, Robert. If there is something out there, they can't see us down in here either."

"Guess that is right, I just like to be able to see."

The stream had run to the northwest most of the day. For a short time it ran due north and then back to the northwest.

"I wish this stream would run west so we can get to the New Mexico Territory," I complained.

"I think, even if this keeps running this direction, we have to hit the Territory of New Mexico. I looked at a book at school and saw a map of Texas and the Territory. If I remember right, we could not miss the Territory if we keep going this direction."

The rest of the day passed slowly, very slowly, and we were beginning to slow down.

"Robert, is that a wall?" asked Lizzie.

We were down in the stream bed, and the walls in some places were several feet high. The deepness of the bed depended on how sharp the turn in the stream was. Most of the time the walls were anywhere from a slope to eight or nine feet tall.

Minnie and I looked where she was pointing. Directly in front of us was a wall. The stream ended and there was a wall. Our spirits sank. We thought we had come to the end of the stream. We were sure that we had taken a wrong turn and that solid wall was the end.

"Robert, if that is the end, and that is just a wall, where is the water coming from? Out of the ground?"

"There's something strange about this." I agreed.

As we approached the wall we suddenly realized that the stream made a hard turn to the left. There was a wall there, but it was not a deadend. The rock made the same turn as the stream. The wall almost was a corner like in a room. The stream and the wall were going to make us take a hard left.

We got up to the turn and were amazed that the streambed had narrowed so much. We made the turn and were almost around the corner when a band of Indians riding fast almost ran over us.

Lizzie squealed and shouted, "Indians!"

I started to run, but they were all around us.

Minnie pulled Lizzie off the mule and held her in her arms.

They jumped off of their horses and crowded around us, talking among themselves. Some of them wore war paint and carried an odd assortment of weapons. The leader, or at least the loudest, kept poking me with his finger and asking me something. All I could do was stand there like a log. The big one yanked my hat off and touched my blond hair. He let out a yell and swung his war hatchet. This did not look good. I was scared to death.

Now they were touching and poking all three of us. There was a lot of jabbering and arm waving by the band. They really got interested in the necklaces that Young Eagle had given us in their camp. The leader of the band kept touching the necklace and again asking questions. They were pushing and shoving. They acted like some of the big bullies in school back home.

The girls were crying, and I had my jaw stuck out. The Indians laughed when they saw my defiance. Without warning one of the Indians picked me up and tossed me on his pony, and he mounted behind me. Without ceremony the girls were picked, up put and tossed on separate ponies. Then an Indian jumped on behind them to hold them captive.

Another rider caught up Number One's reins and shouted. They all turned their ponies and headed back up the draw. They moved at a trot and soon all the sacks of our possessions had fallen off of Number One. As the Indians were riding on the sand banks, all of our goods fell on dry ground, for all the good it does us.

Both girls were hysterical and making it hard for the Indians to hold them on the ponies. Minnie was big enough that she was really fighting her captor. He finally hit her in the side of the head with his fist. She went limp and Lizzie really let it out. She thought the Indians had killed Minnie.

I started screaming at the top of my lungs, and out of nowhere Ol' Bullet was biting the leg of the last Indian in the group. Ol' Bullet pulled him off the horse and immediately attacked the next rider. One by one he was dismounting the riders. Ol' Bullet is big, and he was mad. I had never seen him tear into anybody before. He had dismounted four of the riders before one of the riders hit him in the head with a war club. Ol' Bullet skidded to a halt in the dirt and was still.

Lizzie and I were still raising a ruckus that could be heard all over the Llano. The Indians had had enough. The leader gave an order, we were clubbed in the head and knocked out.

I remember some of the ride, but very little. I did not hear the crying or the yelling of Minnie or Lizzie anymore. I do remember the bouncing of the pony and laying on my stomach on the horse's back. My head hurt, and I was dizzy. I wondered where Ol' Bullet was and if we had lost all of our belongings. Didn't look like it mattered much now.

The next thing I did remember was the buzz in my head. I tried to open my eyes, but my head hurt too much. There was lots of shouting and yelling somewhere in the distance. Then slowly my head began to clear. I looked around and found that I was lying on some skins in an Indian lodge. The dwelling was just like the one at Young Eagle's camp. Next I became aware that I was tied, hand and foot.

My vision cleared, and I managed to roll over. Minnie and Lizzie lay on the pelts at my feet. They, too, were tied hand and foot, and they were gagged. I then realized that a gag was in my mouth. I heard something in the lodge. Startled, I jerked around to see what was there. My head swam and my vision blurred again. After a few minutes my vision cleared, and my stomach stopped churning. I heard the noise again, and turning my head a little further, I saw an old Indian woman.

She looked at me with black piercing eagle eyes. She never took her eyes off me. All the while she was chewing on a piece of skin. Ugh!! Who would put the skin of an animal in their mouth. An Indian I guess. The pain returned, and I drifted off into blackness.

The next time I opened my eyes, Minnie was looking at me. Her eyes were filled with fear. Fear of what would be in store for us. I don't think I had that fear. Probably was just dumb about what Indians do to children when they can capture them. I found out later that Minnie was of the perfect age to become the bride of a warrior. Lizzie would be brought up as an Indian and then become a bride. Me...this part sure put the fear of God in my heart. Young white eyes, they were usually killed.

When I came to the next time, I heard the beat of drums and chanting. I blinked and my head slowly cleared. It was night outside and there was only a little light from the fire in the middle of the lodge. I looked around and saw that Minnie and Lizzie were both awake and looking at me with panic and fear in their eyes. I could only, feebly shrug my shoulders. There was nothing any one of us could do, and there was no help from the outside.

Sleep finally came, despite the noise of the drums and the yells of the warriors. We had been captured about sundown and had been in this lodge all night. I awoke at dawn to the babble of women in the camp. They were preparing the morning meal and probably talking about the three white eyes.

Suddenly I had a real problem. I needed to relieve my bladder. With the gag in my mouth, all I could do was make grunts and groans. The old woman just looked at me and laughed. I could hold it no longer, and I wet my pants. The old woman roared with laughter and pointed at me. I was very embarrassed. I had not done that since I was a little boy. I hid my face from the old woman and the girls.

The old woman got up and put a noose around Minnie's neck. Then she untied her hands and feet. She did not take the gag out of her mouth. Minnie reached up to take the gag out and the old woman threatened her with a raised hand. Minnie left the gag alone. She took Minnie out to the horror of Lizzie and me. Soon she returned leading Minnie and retied her. The old woman took the rope off of Minnie and turned to Lizzie. The rope was put over her head, and then she was untied. Lizzie made no move to take the gag out of her mouth. The old woman was watching to see if she would. When she didn't, the old woman grunted and led her out of the lodge. I learned later that she had taken the girls down in a ravine where the women went for privacy. But all along, the old woman would just look at me, point and laugh.

The cover on the lodge was opened, and a fierce looking man came in. He and the old woman exchanged some comments, and then he left. She stirred up a fire in the center of the lodge, and it appeared to me she was preparing a meal. After she got the meal started, she came over and pulled the gags from our mouths. It took a few minutes for me to work up enough saliva in my mouth to be able to speak. The girls were having the same problem.

Finally, I could speak, and looking at them, I asked, "Are you O.K.?"

They both just nodded their heads, "Yes." I started to speak again, and the old woman backhanded me so hard that my eyes blurred again and my head rang. I shut up and just glared at the old woman. Minnie did not speak for fear of starting to cry. Lizzie was already sobbing, and tears ran down her face. The old woman looked at Lizzie, said something and then slapped her and shouted something else at her. I struggled with my bonds, but could do nothing. Lizzie's tears continued, but she did not make a sound.

The old woman ladled some food into a bowl of sorts and came over to the three of us. She began speaking, as if we could understand her. She jerked each one of us to a sitting position. She was rough, especially on the girls. She took a crude-looking spoon and offered me a bite. The smell was strange, and I started to not take any. Then the hunger in my stomach overruled, and I opened my mouth. I didn't want to know what she had given me. I just chewed and tried not to think about where Ol' Bullet might be right now.

She then moved to Minnie and offered a bite. I was chewing and looking at Minnie to see how she would react. There was fear in her eyes, and she shrank back from the offered spoon.

I mustered up the effort and mumbled around my mouth full, "Eat Sis, you have got to have strength." The old woman was as quick as lightning. She put the spoon in the bowl and backhanded me again, before I could move or blink an eye. The old woman glared at me, and let out a whole string of something in Indian.

Minnie resigned and slowly opened her mouth. The old woman shoved in a spoonful.

Minnie almost gagged, then she started slowly chewing. All the time there were tears in her eyes. She looked at Lizzie, and when the old woman offered food to Lizzie, she nodded her head, "Yes" to Lizzie. Lizzie took a tentative bite between sobs and began to chew. All the time the old woman kept up a running stream of Indian talk. We had no idea if she was instructing us, complaining about us or just talking to herself. The old woman came back to me and gave me another bite, and then she started around and around until the bowl was empty.

When the meal was over, the old woman stuffed the gags back into our mouths. We wanted to talk, but she had slapped Lizzie and had back handed me, and that sure discouraged any attempt to talk. At least for now.

The old woman had taken the girls out in the late afternoon and returned them to the lodge. The routine was quick and without a problem, as the girls gave the old woman no excuse to hit them. The old hag put the rope around my neck and untied my hands and feet for the first time. She watched to see if I would try to take the gag out. I did not. She led me outside right in plain view of the camp and stood there watching me. The urge was so great that the only choices I had was to wet my clothes or go standing right there. I chose to go right there. The women of the camp all stood and laughed and pointed at me. That was probably the worst moment of my life. I kept my eyes down so the girls could not see my embarrassment and shame.

We spent another night tied and hobbled like animals in the Indian lodge. Dawn brought the usual activity to the camp. Cooking was the main event in the camp other than dancing to their drums. I guess there was one other center of interest. That was the ponies. We could hear them. The sound of hooves filled the air most of the day.

Dawn brought the old woman with our first meal of the day. After the meal she would lead us out, one at a time, for a nature call. The girls were taken to the women's place, but each time I was made to stand out in the open in front of the camp. I was really embarrassed by this degrading treatment. We had started back to the lodge and I, to my astonishment, saw a man standing the middle of the camp relieving himself. No one took notice, and he returned to his lodge. I thought I was being punished, but I was just being taken outside. Period!

Late the second day there was a great upheaval in the camp. There was much excitement and shouting. Tied in the lodge, we had no knowledge or idea of what was taking place. The war drums began to beat and a sense of new fever ran through the camp.

We were fed and taken for our outing and put back in the tent in a rush. Even the old woman was in a hurry. We had only seen her poke around and take forever to do a task. Now she rushed everything, especially the feeding of us. She really shoved that food in our mouths. And you could tell that she was in a hurry when she would try to put a spoon of food in our mouths, and it was still full.

We fell asleep late in the night to the throbbing of the drums. There were more of them tonight. From the level of the noise, another band must have arrived at the camp. That would account for the excitement. I was aroused a time or two when the noise level increased, but otherwise, I slept through the racket.

Food came late the next morning. The old woman was grumpy and irritated about something. She took the ropes off of our hands and the gags out of our mouths so we could eat. We fed ourselves, but we still did not speak. After the meal she untied our feet and took us outside one at a time. No rope around the neck. The girls were taken to the same place, and I was shoved outside. The old woman did not even follow me. I returned to the lodge on my own. Our feet were retied, but not our hands. This was very strange. I could have worked the knots loose. If I did get the ropes off, we could not run. We were in the middle of an Indian camp.

Suddenly the cover on the lodge was hurled aside, and to our total astonishment, the father of Young Eagle, Great Eagle, filled the lodge. I mean filled the lodge He was mad and threw the old woman out of the lodge and removed the ropes from our feet. The entrance of the lodge was crowded with people. There was another commotion outside the lodge entrance. Another warrior shoved his way into the lodge.

The two men glared at each other, and there was a heated exchange of words. You did not need to know Indian to know that there was trouble in the air. The two men were very mad. Suddenly they both turned and left the lodge. The crowd outside was pushed and shoved out of the way.

Our lodge covering was not put back, and we could see some of the turmoil going on in the camp. We were left to our own devices.

"Minnie, are you O.K.?"

"Yes."

"Lizzie, are you O.K.?"

"Yes."

Minnie's turn.

"How about you, Robert?"

"My body has a bunch of sore places, but my pride is hurt worse."

"Why?"

I realized that they did not know of my embarrassment, and I had to come up with something quick. "Oh, letting us get in this mess."

The uproar outside continued for some time. We just sat and waited for whatever the future would bring.

The opening of the open lodge darkened and Gray Fox and Young Eagle entered. Young Eagle closed the cover behind him to shut out the curious eyes of the crowd.

We all jumped up and hugged Gray Fox. Young Eagle almost fell over when we all hugged him. Apparently he did not know what to make of that action.

Gray Fox spoke, "Are you all right?"

We chorused , "Yes. We are now!"

"Not so fast. That other warrior that was in here is Thunder Cloud. And that is just what he is. Our band and the other bands try to not have much to do with Thunder Cloud and his band. We are in his camp, and by the Kiowa ways, Thunder Cloud is head chief as long as we are in his camp. He is head chief to the other three bands that are here."

"What can Young Eagle's father do for us?"

"He will keep you alive for one thing. He can keep you from being sold to some other band or carried to the north to our homelands."

"Where is our mule and our sacks of goods?"

"I don't know, but I will have some of the braves look for them."

I spoke up, "The sacks were dropped in the river bed."

"We will see if we can find them."

"Have you seen Ol' Bullet, our dog?" asked Lizzie.

"No, but we will look for him. Now let me see your arms and legs where the ropes were tied."

Gray Fox put some grease on the rope burns.

"Gray Fox, will you look at Robert's scalp? He was hit with a club when we were captured."

She gently pushed the hair back and said, "The skin is only slightly broken, and the blood has covered the wound. I think you will be fine."

Gray Fox and Young Eagle left and put the cover on the lodge door. She had promised to look for the mule and our goods. And, to check and see if Ol' Bullet was around.

At noon Gray Fox came back to the lodge with food. As we ate, she told us what she had found out. "We have your mule with our horses over in our part of the camp. We had to do some real trading to get him. Thunder Cloud's band was planning to eat him."

Boy, that made our eye brows go up. I protested, "Eat our mule?"

"Yes, but we traded them some antelope meat for the mule. We had a lot of meat as our men had just returned from a big hunt. When you were at our camp many of our men were on the hunt. They returned the day after you left."

"What is this place, Gray Fox?" Minnie asked.

"The bands come together several times a year and trade ponies and play games. Games of skill in horseback riding and shooting. We women get to see who is courting who, and who is going to have a baby."

"What about Ol' Bullet?" quizzed Lizzie.

"The braves are looking for him and your sacks."

Gray Fox took the girls out for a nature call. Upon returning, she told me to walk to one side and a little behind her and to keep my head down. Look at the earth. We went out on the prairie away from the camp, and she turned her back. She was both white and a savage. We returned to the lodge, and she said, "I must go. I will come back with your evening meal, and perhaps we will know about your dog and sacks."

We kept the lodge door closed and that made it very hot in the closed lodge. We did sleep, or at least dozed, in the heat. The afternoon passed slowly. We talked a little, but did not have much to say.

Evening came, and Gray Fox returned. She and Young Wolf had all kinds of food. We ate before we talked.

"We have found your sacks, and they are in my lodge. No one had found them or they would have been gone and destroyed. There is little in your sacks that would be of use to an Indian. We have not seen your dog."

"Do Indians eat dog?" cried Lizzie.

Gray Fox did not lie. "Some do. Our band prefers antelope. But from what you told me, the band that brought you in did not stop and pick him up. We found where we think he was hit, but he was gone. I feel he's hiding in the grass looking for you, little one."

"Gray Fox, thank you for finding our goods."

"Children, you are white eyes in the eyes of the Kiowa. They usually sell children, or they keep the girls and they become the wives of braves. If we were in our camp you would be free and on your way. But, we are not. Here is the hard part. Tonight Young Eagle's father, Great Eagle, will fight Thunder Cloud for you. They have argued all day about you, and Great Eagle has challenged Thunder Cloud. If Great Eagle wins you go free, and Great Eagle is the chief of the two bands."

"And if Thunder Cloud wins?" I asked.

"He becomes the chief of both bands, and he keeps you."

"What will happen to Great Eagle if he loses, to him I mean?" Minnie wanted to know.

"He will be cast out of the band and must take his family and live alone."

"This is cruel and not right," Minnie declared.

"In the white man's world it is. Here, it is the way of the people."

"It's still wrong." Minnie declared again.

"You are white eyes. If you had not saved Great Eagle's son, he would not lift a hand to help you. It is honor that makes him fight."

"Is Great Eagle a good fighter, Gray Fox?"

"One of the best, but Thunder Cloud is notorious for his tricks and underhanded ways of winning."

Lizzie spoke, "You mean he cheats?"

"Yes, " was all Gray Fox said. She left, and our spirits were very low.

The braves came for us after dark. We would witness the fight. They put ropes around our necks, but they didn't tie our hands. Then they took us out.

The Indians had built several fires in a circle.

Gray Fox came and stood with us. She was white eyes.

She explained, "As Great Eagle challenged Thunder Cloud, Thunder Cloud got to pick the weapon. Thunder Cloud chose lances. The fight will be inside the ring of fires. See the lances, stuck up in the ground? Each warrior has one lance in his hands and five are stuck around inside the ring of fire. Great Eagle has the feathers of an eagle tied to the lances, so we know the ones belonging to Great Eagle. Thunder Cloud's lances have the tail of a coyote tied on them. If a warrior uses a lance that belongs to the other, he loses. If the warrior throws all of his lances, he can not pick one up off the ground. If he does, he loses. If a warrior is wounded so he can't fight, he looses, and if one is killed......"

The two chiefs came into the ring of light from the fires. Each carried one lance. All the people of all five bands were standing around outside the ring of fires. There were way over a hundred Kiowa in the circle. There were about forty braves. The braves had their women with them and many children. Other than the crackling of the fire, there was total silence.

The leader of one of the bands came into the circle. Gray Fox explained, "He is acting as judge in this fight. He will give the rules. There are few."

After the first leader gave the rules, a second man entered the ring. "This is the most powerful medicine man in the five bands. He has cured many sick. He has driven out devils and demons. He has given medicine to women who could not have babies, and they became mothers. He has medicines for many illnesses."

One single drum started to sound. A slow and steady beat. That sound was all that filled the air. Gray Fox whispered to us, "When the drum stops, the contest will begin." The two warriors stood like stones at the edge of the circle of fires. The drum seemed to go on forever. Then silence.

The two braves moved into the circle. They feinted and faked. One would rush and the other dodge. They jabbed and raked at each other. Suddenly, Thunder Cloud threw his lance. He did it with great ease and power. It flew at Great Eagle, and at the last moment Great Eagle stepped to the side. With that step to the side and in the same motion, he threw his first lance right back to Thunder Cloud. His rapid response almost caught Thunder Cloud off guard. Thunder Cloud barely moved to the side and the lance still sliced through his leather shirt and drew a trickle of blood. A dark cloud crossed Thunder Cloud's face.

They both grabbed another lance and circled each other. There was more feinting and jabbing. Neither man could get the upper hand. Great Eagle faked to throw his lance, and then made out like he stumbled. In that moment, Thunder Cloud threw his lance. They were very close together. Thunder Cloud's lance passed between Great Eagle's arm and body. It drew no blood. In that moment Great Eagle threw his lance at Thunder Cloud's lower body. Thunder Cloud was caught off guard, and the lance went into his upper right thigh. He pulled the lance out.

Blood ran down his leg. The lance had gone through the flesh and had not hit a bone.

Thunder Cloud's voice roared as he grabbed his third lance and threw without any feinting or fencing for position. The lance grazed Great Eagle's cheek, and blood ran down his face. A few inches to the right, and the lance would have hit him in the face, probably dealing a fatal blow.

The fight raged. Neither man could find the opening that would give him victory. Thunder Cloud raced to the edge of the circle, grabbed a lance and without seemingly taking aim or setting to throw, he hurled the lance. This caught Great Eagle completely off guard. The lance hit him in the right side and then glanced off his rib cage. Blood flowed freely from the gash torn in his side.

Thunder Cloud only had one lance left. He circled and tested for an opening. Great Eagle was losing blood at a rapid rate. If this continued he would pass out from the loss of blood. Thunder Cloud began to taunt Great Eagle. There was not a doubt what he was trying to do. Even white eyes could see the ploy. Great Eagle rushed Thunder Cloud and tried to trip him with his lance butt as Thunder Cloud went by. He almost succeeded. Thunder Cloud tripped and rolled on the ground. As he rolled Great Eagle hurled a lance at Thunder Cloud. The lance hit the handle of the lance in Thunder Cloud's hand. The impact broke the handle.

Thunder Cloud did not have another lance. Great Eagle had let his guard down and had not attempted to reach for another lance. The contest should have ended there, except for one of Thunder Cloud's braves. The warrior called Thunder Cloud's name and started to toss him another lance. Suddenly out of the dark Ol' Bullet streaked by the people standing around. Ol' Bullet jumped into the air and bit down on the arm of the warrior. The warrior screamed as Ol'Bullet cracked his wrist bone in his jaws.

Turmoil broke loose. Several of the braves standing close at hand grabbed the hurt man, and several more grabbed Thunder Cloud. The chief that was serving as the judge rushed up to Thunder Cloud and began to shout in his face, and then he shouted in the face of the hurt man.

They were led away. The crowd stood very still as Great Eagle standing alone in the middle of the circle, spoke and Gray Fox translated. "Thunder Cloud and his family are to be banished from any band of the Kiowas. Thunder Cloud has given up all rights to his band and their ponies. Thunder Cloud will be kept in his lodging for three days, and then an escort will take him south to the sands."

Great Eagle turned his gaze on the wounded man, "Also, you, who tossed the spear will be banished along with your family. You will be kept in your lodge and will be escorted back to the Kiowa homeland by one of the bands going north. You will give up all your ponies. Your deeds will be spread through all the bands, and no one will have any contact with you or your family."

Gray Fox tended to Great Eagle's wounds, and then she came to us and said, " You are free to continue your journey tomorrow."

We stood outside the lodge and watched the fires burn down. Ol' Bullet would sleep with us tonight and be safe from becoming some Kiowa's dinner.

Gray Fox said, "All of the other bands will leave tomorrow, and they will take their ponies with them. Great Eagle has let the members of Thunder Cloud's band choose what band they joined. Some had relatives in a band and wished to go with that band. Some of the braves were courting maidens and will go with that band."

That morning the sunrise was beautiful. We prepared to leave. We had our mule and goods. Ol' Bullet stayed close to Lizzie, almost as close as he did last night, sleeping next to her.

Great Eagle and Young Eagle came to the lodge leading Number Three. They offered the mule to us, but we decided that since they had saved our lives and made us welcome, Young Eagle should keep the mule with our thanks.

Gray Fox came to say goodbye. We were a little sad until she said, "Some of the braves say that this stream, Blackwater, goes all the way to the land of the mountains called the New Mexico Territory. It will lead you to your family. The braves say it is only four days walk to the Territory."

The medicine man from one of the other tribes came to meet us. Gray Fox explained that she had told him about the tornado.

Gray Fox translated for the medicine man, "Watch out for tornadoes. I say that when he and the people were told that we had seen two tornadoes at once, they knew that we were special. We had seen the 'Dead Man Walking' and had lived to tell about the event."

She gave us more cured antelope meat. From her medicines, she gave us salve to put on our rope burns and the spot on my head.

We put Lizzie on Number One, along with our sacks of goods, and waved goodbye. Many of the people followed us out on the prairies. Little Eagle rode with us for a distance and then turned back. But, not before he put his finger to his lips and smiled. He was showing us the Indian sign for quiet. Then he rode off waving.

The bands of Kiowa would go their separate ways later that day. By night the bands would be miles from this place called the "The Ground That Runs". Thunder Cloud would be held and then sent to the sand country.

We headed north and reached the edge of the grass and went out on the marshland that lay just to the north of the campground. We could see why the Indians liked this place. There was plenty of water and grass. In the marshes there were numerous birds and ducks. They could catch fish and sometimes an antelope could be taken.

Great Eagle's band would stay at this location for a few days. They would hold Thunder Cloud. After a few days, when all of the bands were gone, Thunder Cloud would be escorted to his new hunting ground. Great Eagle had gained only a few braves and some horses, but the people all said that he had rid the bands of an evil one.

We crossed "The Ground That Runs" by mid morning. We had to use a path that the Indians had shown us, or Number One would have sunk in the mud in "The Ground That Runs." Then the Blackwater turned west, just like the people had said it would. They had never lied to us or cheated us. They were helpful and gave of what they had. They showed us compassion and kindness.

The banks on the stream were not steep nor was the stream deep, so we walked along the banks of the Blackwater and watched all the wildlife in the shallow valley to our left. All day we progressed to the west. We walked parallel to the stream and to the valley. If we ran out of food on this leg of the journey, there was ample for me to shoot or let Ol' Bullet catch.

By sunset we had come farther in one day's walk than any other day. The land was level and flat. The walking was easy along the stream bank. Even with the heat of the day, we had covered a good distance. That evening we found a good campsite in the bend of the Blackwater. The sandy bar made a good bed under the canvas. Minnie was delighted to spend some time preparing us a meal. The antelope, cooked over a slow spit was delicious. Of course Minnie had made our old standby, biscuits and gravy.

I hobbled Number One and spent a lot of time getting the tangles out of his tail and mane. I brushed his coat until it was shining. I tied him to a small tree close to the camp and knew that Ol' Bullet would give us warning if anything came along.

I checked out Papa's shotgun and thought, I have not shot this gun since we left the caprock. I shot the antelope and then I shot two chickens just after we came up on the caprock.

"Minnie, do you realize that I have used Papa's gun only a couple of times on this whole trip?"

Minnie tilted her head and said, "Robert, the Lord will provide."

"Minnie, you are sounding more like Mama all the time."

"Thank you, sir."

Lizzie asked, "If we have walked one day, are there only three days to Uncle John's?"

"Sugar, from what Gray Fox said, we could be that close."

"I wonder if there are Indians in the Territory?" I pondered.

"Papa used to say that there were hundreds of redskins in the New Mexico Territory."

Minnie wrinkled her brow and said, "I read where there are Indian Reservations in the Territory."

We settled down by a dying fire and took turns petting and rubbing Ol' Bullet. He had saved our bacon again. He had taken on snakes, outlaws and Indians. He was a hunter and a retriever. Best dog in the world!

"Minnie, Lizzie and I wondered what Aunt Bess and Aunt Marjie would be doing right now."

"Well, Aunt Marjie has finished supper and is cleaning the kitchen. She is getting all over her kids about their school lessons."

I made a nasty sound, "School lessons?" I had not thought of school in weeks.

Minnie continued, "Aunt Bess is at the supper table planning her budget. She got her crop planted and is trying to estimate how much harvest she can count on. I bet she has cotton, some corn and maybe some sorghum. She will make a ton off that sorghum if she turns it to sugar. She's a planner."

Lizzie looked up at the stars and in a whimsical voice said, "I wonder if Aunt Pettie is O.K. tonight?"

"Sis, if I know anything, she is just fine."

We slowly drifted off to sleep. We slept sound enough, that even though Ol' Bullet heard the coyotes, we did not. They were down in the shallow valley chasing rats and looking for rabbits.

Light had Minnie up and preparing breakfast. I made a run to the brush. Lizzie was just getting awake.

"What's that, Minnie?"

A sound came from the southeast.

"Listen, what is it?" I asked again.

We were all alert and looking in that direction.

"That should be the direction to the camp, Robert."

The wind shifted, and we could hear some better.

"GUNFIRE!" I exclaimed.

"Sh, Robert," Minnie whispered.

The sound came and went. There was a low roar.

When the wind blew from that direction, you could hear distinct shots.

"It is gunfire!" I was shocked.

Lizzie asked, "What is happening to our friends?"

"We don't know, Lizzie."

We stood and listened for a long time. The sounds began to diminish. Then the sounds all stopped. It was very quiet on the prairie. There was an ominous feeling in the air.

The breeze picked up for a few minutes from the southeast, and we could smell burned gun powder.

I explained as if they needed my help, "There has been a gun battle at the camp!"

Minnie looked at me, "The Indians did not have guns, or least not many."

"If they got in a battle with the army......That would be bad , but the army would try to get them to surrender."

"Gray Fox said the army wanted them to go to a reservation and that Great Eagle was holding out."

"If they got into a battle with white men, say outlaws, they would be slaughtered."

Minnie looked at the ground and asked me, "Don't you remember that Young Eagle was being held hostage by some rough types."

"Yes."

"Don't you remember Gray Fox said that Great Eagle had used us as bait to trap the outlaws."

"Oh, My Gosh, Minnie! They are fighting those outlaws where I stole Young Eagle!"

"I think you are right, Robert."

"Do you think we should go back?" I asked.

"We could not do one thing, just get us killed."

Minnie turned back to the breakfast she was preparing, "Let's eat and GET to moving. If they were fighting outlaws, that could be very bad. If the outlaws come this way that would be worse. Let's MOVE!"

We finished breakfast in record time. While Minnie and Lizzie cleaned up, I starting loading Number One. We were packed and going west in perhaps one hour.

I kept watching Ol'Bullet. He sure had heard the noise, and his ears had shot up. Number One had looked around that way and had twitched his ears one way and then another.

The day passed in slow motion. We tried to put as much distance between us and the battleground as we could. We had a cold lunch and kept on moving. Fear that we might meet up with outlaws kept us from growing tired. At least we did not think about being tired. My old heart was pumping hard and fast.

About mid-afternoon Ol' Bullet's ears came up, and he growled a warning down deep in his throat. He looked to the south across the shallow valley.

"Look, Minnie, there are ponies and riders!"

"Robert, they are chasing the ponies"

"Boy, Robert, look at them run."

"Those are the Indian ponies!" I shouted. "They are running from the outlaws."

"Minnie, Lizzie, those horses stampeded during the battle. The battle has ended, and the outlaws are trying to run the ponies down."

"Get down in the streambed and hope they don't see us!"

We turned into the streambed and got down out of sight. I crawled back up the bank on my stomach, just like an Indian.

"Minnie they saw us, some of them are coming this way."

The girls crawled up the bank and watched the riders growing in size with every pounding of the horses' hooves.

Then it happened. They suddenly stopped and began fighting their mounts. The horses had run off into "The Ground That Runs" and they were getting mired down.

We stood up and watched.

Minnie said, "Just the reverse of the parting of the Red Sea by Moses. The mud closed in on the horses and they are stuck. They can't get across 'The Ground That Runs' now."

We watched for a few minutes more and saw that more were getting trapped as they tried to help their comrades. All together there were five men and horses stuck in the marsh.

We watched some more and then brought Number One up out of the streambed and turned west toward Uncle John's.

Minnie started singing and between a couple of songs she said, "The Lord shall provide."

The morning of the first day away from the Indian camp, we had heard the battle. We were scared and trying to put as much distance between us and the battle site as possible. At the end of that day we were perhaps fifteen to eighteen miles from the campsite. We had seen the riders stuck in the marsh, but except for them, we had not seen any other riders or heard any gunfire.

For the next two days we walked. The land was rolling and still covered with grass. The vegetation had not changed for miles and miles.

Minnie spoke, "Robert, Lizzie, there are riders coming!"

We rushed into the streambed and looked for a hiding place, but there was none. We could only hope that they had not seen us, and that by being down in this low place they might ride on by. They didn't!

We could hear them coming, then there was a sound that startled us. It was a bugle blowing. A bugle blowing? Out here in the middle of nowhere. We had hardly heard the bugle when a troop of cavalry rode down on us. There was shouting, and horses were snorting as they surrounded us with guns drawn!

Their eyes became as big as ours when they saw three white kids in the middle of the Llano Estacado. They just sat on their horses and stared. Finally, the officer in charge broke the silence. "How in the Hell did you three kids get way to Hell out here?"

We all started talking at once, trying to tell him how we got out here. He held up his hand for silence and turned to his troop. "Corporal, bring up two horses from the rear. We will put two of these kids on them and the little girl will ride with you Corporal."

"Yes, Sir!"

In a few minutes Minnie and I were put on the horses. The Corporal put Lizzie up in front of him, with the comment, "I've got a little sister back home, just about your age." Some of the patrol took our sacks and threw them across their horses. One soldier led Number One, and the patrol set off to the west at a gallop.

While we rode, we took turns telling the Sergeant about our trip. He just shook his head and laughed, "I'll let you tell that story to my Captain when we get to camp. It is just over there a few hours ride."

It was well after dark when we made the camp. No supper, just let us rest. The three of us were completely exhausted and were asleep as soon as our heads hit the cots. Army cots.

We awoke late the next day. The army orderly assigned to us was really nice. He fed us and told us that our sacks were in the back of the tent. That our mule was in the corral and had been fed and watered. About the time we started eating, an officer joined us at the table. He had coffee and said, "I doubt you remember me from last night as you were all asleep. I'm Captain Long. Finish your breakfast, and then I want you to tell me your story."

That story took most of the day, with him stopping us and asking questions about the Indians and the outlaws. He even listened as to how we had run away and had crossed all of those miles. He only shook his head and said, "I can't put this in a report. They would have me in the stockade for sure."

We rested all day. Late in the evening the Captain came to our tent. "Has the Corporal treated you good? Has he fed you? Do you need anything?"

We assured him that we were fine. Then he gave us the best news we could ever have wanted. "Kids, you are in the New Mexico Territory, if you had not figured that out. These springs are the headwaters of the Blackwater stream. You are almost there, and I think I can help. I have a patrol that needs to be made to the west. You are going with that patrol and should be at your Uncle's in a day or two."

Minnie spoke, "The Lord will provide!"

CHAPTER TWELVE

Nate made another circle though the remains of the camp. Nothing had been burned, but a number of the lodges were destroyed. Some were destroyed completely, and others had received minor damage. He had never seen Indians and was very curious about them.

Nate started examining the lodges for evidence that the brats had been there. He found a man tied to a stake driven into the ground. He had not been able to fight. He had no weapon near him and could not go more than the length of the rope.

Next, he found a warrior with several lashes and cuts on his body, besides the bullet holes. Nate puzzled over this man's wounds for a few minutes. The man must have been in a fight before the battle with the outlaws. From his dress and war bonnet, he must have been one of the chiefs.

Seeing a lodge that showed no damage, he opened the flap and found a dead woman. She had been shot twice. Once in the stomach and then in the forehead. She had long gray hair and clutched a leather bag. Nate pulled the bag out of her hands and looked at the contents. It held only some herbs and roots. He thought for a few minutes and realized she was probably a medicine woman. This medicine woman could not do anything for her people now.

Back out in the open he saw dead men, women and children. They had been surprised, that was apparent. They had not been prepared for a battle. Even Nate could see that things were scattered in disarray from the battle. There was some evidence that some of the children had just been hit in the head and then shot. A few of the women had been violated. No scalps had been taken, so this had to be the work of white men, although strange. No argument about that.

This destruction was the noise he had heard the day before. He was camped on an abutment southeast to the campsite, and the noise came as a roar. He had wondered what could make that kind of noise. Now he knew. The sight sickened Nate, and he had to leave the camp.

His illness passed, and he returned to the camp one last time. He wanted, for some reason, to count the dead. He found eighteen men, sixteen women and twelve children. When he counted the children, he remembered the boy lying beside the mule, a shod mule. He returned to the mule and boy. He tried to piece out what could have happened, that this mule was in the Indian camp. Maybe the mule had gotten away from the kids, and the Indians had found him. If that was the case, why had they not eaten the mule? They, according to information Nate had, liked mule meat. The mule was being ridden, and there was no evidence that they were going to eat him.

He picked thorough the odds and ends of the camp. The Indians had very little. There were some cooking items. He discovered lances , bows and arrows for hunting. The clothes were odd, and he could not figure out what some were. There were a few white man's items in the camp. A pot here, a comb there, some bright objects and a few pieces of white men's clothing. Most everything had been trampled into the earth and was of no use.

Nate returned to his wagon and took one last look at the camp. The buzzards were circling. He had found evidence that they and the coyote had been there the day and the night before. The sight was one of horror, and he would remember each scene as long as he lived.

He followed the stream just a little distance and had to turn west to stay out of the boggy bottom to the valley. He saw a lot of game in the low valley. Birds, ducks, prairie chicken, geese, quail and dove were in abundance. There was no shortage of game along the valley. He could see why the Indians chose this site for a campground. Besides lots of game, there was water and grass for their ponies.

He realized that he was hungry and stopped to fix some lunch. His meat was all gone, and he was afraid to shoot the shotgun this close to the Indian camp. He got out his fishing gear and found that the stream was on the other side of the boggy valley. There were some ponds, but after trying them for a while he gave up. Returning to the wagon, he found one can of beans. Making some biscuits and heating the beans would have to make do for now.

The heat was not causing any problem, but the horses were laboring. By chance, he looked back and saw that the wagon was sinking into the earth and was leaving tracks three or four inches deep.

This caused him to turn south, away from the valley, and move out on hard grass covered ground. He had lost some time from the horses laboring and then having to turn south. He rested the animals often and worried about food and water.

Once or twice he thought he heard noises. With the breeze, he could not decide in what direction it was or what it was. He climbed up on the wagon seat and tried to look out across the prairie, but to no avail! All he could see was grass and more grass. He could have been the last man on the face of the earth.

Sunset came, and he stopped. He unhitched the team and hobbled them. He had no water for them and little for himself. This situation would have to change very soon.

He was still struggling with the problem of food. He finally decided that he would have to hunt. He took the double-barrel shotgun and set out to find some game. He started out over the grassland when a chicken ran out in front of him. With the gun loaded with bird shot, he hit the chicken with one blast from the gun. He remembered the eggs from the chickens, so he hunted around and found the nest, and to his surprise he found six eggs.

Dusk came and he was eating roasted chicken with eggs and biscuits. A real treat. If he could keep finding the chickens, he would not go hungry, but there was still the problem of water. In the morning he would go back toward the stream and see if he could find some water for the team.

To the west there was a cloud of dust covering and making the sun turn red . He wondered what was creating the dust. Had to be lots of horses to create that much dust. He rolled into his bedroll, up in the wagon and went to sleep.

Nate had hardly closed his eyes when the dirt and wind struck. The wind howled, and dust filled the air. The wagon just happened to have the rear to the west and the canvas draw rope was at hand. Nate grabbed the rope and pulled the rear of the wagon canvas shut. If he had not, the wind would have ripped the canvas off the wagon.

The wagon pitched like a bronco in the wind, and he thought that any minute it would blow over. Boy, that was all he needed! He looked out at the team, and they had turned their tails into the wind and had closed eyes in lowered heads.

The wind rocked the wagon all night and into the early morning. Dirt and dust had filtered into everything. It was in his mouth, ears, eyes, hair and clothes. When the wind died, he tried to fix some breakfast. He found he was eating grit with every bite. The wind had only taken a breather and started all over. All Nate could do was hunker down in his wagon and wait for it to stop blowing, if it ever did. He wondered where all the dirt came from out here in this sea of grass.

The wind blew all day and into the night. Sometime during the night, it calmed. Nate had not eaten anything since the roasted chicken. When he tried to have breakfast he had only found grit and had given up and was very hungry. He had looked for something in a can, any old thing, and he found nothing.

He hitched the team and turned back to the north and a little to the west. All the ground he had covered yesterday, or was it day before yesterday, was being lost. About noon he could see the light reflecting off of water in the distance. He approached the water cautiously. This ground could be very boggy and bog down the wagon and team.

He found water close to hard ground. It took a long time to water the horses. He had to unhitch the horses and lead them to water one at a time. He had to be very careful not to lead a horse onto boggy ground. His horses could get trapped. His next job was cleaning all of his supplies and equipment. Evening was setting in when he was finished and had filled his water bags. He would need to stay close to the wetlands to find water for the horses.

His roasted chicken was covered with dirt like everything else, So he took the shotgun and set out to shoot another bird. The fowl ran right out from under his feet and almost scared him to death. It scared him so bad, he missed the first barrel and had to use the second one. The bird was delicious. Also, the fowl's eggs were delicious for breakfast the next morning.

Nate hitched up and turned west once more. He watched the type of ground that he headed the team onto. This took time, but this way he would not get stuck. As he progressed to the west he heard shouting and calling. He stopped the wagon and climbed upon the seat for a better view.

To the north, over in the boggy valley, he could see some men waving their arms and shouting at him. He turned the team that direction and approached the area with caution, the men were stuck in the bog.

They were shouting, "Hey, Mister! Help us. We are stuck in this mud and can't get out!"

One or two were up to their waist. One was up to his chest and the other two were lying in the mud. Their heads were just above the muck enough to get air.

Their five horses were in terrible condition. One was on it's side and only it's head was showing. It's eyes were wild with fear. Two of the horses were only up to their bellies but could not move. The other two were stuck in mud up to their knees. Every time they would try to move they sank deeper. One was exhausted, and his breathing was labored. All of the animals were in peril.

"How did you get in there?' Nate inquired.

They all started talking at once.

Nate held up his hand for quiet. Then he asked the man close to him, "How did you get in there?"

"We saw three kids standing on the north bank of this marsh, and we were trying to ride to them and rode off into the mud. Mister, it's like… You get in and you can't get out. The more you move, the deeper you sink."

Nate looked at them in disbelief. The three kids were just on the other side of the marsh? He watched the men in horror. How could he help them? They all started begging again.

"Mister, do something, do anything. Just help us get out."

Nate held up his hand again. "I don't have a rope in the wagon. Can one of you reach a rope and throw it to me?"

They all began to howl and cry for help. They couldn't reach a rope on any of the horses.

They were already worn out from being in the mud for two days. They had had no water or food. Their actions had taken more energy every hour.

One of the men who was up to his waist leaned back and began to let his body sink into the mud. "I'm tired of standing and fighting the mud. I've got to lay down."

In a few minutes only his arms ,shoulder and head were above the mud.

"Men, I don't see how I can help you." Nate admitted. "We have no rope, and I can't reach you. Do one of you have a suggestion?"

"Shoot us!" One of the men said this in a pleading voice.

"Man, I can't just shoot you. What if I did and a rider came up in the next ten minutes?"

"You have got to do something! You just can't leave us here. Either shoot us or give us a gun, and we will do it ourselves."

They were so deep in the mud they could not get to or use their own guns. The rifles, that were on the horses that were standing, were just out of reach. Just like the ropes.

Nate sat down on the ground and watched the men. Their pleas were driving him crazy. He had not bargained for this. He was hunting kids. All he had found was death of rustlers, squatters, outlaws and Indians. He had seen at least sixty dead people in the last month.

"I'm going up on that high ground and see if there is anyone in sight. Maybe, just maybe, I can see somebody."

They all encouraged him and called thanks for trying to help them. He drove the team to the higher ground and climbed up on the wagon-seat. His heart sank, there was not a moving object in sight. He looked back down the long slope at the men. They were still, but they were watching him. Watching to see if he showed any ray of hope.

It would not be long for them. Two days without water or food, plus all the tension and stress, would do them in, in another day.

He turned the team back down the long slope toward the men. He would stay with them until it was over.

"I did not see a thing on the prairie. I am going to stay with you, but don't ask me to shoot you to put you out of your misery. I'm not capable of doing that. Draw a gun on me, and I would fight. But this....... sorry men."

They were even too far for him to toss out a water bag. If he had, he would have lost it in the mud. They slowly became very quiet and resigned to the fact that this was their last day on earth.

"Mister, will you write a letter to my family?"

"Yes," Nate replied, and he wrote down an address. Nate wrote in the Big Red note book. He had to open the trap door to the false bottom to get the note book. The book was the only thing he had to write in.

The next man, when he was giving Nate an address said, "That's a pretty clever hiding place you've got there. You show it to us, and we all die." And he laughed. "And we are the only other people in the world who know about your hiding place."

"Guess that's right , neighbor."

Nate turned to the third man, "You have someone you want me to write?" He gave Nate an address and thanked him for writing. Then he said, "Mister would you shoot my horse. He is the one that is down, and I hate to see him suffer."

"Sure, I'll do that just as soon as I get the other addresses. By the way, you said you saw three kids?"

"Yes."

"Did you notice which way they went?" Simple question.

"No, but west I think."

"You don't suppose they got in the mud?" The man just shrugged his shoulders.

A small framed man was the fourth one. He was crying and said, "Mister, I was going home to my wife and children right after this raid. I would have had a good stake and could take care of them." He cried some more and then gave Nate the address.

The last man showed no emotion and was gruff. "Probably won't write anybody. You are just doing this to get our minds off what is going to happen. If you weren't so gutless you'd put us out of our misery. Just like shooting a horse." He still gave Nate an address and later thanked him.

Nate went to the wagon and put the note book back in the false bottom and closed the door. All of the men were watching.

Nate got his shotgun and loaded it with buckshot. He walked back down to the men and the horse. He stood for a few moments. The horse was frantic, for the water and mud was almost up to it's nostrils. Nate aimed and the evening stillness was shattered by the ten gauge blast.

Nate didn't look at the men. He walked back to his team and unhitched them. He led them a short distance back up the slope, put their hobbles on and night tied them.

Nate walked back down to the men and asked, "Would you like a fire?"

He was met with only silence. Nate turned away and went back to his wagon. He found a little of his previous meal and out of sight of the men he ate a few bites and had a drink of water. He didn't want the men to see him. He really didn't have much appetite and wished he was in some other place.

That night was the longest in Nate's life. There were times in the hours that followed that he wished he had just shot them all. They were all killers and rustlers. Why treat them with any mercy? But, he could not bring himself to that point.

Nate didn't build a fire. He knew that the men wanted to die in some privacy, and in the dark there was as much privacy as they would have.

Coyotes howled in the night. Once in a while Nate would hear a curse or a cry. He thought he heard some praying, but he wasn't sure.

One at a time Nate heard the gurgling and the last cry of the drowning men. Each faced the hand fate had dealt him in a different way. Some were stoic and silent. Others cried and called for help. But, in the end they were all dead, and the night was silent. Completely silent.

At dawn Nate still did not look down at the mud and marsh. He built a fire and had some eggs with biscuits, gravy and coffee. He took a long time, sitting there on the other side of the wagon. Taking the double-barrel shotgun, he walked back to the marsh.

Another horse had floundered and fought in the dark and was on his side. It appeared he had broken at least one leg trying to escape the trap. The others were deeper in the mud trap, but had not fought. They were just deeper in the oozing mud.

Nate cocked his gun, and one at a time, he shot the horses. There was no cry from the horses as they were shot. Sometimes they would squeal when shot, but with the big double-barrel shot gun, death was instantaneous.

Nate watched each animal either fall on it's side or just collapse in the mud. In a few hours there would not be any evidence of what had happened in this marshy spot.

Returning to his wagon, Nate slowly hitched up his team. The desire to push forward was just not there at the moment, but he drove to the west very slow and deliberately. The day passed without event. The hours slipped by. Nate stopped and rested the animals, made a fire, cooked some food and rode on west. He rode the wagon automatically.

The day ended with Nate camped in a little depression that had water and good grass. The depression was deep enough that his fire would not be visible out on the prairie. With his horses hobbled and night tied, he went hunting. His chicken was gone, and he did like the taste of those wild chickens.

The population of chickens along the marshes made hunting very easy. He had two fowls and a hat full of eggs in a matter of an hour. He returned to his camp and dressed out the two fowls for his supper and some meals ahead.

Nate kicked out his fire and rolled into his bedroll under the wagon. The night sounds filled the air, and he was soon asleep.

The cold gunbarrel being stuck in Nate's ear brought him from a sound sleep. He opened his eyes and was staring into the barrel of another gun.

"Told you I smelled cooking last night, Jack."

Nate looked to see who was speaking. He was the ugliest man Nate had ever seen.

"Friend, crawl out from under that wagon and stand up real slow," ordered Jack the giant.

Nate complied and said, "My clothes are in the wagon. Could I put them on?"

"Right proper gentleman, isn't he?" smarted off the ugly man.

"Let him put on his pants, Shorty, The women may be embarrassed," ordered Jack.

Both men died laughing at the joke of embarrassing the women. When he had his pants and shirt on, the giant said, "Set down here against the wagon wheel, and I'll tie you up."

Nate obeyed and then heard them going through his wagon. There was one thing he did last night that may have saved his bacon. He had opened the trap door and put his double barrel in the false bottom. All the two could find was his standard equipment and supplies.

They took the chicken and went over to their wagon where the women were. They shared the fowl and had a big laugh. The two women came over and went through his things again and cursed him for not having anything worth having.

They complained, "Old wore out saddles and sorry camping items. Why, our pots and pans are better than what he has. Why did we stop and bother with this down and out bum?"

The men came back and checked one more time for anything of value. Nate was thoroughly cursed and slapped a few times for not having something they could use.

One of the women hollered, "Big Jim, is coming!"

There was lots of yelling and cursing about this event. Soon another wagon and a rider showed up. One was driving a wagon and the other was on a horse, "What you found, Jack?"

"Just a drifter, he has nothing worth hauling off."

"Well, I'll be the judge of that."

Big Jim, or that is who Nate figured he was, went through his stuff one more time. "Damn! You are right, Jack."

They all stood around and talked about what to do with Nate and his sorry stuff. They made camp, as if to stay for awhile. The women built fires, and the men went out to hunt.

Nate kept trying to get the rope off his hands. He felt a little slack, but he could not get loose. He tried to think of all kinds of schemes, but nothing came to mind. Then two of the women came over. One untied him while the other held a gun on him.

"Thought you might like some coffee, being as it is yours." They laughed.

"Thank you , Ladies."

"He is a gentleman!" remarked one of the women.

"Thank you, again ladies."

They snickered and said, "If we turn you lose will you be nice to us?" Nate was confused.

"What do you mean , be nice to you?"

"We figure that you have got something of value somewhere in that wagon. So, if we turn you loose, will you give us whatever valuables you have?"

The women were still holding the gun on Nate. Nate looked the two over while he drank his coffee. "I have a better idea, why don't I kill those men, and you go with me. I'm going to New Mexico Territory to my rich brother's place. He has offered me half of the spread if I come out."

Their eyes got big. "Us, go with you?"

"Yes, I will be very wealthy in the Territory, and I could share that with you. Why, one of you might just decide to marry me and be wealthy."

Their eyes got bigger, and their greed matched Nate's or surpassed it.

"You are really going to the New Mexico Territory?"

"That's right, and I'd like for the two of you to come with me. One of you could marry me and the other marry my brother. You would be very rich, and we would have wives."

The sound of horses reached the camp, and the women tied Nate and rushed off. He knew they would be back to talk some more. Nate also knew, if they let him loose, he was only six feet from that double-barrel shotgun.

The men had returned to get some more ammunition and some food, and then they would go back out. They were barely out of the camp, when the women were back. This time they did not have a gun, and they brought him food.

"Tell me ladies, what are your names?"

"I'm Shari, and she's Jenny. "

"My name is Nate, and my brother's name is John."

"Why, I feel like we know you already," said the one called Jenny.

"Well, we need to get really acquainted if you are going to marry one of us." Shari said.

"That's right, and we need to know, how much money will you have?" asked Jenny.

"Well, I don't know for sure, but last year my brother went to Denver for a month's vacation. And he told me, if I would come out, we would be taking lots of trips for business. So, to do that, we will have, to have plenty of money. You would be going to all those big cities and buying fancy clothes and things."

They were in stitches "Why would you want to marry us?'

"My brother told me to find two fine women and bring them to the New Mexico Territory, and I had not found them until I saw you. I feel like this is just what he would want."

"We are going to think about it for awhile. But, we will have to tie you back up. Not tight. Just tight enough that the men will not notice."

At noon they brought him food and water, and one of them rushed off. Jenny stayed with him. She said, "We are really thinking about going. I'm staying here in case the men show up so I can tie you and go on about my business. I probably will be the one to marry you. I like big men!" The other one came back in a few minutes. They tied him and left.

Nate had already tested the ropes and unless one of the men checked them, he could get away or get his gun anytime.

The men returned late in the day with no game, but with lots of talk. There had been a fight with some Indians, and they were wiped out. They had run into a friend that had seen the battleground. And Nate had thought that the Llano Estacado was empty. That was all they could talk about the rest of the day.

They had supper, and the women brought him some food after the men went to sleep. The women whispered and made plans. As they left, Jenny said, "I wish I could stay with you, but Jack might miss me."

Nate let the camp really get to sleep and he slipped his ropes and rolled under the wagon. It took only a few moments to open the trap door and retrieve his shotgun and some ammunition. Gently he closed the trap door. Then he circled the camp and crawled up in one of the other wagons and covered up with some of the contents.

"He's gone!"

"What do you mean he is gone?"

"HE'S GONE, that's what I mean!"

"How did he get away?"

In the early morning fog, the four men ran around and around in circles looking for Nate. Looking around the wagons.

"Jack and Shorty, you look in the wagons and see if he is hiding in one of them. The two of us will ride out on the plain and make a circle, and see if we can see him."

They had all slept on the ground, and in their minds he could be in any one the wagons or he had gone out on the prairie. Jack started searching the wagons.

"He's not going to hide in one of our wagons. He is in his own," declared Shorty.

"Let's look real quick, and then we will look in his. He sure can't have gone very far on foot. Not as fat as he is."

Jack climbed up on the seat of the wagon and was taken completely by surprise when Nate sat up and cut him in half at close range with one barrel of his shot gun. Shorty ran to the wagon and climbed up in the other end. That was what Nate had hoped he would do. Jack was at one end and Shorty would come in the other. The man never knew what hit him. Nate was still partially covered up, and Shorty did not see him. The blast carried him up and out of the wagon. He, like Jack, hit the dirt dead and near cut into.

Nate reloaded and moved quickly to his wagon. The women were screaming and had fallen on the ground and hidden their faces in the grass. The women never saw him go to his wagon.

The other riders came racing back into camp. "What's happened?"

"He's in that wagon!" screamed one of the women, pointing at one of their wagons.

The man climbed up in the wagon and shouted, "He's not here! Where is he, woman?"

The women were hysterical and were screaming at the top of their voices.

One of the men rode his horse around to the front of Nate's wagon. He climbed over the seat and was blown completely out of the wagon, landing on the tongue and his weight broke it. One barrel of the shotgun had done the trick.

The last man raced his horse at the wagon shooting his handgun. His bullets were all going wide of the mark. He emptied his gun, and there was a pause. Nate had counted the shots. Nate heard him curse, and that is when the cover on the back of the wagon was thrown open, and Nate jumped to the ground. The rider was almost on him and was screaming at the top of his lungs. Nate swung the shotgun and blasted the last rider out of the saddle.

Nate paused, checked his gun and reloaded. He walked around to the front of his wagon and looked at the tongue. It was broken. He turned to the other two wagons and discovered that one of the other tongues would fit his wagon. It took only a few minutes to change the tongue.

It took more time to find his belongings that had been scattered through the camp than it did to fix the wagon tongue. He located his coffee pot and coffee first. Picked up his bags of flour, baking soda, salt and his Dutch oven. The rest of his equipment was just tossed on the ground around the tail of his wagon. No effort was made to sort or clean his belongings, he just threw them in the back of the wagon.

Nate hitched up his team and climbed aboard. He looked at the two women and turned his wagon west. They were bawling so hard, they did not know that Nate was gone.

Nate returned to the trail he had been following and caught his breath. He had gone a few miles and just happened to look back down the trail. Two riders were coming after him, and they were whipping their horse. He whipped up the team and started looking for cover. He heard gunfire and looked back, and they were gaining fast. He whipped the horses some more, and the team went over a rise and ran out into the "The Ground That Runs." They were several strides into the mud before the horses and wagon were trapped and slowed and then stopped in the "The Ground That Runs".

He was stuck and the riders were shooting at him from the rear. He crawled through the wagon and poked his shot gun out the through opening in the canvas. The riders came barreling down on the wagon, firing as they came.

The first blast of one barrel knocked the lead rider from his horse. Nate swung the barrel to the left and pulled the second trigger emptying the second saddle. Nate reloaded and crawled down from the wagon. The two men weren't dead , but they both were seriously wounded. A gunshot from a ten gauge at close range was not only effective, it was usually deadly. He approached them and saw that one was unconscious but the other one was fully awake.

He stooped down and gazed into the face of the conscious man, "Who are you, and why were shooting at me?"

The man had a hard time speaking, "We are friends of the men you killed earlier, back at that camp you just left. You killed all four of my friends. I guess you have killed me and my buddy."

Nate squatted there by the man for a few minutes, "Anything I can do to make you more comfortable?"

"Some water, there is a canteen on my horse."

The man drank, slowly and with difficulty, from the canteen, "Thanks, Mister."

Nate examined the other man and found that he was dead. "Your partner is dead."

"Yeah. I saw him take that first shot. He was close to you and figured that he had bought it."

"Sorry."

The man coughed a little and a thin smile crossed his face, "Hell, we would have killed you. Why should you be sorry."

Nate offered him some more water, and the man declined, but he looked up at Nate and asked, "What kind of gun are you shooting?"

"It's a ten gauge double-barrel shotgun."

"Mighty powerful weapon."

"Say, I'd like to ask you a couple of questions, if you are up to it?"

"Fine, I'm not going anywhere."

Nate sat on the ground beside the wounded man, "What were you and your friends doing out on the Llano Estacado?"

"We used to hunt buffalo for the army. Lately we have been hunting Indians for the them. They pay twenty-five dollars for a scalp."

"That is the reason your friend was so interested in the battle that he had heard about?"

"I told Jack about the battle."

"I wondered how your man found out about the Indians."

"I met Jack out on the prairie hunting and told him. He said I should go find the rest of our bunch and then come to his camp."

"How many are there of you?" Nate inquired. He did not want to be surprised again.

"One more wagon, is coming to Jack's camp."

"How did you find out about the Indians?"

"I rode into a camp south of here. They said that they had just had a shootout with a bunch of Indians. Left them for dead. Best of all, they didn't scalp a single one. I came for Jack and his bunch so we could go scalp them."

"I was rounding up the boys so we could go scalp the Indians when you started shooting. Oh, I would so much like to see my mother." With that statement the man died.

Nate sat there for some time thinking about what the man had said. They were scavengers, just like the buzzards and the coyotes. Then he remembered that there was another wagon of the scalpers, and he had better move on.

It took some time to catch the two rider's horses. They were skittish and scared. Nate might not have caught them if one had not gotten the reins tangled in some brush. Nate eased up to the horse and tried to calm him. He talked softly and stroked the horse's neck. The horse calmed, and Nate adjusted the stirrups and swung up in the saddle. Riding the first horse made it fairly easy to catch the second one.

He found a rope on one of the horses and shook out a loop. He climbed down and put the loop around the feet of one of the men. He dragged the man some distance from the wagon. Then he returned and repeated the task. With the two men away from the wagon, he could begin to sort his stuff. What was ironic was the fact that only the other day, he had needed a rope to save the five men in the marsh. Now he had a rope and had used it to drag two dead men away from the marsh.

Returning to his wagon, he realized that his two horses were trapped in the mud, and he could not get them out. The front of the wagon was sinking a little at a time. The rear appeared to be on solid ground. If he worked fast, he could salvage most of his equipment and goods. His horses were doomed to the marsh. They had thrashed about some, but were standing docile at this moment.

Tying the two saddle horses to the rear of the wagon, Nate rapidly unloaded the contents. The scalper bunch had thrown all of his stuff out on the ground. Then when he picked it up he just threw it back in the wagon. It was a mess. And now he was throwing it back out on the ground. A bigger mess.

He took his time and went through the camping gear. He would be traveling on two horses and would have to leave some things behind. The two rustler's saddles he tossed to one side. Maybe some traveler would come along and could use them. He emptied the saddle bags on the horses. The only thing he found of value to him, was some coffee. Having emptied the saddle bags he loaded baking soda, flour, salt, coffee, gun shells, some clothes and his money packet from the false bottom.

With the wagon sinking and Nate's bulk, he almost couldn't get in under the rear of the wagon. It was a very close place to work, to get the trap door open. The other problem was Nate would sink a little in the soft soil on the bank of the marsh. He wasn't too worried about getting stuck, but it made him uneasy. He had seen five men sink in the goo.

He had retrieved the packet with his money, letters of credit, the pair of boots with three hundred dollars and his bank book. The only other thing he took from the bottom was his brother's rifle. There was a long gun scabbard on both saddles. The scabbard was a place to carry the rifle. He put the shotgun in one of the scabbards. The shotgun did not fit very well, but because of it's weight, it was better than carrying it in his hands all time.

He took the canvas off the wagon. He rolled it and the torn canvas from the tornado into a bundle. He tied the bundle behind the saddle of one horse. His bedroll he tied behind the saddle of the second horse. He made some sacks from the torn canvas and placed the remainder of his gear in two of them. Tied together and to the saddle horn, they would hang over the saddle horn of the extra horse.

Nate took one last look around. There wasn't much left. He had thrown the extra guns from the false bottom into the marsh. He had changed out of his muddy clothes and thrown them into the marsh. Nate put on the rustler's boots with the three hundred dollars hidden in the pocket inside the boot top. The boots were near new, and they fit

Nate. A fine place to hide some extra cash. His old boots and the other pair of rustler's boots he threw in the marsh. Everything else of value was packed on one of the horses. There remained one more thing to do.

Nate walked around to the driest spot beside his wagon. He stood for several minutes before he cocked both barrels of the shotgun. Raising the gun he fired one barrel at a time. One shot for each of his horses stuck in the mire. What a waste, two fine horses and his wagon with it's false bottom and trap door. What a waste!

Nate checked the cinches on the horses one more time. He adjusted the stirrups on the second horse. He would ride one horse for two hours and then change to the other. He wasn't a horseman, but it was better than walking. Besides, he was in a hurry and with two horses and no wagon, he could make good progress.

He had to find the brats!

It was past noon when Nate had all of his gear ready to go. He had not eaten since last night, but he had no appetite. That did not matter, he just wanted to get clear of this scene.

Dusk found Nate ten or twelve miles west of the carnage. He had witnessed another display of the brutality of the prairie yesterday and today. In the last two days he had seen more people die from ignoring the dangers of the prairie. Or they had died from ignoring the traps of the prairie.

He made camp down in a ravine. He had no misconceptions that he was out of danger. Nor did he think that being down in a low place would give him much protection.

He put bird shot in his gun and shot a chicken for his dinner. While he was on the prairie he hunted eggs for his breakfast. A lot of things could go wrong, but Nate intended to eat the very best possible. The chicken roasted over an open fire made a delicious dinner. He sipped his coffee and was glad to be alive.

When he got ready for bed, he took some precautions for safety. He hobbled one horse at the fire. He then took his bedroll and the other horse some distance from the fire. Out in the dark, he hobbled the other horse and rolled out his bed. Nate then tied a rope around the horse's right front foot. After that Nate tied the rope to his own wrist. Nate hoped that if the horse stomped, or something bothered the horse, he would be warned.

Nate awoke early and was in the saddle by sunup. The horses were well broken, and they did not mind his weight, especially since he was changing horses every two hours. Yesterday afternoon he had changed twice. He could feel the difference in the fresh horse. The horses had carried him west for six hours yesterday. He didn't run or even trot the horses. He did keep them at a fast walk and tried to cover as much ground as possible. He needed to save their strength in case he needed to run.

Night found him camped out in the open. He built a fire and hoped for the best. The terrain had become very flat. The stream was off to the north, and he had no way of knowing if there was shelter there. He had found water easily enough. His shotgun had provided him chicken for another night and day. He estimated that he was near the New Mexico Territory. By following the stream and the wet lands, he should find some sort of trading post or village when he came to the west edge of the Llano Estacado.

The next afternoon Nate could see sunlight reflecting off some water to the west. The sun was sinking low, and the water turned orange and red as the sun settled. He had to work around some more marshland to get to the water. By sunset he was only a few miles from it.

He squinted his eye. Was that campfire smoke? Or maybe, dust? He continued on at a little slower pace. He did not want to ride up on some unsavory people. He had had enough of that for one lifetime. Nate never thought of himself as unsavory. He was just trying to look out for himself.

Nate was concentrating on the water and the dust or smoke so hard that he did not see the riders coming from his rear and to his left. There were eleven, and they were closing in on him fast. The first hint to him that there were riders to his left and rear was the sound of the horse's hooves. The sound suddenly filled the air, and Nate jerked his head around to see what was causing all the noise.

Eleven blue coated riders in two neat columns, with one man out front. It was a troop of U.S. cavalry. They swept up to him in a rush. The leader pulled alongside and commanded, "HALT!"

Nate halted the two saddle horses and said, "You are a sight for sore eyes, soldier."

With pulled gun the officer commanded, "You just keep your hands where I can see them, while you do some fast and tall talking. Corporal, guard this man."

A Corporal saluted smartly and aimed his pistol at Nate, "Mister, don't do anything that will make me sorry for having to shoot you. Move, and I'll blow your head off!"

Nate's eyebrows shot up. Why was the officer talking to him in that tone of voice?

"Now, dismount and move over away from your horses!" commanded the Corporal. "Trooper go though these saddle bags and sacks and see if there are any guns."

Yes, Sir!"

The lieutenant barked some orders, "Pickets out and keep a sharp eye. Trooper, search this man! Mister, keep you hands in the air!"

Nate did as he was told, as he was searched by one of the soldiers.

The Corporal reported to the Lieutenant, "No weapons on him or in the saddle bags, Sir."

The Lieutenant returned to where Nate was standing with his hands in the air. "Good. Now, mister, let me hear in as few words as possible who you are, and what you are doing on the Llano Estacado."

Nate stuttered, "I...I...Don't know where to start."

"Corporal, if this man doesn't give a straight answer with the next question, shoot him."

"Yes, Sir!"

"Now Mister, I will ask you one more time, Your name? "

"I'm called Nate."

"No last name?"

"Nate Carter, sir."

The Lieutenant frowned, "And, why are you out here?"

"I'm chasing some runaway kids. They stole animals and valuables and ran away from home." Nate rushed out the words.

"How many kids?"

"Three. Sir."

"Would one of them be a boy and the other two girls?"

"That's them. Have you seen them?"

"Yes, we have."

"Where are they?"

The officer did not reply. Instead he gave the order to mount. "You, too, Mr. Nate Carter."

They rode toward the water and their camp. Nate could only go along.

The officer spoke when they were on their way. "We are out of Fort Sumner. We have been on patrol for Indians in this area. We are trying to round up the last of the Kiowas and put them on a reservation."

"I saw some Indians back on the trail…! Oh three or four days ago!" He was very excited.

"That is good information, and you can tell your story to the Captain when we get to camp. Our camp is at some springs that are the head waters of the Blackwater. You were, I guess following the Blackwater."

The camp came into sight. There were several tents pitched and some soldiers moving about the camp. Smoke rose from a cooking fire, and Nate thought, I wonder what army food tastes like?

They arrived at the camp, and the officer told Nate, "You stay right here, and I'll report to my Captain."

The officer returned and said, "The Captain will see you now."

Nate was escorted to the Captain's tent, and the officer said to the Captain, "With your permission, Sir, I would like to see to the welfare of my men."

"Dismissed. Mr. Carter, I am Captain Long. We are out of Fort Sumner and looking for Kiowas. I understand that you may have some information for me. We will have some supper, and you can tell me what you know. "

A table was set for one, but an orderly came with a field chair and another setting for the table.

Nate was offered the field chair. "Tell me of your experiences with the Kiowa."

"I only found their camp after they had all been killed."

The Captain's eyes bore into Nate, "After they were killed?'

"Yes, Sir. I was down farther southeast from their camp, and I heard this awful roar and noise up the trail. It was the next day when I got to their camp and found them dead."

"Tell me all you can remember about the camp. It might give us a clue as to what band they were."

"I saw so many dead, it is hard to remember."

"Let me ask you some questions. Did you see any guns?"

"No. only lances and some bows and arrows."

"Was any Indian wearing any special clothing?"

"None that I can describe."

The Captain lighted his pipe, "How about the lodges? Can you describe them for me?"

"Only that some were destroyed and others were not. There was only one that had little or no damage. "

"Describe it."

"I can't describe it very well, but there was a dead Indian woman in the lodge"

"What did she look like?'

Nate thought for a moment or two, "There are two things I remember . She had long gray hair, and she was clutching a leather bag. I looked in the bag, and all that was there was herbs and roots."

The captain's brow furrowed, and he looked at the far horizon, "Damn, that would have been Gray Fox. She was Great Eagle's medicine woman. Great Eagle was our best contact with the Kiowas out on the Llano Estacado. He was ready to come in and go to the reservation, but he was holding out to find out where they would be sent, and what reservation would be their home. They had lived on the upper Llano for centuries, I guess."

They sat in silence for some time. "How many do you think were in the camp?" the Captain asked Nate.

Nate vividly remembered going back and counting the dead. That he would never forget. "I counted them, Captain. There were eighteen dead men, sixteen dead women and twelve dead children."

The Captain sat for a very long time and puffed on his pipe, "If they had come in last month, they would be alive. We were going out to see them in about two more weeks. Damn!"

Dusk was settling over the camp. The men were hushed and all activity had slowed for the evening meal. Taps had been blown and the colors struck.

The orderly returned with supper. The captain thanked the orderly and invited Nate to pull up to the table and join him. The chow was typical army chow, but Nate thought, "I didn't have to prepare it."

As they ate the Captain said, "Tell how you have come to being on the Llano Estacado."

Nate's story went all the way back to the kids running away. He told the officer about the rustlers, the squatters and the outlaws. He told him that he had had gun fights with them. That the Indians were all dead when he found them, and that only in the past two days he had run into some scalp hunters.

The Captain interrupted Nate, "What you have told me about the Indians was very interesting. The rustlers and the outlaws are not in my patrol sector. That area is patrolled by men from Fort Richardson at Jacksboro. I would, after dinner, like to hear about the scalp hunters."

With the meal finished and a fresh pot of coffee at hand, the Captain turned to Nate and said, "Please, tell me about the scalp hunters."

Nate filled him in on his run in with the scalp hunters. Nate also told him about the five outlaws, who probably had killed the Kiowas, who were dying in the marsh mud.

"We lose quite a few men all along in the marshes. That marsh is about four miles wide and maybe forty miles long. Many a man and beast have fallen into that trap. Mr. Carter, could you give me some directions to the Indian camp and to the scalper's camp?"

Nate gave as good directions on how to find the Indians as he could. "Captain, the Indians were camped right on the edge of the marsh. I don't know how far east that is. I didn't have any reference to go by."

Captain Long stepped outside the tent and called, "Sergeant, get your butt up here and now!"

The Sergeant appeared as if by magic, out of the dark. "Yes. Sir!"

"Prepare a patrol for tomorrow. You are to ride the south side of the marsh until you find the remains of Great Eagle's camp. They were ambushed and bush whacked several days ago."

"Yes, Sir!" A Sergeant appeared and saluted.

"Also, you are to be on the lookout for some scalp hunters. Mr. Carter had a run in with some of them in the last few days and left six dead ones out there somewhere. Also, there may be two women stranded at a camp." The Captain did not ask Nate for directions to the scalpers camp, nor did he give any instructions to the Sergeant.

"Dismissed, Sergeant."

"Thank you, Sir!" The sergeant saluted, and disappeared back into the dark.

"Well, all that you have told me seems on the up and up, Mr. Carter. We had three kids here a few days ago, and they told us of seeing rustlers and outlaws. They did not have any dealing with them. They also told me that they had been in the Indian camps, and that they were treated very kindly. Hard to believe, knowing the Kiowas. The only place that the story is different is the part about them being runaways. They said that you stole from them and their Uncle John who lives over yonder by that mesa."

Nate's mouth was hanging open, "That I stole from them! Why.. I... Never!"

The Captain held up his hand, "That's between you and your family. That is a civil matter, and my concerns are military matters."

Nate was still sputtering, "Well, I never...."

Captain Long again stepped to the entrance of the tent and yelled, "Sergeant!"

Again the sergeant appeared out of the dark and saluted, "Sir?"

"Sergeant, show this man where he can sleep tonight. Feed him in the morning and escort him out of my camp! Is that clear, Sergeant?"

"Yes, Sir, Captain!"

The Sergeant said, "Follow me!" Nate was shown to a tent.

"Captain's orders, you are to stay in this tent unless someone comes for you. Your horses have been fed and watered, and your gear is in a safe place."

At dawn when the bugle called the soldiers to reveille, Nate was up and had had his breakfast. He was shown his horses. He saddled and rode out the camp to the west and in the distance, the Mesa.

CHAPTER THIRTEEN

The next morning after breakfast the orderly brought our mule to us. "I hope you kids find your family O.K."

We thanked him and watched as some other soldiers brought mounts for us. The patrol was made up of forty men , plus the Sergeant and the Corporal. They formed up, and we were put on horses. Number One was led by a trooper. There were six pack animals in the column, and our sacks had been tied to their pack racks. Again the Corporal put Lizzie up in front of him. "You will be safe here," he said.

Captain Long came to tell us goodbye and added, "I know your Uncle. Give him my regards. I hope for the best for you, kids. I know you have come a long way and deserve some breaks. I think you will find them here in the Territory with your uncle and aunt. God's speed!"

The Sergeant saluted the Captain and hollered, "Forward Ho!"

We were on our way. We were all just bubbling and giggling about getting to Uncle John's. This part of the journey was going to be very easy. Me, riding an Army horse! Boy, would I like to show my school teacher now! I have been to an Indian camp. I have seen rustlers. I have seen outlaws. AND, I have ridden with the good old U.S. Cavalry. Boy, I bet all the boys in my class would be green with envy.

The ride was not easy. The ride would take hours and hours, and the patrol had other business to attend to besides getting us to Uncle John's.

The patrol rode south from the springs, not west like we thought.

The sergeant explained, "There was a report that some of the Kiowas may be camped about ten miles south of the Army camp at some marshes and springs. They are hiding out, even on the prairie. They don't want to go to the reservation."

The Cavalry made good time, And they sure did things different from the rest of us. For one thing, they didn't stop much. They rode, for miles, and then walked for twenty or thirty minutes. Then back in the saddle for another stretch of miles.

The Corporal had adjusted the stirrups for Minnie and me. We were comfortable on the horses, but we were not used to riding for miles and miles.

We had been out about two hours when, thank the Lord, the Sergeant called a stop. "We'll send out some scouts to look for the Indians. No need to let them know that a troop is in the area."

Four scouts rode off. They broke up into pairs and disappeared to the south. That is another thing about the Cavalry, they sure do a lot of hurrying up so they can wait. We waited perhaps an hour before the scouts returned. The Indians were camped at one of the marshes. There were about twenty, counting the women and children.

"Corporal, select four troopers to stay here with the children and give the girl to one of the troopers. Leave the pack animals. I'll lead half of the column, and you lead the other half."

The troop moved off with precision and split up into two groups just as they went over the horizon. There was no gunfire that we could hear. Just a lot of waiting for news of what was happening over the hill.

A single trooper came riding back to where we waited. "The Sergeant says to move up to where they have a camp."

We mounted, and with Lizzie in front of Minnie, we moved out. The five troopers had put the pack animals and Number One on lead ropes so they could ride. We joined the troop, and the soldiers began to pitch camp. The sergeant came over to our tent and said, "We will be here for the rest of today and some of tomorrow. The Indians did not put up a fight. They are hungry more than anything else. When we get camp pitched, we will feed them."

The troop was not long pitching the tents and building campfires. They broke out rations and started feeding the Indians. The Indians did not like the rations, so the Sergeant sent out some hunters. They were back in an hour or so with chicken and rabbit. When this was cooked the Indians cleaned it up in a hurry. Like hungry dogs.

After the Indians had eaten, the Sergeant ordered the Corporal, "Stay behind with ten men and the pack animals. The kids are to stay behind. I will take the Indians back to the main camp. Walking will be hard on their feet and their egos. It will take all the rest of this day, but I should be back some time tomorrow. Send out scouts and be checking the small lake and ponds scattered all over this area. There may be other Indians around."

All the Corporal said, was, "Yes, Sir!"

The Indians had packed their few belongings, and the column moved off to the north. The entire Indian band would have to walk, and walking would hurt the dignity of the braves. Out of the band there were some nine men and the rest were women and children. There were only five horses, and they were pressed into service as pack animals. The column could move a little faster if the people did not carry belongings.

We watched the column move out of sight. Soon nothing could be seen except the dust in the distance. We talked about our friends at Great Eagle's camp. We told the soldiers in the camp about our meeting with Great Eagle and his band.

"You were in Great Eagle's camp?" asked a soldier.

"Yes, we stayed for two nights." Minnie replied.

"Nobody hurt, you?" asked another soldier.

"No, they were very nice," Lizzie declared.

There was a lot of talk about that.

The Corporal asked, "You were in their camp and were not murdered or worse? They let you go?"

I spoke up boastfully, "The reason they were nice to us was I saved Great Eagle's son."

The men had a good laugh over that statement.

"Why, sonny, those redskins would cut your ears off and feed them to the dogs in their camp."

I got huffy. "Well, believe me, I did, and here is the necklace that his son gave me." I jerked it out from under my shirt and held it out for them to see.

"My God, that is Great Eagle's symbol, and his eagle."

"They gave one to each of my sisters, too." I was indignant.

The Corporal broke up the discussion and sent three pair of soldiers out to scout the small lake to the south and west. He put the others to working on harness for the horses and any other job he could find for them. He kept them busy.

We rested in the shade of the tent and watched big white puffy clouds float by. Ol' Bullet and I went hunting in the late afternoon. When we returned with four chickens, the cook was grateful. The men wanted to know how we got the chickens when they had not heard any shooting.

"Ol' Bullet. He runs them down and brings them to me," I bragged.

"Well, buster, we might just keep Ol' Bullet for ourselves and use him to hunt."

That made Lizzie start to cry. The men laughed and suddenly Ol' Bullet was standing right in front of the three men. The growl came from down deep in his throat, and he showed those big ugly teeth of his. The men backed off, and one of them said, "That dog would tear you up if you touched one of those kids." If he only knew! Ol' Bullet had taken on a whole Kiowa band.

The scouts returned and reported that there had been a band of Indians at two of the waterholes. They were moving to the west along a line that should take them to a lake that was about twenty five miles west of here. That lake was only about ten miles from Mesa.

Our hearts went up into our throats. Ten miles of Mesa and Uncle John's? We had no idea that there were hostile Indians in this area. Boy, were we lucky to be with the Cavalry and not out on the prairie alone, trying to get to Uncle John's.

"Corporal, are the Indians you are chasing wild?" I asked.

"Son, every Indian that I have seen has been or is wild and savage."

"The scout said that the band could be as close as ten miles of Mesa?"

"That's correct. They have at least a one day lead on us, and we may lose them."

At sunset the camp grew quiet. We watched the sky get dark and the stars come out. Then the quarter moon came up. The evening was still and only the night birds sang in the brush.

All we could think about was that there might be Indians close to Mesa. The cook brought some chicken with beans and biscuits. This was one of the few meals we had had that Minnie did not cook. After the evening meal the Corporal came and sat with us children.

"We all know your Uncle. He was stationed at Fort Union. That fort is north of here some two hundred miles. We are out of Fort Sumner. That is off to the northwest about forty miles. Each fort has the responsibility of patrolling hundreds of square miles around the fort."

"How do you not get lost?" Minnie asked.

"We use a compass and an instrument just like they use on a ship. We can take readings from the sun several times a day and draw a map. This can tell us where we are within a few miles."

"Boy, that is magic!" I exclaimed.

"The Indians know the territory and go anywhere they want. We wonder how they seem to know right where to find water and right where they are. You would think they had a map of this whole country. Very strange."

"How long was Uncle John in the army?" Minnie inquired.

"He served in the northern army during the recent unpleasant conflict."

"Were you in the war?" I asked.

"I was in your Uncle's regiment. Several of these men were with him. He has four men at his place that were with him all during the war."

"With those men there, can they fight the Indians?" Lizzie wanted to know.

"Yes, they are well fortified at that place They have water and a good compound to fight from. Your family is very safe. They have been in that place for at least ten years, and the Indians haven't bothered them much. These Indians know your Uncle. He was with the regiment out of Fort Union for a number of years, and he is a well known Indian fighter "

"Gosh, my uncle is famous!"

"Robert you used that word , I heard you use that word the other day. You had better stop. When we get to Uncle John's, he might have something to say about that."

"Oh, Sis, I just forgot."

We turned in, and I was asleep in a heartbeat. Having all of these men guarding all around us made us feel safe. More than that was not having to worry about food, Indians, outlaws or rustlers. I became a real sleepy head.

There was not a bugle to wake me up, but a good full faced lick from Ol" Bullet will do just as good as two bugles.

Breakfast was great. We had eggs, gravy, biscuits, meat and some jelly. Army issue. I did enjoy that treat. I could eat that every morning of the year. And especially if Minnie could do the cooking. She is better.

The rest of the patrol returned right before lunch. The scouts were out, and the Corporal was expecting them back soon. They had found some more tracks yesterday and were convinced that the band was heading for the Biggest Lake.

I asked, " Why, is it called the Biggest Lake?"

"This area is covered with a series of little lakes and this one is the big one, so the name Biggest Lake."

The noon meal was almost ready when the balance of the troop arrived. The Sergeant ordered the patrol that had been in the saddle to rest and the remainder of the troop to prepare for a forced march.

He came over to us, "This may get to be rough. We will be riding hard and long. When the scouts get in, we will head for Biggest Lake. We will track the Indians all the time to see that they don't double back on us."

Scouts started arriving right after the noon meal. They were all in by two o'clock, and the Sergeant ordered, "Get these men some food and prepare to move. We move out in thirty minutes."

I can say that there is something else that the cavalry is good at. When they need to move, they can do it. They were packed, loaded, mounted and in formation in exactly twenty-five minutes, by the Sergeant's pocket-watch.

The column moved out at a gallop, with the scouts spreading out in front the them. All during the afternoon scouts would return, give reports and be sent back out on the trail of the Kiowas. The column never slowed. There were now ten minute breaks and short walks and then back into the saddle. The Sergeant was pushing hard, as he had a lot of ground to cover to catch the Kiowas.

The scouts reported that they had seen the Indians, and that the troop had cut the Indian lead in half in just a half day. The Sergeant got some good news from another one of the scouts. The Indians were short of horses, and they could only go as fast as the slowest persons could walk. The scouts reported there were a number of children in the Indian band, and that they were almost crawling.

The column ate supper in the saddle. Cold beef jerky, cold biscuits and water. We would ride until sundown. At sundown we made a cold camp. No fire for fear the Indians would see it. Canned and packaged rations were passed out, and that was supper. I saw why the Indians did not like the rations. Ugh, they were terrible. We ate them anyway, that was all there was. The chicken from last night was gone. One of the solders said, "Beats hard tack and water."

We slept on the ground, with no tents for protection. I wondered what a tent protected you from. Rain was the only thing I could think of where a tent would protect you.

One scout did not come in last night, and the Sergeant was worried about him. Not like him to not report back. Bad sign.

The column was up and had had more rations before sun up. The camp was struck, and the column was on the move just as the sun came over the eastern horizon. The column rode hard all morning, and, according to the scouts coming in to report, we were gaining on the Indians every step of the way. The Indians were barely moving. They were having to carry children and the older people.

I was enjoying the excitement of riding with the U.S. Army Cavalry. I looked at the girls and saw that the hard riding was bothering them.. Minnie was holding up pretty good, but Lizzie was really hurting. Her legs were so short that she could not straddle a horse without it hurting her after a long ride. Finally one of the troopers came to her rescue.

At one of the breaks he pulled a saddle off a horse and put the saddle on Number One. I started to protest that Number One had never had a saddle on him, and he might buck. Minnie caught my arm and shook her head "NO". I watched the trooper put the saddle on Number One. Old Number One did not twitch an ear. The trooper shortened up the stirrups for Lizzie. Instead of riding straddle, she was riding up on top of the mule with her legs pulled away up. This way she was not stretched out so.

When we started, they had to put her up on the mule. She grinned and said, "I bet Number One will be easy to ride." I don't know if it was in her mind or if the stirrup change did that much good. One thing was obvious, she was not tiring out so quickly. Then the trooper pointed out that the mule's gait was much smoother than a horse. So, with this combination Lizzie was doing great.

The trooper rode up by me and said, "I got a family of all girls back home. When my tour is up, I'm bringing them out. We are going up where your uncle is and get us some land. I got five girls from three up to fifteen. I sure miss them."

The troop was stopped for another break when the trooper that had not shown up last night rode in. He saluted and reported, "I got real close to them last night when they camped. They are arguing about going to the reservation. Some are hungry and tired. Others want to fight and not go to the reservation. They are meeting up with another band at the Biggest Lake. If they do go, there could be as many as thirty warriors. No guns in this band, but the other band may have guns."

"Good report, soldier!"

"Thank you, Sir! Sorry about not being back, but thought you'd want to know as much as possible."

"Good thinking, soldier."

"Thank you again, Sir!"

"Get you some food, and we will be moving in a few minutes." The soldier saluted and moved off to see about something to eat.

The Sergeant and the Corporal held a conference. They had rounded up two other bands before the one yesterday. With Great Eagle dead, or so they thought, that made four bands out of circulation. These two bands were about the last of the Kiowas. The odds did not disturb them. The soldiers had the fire power, and the Indians only had a few rifles.

A plan was agreed upon. One trooper was to cut across country to Uncle John's and warn him that there were two bands of Kiowas in the area. They might be headed his way. The Sergeant was afraid that if the Indians ran north from Biggest Lake, they would hit Uncle John's place. With the extra trooper there and an early warning, they would have a good chance of defending themselves. They would have six guns and a good fort to fight from. They could fight off any band until the troop arrived.

The trooper headed northwest at a gallop. The main body took back up its pursuit of the Kiowa band. Maybe they could catch them before they got to Biggest Lake. They could not leave the trail and cut across to Biggest Lake. They feared the Indians might change their minds and head some other direction. To cut across to Biggest Lake and leave the Indian trail was a gamble, a bad gamble, so they just had to push hard, really hard on the trial.

The troop ate lunch in the saddle. Ate rations and had water this time. They had to be getting close to the Kiowa band. Just at sundown, the troop caught the Kiowas. That is they caught the women and the children. The men had disappeared into the brush country. The trackers said that it appeared that the men were going to Biggest Lake.

The Sergeant figured that the Indians wanted the column to find the women and children. They knew that the column would feed and care for them. The final thing the braves were probably wanting was for the column to stop all together. The Sergeant decided to fool the Indians, this time. He would leave a small section with the women and children, and he would head for Biggest Lake. He had to gamble that that was where the men were going. That they were going to meet the other band.

The column moved off leaving food for the Indians. It was rations, and the Indians probably did not like the them, but If they were hungry, they would eat them. The Indians would stay at this position with a guard of four men. Sergeant ordered that another four troopers, the pack mules and the children would follow at a slower pace. The ride was going to be even harder, and he could not split his command any further. Everyone was getting ready to ride when Minnie approached the Sergeant.

"We have been through a bunch of trouble getting this far. We don't feel right making you leave four of your best men with us. You need every gun you have. May I make a suggestion? Let us follow with the pack horses. We can ride and rest . We have Ol' Bullet to warn us if there is trouble. We are not afraid, and we want to help. That is our Uncle and his people out there who need your help. Give us directions. Tell us what stars to follow, whatever. But, let us help. We will be behind you and the Indians in front of you, so we should be very safe. Just Leave two soldiers, the older man and the new trooper. With them and Ol'Bullet we will be safe and you can take the four good guns with you."

The Sergeant was taken aback that one of these three children could come up with such a good idea. One that would be so much help. It would give him four more guns. The older man was due to muster out, and the young recruit was not of much use yet. He made the hardest decision of his life. If it failed, he would be in the stockade for the rest of his life.

He drew a rough map and handed it to the older trooper and looked at Minnie, "I hope you know what you are doing. I think I know what I am doing." He looked at the children and then the two troopers "For tonight keep the moon at your back until it is over head and then stop and rest. Let it sink and then follow it. O.K.?"

The order was passed that there would be a night ride. The men would eat at the next break or in the saddle. They would try to be at Biggest Lake before the Indians. They rode off into the evening dusk. Silence filled the air except for the occasional stomp of a horse hoof.

Lizzie put her finger on the matter that was bothering me. "Are we going to ride all night, Minnie?"

"If we have to."

"How will I stay in the saddle?"

"I'll hold you if you need to sleep."

"Robert , how are you going to make out? We have a long night ahead of us."

"Gee, Sis. I don't know, just do the best I can."

The older trooper led out, and we started riding. Minnie took out the pocket watch and looked at the time. "It is eight o'clock." She made a suggestion to the trooper, " We could ride until ten and then take a break."

The older trooper nodded his head in agreement, "Good idea." You would have thought that Minnie was the commanding officer. We had been on the trail for so long with her giving orders, it was natural for her to continue.

Ten came and then twelve. We were sure getting tired. The older trooper said, "Let's stop here and have a long rest, we have been in the saddle all day, plus for four hours tonight." We lay down on one of the canvases, and Minnie and the trooper let us sleep for thirty minutes. Then they had us up and mounted and on the way. At two I was asleep in the saddle, weaving back and forth. I knew I would be O.K. if I didn't fall out of the saddle.

Sometime around four we could hear a soft whistle. It sounded like a night bird. But, the "bird" got closer and closer. The bird would call, and then there would be silence. The "bird" was almost to us. We got off to one side and waited for the "bird" to go by. We did not know if it was Indian, cowboy or soldier. It was a soldier, the one that had ridden away to notify Uncle John.

He had met another scouting party from the fort, and they said they would double back to Major John's to give them a hand. The rider had turned around and was back. He was surprised that we were out there all alone, just three kids and two troopers, one old and one very new and scared trooper.

I spoke up, "We are not alone, we have Ol' Bullet."

"I have a feeling he could take on the whole Kiowa nation."

We kept riding. The soldier led the pack train and our animals while we slept in the saddle, with the older trooper and the new recruit bringing up the rear. He had tied our reins to the horse in front of us, That way we could sleep. We dozed and rode and stopped and dozed. During the night Minnie had held Lizzie. At dawn Lizzie wanted back on Number One. We had ridden for almost ten hours that night.

Day break found us only three miles from the Biggest Lake. We stopped and made a nature call and had some army rations. UGH! They are worse today. Just as we were about to remount we heard gunfire in the distance. It sounded like it came from the direction of Biggest Lake according to the trooper.

We rode forward, the trooper, six pack horses, one mule with Lizzie, one horse with Minnie, one horse with me, one old trooper and one new recruit. That was a total of twelve animals. And of course Ol" Bullet. We were approaching the lake from the east with the sun behind us. The gun battle was still raging on. Then something in the early morning mist scared Ol' Bullet. I should not say scared him. He saw or heard something that made him bark and raise cane like I have never heard.

But, that was the wrong thing to do around a bunch of horses. They bolted for the lake at full speed. The lead trooper's horse was the closest to Ol' Bullet when he started all the barking, almost right under the horse. That poor animal was the lead animal, and our horses were all tied on behind. In a heartbeat the nine horses, one mule and two trailing troopers were thundering down the hill toward the lake.

We didn't know it, but the troopers had found a much larger band of Kiowas at the lake. The Kiowas were putting up a real fight. That is until they heard the thundering of our horses down the hill toward them. They thought it was fresh troops, charging. All the Indians could see was the dust from the horses and mules against the morning sun. The troopers were yelling at the top of their lungs trying to stop the runaway horses and mule. All that did was make more commotion and spook the Indians, and they fled on foot. When the Indians started to run, we added our voices to the melee.

The trooper managed to pull his horse to a stop right in front of the Sergeant. "Trooper Hall reporting for duty, Sir."

The Sergeant could only stand there with his mouth wide open. We all started laughing, and Ol' Bullet started barking.

"Corporal!" shouted the Sergeant, stopping all the laughing. "Get these men mounted, and let's get after those Indians. They are retreating to the north."

"Yes. Sir!"

"Trooper Hall, what are you doing here?"

"Sir, I met G Troop about two hours after I left the column. They have moved to John Carter"s place. They will help defend that position, if necessary. Also, Captain Shirley of G Troop asked me to relay to you, that if you can push the Kiowas to the north, you will have them between his forces and yours coming from the south, Sir!"

"Thank you, Trooper!"

The troop was mounted in a few minutes. "Corporal, you, section two and these two brave troopers stay here. You are in charge of the wounded, the pack train and the children. You come slowly behind us. We will move to trap the Kiowas. See to the wounded." The corporal saluted.

The column moved out with the Sergeant in the lead. We dismounted and found a place to rest. We would be heading north soon. The Corporal made the rounds checking on the wounded. There were no seriously wounded men but there were three dead. They were wrapped in their rain gear and tied to their horses.

The second column was ready to move north. We traveled at a slow pace for the benefit of the wounded. Within the hour we could hear shooting to the north, and then it was quiet. The column pushed on, and as we topped a small rise, we could see two riders coming toward us.

"Corporal," one of the troopers called as he saluted. "The Sergeant's compliments, Sir. The Kiowas have surrendered. When they found troops on two sides of them, they threw down their weapons. The main column and G Troop are at John Carter's. The Sergeant ordered us to bring the children on up. You are to take all mounts and pack animals under your command and move to the south side of the mesa to establish a camp. The Captain will meet you at that point."

"Very good," the Corporal replied. "Children, go with the trooper. We will be moving very slow, and you can go on up and see your family. We will need your horses. You can ride three on your mule from here to Major Carter's." Minnie and I dismounted and Lizzie was helped down from Number One. The saddle was removed from Number One, and all eight of our sacks were unloaded off the pack animals. The column moved off.

The second trooper helped us put the four pair of sacks on Number One. Then we put Lizzie on Number One, and the trooper helped Minnie and me up on him. Lizzie was up front with me in the middle and Minnie on the rear of Number One. That was a pretty big load on Ol' Number One.

As we rode, the trooper was very talkative, "I was in your Uncle's outfit up at Fort Union. He was the best officer I ever had. Your Uncle is a great Indian fighter, and we sure hated for him to muster out of the Army. He has been living here for about fifteen years" He concluded his comments by pointing at a long low structure in the distance. He continued, "That is your Uncle's compound. Sure is a good fort. The building has expanded over the years. The first time I saw it there were only two rooms and some walls. Then your Uncle kept adding rooms as one thing and another happened, and now it is that big."

We arrived at Uncle John's compound at noon. There were troopers everywhere. A corral had been turned into a temporary stockade. The stockade held about forty-five Kiowa braves. We learned that riders had been sent out to bring in the women and children of both bands. They had been left, when the men started their last fight with the Cavalry.

We three rode up on Number One and sat there in front of the long low structure. "Where does Uncle John live?" Minnie asked the trooper.

"Here." He replied.

At that moment the gate opened and John Carter's whole family rushed out of the compound. There were our Uncle and Aunt and five children, twin girls, and three boys.

We dismounted and all just stood still. We just stared at each other. Finally Uncle John shouted, "I can't believe it. Minnie? This is Robert, and you must be Lizzie!" I'm your Uncle John, this is your Aunt Mary and these are your cousins. We were grabbed and hugged by our Aunt and Uncle. The children danced around us and yelled. Even some of the troopers gathered around. Uncle John asked, "Did you three kids ride all the way from Texas on that one mule."

Minnie answered, "No, we started on four mules." Her shoulders sagged. "It's a long story, Uncle John."

Aunt Mary spoke, "You can tell us later. Let's go inside."

In the compound we were escorted to a long table under a canvas awning. "This is where we eat most of our meals. Out here in the open. Not enough room in the house for this many people."

After a great meal, Aunt Mary took us inside. "The Sergeant has told me some about your long and hard ride. So, let's get you a bath and to bed. You can have a good rest. Sleep as long as you want to. There will be plenty of time to tell us about your trip."

I didn't think I could go to sleep with all the activities going on around the compound. I wanted to see and hear everything. I wanted to see and watch the Indians and then the soldiers. I wanted to be in the middle of things. I don't really remember laying my head down.

When I awoke, I was confused. I had forgotten where I was. Then the memories rushed back, and I jumped out of the bed. I pulled on my clothes and rushed outside. There was no noise or movement. It was very quiet. I ran out the compound gate and turned to my right to see the soldiers and Indians. They were gone. No wonder the place was so quiet. I went back inside the compound.

Uncle John was coming out of one of the rooms, "Robert, you are up! Did you have a good rest?"

"Yes, Sir. Where did the soldiers and Indians go?"

"They have been gone since day before yesterday. They pulled out the afternoon you got here, along with the braves. The women and children were being escorted by other troopers and took different routes. That was almost forty-eight hours ago."

I came to a halt, "Forty-eight hours ago? I slept that long?"

"Yes sir, young man. You slept that long, and your sisters are still asleep. Come on, and we will find you something to eat."

The girls came out of their room about sundown. I had explored the compound with my newfound cousins. There were ten rooms in the compound. It was in a square, with rooms all the way around three sides. There was a high solid fence across the fourth side. That made the compound complete. A great fort. There was a stream that ran out of the mesa on the west side of the compound. Uncle John had channeled the stream to run right through the kitchen and out into the compound . They had water in the house and could raise a garden and trees in some of the compound area. It was great! The cousins said we would go up on the mesa tomorrow.

We were gathered around the table in the yard. There was us, Uncle John's family, the four men who had served with Uncle John and the U.S. Marshall, who had come by on his monthly rounds. Uncle John said, "Time for you to tell us what happened and why you are in the Territory. You know it was quite a shock to find you at our door. I would have not recognized you if your Mama had not been writing to us all these years and sending us tin-type pictures."

It took the better part of a half day for us to get the whole story out and for them to understand all that had happened. They sat very quiet and still after we finished. Finally Uncle John spoke, "It is sad to hear of all our loved ones gone. Grandma and Grandpa, your parents, my brothers and so many cousins." He paused and there were tears in his eyes. "I had not seen Grandpa and Grandma in years. I came by to visit at the end of the war, on my way west to Fort Union. We will miss them."

He slowly got up and put his arms around the three of us and said, "You have a home here. No question about that." Our cousins cheered. "You, are more than welcome. Now, we have got to see what can be done about your inheritance, and see if there is anything else back home that should be yours. Now, the marshal here can send wires from Fort Sumner to the sheriff in Texas. That way we can let the law handle the problem."

The Marshall agreed to help all he could. He was very nice and wanted to meet this Uncle Nate. He believed that he just might put Uncle Nate in jail, for a number of things.

The discussion went on for the rest of the day. After supper that day, Aunt Mary commented, "There are some things I want to know about. What is in those eight sacks that were on the back of your mule? Did you think you would make it on one mule, named Number One? And, last, where is the skunk, Uncle Nate?"

We really did like this aunt, right off. When we opened the sacks and showed her the contents, she nearly fainted. We had three sacks of ruined bedding. There were two sacks with some mighty worn wagon canvases. One sack had our cooking and eating utensils, not in too bad shape. One sack had what was left of our food. That was bad, and Aunt Mary's nose really turned up at the contents. And the last sack, had our clothes, Minnie's and Lizzie's Christmas dresses, the Bible, Papa's 4-10 shotgun and Lizzie's two dolls.

Lizzie looked at them. They had faired the trip fairly well, considering all they had been though. "Aunt Mary, if you could wash and mend them, I would like to give them to the twins."

"Oh, Lizzie, you can't give up your dolls, they were Christmas and birthday presents from your Mama and Papa and Grandma and Grandpa."

"Aunt Mary, I want your twins to have them. Not some other twins."

We all understood exactly what she meant. That was settled and no argument.

The next morning one of the former troopers shouted, "Rider coming! It's a trooper, and he is leading a horse."

The rider arrived at the gate to the compound leading a saddle horse. "Major Carter, the patrol found this horse running lose. The Sergeant found some papers in the saddle bags that had your name on them. So, he sent me to deliver this horse to you. Thought that it might be yours. He may have been snake struck, for the looks of that place on his leg. The papers seemed important. Here is the horse and the papers are in the saddle bags. With your permission, sir, I will return to my troop."

In military fashion Uncle John said, "Good report, soldier. Thanks for the courtesy, and my compliments to your commander." They saluted, and the trooper rode east.

Uncle John tied the horse and took the saddle bags. He walked back into the compound with all eight children following. We gathered around the table, and he sat down beside Aunt Mary. He opened the saddle bags and took out an oil skin wrapped packet. Upon opening the packet several things fell out on the table, letters, a little book and a bunch of money. The money was between the package wrapping and the oil cloth. Unless you took it out and shook it, the money might not be noticed.

"I'm surprised that the troop didn't take this money, if they saw it," Uncle John said. Then he started opening some letters and a bank book. His eyes went wide, and he swore under his breath.

"John Carter!" Aunt Mary exclaimed.

"Sorry, Mother." He continued to read through the contents, and then he counted the money. "Lord, there is almost a thousand dollars here." Then he turned to the three of us. "These letters are letters of credit. This bank book shows that you have almost fifteen thousand dollars in a bank in Texas." Then he turned to Aunt Mary. "And, we have almost eleven thousand dollars in the same bank. And Nate has almost eleven thousand dollars in that same bank."

"How do we get it out here, Uncle John?" Minnie inquired.

"I don't know, but I can get the military to help us. Tomorrow I will ride up to the fort. There I can use the telegraph, and I will send some wires. We know the army will help. I may have to be gone for several days, with the ride and a couple of days waiting on answers."

Minnie had her brow all wrinkled and muttered, "I'm sure that this stuff from the saddle bags has something to do with Uncle Nate."

"How do you know that, Minnie?" asked our aunt.

"Robert found a little notebook with numbers, or numbers just like those, and we put them in my Bible. Let me get the Bible, and we will see."

Minnie returned and handed the little notebook to Uncle John. "The same numbers, you can see for yourself. These papers from the saddle bags have something to do with Uncle Nate. I just knew it!"

Uncle John and one of the troopers that worked with Uncle John were gone to the fort when I got up. I had not gone back to being a sleepyhead, but I wasn't getting up with the chickens.

My cousins and I explored the mesa to the west of the compound. I asked about the town of Mesa.

The family laughed. "There is no town, that is just a place. We say we live at Mesa and everyone knows where that is. The "Town" of Mesa, if that is what you want to call it, is a church-school, a livery stable with a blacksmith and a mercantile store."

I was disappointed that there was not a town. The nearest town was the village around Fort Sumner, forty miles from here.

Uncle John was back in four days. We were all surprised. They had ridden to the fort in one day, can you imagine, one day and forty miles. Spent two days on telegraph wires and answers, then one day home and forty miles back home. That is the cavalry for you. Boy, these old cavalry men can sure cover the ground.

When he arrived late at night, we were all asleep. The next morning at breakfast he gave us the good news.

Uncle John explained, "The Army had indeed helped us. They had sent wires to various forts to be on the lookout for Uncle Nate. They had also sent wires to various sheriffs in West Texas in as many county seats as had a telegraph. As luck would have it, there was an army patrol in the town where Uncle Nate had deposited the money. The Army Captain and the Sheriff walked in the bank, and the little weasel banker almost passed out. He was more than glad to help."

Uncle John placed Lizzie on his knee and continued. "Best part, the money had been sent by wire, with the help of the Army, to a bank in Las Vegas in the New Mexico Territory. The money, all of it, is out of Nate's reach. Oh, by the way, that includes Uncle Nate's. It is being held, until the proper authorities can look into his activities. The money in the packet...... the Marshall said to give it to you three kids for your effort to get to the Territory." He handed Minnie the packet as he was talking, and Minnie only held it for a moment.

Minnie just handed the money right back to Uncle John and said, "You use it!"

"What ever you say, Minnie. I may put it in the bank at Las Vegas for you three, and we can use some of it in the future. Is that all right with you?"

We all nodded "Yes."

Minnie spoke up, "Uncle John, does Aunt Marjie and Aunt Bess know where we are?"

"Yes, they do. I sent them a long telegraph that you were here and O.K. Then I wrote them a long letter. I told them about your trip and all that had happened to you. They will get the letter in a few weeks."

"Thank you, Uncle John." Minnie gave him a hug.

Uncle John put Lizzie down and pulled out an Army map of West Texas and the Territory of New Mexico. "Now, let's take a look at where you have been, and I have some more story for you."

We all gathered around the map. "You started right about here, right?"

We nodded, "We guess so."

"Well, brace yourselves. Your Uncle Nate has been on your tracks all the way from there to the Territory."

Our eyes got big and round. "All the Way?" we wanted to know.

"Yes, and here is how I know. You ready?"

We all nodded.

"When I got to the fort I met with the sheriff, and we discussed your journey and all the dangers you went through. While we were in the commander's office an orderly from the doctor came running in and told me that they had a man in the infirmary that had the same last name as mine.

The doctor had sent the orderly to see if I wanted to talk to him. I asked the man's name, and the orderly told me it was Nate Carter."

We all sucked in our breath. Uncle Nate was at the fort. What was going to happen now?

CHAPTER FOURTEEN

Nate rode hard all day, at least it was hard for him. He was really too big for a horse. He had to stop and rest once an hour. He changed horses every two hours. If he had not had two horses his progress would have been very slow.

The soldiers had been stiff and formal with him, but he had learned that John's place was to the west just one hard day's ride. He thought that he could be close by sunset. He had to stop, so he rested an hour at noon.

After his noon rest, as he stepped up to straddle the horse, a rattlesnake rattled. The horse shied from the rattlesnake that was almost under the horse's hooves. Nate thought that the snake had rattled and struck the horse. The horse reared and bucked. Nate stayed on him for a few jumps, and then he hit the ground. The snake crawled away in the grass, but Nate wasn't moving. He was out.

The horse that was bitten ran way. That other horse just backed off and snorted a few times, but he did not run away.

It was dark when Nate came to the first time. His head was splitting, and he was disoriented. He had no idea where he was, nor could he move one muscle. Then he realized that he was in a wagon. His head split every time the wagon hit a rough place in the road. And that was often

Nate heard voices, but they were muffled. He tried to listen, but his head was splitting, and he passed out as darkness came again. When he awoke the next time, he heard the wagon drivers.

"Sure was hard loading that fellow."

"He is big."

"Wonder how he got on the ground?"

"Dummy, he either fell off his horse or the horse pitched him off. You tie that horse on good back there?"

"Yes, What are we going to do with him?"

"We'll let the doctor see him at the Fort. Then the doctor can decide what needs to be done."

"Did you go through his pockets, to see if he had anything of value?"

"Yeah, he is busted. Not one thin dime on that drifter." Nate reached down and felt the inside of his right boot. The money was still there, they just thought that he was busted.

They would have robbed him if he had had any money that could have been found. The wagon rattled and banged all day. He floated in and out of consciousness. When he awoke the wagon was moving, and he guessed that if the drivers had looked in on him, he was out.

He heard the drivers talking as they pitched their camp, "Sure glad we made it to Sock Lake."

"You're right. We can water our stock, have some trees to get under and be out of the sun."

"Don't you think that we should make the fort tomorrow?"

"Sure do, and we can turn that fellow over to the doctor."

"If this drifter is busted, why did we even bother to pick him up?"

"Why, you never know, there might be some reward money for him."

Nate was still drifting in and out of darkness. He tried to remember what had happened. Slowly his head cleared and the events came rushing back. He remembered knowing that it was dark and wondering if the snake had struck him. There in the darkness of the wagon he felt of his head and then ran his hands over his body. Just his head had been cracked and apparently there was no snakebite. Then he drifted back into unconsciousness.

The drifters had arrived at the fort and reported to the Captain of the Guard. "We have a sick man in the back of the wagon, and we want to take him to the doctor. Can you tell us where to find the doctor?"

The Captain looked in the rear of the wagon and asked the drivers, "Any idea who he is?"

"Nope. He didn't have any papers on him or in his saddle bag."

"Did you go through his things to find some identification or to see if he had money?"

"We just looked for some identification, but he didn't have any or any money either."

"Yeah, I'll bet. The doctor is in the building on the right at the end of that row of buildings."

"Thank you, Captain. Will you notify the sheriff that we brought this man in, in case there is some reward money for him?"

"Sure, he'll be here in a day or so, and I'll tell him."

"Thank you, Captain." They drove away. "The nerve of that Captain, to think we would take money from a hurt fellow."

"Well, we would wouldn't we?"

"Sure, but don't tell anybody."

They dumped, literally dumped, him at the doctor's and drove away to tend to their business.

Nate awoke some time later in an army bed. He looked around and realized that his head was much better. He sat up on the side of the bed and heard a voice behind him.

"Good, you are awake. How do you feel?"

"So, so."

A man walked around in front of Nate.

"I'm Doctor Brazwell, the fort doctor. Would you liked some coffee?"

"Please."

The man returned in a few minutes with a hot steaming cup of coffee.

"I didn't catch your name, stranger."

"I'm Nate Carter, late from Texas."

"Who did you say you are?"

"Nate Carter."

"Why, would you believe! We had a major in the cavalry who was named Carter, Major John Carter. Are you any kin, by chance? Matter of fact Major Carter is over at the commandant's office right now."

Nate tried to not show any emotions. It seemed like a dream that his brother, John could be here in this fort, of all places. Was it possible?

"That is an odd thing." Nate said to the doctor.

"I'll get him, and you can visit."

Before Nate could react, the doctor was out the door hollering for an orderly, "Go over to the commander's office, and tell Major Carter that we have a man here in the hospital who is named Nate Carter. See if he wants to come over and visit, might know him or even be kin."

The orderly was gone less than a minute when the door of the hospital burst open and in charged the commander of the fort, the U.S. Marshal and of all the people in the world, Major John Carter, former major in the U. S. Cavalry.

The marshal was ahead of the other two. "Are you Nate Carter?" demanded the Marshal.

"Yes, I am." Nate replied.

"You are under arrest, Mr. Carter."

"What for?" Nate huffed.

"I'll let the circuit judge file the papers and charges, when he gets here."

"Nate?" John spoke to him for the first time.

"John?" He was completely tongue tied. It was John.

They stared at each other for several minutes. Each started to speak and then would stop.

Finally, John said, "Nate, I have a question or two for you, and I think you had better give it to me straight."

"All right," was all Nate could say.

"Why, did you try to cheat Minnie, Robert and Lizzie, not to mention me, out of the money that came from the sale of Grandma's and Grandpa's land and stock?"

"I was coming to the Territory to deliver you yours."

"If that is so, why did you deposit all the money in your name in a bank back in Texas?'

Nate's mouth fell open, and he began to sputter, "I..I.. I…now…. I"

John Carter's mouth was turned town at the corners, "Why didn't you tell me about Ma's and Pa's death when you wrote. I got two letters from you and you never mentioned the illness that spread through the country. Nor, did you tell about all the deaths."

"Well…I…I.. didn't…want to .."

"Mr. Carter," the marshal cut in. "We have your bank books and letters of credit all made out to you and not to the rightful owners. This is called theft in the Territory. And if you can't come up with a better answer than I have heard, you are going to the stockade."

Nate could only sit there in silence.

John asked the marshal, "If I don't press charges, then you will not have a case. Right?"

"Well, right. But you are not going to let this skunk walk away are you?"

"No, but he is broke, and but for one horse he is afoot. Can't we just escort him out of the Territory and be done with him?"

"If that's what you want, we can take care of it," replied the Marshal.

"I think that is what I would like to have happen."

"Mr. Nate Carter," the marshal thundered. "Let me fill you in on a couple of things. Number one, all the money in the bank in Texas has been moved to a bank in the Territory. Yours included, if it is yours." The marshal held up his hand stopping Nate. "Further this matter will be decided by the authorities, here and in Texas. We have wired all the sheriffs in your fair state that might have something to do with this matter, and I have wires from two of them who want to talk to you. Now you put your boots on, and I'll get you an escort out of the Territory."

The commander spoke for the first time. "Marshal, allow me. I have a troop forming up right this minute. They are going to Fort Richardson in Texas. That fort is being closed and these men are going there to bring back a wagon train of supplies. There are a bunch of Major Carter's friends in that troop, and they would be happy to get this 'Gentleman' out of the Territory. They can escort him to Texas, and then he is on his own, to deal with the Texas sheriffs."

"Good! Then Mr. Carter, get your boots on and never, and I mean never, set foot in this Territory again. Clear?"

Nate shook his head, " Yes."

"Then get your boots and let's go."

As Uncle Nate pulled on his boots, he felt of the slight bulge on the inside of the right boot. There was three hundred dollars in that secret pocket. He wasn't totally broke as his brother thought. Things could be worse. He could be run out of the Territory, totally broke. The marshal led him outside, and the soldiers almost threw him on his mount.

The fort commandant turned to the officer in charge. "It is going to be interesting to see how Mr. Nate fairs, trying to keep up with your troop. Plus, Captain, this man is to be escorted out of the Territory, all the way out. Understood?"

"Yes, Sir. Sir?" The Captain of the troop responded and asked, "Did this man have anything to do with those children being out on the Llano Estacado by themselves? And, are they kin to Major Carter?"

The commander answered the Captain, "You are correct on both accounts!"

"Thank you, Sir. We will be happy to escort this scum out of the Territory!"

The commands were given, and the troop along with Nate Carter moved out, headed east to Texas.

CHAPTER FIFTEEN

"Kids, I did talk with Nate for a few minutes, just before the troop pulled out. He said that he had followed you all the way from home. He was always just behind you and could not quite catch up."

Uncle John pointed to the map, "That ranch is right about here. He was at that ranch house, Robert, when you got supplies."

Uncle John moved his finger to a different place. "And right along here is where he had a run-in with the rustlers." Uncle John pointed to another place on the map.

Then he pointed to another spot on the map and said, "In this general area of the Llano, he was in the outlaw camp for several days. Not far from where he found your mule at the ambushed Indian camp. You know you said you saw some men stuck in the marsh? He saw those men. Then he lost his wagon and two animals to the marsh."

Uncle John ran his finger over the area that reached from the caprock to the spring in the Territory. "All of that occurred somewhere in here. The Army has not mapped that part of the region and knows practically nothing about the area. An area that is over a hundred or so miles wide and several hundred long."

Uncle John indicated a place just to the west of the border of the Territory. "Finally, he ran into an Army patrol, and they took him to these springs. You know the ones, the ones that are here. That is where you spent the first night in an army camp." He pointed at a spot on the west side of the line between the Territory and Texas. "Right?"

"Yes," Minnie replied.

Uncle John paused and looked at the three of us and said, "Now the best news of all. Your Uncle Nate is now long gone from the territory and should be in Texas!"

There was a period of cheering and hand clapping at the news.

I spoke up and asked, "Does that mean I can have that ten gage double-barrel shotgun to go with Papa's four-ten?"

"It does, Robert."

Lizzie asked, "Uncle Nate was sent back home?'

"Yes, Lizzie."

Minnie said, "I told you all along, 'The Lord Will Provide!' "

"Yes, Minnie," I smiled and said, "for three kids on a mule."

Printed in the United States
4383

9 780595 178162